PROMISING

Book Two of Kira's Story

The Realm Series

By Rebel Miller

Editor: Stephanie Fysh

Cover art: Russell Morgan at www.goodsandcargo.com

For mature audiences

ROMANCE, SCIENCE-FICTION, NEW ADULT

ISBN 978-0-9947702-1-9 (EPUB)
ISBN: 978-0-99477-024-0 (PRINT)

To my two beautiful sons

MILLER BOOKS

Thank you for purchasing a Rebel Miller Book!

As an author, nothing is more exciting than knowing that readers are discovering my novels and enjoying them, so please take a second to connect with me on <u>Facebook</u>, <u>Twitter</u> and <u>Instagram</u> to learn about my upcoming releases and share your reviews.

~

Finally, look out for details at the end of this book about how you can receive a **bonus scene** from *Promising*.

Sincerely, Rebel

Other Books by Rebel Miller

Awakening

CONTENTS

CHAPTER ONE

"Don't you find it odd?" I asked, sensing Tai's presence, as usual, before he was near.

"What?" He knelt in front of me. In my periphery, his hazel eyes scanned my face.

"That we treat death the same way we do birth," I replied, watching my cousin, Adria, over the bulk of his shoulder. The two-year-old dashed across the sitting area, waving a fistful of purple and red ribbons as she went. Heartache and an unrelenting sense of guilt burned a stinging path through me. "Addy thinks everyone's here for someone's festival day or baby welcoming."

Tai glanced behind him. Adria was twirling about in front of Ma, the ribbons she held high dancing about her dark blond hair.

Despite a month having passed since my Aunt Marah died, Ma insisted that we keep to protocol and hold a farewell. She believed it would be disrespectful to my aunt's soul for us not to acknowledge in some way her life and the joy she had brought to ours. After managing to get Khelan to agree, she had placed the customary bouquet of purple and red ribbons outside the front door, signaling the period of mourning. Since then, our home had been filled with neighbors and friends who offered heartfelt condolences for the loss of a loved one following, they believed, an unfortunate accident.

But they didn't know the truth.

Ma gave Adria a small, indulgent smile then smoothed down the creases of her bright red dress before greeting yet another group of guests.

Tai turned to me with a scowl. "Are you doing penance?"

I blinked into his hard stare. "What?"

"Come on," he said, holding out his hand. I saw the criss-cross pattern of scars in the center of his palm, telling me more than he ever would about the level of aggression required to put it there. "You've been here long enough," he added.

When I didn't respond, Tai took my hand and rose to his feet, pulling me up with him. I followed his lead without resistance. A break was probably a good idea. After all, I planned on being at the farewell for the entirety of the customary three days. It was the least I could do.

We were in the middle of the hallway when my brother appeared, having just stepped out of his old bedroom at the end of the hall.

Rhoan's expression darkened. "Where are you two going?" he asked, standing in front of the door to the study, arms crossed.

Tai's only response was to sidestep Rhoan, but he had to stop abruptly when my brother shifted to block his way.

Tai exhaled deeply as a scowl filled his face. "I need to speak with your sister."

"Can't you speak with her in there?" Rhoan dipped his chin toward the sitting room.

"What do you think, Rhoan?" Tai said with a curl to his lip. "That I'll defile your sister in the middle of your aunt's farewell?"

My brother's nostrils flared. "I don't know," he said with a shrug that did nothing to lessen the contempt in his eyes. "You've defiled her before. Who knows where or when the mood will strike you next?"

"Rhoan, Tai, *please*," I whispered, looking pointedly at a guest passing by.

Both of them ignored me.

Tai leaned into Rhoan, still holding my hand. "I thought we were past this," he stated, assessing my brother.

Rhoan was a large man, but even *he* should have been intimidated by Tai. Nevertheless, he lowered his arms and leaned into Tai's face. "My family and I have thanked you repeatedly for protecting Kira during and after the attack on Septima," he said, his light green eyes sharpening as he bore holes into Tai. "Don't take that as permission to continue fucking around with my sister."

Tai's hand tightened painfully around mine, and I glared at my brother. That was it. I'd had enough of his snide remarks over the last few weeks.

"Rhoan, this isn't the time or place," I hissed. "It's in the past! Get over it!"

"Everything all right over here?"

Startled, the three of us swung around to find Khelan approaching. Tai gave my hand a gentle squeeze before releasing it.

Khelan glanced between us, our sudden silence making him frown. "What's wrong?"

Rhoan slid his hands into his pockets, shifting his gaze from Tai to Khelan. "I was just thanking our resident protector once again for watching over Kira on Septima during the attack," Rhoan said smoothly, his eyes returning to Tai. "He's been such a *good* friend to our family."

Tai's eyes darkened to nearly black as he looked at my brother.

Khelan nodded, thankfully oblivious to the undercurrent of tension between Rhoan and his alleged best friend. "There's certainly no limit to how much we can express our gratitude," he said with a grave expression.

Tai frowned and tightened his jaw. "You've thanked me enough, Khelan."

Khelan shook his head. "It will never be enough," he said. "It's not just for protecting Kira on Septima. It's for everything before that as well."

Tai hesitated, then gave a short nod, accepting Khelan's thanks.

Khelan glanced toward the sitting area before stepping close, tightening our circle. "Have you heard anything about who caused the attack?" he asked in a low voice.

Tai braced his shoulders back. "Not much," he said, matching the volume of Khelan's voice. "Mostly speculation and rumors. Nothing worth repeating."

"What about the factions?" Khelan pressed.

Rhoan and I exchanged an uneasy look.

Since Khelan had decided to avenge my aunt's death by supporting the factions through Uncle Paol and a man named Maxim, we had heard very little of what had been going on with the three of them. Despite our attempts to change Khelan's mind, Rhoan and I suspected he had been in constant communication with the other two.

It certainly wouldn't have been the first time he'd kept the truth from us.

Tai studied Khelan. "They've started establishing more command centers, throughout the Realm," Tai said. "Usually in remote but resource-rich towns."

"Like Tholos," Khelan noted, referring to the town where my aunt, his sister, had been killed.

Tai nodded, appearing deep in thought. "There's a town called Tork, on Hale Three, that we're monitoring closely," he said. "Since their minister was killed, activity at that site has become more aggressive than anywhere else we've been monitoring."

Khelan appeared grim. "And what of Prospect Eight? Any news about the rebels close to Merit?" He held Tai's gaze as he asked about the town where *we* lived.

Tai's eyes cooled. "No, I haven't heard anything."

The lines around Khelan's mouth tightened as a knot formed between his brows. He glanced over his shoulder to Ma. She and Da were speaking with a neighbor. He turned to me with bleak eyes. "Your Ma is having a hard time explaining where Paol is."

I frowned. We had all agreed to say that Paol had been called away on business for an extended time. It was the best excuse we could come up with for his prolonged absence and the need for us to watch over Adria.

"Maybe you should go to her," I said, reading the concern for Ma in his eyes.

Khelan nodded but his expression was rueful. "I don't know why I agreed to this blasted farewell," he said. "I'm lying right to the faces of men and women I've called friends for years."

The three of us watched as he walked over to Ma, who extended a hand toward him but then seemed to change her mind. She clasped her hands at her waist instead and stepped between him and Da, close to Khelan's side.

A bitter taste filled my mouth at the irony of what he had just said. He had been lying to my face for *years*, hiding the truth that he was my biological father. My parents had explained their justifiable reasons, but the fact still remained that they had deceived me.

"I've been monitoring Khelan," Tai said in a low voice.

I swung around, certain I had heard incorrectly. The only reason Tai would be monitoring Khelan was if Rhoan had told him about his support of the factions. I couldn't believe Rhoan would go back on our agreement to keep that information from Tai. He had already done too much in the name of protecting our family. I didn't want to add to the burden he was helping us carry.

I settled a scathing glare on my brother. "You *told* him?"

Rhoan gave me a disdainful look. "I didn't tell him anything, Kira."

I continued glaring at him, not believing a word.

"He's in the blasted *Protectorate*," Rhoan said through clenched teeth, then drew back his shoulders, staring down at me. "Makes you wonder what a citizen in a higher caste would be able to discover, and how quickly, doesn't it?"

I froze. *Does Gannon know about Khelan as well?*

Like Tai, I had wanted to keep this information from Gannon, but Rhoan had been skeptical that Gannon wouldn't simply find out on his own, especially since he had been already monitoring our family as closely as Tai. I had told Gannon that my aunt had been killed in the middle of a battle between factions, but not about Khelan's resulting desire for revenge.

I saw Tai's growing confusion as he looked between Rhoan to me. "I'm getting the feeling that I'm missing something," he said, narrowing his eyes.

I avoided his gaze and disengaged the door to the study. "We shouldn't be having this conversation here," I said, grateful when Tai and Rhoan followed me into the room without argument.

"Explain," Tai ordered no one in particular as soon as the door slid shut behind us.

Rhoan glared at Tai. "First, tell us what you know."

Tai leveled him with a look. He was a man used to giving orders, not taking them.

I tensed, readying to silence another quarrel, when Tai exhaled deeply, as if he had decided to swallow his pride. "For some reason, Khelan has been in regular communication with someone named Maxim," he said, then frowned. "I've never seen anything like it. I can't find out anything about the man. Nothing about his caste or family, or what he did before getting involved with the rebels."

Rhoan caught my eye, and in doing so, Tai's attention as well.

"What are you not telling me?" Tai demanded, bearing down on me now.

I shook my head and stole a glance at Rhoan, hoping for help.

"He's going to find out anyway," my brother said with a sigh. "Let's just tell him. At least now we'll know what Uncle's up to. *He's* certainly not telling us anything."

Rhoan was right. If Tai was on Khelan's trail already, it was only a matter of time before he found out the rest of it.

I sighed deeply, facing Tai. "Maxim's an elite. At least, I think so."

Tai appeared baffled.

"His accent," I explained. "It's the same as Liandra's."

Tai frowned. "How do you know that?"

I shot a look at Rhoan. "Maxim and Paol came to our home shortly after the attack on Septima," I said, wincing at the alarm that leapt into Tai's face. "Paol wanted to leave Adria in our care, and Maxim asked for Khelan's help supporting the factions. *That's* why they've been in contact with each other."

Tai's eyes became as hard as granite. "You were going to keep this from me?" he bit out.

My shoulders slumped. "You've done enough."

Tai stepped forward, looming over me. "That's *my* decision to make."

I peered up at him, watching the tension ripple through the muscles along his neck.

"Back off," Rhoan said, eyeing him. "She was only trying to protect you."

But Tai wasn't moved in the least. He continued to glower at me.

"Why were you monitoring Khelan?" I asked. "Do you think Paol and Adria are still in danger of being discovered?"

Tai shook his head. "Between the delays in the deportation of Argon citizens and the fallout after Septima, the last thing the Realm would be interested in is a subordinate and his child, both of whom were to be placed in neutral status."

I released a breath of relief.

"I only just started monitoring Khelan," he continued. "I've been keeping tabs on Paol's activities and noticed his interactions with Maxim."

Just then, Khelan's voice filtered through the door, calling out for my brother from somewhere beyond the hallway.

Rhoan cursed then looked at Tai. "Come see me before you leave," he said. "I want to know everything you do." With that, he threw a look of warning at me before striding out of the room, leaving the door wide open. I tracked his steps and disengaged the door.

Of course, Rhoan wouldn't think to close the door and offer us any privacy. No doubt, he thought Tai was so mad with lust for me that he would take me passionately behind any closed doors.

Little did he know.

"Why are you blaming yourself for your aunt's death?"

I whirled around, surprised by the question. "What?"

Tai's shoulders lost some of their tension as he approached me, his head hanging low to meet me eye to eye. "You've been sitting in that chair in the sitting room looking more repentant with each passing second," he said.

I had opened my mouth, ready to dismiss his observation, when I realized he was right.

"I just wonder if there's something we could have done," I said finally, wrapping my arms about my waist.

Tai frowned. "We *did*, Kira," he said, searching my face. "We were monitoring her and her family, protecting them as best we could. Your aunt was killed while we were under attack on Septima. If you're to blame, then you had better blame me as well."

I knew that what he was saying was rational and the truth, but a sense of responsibility stubbornly gnawed at my mind.

"Why didn't you tell me about Khelan?" he asked, running a palm up my arm. "I could have helped."

I shook my head, considering him. "You could lose your rank and be imprisoned if your superiors found out that you were aware of a citizen helping the factions and chose not to report it," I said.

He rested his palm just below my jaw, hesitating a fraction of a second before placing it there. "Helping you is *my* choice to make," he said simply. I stared at him, indulging in the feel of his hand against my skin and wondering at the depths of his selflessness.

"Rhoan's not leaving for now," he said. "Let me take you home. You can come back tomorrow."

I sighed, fatigue setting in. Grief and worry were taking their toll, but I had committed to staying at the farewell with my family, and I wasn't about to change my mind.

Ping.

I startled at the sound of the incoming message on my comm, and my heart skipped a beat. Grimacing an apology to Tai, I turned away to check my device.

`Call me when you get home.`

Gannon.

I smiled, and quickly replied.

`As always.`

His response was immediate:

`I love you.`

My smile grew, and I ran a finger over the three words as they faded to black.

Since Septima, Gannon had become increasingly verbal about his feelings for me. In addition to leaving me breathless, however, his declarations of love left me frustrated, initiating an internal battle. The truth was, when he said or wrote things like that, I felt like I ought to respond in kind but always resisted.

I turned slowly to Tai, still lost in thought. The intensity of his expression jolted me to the present, and I dropped my wrist.

"Gannon's been worried about me," I said, acting on an irrational urge to explain myself. "If I don't respond, he'll just call."

Tai nodded, his guarded look slipping back into place, the change in his eyes revealing more than if he had explained the shift in his demeanor with words. As a protector, Tai was trained to be in control of all things — actions, emotions and thoughts. But since he had revealed his true feelings for me, and as our lives became more intertwined due to my family's secrets, I found it much easier to see through his protective exterior.

He pivoted and headed toward the door, his gait so stiff I knew something was off.

"Tai," I said, stopping him. He turned to me, his face perfectly blank. "What's wrong? Why are you acting this way?"

His eyes narrowed, but the mask he had donned stayed put. "What way?"

I searched his face, trying to put into words what I had picked up in his expression. "Angry."

"What do you expect?"

I cocked my head and gave him a questioning look.

"He doesn't deserve you," he said flatly.

I balked. *That* was why he was in a foul mood all of a sudden! "You have no right to be *angry* about that," I said, disbelief nearly choking me. "You said you don't want to be with me."

He stepped toward me, fists clenched. "I *choose* not to be with you. I would never say I don't *want* to be with you."

I stood firm against the rising tide of anger that was overcoming his face. "It's the same thing in the end," I declared.

"Oh, there's a difference, Kira," he said, glowering now. "*I* know my limitations, while Gannon is choosing to *flout* his. He's stringing you along!"

I shook my head. "He cares for me. You've said so yourself."

"Yes," he conceded, his shoulders set. "He does care for you, and more than I want to admit, so it drives me fucking insane that he'd continue with you like this. Hallowed Halls, how do you think this is going to end?"

I turned away, but he came to stand before me. I stared at the wide expanse of his chest, unwilling to look into his eyes as the walls of the room suddenly pressed in on me.

"Let's play this out," he said. "You and Gannon continue your affair in secrecy, managing to dodge family, friends, peers, officials and the rabid media. Then, five years from now, at the end of his father's last term, he's appointed high chancellor by Realm Council. Are you prepared to be his mistress? Because that's all you'll be."

Every part of me begged to reject what he was saying, but my head couldn't summon a solid argument.

"I'm not his mistress," I whispered, studying the folds of his dark gray shirt.

"You certainly aren't his girlfriend, and you'll *never* be his partner or wife."

I looked up at him, tears springing into my eyes, speechless at the ferocity behind his words. "I never said I wanted anything as permanent as that." Actually, I had never allowed myself to even *think* so far ahead.

Tai shook his head, clearly unconvinced. "And what about when he finds out that Khelan, your father — the one who's a senator in hiding — is supporting the factions?" he challenged. "What then?"

I stepped back and held a palm over my mouth, the truth of it all spreading a deep ache through my chest. I blinked back my tears, but a few still managed to fall past my lids and onto my cheeks.

"Fuck." Tai reached for me, enfolding me in his arms. He ran a hand up my back and lowered his head so his mouth was close to my ear. "I hate that I'm hurting you, Kira, but I need to show you the truth," he said, his lips brushing my cheek.

I didn't want the truth, so I buried my face in his chest and inhaled the light scent of coffee and soap that lingered there. For a few moments, I let my tears flow and dampen the soft fabric of his shirt.

I had almost pulled myself together when the door slid open. I jumped and took a hasty step back, the abrupt movement causing Tai to release his hold on me. We both spun to face the door.

Ma stood, wide-eyed, at the threshold, holding a large box at her hip. "Forgive me," she said, looking between Tai and me. "I didn't know anyone was in here."

After another quick glance at Tai, she entered the study and placed the box on the desk. Inside it was a collection of colorful objects. Avoiding my mother's odd expression, I stepped closer, reached in and pulled out a small notebook that looked like a journal. It was leather-bound and had a fanciful floral pattern embroidered on the material. The box was filled with a number of other books just like it.

"They were your aunt's," Ma explained.

I looked up from the journal. "They're beautiful."

Her brown eyes, so much like my own, continued to assess me for an uncomfortable length of time. I shifted my feet and stole a quick look at Tai, who stood silent and observant just behind her.

"I'm planning to have them protected with a seal," she said, drawing my focus. "I think Addy would like to have them one day."

I nodded and smiled tightly as she turned to leave. Just before she did, she shot another look at Tai and disengaged the door, allowing it to slide shut behind her.

Tai sighed and came to me, running a hand over his short-cropped hair. "Kira," he said, "please just think about everything I've said."

I stiffened and glanced at him from the corner of my eye. "This is *my* choice, Tai," I said, throwing his words back in his face. "You made yours. Let me make mine."

* * *

"How is it that with all our system's technology I can't make love to you from thousands of light years away?"

I snorted, but my lips tilted up at the corners nevertheless. "I'm sure the Protectorate has some sort of virtual reality device that could be refashioned just for that purpose," I offered, rearranging the wool blanket on my lap.

I was curled up in bed, facing my monitor and resting against a pile of pillows. It had become a familiar position over the last few weeks, one from which I would relay the day's activities during my nightly call with Gannon. Well, it was a nightly call for me. The sun had already risen where Gannon lived, on Dignitas One.

Suddenly, Gannon seemed to be deep in concentration. "No, on second thought, there's no technology that could ever measure up to the real thing." He grinned.

I smiled, heat rising to my cheeks.

"There's the smile I was looking for," Gannon said, leaning closer to his monitor, and so closer to me.

He was sitting in his office. He had been holding our calls from there more frequently over the last month. From what I could see, his office was a large, well-lit space. A wall of floor-to-ceiling glass ran its expanse directly behind him. Through it, I could see citizens of every caste striding by in obvious haste to get things done, more than likely at Gannon's bidding. During these nighttime conversations with Gannon, and within the intimate surroundings of my bedroom, it was easy to forget who he was and his status. As chancellor, he surely had, every day, a checklist as long as my arm, filled with tasks.

I frowned as I noted the time. "I should let you go," I said, sitting up.

"Why?"

I glanced pointedly behind him, fiddling with the thin strap of my top. "Your office looks incredibly busy."

He blinked then swiveled in his chair to look at the steady stream of people behind him.

"Oh, my support always look like that," he said, mischief glittering in his clear blue eyes as he turned back to me. "They think it'll prevent me asking them to do anything else." He winked, and I laughed, loving his cheekiness.

If his office was anything like the Judiciary on Prospect Eight, where I worked, there would have been, since Septima, a heightened state of activity and an added fervor underscoring every project. The Corona had wasted no time gaining approval from Realm Council to initiate an investigation that would seek out who was responsible for the attack. In her own words, it was an act of war against law-abiding citizens that would not go without justice.

A shiver rippled through me as I recalled her remark.

"Gannon," I said so sharply that he became somber at once, "promise me you won't monitor my family anymore."

He narrowed his eyes. "Why would I do that?"

I swallowed. "Uncle Paol made his decision, but my cousin, she's safe with my parents," I said. "He'll need to answer for his own choices."

"I would rather be aware of what your uncle's up to," he said. "If he's still aligned with the factions, then, depending on what he does, you or your family could be in danger."

I was shaking my head before he finished speaking. "It would be best for Adria and my family if we just let things lie," I said.

Gannon scowled. "That's not something I normally do, Kira," he said. "*Things* have a way of coming back up to haunt people."

I leaned toward him, clenching my fists. "*Please.*"

Gannon must have seen something in my expression because he nodded, though with a great amount of obvious reluctance.

He ran a hand through his hair, disheveling the blond locks, as he lowered his gaze to his desk. "How'd it go today?" he asked.

I thought for a moment then ended up with "Good." It was odd to describe a farewell as such, but there was truly no other way to describe it. I sighed. "A lot of people came by."

He glanced up from under his lashes. "Was Tai there?"

I hesitated then nodded.

Gannon lowered his gaze again, this time to his hands, which were now clasped tightly in front of him on his clear glass desktop. "And how is the newly appointed commander of Prospect Council?" he asked, still looking at some point around his wrists.

I blinked. "He…seems fine."

Gannon nodded, still not looking at me.

I studied the crown of his head with a frown. "When will you be back on Prospect?" I asked, hoping to change his mood.

Finally he glanced up, with apology clear in his eyes. "I was hoping to be there in the next few days," he said, cringing, "but my father just asked me to lead discussions on Hale Three. Since their minister's murder on Septima—"

My pulse spiked. "*Where* on Hale Three?"

Gannon drew back, frowning, no doubt at my sharp tone. "A town called Tork."

I shot up to my knees, gripping the blanket on my lap. "Don't go."

Worry flickered across his face. "Kira, what's wrong?"

I licked my lips. "The factions," I said. "They're using Tork as a command center. You could get hurt." *Or worse.* Oh gods.

Gannon's shoulders dipped as he frowned. "*Lahra*," he began, and I melted a little at the endearment. "There's violence everywhere. I'll be well protected."

That wasn't enough. "Can't someone else go instead?"

He shook his head, regret clouding his eyes. "It's not that sim—"

"Please," I said, holding back a swell of fear. "I can't have what happened to my aunt happen to you."

Gannon ran a hand across his mouth and he leaned back, studying me. For a few beats, we were silent as we stared at each other. My heart jackhammered. I knew I was being unfair, but I couldn't care less.

He crossed his arms. "How do you know about Tork?" he finally asked. "I've only just learned of the trouble there, in a report."

I opened my mouth, but hesitated for some reason before responding. "Tai told me."

"Tai?"

I took a deep breath. "Yes, well, at the farewell, Khelan asked Tai for information about the factions and..." I dropped my gaze to my lap as I rubbed my temples. "Why do I feel like I'm apologizing?" I lowered my hands, raising my head.

Gannon sat forward in his seat. "He's so blasted ingrained in your life," he ground out.

I exhaled a puff of air. "He's my brother's best friend. Our families are close."

"Must he always be so close to *you?*" The light blue of his irises was almost translucent, his eyes were so bright.

This didn't make sense. "What's going on, Gannon?" I asked, searching his face for clues. Surely he knew by now that I was his even if it was acknowledged only between us!

Gannon exhaled deeply, leaning onto his elbows. "I'm sorry," he said with a depth of gravity that filled me with concern. "I — I'm taking things out on you."

"What things?" I asked, taking in the stiffness of his shoulders.

He glanced about the room before coming to rest on me again. "It's Realm Council and these ongoing meetings since Septima. I just—"

"No," I said firmly as I crawled closer to my monitor to assess him closer.

Gannon relished what he did. If anything, his work was invigorating, not irritating. Since leading the task force that established a special committee on exploration, Gannon had been called on to oversee a broad range of projects, from managing trade negotiations to offering opinion on security measures. Whenever we spoke, he gave me a rundown on his day that had my head spinning but seemed to only leave him more energized.

I narrowed my eyes. "This isn't about work *or* Septima," I said.

He looked at me for a moment then sighed. "I had an argument with my father."

I studied him, expecting more. An argument with his father wasn't new. Gannon and his father regularly exchanged terse words. I suspected they were too much alike to do anything else.

"About what?" I asked when it became apparent that there was no explanation forthcoming.

He thrust a hand into his hair, seemingly searching for words. After a long moment, he lowered his arm. "About things I want and can't have," he said finally, holding my gaze.

It took me a few seconds to understand he was talking about me. My eyes widened. "Oh," I said for lack of a better response.

Gannon shook his head. "I wanted to be there with you, *for* you, at your aunt's farewell. I almost ordered Talib to take me to an arc station at least five times," he said. "But I couldn't figure out how to explain why a senator — the Realm's chancellor, no less — would be attending the farewell for a subordinate woman he never met."

I tossed off the blanket that was tangled around my knees. The cool air skimmed my bare legs as I sat directly in front of the monitor, my hands fisted in my lap. "There's no way you could have come, Gannon, and I'm glad you didn't," I said, causing his eyes to narrow even as they ran a heated path over me.

"You would prefer to have *Tai* stand by your side, instead of *me*?"

I frowned. "That's not what I meant," I said. "You being there would have only brought more complications to your life than I already have."

"You've brought nothing but meaning and happiness to my life," he said, steel in his voice.

I stared at him with my heart in my throat, clenching my jaw until it hurt so I wouldn't say something foolish, like how deeply I cared for him. Heart aching, I raised a hand and placed it on the screen, just over his cheek. He sighed so deeply I could have sworn he actually felt my touch.

"I can tell you know," he said, watching me as I ran my fingers along the lines of his lips. "No matter what you will or won't say, I know how you truly feel about me."

I smiled, tilting my head and lowering my hand. "Well, that should reassure you then, shouldn't it?"

He studied me for a long moment, rubbing the pad of his thumb back and forth, across his bottom lip.

"Excuse me, Chancellor."

Gannon turned in his chair. I looked beyond him at an older man, a senator, standing by the door. He had a shock of white hair that complemented the wisdom plain in his face.

"The marshal is here for your meeting," he said, flicking a glance my way before looking back at Gannon.

"Thank you, Arthur." Gannon turned to me as the man walked out of my view. He grimaced. "Time's up."

I smiled ruefully. All of a sudden, I had a horrifying thought and hiked the blanket up over my chest.

"Gannon, can everyone see me through your monitor as easily as I can see them?" While no one would be able to determine my caste in my nighttime attire, the scantiness of it had me alarmed.

"No, not everyone," he said, then smirked. "Though poor Arthur is sure to be tongue-tied for the rest of the day."

CHAPTER TWO

Thankfully, the gods were on my side.

I dashed across the marble floors of the Judiciary's lobby and managed to slip into an elevator at the last moment. I checked the time on my comm and released a breath, grateful that I wouldn't be late.

"Fancy meeting *you* here."

I raised my head, a smile growing on my face. I would know that quirky charm anywhere!

"Where are you?" I asked, peering over my shoulder.

Just then, the elevator stopped at my floor and the group of us spilled out into the reception area. I turned and found Asher giving me a gallant bow.

"My lady," he said, straightening.

I smiled and looped my arm through his as we entered the main work area. "Are you ready?" I asked.

Asher's usual grin flattened on the spot. "You know," he said, "Mila asking us to be in a meeting this early in the day can only mean one of two things: we're about to be dismissed, or she's going to hand down new directives from Realm Council about the special committee meetings. Either way, I'm about to lose my breakfast on these marble floors."

I laughed and nudged him with my shoulder, hoping to bring back his smile. "I think it's probably something closer to new directives than a dismissal, Asher."

"You never know," he said with a sigh. "She's a terribly unpredictable and demanding woman."

I snorted. "She's not that bad."

"*Not that bad?*" Asher repeated, his dark eyes wide. "She's freaking bionic!"

I would have laughed again, but he looked so distressed, I had to hold back. I released him and began taking off my wool coat as we approached the boardroom where Mila had arranged for us to meet with her.

"Has she assigned you to yet another project?" I asked as we walked into the room. The lights flickered on automatically.

Asher nodded as he removed his short leather coat. A "bomber jacket," he called it. As usual, Asher's retro clothing reflected his own uniqueness.

He flattened out his tablet on the wide table that ran the length of the room, sat down, then looked at me over the top of his wire-rimmed glasses. "She says it's a testament to — and I quote — how much *fucking confidence* she has in my abilities." He shook his head. "All Above, I didn't know it was possible to resent one's own talents."

This time I couldn't help it: I laughed.

Over the past few weeks, Asher's interactions with our direct and uncompromising interim minister had become a source of great amusement for everyone in the Office of Exploration. The truth was, it was a nice for a change to have something to make light of. Since the attack on Septima, the usual buzz of activity at the Judiciary had carried a somber undercurrent. Nevertheless, Mila was under strict orders to move projects forward. With Realm Council refusing to pause or even slow down our regular affairs in the face of the factions' violence, the Corona had accelerated the process of appointing members to the special committee on exploration.

"I'm so flipping glad you're supporting Mila on this project too," he said, still focused on his tablet. "Maybe you can get her to ease up. You're the only one who has a good rapport with her."

"Yes, well…" I said with a frown, trying to squelch the sudden memory of those terrifying moments during the attack. "I suppose that's the benefit of surviving an attack together."

Asher raised his eyes. "Sorry," he said. "That's the last thing you want to be thinking of."

I managed a small smile and a shrug, dismissing his apology as unnecessary because it was.

Asher returned to his tablet at the same time as my comm signaled an incoming message. I tapped at the device, my mood lifting at once.

I miss you.

My body hummed at Gannon's words as I replied.

I miss you too.

I've good news. I should be able to get out of my trip to Tork.

Really?!

Would I lie to you?

I beamed as he continued:

I'll be with you on Prospect in a couple days if it's the last thing I do.

I rubbed my lips together to stop myself from bouncing in my chair.

Be warned, Kira Metallurgist…I have a desperate need to fuck you.

And just like that, right there in my seat, I melted into a puddle. Good gods, he could have given me flowers and I couldn't have felt any weaker in the knees.

After a few moments drinking in Gannon's message, I remembered myself and raised my head to find Asher watching me from across the table. I hoped my face wasn't as flush with heat as the rest of me.

Asher gave me a knowing look capped off with a smirk. "So, how's *that* going?"

I gave him a small, awkward shrug, hoping to downplay the riot of my emotions.

"Ya. No need to answer," he said, grinning and focusing on his tablet again. "A look like that says it all."

I watched as Asher worked on his scroll. It was odd having someone at work know about Gannon and me. Asher found multiple opportunities to tease me about my "secret affair." On the one hand, his teasing added a sense of normalcy to my relationship with Gannon, but on the other, it emphasized its illicitness and uncertainty.

After tapping out a quick reply to Gannon, telling him to get some sleep and to stop seducing me via comm, I noticed the time. Our meeting with Mila had been scheduled to start ten minutes ago, but she had yet to arrive. As soon as I had the thought to contact Theo for an update on her schedule, however, Mila strode in, mug in hand.

"Kira, Asher," she said by way of greeting.

Both Asher and I sat up in our seats and said our good mornings.

Mila was intimidating on the best of days, but today she had a more urgent and commanding air than usual. She sat at the end of the table, leaning on one arm of her chair, her hand wrapped around her steaming drink. I had assumed it was coffee, but the smell was pungent and somewhat pleasant.

"Are you drinking *hurim* now?" I asked, eyebrows raised.

Hurim was a tea from Hale that was used most often by members of the Protectorate for a boost of energy or to offset drowsiness following arc travel. Its strength made it a heavily regulated item by the Realm, but that didn't mean those in senior positions couldn't find ways to get it in batches.

Mila narrowed her eyes on me. "If you had both the Corona and the Prospect ambassador up your ass on a daily basis," she said with a shake of her head, "you would need something with a little kick as well."

That sounded like a worthy excuse, so I grinned and nodded dutifully as she turned to Asher.

"Thank you for your quick work compiling the list of possible special committee members," she said to him. "If you check your scroll right now, you'll see that I've boiled the list down to a minister from each dominion, including myself."

I leaned forward. "Have you made a decision about the subordinate representative?" I couldn't help but ask; I felt responsible for the position I had played a role in establishing.

She frowned and set her mug on the table. "Unfortunately, I'm still trying to decide who the sub rep will be," she said, then glanced at Asher. "See if you can pull more detailed backgrounds on the two region councillors I highlighted, Analyst. That should help me make the decision."

Asher nodded and bent over his tablet to make a note.

Mila rested her elbows on the table. "Now for the reason I brought you two in," she said. "The special committee's first meeting will be held here on Prospect Eight two weeks from now, but future meetings will be held on Dignitas One."

Excitement coursed through my veins.

Traveling to Dignitas One would mean I could spend more time with Gannon! Of course, it would also mean boarding an arc craft again. My stomach turned over as my eagerness abated.

Mila looked at me, her features set sternly, but with shades of sympathy. "I know this first arc trip since Septima might be a little traumatic," she said, reading my mind. "Let me know if you'd feel more comfortable traveling with a protector."

"Thank you," I said with a weak smile.

Mila rubbed her hands together, leaning on the table. "I've been asked by the high marshal to give an eyewitness account of the attack on Septima, and I'm happy to do it. Those sick rebel fucks killed Finch, and many others." She looked between the two of us, desire for retribution burning bright in her dark brown eyes. "I've been advised by our ambassador that no matter how much *hurim* I drink to keep my head above water, I'm going to need more help, so he's ordered me to obtain additional support for the special committee." She glanced my way. "More specifically, a director."

I studied her, trying to read between the lines. Was she saying that she wanted Ana to join the team? I frowned, worried that once again I would be ousted from a project I loved because of Ana's seniority, or rather, *my* lack of any significant rank.

Mila thrummed her fingers on the table. "Why is your caste name Metallurgist?" she demanded.

I blinked, surprised by the change in subject. "I guess…" I swallowed, then grasped onto a reason. "I just haven't had a chance to change it yet."

Mila stopped moving her fingers and assessed me with a frown. "Your name doesn't reflect your skill or your profession," she said.

I threw a look at Asher, who appeared as lost as I was.

Suddenly, Mila straightened her back and nodded, as if coming to a decision. "As of today, you're a director," she said.

I nearly fell out of my chair. "P-pardon me?"

"You heard me," she said, nodding as if the more she thought about it, the better her idea seemed. "You've been working on this project since it started, the office respects you and you get things done. Plus, you have your own bloody office, for fuck's sake." She stood up, tugging at the lapels of her black, red-trimmed jacket. "Asher, you'll support Kira until the special committee presents a recommendation to Realm Council."

I figured Asher's wide eyes were a direct reflection of mine.

"Mila, I-I don't know what to say," I said, coming to my feet. "Thank you."

She snorted and picked up her mug. "Don't thank me yet," she said. "In your new role, you'll be supporting the sub rep. Protecting that poor soul from the spiteful tongue of leadership and the harsh scrutiny of the media will have you cursing me to the underworlds in no time."

She strode toward the door but stopped before she quit the room. "And another thing," she said with what looked like a bitter taste in her mouth. "The media have been hounding me for information about the special committee. See if you can find out what they want, and get them off my bloody back."

With that, she left.

Asher and I remained silent for a few moments, staring at the door.

"Would you please explain what in the worlds just happened?" I asked, glancing down to where he still sat.

Asher deactivated his tablet and stood with a grin. "Kira Metallurgist, I believe you just gained seniority."

* * *

"You know, they've written about conditions like yours in medical records," Sela said, folding a tiny floral sweater on her lap. "I thought it was a myth, but it seems you do, in fact, have the gene."

I snorted. "I don't think it's a particular *gene* that gains one seniority."

"Be that as it may," she said, standing up and placing the sweater in an intricately carved chest of drawers, "I think gaining seniority less than a year after leaving Primary Academy qualifies for some sort of medical inquiry."

Since I'd arrived at her house after work an hour or so earlier, Sela and I had been hidden away in her guest room — no, her *nursery*. The space had been transformed into an infant's paradise, with brightly colored furnishings and whimsical art hanging on the walls, ready for her daughter's imminent arrival. Though there were still a few months before Sela would give birth, her in-laws were due to arrive within the next week for an extended visit. As a result, Sela and her partner, Derek, were in full preparation mode.

"So, what do you think?" Sela asked, glancing around the room with a hand on her hip. With her round belly, her floral dress and her auburn hair piled in a messy knot atop her head, she looked more homemaker than medic.

I surveyed the space and decided on "It looks really good."

In truth, I wanted to tease her and say something about the overwhelming amount of pink in the space or the domestic air she was giving off, but Sela was agitated and had been since my arrival. I could tell by the way her eyes avoided mine that it wasn't about her upcoming family visit, either.

I sat down on the small bed Sela had kept in the room for guests and pulled a small pillow onto my lap, watching her work herself up to what she wanted to say.

"I'm sorry Derek and I couldn't be at your aunt's farewell," she said, still puttering around.

"That's all right."

She glanced at me. "Who knew morning sickness could rear its ugly head so terribly more than halfway through pregnancy?"

I grinned. "Aren't *you* supposed to, being a medic and all?"

She smirked. "Yes, well, I must have missed that during my training."

I smiled.

Sela took a deep breath before she came to sit beside me. "I'm happy Tai could be there for you."

I nodded.

"He's been a steady shoulder to lean on during these uncertain times," she added.

"Yes…," I murmured before adding, "Gannon too."

Sela went still even as her gray eyes searched my profile. My shoulders tensed, waiting for the inevitable.

We hadn't spoken of my relationship with Gannon in any detail since before Septima. Sela had been beside herself when she'd learned that I was on the arc craft that was attacked, but with everything that had been going on with my family and at work since then, we hadn't had much of a chance to see each other, much less engage in any meaningful conversation.

"I know that," she said carefully. "But Tai's the one who will stand by you should the truth about your aunt and uncle hiding from the authorities come out."

I glanced up, eyebrows raised, and found her looking at me steadily. I had suspected that Sela knew that my Aunt Marah and her family had been running from the Realm, but I had never sought confirmation, concerned that doing so would only put Sela in an awkward position. Looking at her now, any confirmation I needed was clear in her eyes.

I frowned. "I told you Gannon loves me," I said. Sela made a face of irritation that clawed through me. I gripped her hand. "He *does*, Sela," I said. "You'll just have to trust me."

Gods, I wished I could tell her more — that Gannon had been helping me to protect my family — but I held back for the same reason I didn't tell her about my fugitive aunt. It would mean asking her to deny knowing about Gannon's illicit activities.

Sela sighed. "Kira, our worlds are set up according to strict order, all for advancing our system," she said. "The rules restricting relationships between castes are meant to maintain a balance in roles. You can't exp—"

"I'm *fully* aware of the boundaries and expectations of the Realm," I reminded her.

Sela studied me with the cool detachment of a physician deciding how best to treat a patient. She appeared to think I had become afflicted with some sort of malady.

"Okay," she said finally, extricating her hand from under mine to run her palms down her thighs, in that determined way of hers. "Maybe Gannon's sincere in his feelings for you, but a man in his position? It's only a matter of time before he has to do something that will hurt you and your family, whether intentionally or not."

I rolled my eyes and stood up, tossing the pillow behind me onto the bed. Tai and Rhoan had said something along the same lines. I was getting tired of hearing the same thing in different voices. I approached the window, where I glared at some imaginary target outside, my arms crossed.

"Tai has *always* been there for you," Sela said quietly.

I spun on my heel. "So I should be with him out of gratitude?"

"You *know* that's not what I mean."

"That's what it sounded like."

Sela eyed me, hands gripping the edge of the bed. "Kira, you *love* Tai. You should tell him."

I hated the ache that spread through my chest. "He'll just run the other way," I said, exhaling long and deep.

She sat forward, appearing encouraged for some reason by my response. "Tai loves you too. He won't run. He'll stay if you want him to."

I shook my head, sorry for her. My best friend had no idea how wrong she was.

Sela frowned. "You *do* want him to stay, don't you?"

"It's not a question of whether I want him or not," I said with a sigh.

Sela thinned her lips then glanced down at her hands, a tight knot on her lap. "Have you ever thought," she said slowly, looking up, "that maybe if Gannon wasn't in the picture, Tai would act on his feelings for you?"

I frowned.

Sela shrugged. "I mean, which man would declare himself in love and become vulnerable to a woman who's so obviously caught up with someone else?"

I narrowed my eyes. "This isn't about Gannon, Sela." I couldn't keep the bitterness out of my tone. "Tai's had *five years*."

Sela raised an eyebrow. "I didn't say he was *quick* about it." She quirked her lips. "But he *did* tell you he wants you."

I sighed. "And then in the same breath told me he couldn't — no, *wouldn't* — be with me."

Sela snorted. "Oh, please. So what?" she said with a wave of her hand. "Derek told me we should wait a few years before partnering. I told him good luck finding another woman."

A reluctant smile came to my lips. Yes, I could easily imagine the soft-spoken Derek submitting to an irate Sela. I didn't think making demands would work on Tai, though, considering how poorly my attempt at forcing the issue had gone once already.

Heat rose to my cheeks. "I tried seducing Tai once," I said.

Her gray eyes went wide, filling with sisterly camaraderie.

"Don't get too excited," I said, cutting off her inevitable bombardment of questions. "It was a bad scene. We ended up in yet another argument."

"Well, try again!"

I balked. "All Above, Sela! There's only so much rejection I can take!"

Sela deflated, but only a bit. "A man who doesn't want to be with you wouldn't hang around your family home the entire *three days* of your aunt's farewell."

I crossed my arms. "Tai is dutiful in all things," I murmured. Meanwhile, a spark of something that felt agonizingly close to hope lit inside me. I bit my cheek, tamping it down.

Sela sighed and stood up, searching my face. "I just don't want you investing too much in a relationship with Gannon."

I almost laughed out loud. Good grief — it was *way* too late for that.

"If you won't think of yourself, then think of him," she implored, approaching me. "Gannon's a man on his path toward becoming high chancellor. The actions of your aunt and her family are a liability to him. It can't end well, Kira — not for you *or* for him." When I didn't respond, she gripped my hands. "You didn't answer my question. Do you still want Tai?"

I glanced down at our hands. Sela had been my friend for so long, I couldn't lie to her any more than I could lie to myself. After a deep sigh, I raised my head to look her in the eye.

"Of course, I do," I said, then added, "but I just wish…" I trailed off, not certain how, or whether, to articulate the thought that had just snuck into my head.

Sela cocked her head, eyes narrowed. "Wish what?"

I studied her. This was *Sela*. If there was anyone I could be honest with about my feelings, it was her. "I wish I didn't have to choose," I whispered, wincing as the words came out. "That I could just be with both of them."

Sela shook her head slowly, seemingly forlorn that her best friend had finally lost her mind. "I was wondering when that idea would come up," she muttered with her mouth turned down. "It's a rational thought, Kira, but based on what I know, those two men would never agree to be in a multiple with you, and would you really want that anyway? My gods, you'd be the referee in the middle of a constant battle of wills!"

She was right, of course. I had a hard time imagining Gannon and Tai agreeing on the weather, much less committing to a relationship where they would have to agree on how to share a life with me — not that I was thinking that far along.

Sela eyed me. "Plus, you and Gannon would *still* be in restricted castes," she continued. "What kind of relationship could you truly have if one half of it was hidden from the worlds?"

I frowned. Caste restrictions on relationships hadn't stop my parents from being together, but then, that didn't make the idea of a multiple any more appealing. In fact, when I considered the heartache and deception intercaste restrictions had caused in our lives, the very thought of entering into a similar relationship was unsettling.

Sela gave me a stern look, one she reserved for the delivery of meaningful advice. "Tai just needs to know that you're open to him," she said, holding my gaze, "then he'll come around."

* * *

The apartment I shared with Rhoan had a warm and hazy glow when I returned to it later that evening. That was hardly unusual. The light in the sitting area was dim, the way we normally left it when the space wasn't in use. It was the scent of sweet perfume that made me pause by the door.

Tossing my coat and bag on the nearby bench, I glanced toward Rhoan's room. His door was closed, but that did nothing to block a high-pitched squeal that came from the other side of it.

Oh gods. I checked the time. If I took a hover, I could be back at Sela's in less than half an hour.

I was reaching for my bag when Rhoan's door slid open. He stumbled out, dragging a shirt on, before coming to a stop.

"What are you doing here?" he demanded, disengaging the door behind him. "I told you I'd have someone over."

I cut him a look before striding into the kitchen. "You also told me whoever it is would be gone by now."

"What are you talking about? It's only—" He glanced at the time on the wall-to-wall monitor in the sitting area. "Shit."

"Exactly," I said, selecting a bottle from the cooler. "I have a call soon and I'd rather not have the *sound* that is your lovemaking in the background."

Rhoan shrugged, a smirk on his face. "What can I say? The woman's insatiable."

I groaned and started for my room at the same time as the door to Rhoan's opened, revealing the woman in question. I had to admit, she was certainly my brother's type: curvaceous, tall and redheaded, with a look of all things innocent, bright and sweet.

Rhoan pecked her on the cheek and walked into the kitchen. "Kira, this is Bethany Curator," he said over his shoulder. "Beth, my sister, Kira."

"Hello," I said, noting the way her eyes widened as she looked at me.

Beth approached, her dark blue eyes brimming with excitement. "*I know you,*" she said, pointing a finger at me.

I was *this* close to looking behind me. "You do?"

"I saw a photo of you on the newsfeed today." She tossed one of her reed-thin dreadlocks over a shoulder and turned to my brother, who was now leaning against the kitchen counter with a large quidberry in hand. "Rhoan, you didn't tell me your sister's supporting the subordinate representative on the special committee."

Rhoan raised an eyebrow. "I would have, had I known," he said, then glanced at me before taking a bite. He chewed the fruit with a contemplative frown.

Beth, I realized, must have seen a report sometime after my phone call with a member of the media who had wanted information from Mila. She stared at me now with wonder in her eyes. "It must be so exciting!" She fairly bubbled, crossing her arms under her ample bosom and looking me over with a smile. "How did you get involved in such an incredible project?"

I flushed, uncertain for a moment how to respond. *My father — the senator one, that is — took advantage of the system and managed to get me a position far above my qualifications.* I settled on "With a stroke of luck and some hard work."

Beth grinned. "Well, you're an inspiration and more than a bit modest, I'm sure," she said. "My brother, Heath, would *love* to meet you. He's just starting out as a reporter, but he's on his way up, you know what I mean. Just like you, I suppose."

I smiled, fidgeting with the cap on my drink, as she beamed.

Suddenly, her comm sounded, thankfully releasing me from her wide-eyed regard. With a gasp, she glanced at her device. "I guess I should get going," she said, pouting in my brother's direction.

After Beth had collected her things and donned her coat, she and Rhoan said their goodbyes with a lusty kiss. He disengaged the door and returned to the kitchen, where I had been drinking my fruit beverage.

"You should be proud," I said, grinning. "This one seems to be a natural redhead." I enjoyed reminding my brother whenever I could of his love for redheads and his inability to spot a true one from one created by cosmetic optic.

Rhoan snorted and leaned against the doorjamb. "So I would have expected a more senior person to be supporting the sub rep," he said, crossing his arms.

I straightened. "They *do* have a more senior person," I said, then paused for effect, my grin broadening within the silence. "You're looking at Prospect Eight's newest director."

Rhoan drew back, pride and wonder overcoming his cynical expression. "Halls, Kira," he said, looking me over. "It's a wonder you haven't become *my* superior yet."

I laughed then brushed past him to go to my room. Gannon would be calling soon, and I had a manual about my responsibilities as a director, filled an intimidating amount of content, that I needed to read through before then.

"Let's just hope they don't appoint me as sub rep," he said, stopping me in my tracks. I turned to face him. "The last thing we need is to be living *and* working together."

I stared at him. "You're kidding."

He shrugged. "I've been shortlisted for the position."

I gasped and was about to launch into an excited round of congratulations and hugs when I noticed his expression. This was great news, a major step in Rhoan's career, but he appeared less than enthusiastic. In fact, he seemed downright annoyed.

I frowned. "You don't want the role?"

He twisted his lips with a heavy sigh. "I don't really have a choice," he said. "My superior told me that the role's going to either me or another region councillor. I suppose the reward for good work and a stellar reputation is becoming a part of this shit show."

His disdain for the position stung. "I worked hard to help give the Subordinate caste a voice on the special committee," I said.

I knew, though, that despite the fact that Rhoan was well regarded by his peers in governance, he was a skeptic of any form of authority, especially Realm leadership. And considering how they had tried to expel members of our family, I couldn't blame him. Still, I had figured Rhoan would appreciate the chance they were giving our caste to take part in a high-level project such as the special committee on exploration, the very first of its kind.

Rhoan immediately appeared contrite. "I'm sorry," he said, pushing away from the doorjamb. "Don't get me wrong. The role's important and all — I just don't think I or any other subordinate is going to actually be heard. I just don't know how comfortable I am with being nothing more than a token."

He was only speaking the truth. I knew for a fact *that* was exactly why Realm Council had agreed to having a subordinate play a role. With the factions mostly filled with citizens from my caste, giving us a voice was a way to ease rising tensions. But this truth didn't negate the fact that how the sub rep performed would set a precedent for our fellow caste members' future involvement. Perhaps there was another reason he was hesitant to be a part of the process?

I stepped toward him, a flicker of uncertainty pinching the muscles around my neck. "Do you think it would be a problem, you and I both working on the special committee?" I asked.

Being part of the special committee *would* bring a lot of attention to Rhoan and me, it was true — attention we didn't need considering the unlawful activities of our family.

Rhoan ran a hand through his curly hair. "Tai said that the Realm wouldn't be so interested in our family now," he said with a sigh. "The last thing I want to do is reach out to that asshole, but I'm going to give him call just to be sure."

The false sense of security I hadn't realized I had been holding onto fell away.

Ping.

I glanced at my comm, expecting a message from Gannon. The smile that was growing on my mouth fell away.

Two days.

I frowned and tapped at the device, looking for sender identification.

"What's wrong?" Rhoan asked.

"Nothing," I mumbled, shaking my head. "I just received an odd message."

He stepped toward me. "What does it say?"

I showed him the device.

Rhoan shrugged. "Looks like an event notification." He ambled off to the sitting area.

I would have agreed with him, but the only event I had scheduled within that timeframe was Gannon's visit to Prospect, and I hadn't set a reminder. Dear gods, I *needed* no reminder for that.

I swiped through the device again, determined to figure out what was going on. My comm was my primary means of communication with Gannon. If it was about to break down, I would need to take care of it, and quickly.

"So are you going to change your caste name now?" Rhoan asked.

I blinked at his question and glanced up to find him sitting on the couch, browsing through video options on the monitor.

Having gained seniority, a caste name change was expected of me. I should have been happy to release the one I had for the mere fact that it was a reminder of the lies I had been told by my parents. If I'd used my biological father's caste name, I'd have been going by Solicitor for the past twenty-one years. But I couldn't quite see myself with that caste name, much less Director.

"The grace period restarts now that I've gained seniority," I said with a shrug. "I still have time."

CHAPTER THREE

Five weeks, three days and — until twenty minutes ago — eighteen hours.

That was how long it had been since Gannon and I had been in the same room. The need to be with him had been so strong, I could taste it on my tongue. He had said he would come, but some part of me expected him to send a message apologizing for some urgent matter that would take precedence over our need to be together. Instead, as promised, two days later, Talib picked me from the Judiciary and took me to Gannon's private residence nearby.

I strolled the perimeter of his sitting area, enjoying the scent and feel of him that lingered in the familiar surroundings as Talib droned on.

"You have a number of meetings on Dignitas before and after you meet with the ambassador tomorrow," Talib said, standing in the middle of the room, tablet in hand. "This will make movement between dominions complicated, so I'll be speaking with Arthur about security at each location."

"Good," Gannon murmured with arms crossed. Though his body was turned to face Talib, his eyes were fixed on me, and had been since I had arrived. He narrowed them, but not enough to prevent me from seeing a flash of impatience.

I smothered a smile.

"Your father has asked to meet with you following his visit to Hale Three," Talib continued, still looking at his device. "He plans to issue a report about the way trade is being impacted by the recent rise in violence in Tork and wants to run it by you first."

"That's fine," Gannon said, still tracking my steps but now with a clenched jaw.

I sauntered over to a desk in the far corner. It was an ornate, antique-looking construction, covered in sheaves of paper and two tablets, one flat, the other rolled up into its portable scroll form. A glass bottle filled with what looked like water sat atop it as well. I ran my fingers along the edge of the desk, looking over my shoulder at Gannon. He threw a pointed glance in Talib's direction before rolling his eyes, and I couldn't help the laugh that slipped out. I tried to bury it by covering my mouth with my thick silk scarf, but it was still loud enough to be heard. Thankfully, the protector was more engrossed in his duties than in the rising need between Gannon and me.

The moment Talib had ushered me through the front door, Gannon had enveloped me in a passionate embrace. We gripped each other so tightly, tears came to my eyes. It was overwhelming to again be in his arms. But when he started laying kisses across my face, I had to draw on a deep well of strength to pull away. Talib was incredibly loyal to Gannon, but flaunting our clandestine relationship in the protector's face didn't seem the wisest or most respectful thing to do. With a sullen expression, Gannon had held back, allowing Talib to go through the motions of his expected end-of-day report. Since then, a hungry anticipation had risen fast and thick in the room. Talib, though, for all his attention to detail and all his superior's terse replies, seemed completely oblivious to what was happening.

"You also have a meeting with Thaddeus Centurion," Talib continued in the neutral, clipped tone of his caste. "The high marshal and all members of the investigative committee have been confirmed, so we'll escort you to the meeting once its location has been determined."

I raised my head at the mention of the Protectorate caste's leader and found Gannon's eyes still on me, his eyes becoming more hooded as the seconds passed by. Enough was enough.

I turned to the desk. Rather than opt for liquor, I reached for the water bottle and filled a glass. Then I faced Gannon, rested a hip against the desk and licked the rim of the glass slowly as I held his gaze. It took everything I had to keep a straight face at his reaction.

Gannon's eyes flared with heat a moment before he cleared his throat. "That'll be all, Talib," he said, striding toward the front door.

The protector frowned and gestured to his tablet. "Chancellor, your father has also ask —"

"Talib," Gannon said firmly, drawing the other man's full attention. "Anything pertaining to my father can *certainly* wait until tomorrow." He raised an eyebrow, shooting a glance at me.

Talib looked my way then back at his superior as understanding loosened the knot between his brows. "Of course," he said before meeting Gannon at the door.

I struggled with guilt — not because I was filled with it, but because I lacked it. The need to get my hands on Gannon was all-encompassing.

After a final parting word to Gannon, Talib made a quick exit. The moment the door slid closed, I put the glass back on the desk and started unbuttoning my jacket.

"He's one of my most trusted confidants," Gannon said, his legs eating up the short distance between us, "but a greater cock blocker I've never known."

I laughed as Gannon tugged my jacket down my arms and threw it on the ground before tackling the clasp at the waist of my skirt. "And you're no help," he said, eyes focused on his task, "teasing me like that."

I smiled as innocently as I could. "I didn't do anything," I said, pulling at the buttons of his jacket.

He leveled me with a look. "You couldn't be more obvious in your seduction."

"Is that right?" I said, wriggling out of my skirt and unwinding the scarf from around my neck. I shrugged. "Well, I don't think it matters. I was successful."

He snorted. "You could have simply stood there and you would have been a success," he said, removing his jacket and tossing it and my own clothing somewhere behind me, into the middle of the room.

"Remove those," he said, gesturing to my boots with his chin.

I nodded, already pulling at them, prepared to do whatever he wanted if it meant he'd act on the hungry look in his face. By the time I'd kicked my shoes and leggings off, he was on me again, wrapping his arms around me as we surrendered to each other's kisses.

After a few moments I pulled away, needing both air and the sensation of my naked body against his. I tore out of my sweater and it too found a home somewhere on the floor. I was reaching for Gannon's belt buckle when I caught the look in his eyes. Lust, love and everything in between flared hotly within them, and I flushed, surely matching the level of heat I saw there.

He stepped back and ran his eyes over me in my half-naked state. My heart raced as I took in his reaction to the sheer, blush-colored lace lingerie that I had bought just for today, this very moment when we'd be together again.

I took a deep breath. "Do you like it?" I asked, simply because I wanted to hear him say so.

Gannon raised a hand and trailed a path with his fingers across the top of my bra, between my breasts then down to my waist. He swallowed thickly and nodded, and glanced up at me, unadulterated need in his eyes.

"You look beautiful," he said, and I smiled, thoroughly pleased that he'd said I looked as wonderful as I felt.

I expected him to ravish me, but instead he backed away, eyes glittering as he walked to the middle of the room, where he began yanking cushions from the large leather couch and dropping them on the floor. It took me a moment, but I soon understood what he was doing.

I hurried over and laid the cushions in front of the fireplace, where the flame crackled quietly and casted a warm glow into the dimness of the room. I was making a space for myself in the center of the pile of cushions when Gannon stood over me, desire etched in every line of his face. Then the gods answered my prayers, and he began removing the rest of his clothing. When he was done, he grinned, and I realized then just how much he knew I had enjoyed the show.

I fell back onto the cushions, laughing. "You're lucky your arrogance isn't unfounded, senator," I said, watching him bend down and crawl over me. "Otherwise, you'd be incredibly obnoxious."

He was on all fours, looking down at me, when he said, "The day I don't hear my name associated with the word 'arrogant' is the day I know the apocalypse is near." He smirked, nowhere near ashamed of himself.

I frowned, not liking the way he shrugged off the reputation but rather perpetuated it. "I wish you would stop giving people that impression."

"Why?" he asked, smirk still in place. "Arrogance is my one defining trait."

I brushed strands of dark blond hair away from his face and held them back with my palms on the sides of his face. "You're much more than arrogant, Gannon."

He dipped his head and lowered his mouth to mine. "With *you* I am," he said against my lips.

I smiled, warmth suffusing my body, and wrapped my arms around his neck, deepening our kiss. After a moment in which we luxuriated in the taste of each other, he pulled away.

"I want you on top," he declared, shifting down my legs.

I blinked as he gripped my poor excuse for panties and began dragging them down my hips. Gannon was a man who needed control and during lovemaking. I enjoyed that as much as he did, so hearing him give up a position of power surprised me even more.

"Are you sure?"

He chuckled, flinging my underwear over his shoulder. "Yes, I'm quite sure that I want to fuck you."

I made a face. "No…I mean…"

He sobered. "What is it?"

"I thought you liked — needed — to be, you know, dominant." I really shouldn't have flushed, but good gods, I couldn't help it.

He cocked his head. "I do."

I sighed. He had challenged me to do something similar in the past and I didn't want to repeat the lackluster result. "Then I don't think this is going to work."

Gannon rolled his eyes before shifting beneath me and gripped my hips, repositioned them directly above him, then thrust inside me. I gasped at how far he reached when I sank down on him.

Oh. So silly of me to think that me being on top meant he would relinquish control!

He smirked, apparently reading my mind. When he sank his fingers into my thighs, I followed his wordless command and bore down, allowing the weight of my body to drive him even deeper inside me. It felt like years, not weeks, since we had been like this, and my sex responded eagerly, softening, readying itself for more.

Gannon ran his hands up my back then unlatched the clasp of my bra. After stripping me of the flimsy material, he cupped my breasts, appearing fascinated with weighing them and molding their full shapes.

"Halls, I love your breasts," he murmured more to himself than me before smoothing his palms around my back and down to my behind. "And don't get me started on your ass."

I feigned indignation. "I knew you only wanted me for my body."

His blue eyes widened, filled with exaggerated appreciation. "And my gods what a body it is!"

I made a face and swatted him on the shoulder.

With a laugh, he flipped me over and started a lazy path of kisses down my belly. I knew where he was headed, and my heart skipped a beat in anticipation. I raised my hips, trying to hurry him along, but he held me with a firm grip, a bite of pain lighting up my skin as his fingers dug in. He rested between my legs and began playing between the folds of my sex, his fingers grazing the hard nub of my clit.

"I've been thinking about a lot of things since Septima," he said, still fondling me.

I angled my hips, trying to give him access to more of me without seeming too obvious about it. The last time I had tried to force his hand, I'd earned a swift and stinging slap on my hip.

"Almost losing you made me realize that, while we have our roles to play," he continued, sliding two fingers deep inside me, "we can't let them dictate who we choose to be with."

I gripped the cushion beneath me, my need for him spreading a painful ache through me. I whimpered, writhing against his hand as he stroked a spot inside that had the walls of my sex grasping at his fingers.

"I want you to know that you're everything to me," he said.

I groaned, reaching down to fist a handful of his hair. "Gannon, those are the most beautiful words I've ever heard, and much later — perhaps when I'm alone and pining for you — I'll think on them fondly, but right now, I *really* need you to fuck me!"

He smirked, a twinkle in his eyes. "Now who's after someone's body?"

I dropped my hand and exhaled. "Actually, right now, all I need is your cock."

"Well," he said, becoming predatory again. "I can certainly accommodate that."

Gannon climbed up the length of me and gripped my thigh. His gentle tug told me that he wanted me to turn over. When I did, he slid his hands up to my waist then, a moment later, positioned a pillow resting by my side under my hips, tilting me up to him, as he settled himself closer between my legs. My pulse leapt when he suddenly shoved into me and began fucking into me with sharp, tight thrusts.

Soon, Gannon and I were panting from the passion and force of the need between us. The sound and feel of him behind me filled me with a new sense of urgency, and I pushed back, meeting each of his thrusts, demanding more even as he filled me completely.

"Fuck," he groaned, driving into me and taking up my challenge.

Gannon shifted and recommitted to his torturous assault, pummeling into me. I moaned, enjoying his demanding touch as he slid a hand up my back, applying increasing pressure until it ended high up between my shoulders where he wrapped his fingers around the back of my neck. I should have felt vulnerable, but the power and control he had over me, in the throes of his passion, only empowered me.

Gods, I was already so close, but for some reason I hung at the precipice, waiting for something. Arching my back, I cried out his name, shocked by how hoarse and desperate my voice sounded. I didn't know what I was begging for, but I knew he had it.

After a few insistent strokes, Gannon leaned down, bringing his mouth to my ear, and whispered the word I needed to hear.

"Come for me, *lahra*."

My eyes widened at the power of the orgasm that gripped my body. My sex clenched hard as I hurtled over the edge and came in a blinding rush, groaning my release into the cushion. Gannon growled as I tightened around him, and the sensation of his cock dragging through the thick, aroused walls of my sex sent me spiraling into another orgasm.

I was still floating, coming back to earth, when he eased away from me and slid a hand down to my waist. He tugged, urging me to turn over. With muscles trembling from climax, I rolled onto my back, and closed my eyelids, too sluggish to keep them open, as he pressed into me again.

"Open your eyes," he demanded.

Sighing, I opened them and watched him drive into me over and over until a few beads of his sweat fell onto my chest. I ran my forefinger through the drops on my breast and left a wet path around the nipple. Gannon's eyes narrowed almost desperately on my movements. When I brought the finger to my lips and sucked it, he closed his eyes and quickened his thrusts between my legs, his cock swelling even larger inside me. Suddenly, he shouted out and rutted into me as he came long and hard. I watched, wide-eyed, as he gave everything he had to me.

Gannon kissed me hard before lowering himself with unsteady movements to my chest. I wrapped my arms around his sweat-slick shoulders and enjoyed the feel of our skin melding and the sound of our ragged breaths. After a while, Gannon eased to his side, no doubt remembering my need to breathe. I smiled, realizing that I would rather have the comfort of his weight than satisfy the need for air any day. He looked down at me, and we simply stared at one another.

Already, I was starting to miss him.

He was scheduled to leave the next day. I squashed the thought and turned my mind to the exciting news I wanted to share with him but had held back, thrilled by the idea of telling him face to face instead.

"Guess what," I said, toying with his hair.

"Hmm," he said, pressing kisses into my neck.

"Mila appointed me a director."

Gannon raised his head. Pride filled his eyes, making them shine bright even in the flickering light of the fireplace.

"And…," I continued, "my first duty is supporting the subordinate representative on the special committee…who could be my brother."

He raised an eyebrow. "Your brother?"

Heat filled my cheeks as I nodded.

Gannon grinned, pressing his pelvis into me. "Aren't you happy now that I got rid of that prick?"

I chuckled. "Prick" was certainly one way to describe my former superior, Gabriel Minister. When I had told Gannon and Tai that Gabriel had assaulted me after accusing me of being a manipulative whore bent on taking over the Judiciary, they had wasted little time exacting revenge and arranged to have him beaten up and dismissed from his position. It was what Gabriel deserved, but I tried not to think of how much they had risked by using their rank to defend me.

I drew back, just then registering what Gannon had said. "Are you trying to say that I gained seniority thanks to you?"

He planted a kiss firmly on my mouth, softening the tension there. "No," he said. "Anybody with good sense can see how incredible you are. It's only a matter of time before you've gained rank on me." He winked.

I shook my head, laughing, and we indulged in a kiss for a blissfully long while. Finally, we came up for air.

"Why are you—?" I cut myself off. I had such a short amount of time with him, I didn't want to ruin the mood. "Never mind," I said, raking his hair away from his face.

He held my wrist. "You can ask me anything."

I considered that, then asked, "Why do you have to meet with the high marshal? Talib said you have a meeting with him."

He inhaled deeply and pushed back and up into a seated position between my thighs. He reached for my hands, pulling me toward him so we were face to face, my legs wrapped around his waist. "I'm working with him on the investigation to identify those responsible for the attack on Septima."

I took in the pinched lines around his mouth. "You didn't want me to know?" I asked, reading the uneasiness in his expression.

Gannon shook his head. "It's possible that I'll have to visit some violent locations." He ran his hands up and down my back. "You're already worried about me as it is. I didn't want to give you more reason to be."

I swallowed back a selfish demand that he not become involved. Gannon had a life to lead, a large one that didn't, *couldn't*, involve me. I wouldn't try to dictate his every move, no matter how much I wanted to.

"The Corona and your father must think quite highly of you to ask for your participation," I said with a tight smile, willing my anxiety away.

"They didn't ask. I petitioned for it." The blue in his eyes darkened. "This isn't technically in my jurisdiction. I just feel like I have to *do* something. I won't allow rebels to hurt innocent people."

My hand trembled as I ran fingers across his brow. "It's a complicated matter, though, isn't it?" I said. "The factions haven't formed without reason. They're retaliating against Argon's expulsion for going against a ban on exploration that they think should be lifted."

His eyes narrowed. "They almost killed you and my father, Kira," he said. "They *did* kill your aunt. Anyone who played a role helping the factions should be brought to justice."

I stared at him, eyes wide, not knowing what to say. What *could* I say? There I was, the daughter of a man who was supporting the very people he was arguing against.

He thrust his hands into my hair, cradling the back of my head and bringing me close. "Don't worry, *lahra*," he said, his breath hot on my lips. "I'll be all right."

He had misread the look on my face for fear when it was guilt that wound through me.

I swallowed to loosen my tongue. "Is this why you're not leading the special committee?"

Gannon had been overseeing the task force to establish the special committee, so, to my mind, it would have made sense for him to continue. Instead, the high chancellor had been appointed to manage it.

"I was always supposed to hand the committee over to my father," he said with a shrug. "I do the grunt work. He takes the glory." Gannon grinned, and I knew his flippant quip was meant to lessen the tension between us. He lowered his hands to hold my own. "Though I do have him to thank this time around. Because he agreed to handle affairs on Hale, I'm here with you now."

I laughed. "I'm not sure your father would have been so accommodating if he knew the true reason you wanted to duck out of your duties."

"He's a smart man. I'm sure he has his suspicions." Gannon's head was bowed now, looking at our joined hands, so I couldn't see his expression. All of a sudden, he tightened his hold and glanced up, his blue eyes glimmering. "I have something for you."

I raised my eyebrows as he leaned over to reach around me to his jacket. He rustled there, inside a pocket.

"Close your eyes and open your hand," he said, returning to me.

I did so without hesitation, then waited for what felt like an eternity. Nothing happened. "Are you still there?" I whispered with a smile.

Gannon chuckled, but it sounded off, coming out short and tight. He drew in a ragged breath, and something small and light tumbled into the middle of my hand.

"Open your eyes."

When I did, a torrent of emotions and words rushed forward, but none was definable enough to express. Instead of trying to put thought into words, I blinked and just stared at the sparkling ring resting in my palm.

It was the finest piece of jewelry I had ever seen, and probably the finest I would ever know in my lifetime. Large round-cut stones, which must have been diamonds, given their clarity and the brilliance of their shine, sat in an intricate pattern that swirled around a delicate rose gold band. My hand started to shake, causing the dim light around us to bounce sharply off the edges of the gems.

I wrapped my fingers around the ring and held it to my chest, looking at Gannon. "Why are you giving me this?"

Gannon's eyes fell to my clenched fist then rose to meet my gaze. "My father gave it to my mother when they married, which they only did to appease traditional Septima leadership after he became high chancellor."

My eyes widened. *All above!*

"You're giving me your mother's *wedding* ring?" My breathing became shallow, making me light-headed. I knew the sensation wasn't a sign of one of my panic attacks, but it felt very close to it.

"She's never worn it." He studied me. "It's part of my inheritance."

I stared at him. "It's a *wedding* ring!"

"It represents my commitment to you." He hesitated. "We can call it a promise ring, if you prefer."

My pulse slowed a bit, but when he spoke next, my heart galloped again.

"I expect you to wear it at all times."

"Gannon, you can't be serious!"

"I'm nothing but."

"I can't accept this, much less *wear* it."

He scowled. "Why not?"

"For one, I would have a hard time explaining how I came to own such a piece of jewelry."

"Say your long-lost relative gave it to you."

I laughed. "Anyone who is even *remotely* familiar with me knows there is no such wealth lurking within my family."

He raised an eyebrow. "Is that so?"

My smile slipped at his reminder of my recently discovered lineage.

He brushed the back of his fingers along my jaw. "I want you to have something that reminds you of how much you mean to me."

"I don't *need* to be reminded."

"Halls, Kira!" he cursed, dropping his hand. "Give me this one thing!"

I lowered my gaze with a sigh, opening my palm to look at the ring again. It shone bright even in the day's fading light. As much as I wanted to deny him for a number of selfless reasons, I couldn't for all the selfish ones. After a long moment, I looked at him with a wobbly smile.

"All right," I said. I would wear it on my hand when with him, and on a necklace beneath my clothing otherwise.

A look of pure satisfaction swept across his face. He immediately plucked the ring from my palm and took my left hand. When he slid the ring onto my fourth finger, we stared at it, watching it glimmer against the warm complexion of my skin.

I chewed a corner of my lip, still looking at the jewelry. "How did you know it would fit?" I whispered, irrationally worried that a loud voice would disturb the reverence of the moment.

"I measured your finger while you slept on Septima."

I must have been sleeping like the dead because I hadn't felt a thing. I shook my head, glancing up. "You are a cunning man, Gannon Consul."

He smiled, making no attempt to argue with the truth. "I love you," he said.

The sincerity and depth of emotion in his eyes did more to melt my heart than the words he spoke. I wrapped my arms around his neck, burying my face into the warm space between his jaw and shoulder.

"Thank you, Gannon."

When there was no response, I steeled myself and pulled away to meet his eyes. Instead of anger or disappointment at my reticence to return his sentiments, I found resignation lying there. It was the worst of all possible emotions. Tears filled my eyes.

"Don't," he said, wiping away a tear. "You're mine. That's all that matters."

* * *

The coolness of the sheets woke me later that night. I reached across the bed, eyelids closed, feeling nothing but a dip in the mattress and an unwelcome lack of heat. A clattering drew my attention to the bathroom door. When a shadow moved past it, I lifted my head, looking through sleep-drunk eyes.

After Gannon had given me the ring, I had made a show of it, tilting my hand to and fro to make sparkling patterns dance across the ceiling and walls. Once the light became too faint to see the ring's reflections, we went up to his bedroom to entertain ourselves with kisses and caresses that ended up in urgent lovemaking. I had fallen asleep with my cheek on his chest, feeling the steady rise and fall of his breath.

That felt like it had been only an hour ago, but I blinked at the monitor at the other end of the room, surprised to see that it was already very early morning.

"Gannon?" I rolled to my side, shoving hair out of my face. I should have tied it in a bun before falling asleep. I would pay for my negligence with a tangled head.

I called out for Gannon again. "Do you need a lapse kit?" I asked. A sleep aid had to be the reason he would be rummaging around what was still effectively the middle of the night.

Suddenly, Gannon staggered out of the bathroom with a duffel bag in hand. His face was pale, eyes wide and unfocused.

I shot up into a seated position as he propped himself against the doorjamb. Ice filled my veins. "What's wrong?"

He shook his head as if trying to organize his thoughts. "There's been an accident…My father…"

I scrambled out of the bed, wrapping the sheet around my naked body. "What happened? Is he all right?"

"I don't know." Gannon shoved away from the doorjamb and rifled through his chest of drawers. After placing a few items I couldn't see into the bag, he pulled out a wool shirt and pants then began struggling into both. "There's an arc craft leaving for Dignitas in less than an hour."

"Of course," I breathed, clasping my hands around the sheet and holding it at my breasts. "I understand that you have to go."

He glanced at me then reached for my sweater and skirt, which lay atop the chest of drawers. He handed my clothing to me, and I took it reflexively.

"Talib's on his way to take us to the station." Gannon ran an unsteady hand up my arm before pulling more items from a drawer and packing them in his bag.

He must have spoken in error, I thought. More than likely his mind was so muddled by worry for his father that he wasn't thinking straight. I sat on the edge of the bed, holding the clothes in my lap. The cool air in the room brushed my bare shoulders and I shivered.

A moment later, Gannon stilled, then turned to me. "Why aren't you getting dressed?"

I frowned. "Why would I?"

"Because you're coming with me."

I stared at him. "No, I'm not."

He approached the bed, alarm drowning out the worry that had filled his face. "Why?"

I searched for words that would explain the obvious. "This is a time for you and your family, Gannon," I said, shaking my head. "I can't go."

"You can, and you will."

A puff of air slipped out of my mouth. "How would we explain my being there?"

"We wouldn't *explain* anything," he said through clenched teeth, eyes narrowing. "Did last night mean nothing to you?"

I searched his face, shocked into silence. I had promised to wear his ring, but he had to know that that this wouldn't change the worlds we lived in.

The sound of the front door opening and closing downstairs, followed by heavy footfalls, signaled Talib's arrival. I shook out my sweater and skirt and hurried to put them on. As I did, I studied Gannon, who watched me with confusion on his face. It was clear he wasn't thinking straight; I would have to walk him through this.

"Gannon," I ventured, standing in front of him, now dressed, "just a week ago you told me the reasons you couldn't come to my aunt's farewell. Those same reasons apply now."

A shuffle of footsteps slowed at the door. "Gann—" Talib drew up, seeing me, and cleared his throat. "Chancellor, are you ready?"

Gannon nodded. "We both are." His body stiffened. "How's my father?"

The protector's expression shut down, shifting in a flash from impatient to guarded. "They won't say until you arrive on Dignitas," he replied.

Gannon clenched his fists so hard they began to shake. Not caring about Talib being in the room, I wrapped myself around Gannon, holding him close as tears welled my eyes. For a long moment, Gannon stood stiffly within the circle of my embrace, allowing me to comfort him. Suddenly, he shrugged out of my hold and gripped the top of my shoulders.

"Come with me!" A light sheen glossed his eyes.

My heart squeezed so hard, I was sure it would stop. I glanced beseechingly at Talib. He would understand, maybe more than Gannon. Perhaps *he* could convince Gannon that my going with him was a bad idea.

Talib stepped forward. "It would only reflect badly on her," he said with a frown. "They'll know the reason you weren't in Tork was so you could be with her."

Gannon tensed, the faint lines around his eyes pinching together. After a heavy beat of silence, he released me then turned to collect his bag. I watched him, arms wrapped about my waist, as he handed it to Talib and came back to me.

"I'll message you once I know more," he said. "I'll have Jonah take you home when you're ready."

I nodded readily, eager to have him know it was all right for him to leave me to take care of his family.

Gannon gave me another kiss, this one swift and hard, then left the room with Talib.

My heart pounded painfully as I listened to them go out the front door. After activating the monitor on the opposite side of the room, I hurried over to the bed, where I sat cross-legged in the middle and allowed my mind to dive into frantic tailspin. To keep my sanity, I calculated the time.

It would take him twenty minutes to get to the nearest arc station, then another ten to pass through security. That would be followed by an hour in flight, and possibly another thirty minutes to disembark. I wasn't sure where his father's residence was on Dignitas One, but as he was a Realm councillor, it couldn't be very far. Nevertheless, I gave that trip a generous thirty minutes.

I removed my comm from my wrist, opting to hold it like a life source in one hand. As I watched the stream of updates on the newsfeed, I unraveled a knot in my hair. News had broken that the high chancellor had been hurt en route with his delegation to meet with local ministers. There was no definitive word on his condition.

I knew my calculations were right when just under three hours passed and the newsfeed reported Gannon's arrival at his family residence.

Ping.

I almost dropped the comm in my haste to activate it.

"Gannon?"

"Good," Tai said. "He's not with you." A door slid shut, silencing the surrounding chatter and commotion in his background.

I frowned. "Tai?"

"Have you heard?"

"About Gannon's father? Yes."

"Where are you?"

I hesitated. "I'm at Gannon's."

A pause.

"So he's on Prospect?" he asked.

"No, he left," I said, shaking my head, even though he couldn't see me. "Tai, I need to keep this line open for Gann—"

"It makes sense now," Tai said, but it sounded like he was speaking to himself. "The official itinerary says Gannon should have been in Tork, so it threw the Protectorate for a fucking loop when they didn't identify him among the bodies."

My stomach turned in on itself. *Oh gods!*

I shifted on the bed, sitting on bent knees. "The bodies?"

"The media are already looking for a reaction from his family and will more than likely go by Gannon's residence there," Tai said. "You need to leave. I don't want you caught in the middle of this."

"In the middle of what?"

Tai hesitated. "Kira, what did Gannon tell you about his father?"

"Nothing," I snapped, becoming impatient. "He *knew* nothing. Gannon said there was an accident. Talib said they wouldn't tell him anything until he returned to Diginitas."

Silence.

My heart clogged my throat. "Damn it, Tai! Tell me what happened to Gannon's father!"

He cursed. "He's dead, Kira," he said. "The high chancellor was killed last night on Hale, by rebels."

CHAPTER FOUR

In a hall in Prospect Seven, Mila gripped the sides of a podium. On the full-wall monitor in our Judiciary's media room, where my peers and I had assembled, she appeared larger than life. "Death is spreading like some wretched disease," she said.

I clasped my hands, pressing them against into my waist and trying to hide their constant tremor from colleagues sitting close by. Still, Asher kept darting anxious glances at me.

Days after news had broken about the murder of the high chancellor and his entourage, work across all Judiciaries in the Realm remained at a standstill, with everyone glued to the newsfeed, trying to make sense of what had happened. Attempting to alleviate the tension and uncertainty, Mila had called for everyone in the Judiciaries of her world and ours to assemble, so that she could say a few words.

She continued: "Between the recent attacks on Septima and now this on Hale, the Realm has taken terrible blows at the hands of rebels whose sole goal is to destroy everything our system was built on.

"I echo our sovereign's sentiments in her remarks yesterday. The Realm's achievements and progress are grounded in our ability to thrive *despite* adversity." Mila paused, shaking her head, mouth turned down. "High Chancellor Marcus Consul was a fearless, fair and revered leader who will be greatly missed by his peers and, most especially, by his family. But the reality is we must go on. We're made stronger by moments like this. Lean on the words in our system's motto: Strength, Resolve, Adherence." Her face tightened as she sighed. "I always do."

Murmurs filled the room as the transmission switched from Mila to a newsfeed that was looping reports about the high chancellor's death.

I turned away and took in a shuddering breath as Asher eyed me.

Simeon Administrator, sitting behind me, leaned forward in his seat. "There were no survivors," he said in a low voice as he stared with wide eyes over my shoulder at the screen. My stomach heaved at the thought of looking at the footage one more time.

"It's so strange," Andres Proctor said, shifting in his chair in front of me and pointing at the screen. "That airspace is monitored and limited to official transportation. No one but authorized persons should even be there, much less *know* that the high chancellor and his party would be traveling through the area."

I risked a glance at the monitor. The newsfeed switched from an aerial view of the wreckage to a reporter on the scene. He trampled over the debris while speculating on the final moments of Gannon's father's life.

There was only so much I could take.

I jumped up and skirted around the back of Asher's chair, causing him to jostle forward. With a hasty apology, I rushed out, praying I would make it to my office without breaking down. Asher called my name from somewhere behind me, but I was seconds away; if I stopped now, I would only make a bigger scene and raise questions that I couldn't answer. As soon as I passed through my door, I disengaged it and let everything go.

Sobs so thick they cut off my breathing rose up to the surface in heavy waves. I couldn't hold them back and I didn't want to. I'd been holding them at bay all morning, all the past few days; acting as if the high chancellor's death was nothing more than the unfortunate loss of an official leader was taking its toll.

I staggered to my desk and clutched the edge of it, trying to breathe around my gasps.

A light rap at the door was accompanied a voice laced with concern. "Kira?"

I sniffled and swiped at my cheeks with the back of my shaking hands before going to disengage the door. On the other side of it, Asher's brown eyes were so full of sympathy for me that my lips started to tremble.

He stepped in quickly and, after the door slid shut, wrapped an arm around my shoulders. "Is there anything I can do?" he asked, leading me back toward my desk.

I shook my head, leaning into him.

He frowned. "Why are you even here? Maybe you should go home."

"No," I said through a mouthful of tears. "I'll just go insane watching the newsfeed and waiting for Gannon to call."

He paused then asked with a wince, "How's he doing?"

I pressed a fist to my mouth, looking off somewhere to his side as I succumbed to another fit of tears.

When I had finally spoke to Gannon, hours after Tai had relayed the news, he'd sounded like a hollow version of himself. I spent the first half of our call crying while he sat silent on the other end. His silence only made me sob even harder, because in it I sensed the depth of his grief. When he did speak, it was to tell me that his family had wanted to get the news to him before the media got wind of it. Apparently, they had been frantic over his whereabouts for a few dreadful hours.

"I'm so sorry, Kira," Asher said now, his face grim.

For a long while, he simply stood at my side, arm firmly around me, as I cried long and hard. I felt for the ring Gannon had given me. It rested just below my throat, hidden behind my blouse.

When my sobs abated, Asher sighed, releasing me. "Look," he said. "Nobody's going to do much work around here today. A group of us were going to head out for something to eat. Do you want to come? It might be a good idea to get some air."

I thought about it, but all I really wanted to do was hide from the worlds. Every time I thought about the high chancellor's death, a war of emotions began to rage inside me. There was a deep sense of guilt from knowing *I* was the reason Gannon hadn't gone to Tork, and an overwhelming thankfulness that it wasn't him who was killed. Underlying all of that, I carried Gannon's grief as my own.

Asher shifted his feet. "I'll understand if you don't want to go."

"N-no," I said, sniffling myself into shape. I needed to be around people or I'd just continue to fall apart. "I just…needed a minute."

"Okay," Asher said, bobbing his head. After a moment, he reached into his back pocket and pulled out a scrap of white material. "Here."

I took it before realizing what it was. A wobbly smile came to my mouth. "You carry a *handkerchief*, Asher?"

He shrugged then puffed out his chest. "You never know when there'll be a damsel in distress."

I snorted. "Yes," I said drolly even as I used it to wipe away my tears. "A handkerchief does solve all problems."

He smiled with a small shrug. "Most of them, at least."

I released a deep breath. "Thank you," I said, hoping he knew it was for not just the bit of fabric, but the pick-me-up as well.

Asher smiled and gave my hand a squeeze. "Come on," he said, and I followed him out of the office, tucking the handkerchief into my jacket pocket.

The Judiciary was normally a hive of constant activity, but for the last few days the place had been like a tomb. As Asher and I walked back into the main workspace, I saw that it was empty save for a handful of people loitering at their desks. Everyone else must have had the same idea as Asher and was opting to take a break. The shock of the high chancellor's murder had been felt across our system. It was no wonder that we would need a moment to catch our breaths.

We were almost at reception when Theo called my name sharply. With a quick word to Asher that I would meet him in the lobby, I headed toward Theo, wondering what I had done that he would summon me.

"This just arrived," Theo said when I reached him. "I was told to hand-deliver it to you." He gave me a slim, dark purple envelope decorated with the gold embossed seal of the Realm. It seemed far too official.

"This is for *me?*" I asked, turning it over in my hand. "Are you sure it's not for Mila?"

He peered up at me. "I already delivered one to her," he said then pointed to my name printed in bold type on the front of the envelope. "You're the only one in our entire Judiciary with *Metallurgist* for a caste name."

Theo pivoted on his heel and walked away. Why the man always had to be in a foul mood, I would never understand.

Dismissing his attitude, as I had learned to do, I tugged gently at the sticky closure along the edge of the envelope and pulled out one of two crisp pieces of paper.

Dear esteemed friend of the family,

It is with heavy and broken hearts that we invite you to the ash ceremony for a loving husband, dedicated father and our esteemed High Chancellor, Marcus Consul of the Realm. This celebration of his life will be held at the Grand Hallowed Hall in the town of Commune on Septima Two.

We would be deeply honored by your attendance. Please find instructions for the confirmation of your attendance in the enclosure.

His loving family,

Lenora Magistrate, Gillian Principal and Gannon Consul

Tears were in my eyes by the time I finished reading. Only one person would have sent this to me.

Hands trembling, I reached inside the envelope to pull out the other enclosure, looking for unnecessary confirmation. I found it anyway in the three words handwritten in tight, bold script at the bottom of the paper:

Lahra, please come.

* * *

I had thought about it long and hard, but there was really no way around it. I had to ask Tai.

I sat on a bench in the lobby of the Judiciary at the end of the day, waiting for him to message me when he arrived. The place was dark and quiet now, the usual hustle and bustle long gone an hour after most people had gone home. The only sound was the steady whirring of an automated cleaner running close to the ground, eating up everything its path. It bounced off a bench on the opposite side of the lobby, spun around, then droned on.

After receiving the envelope, I hadn't been able to speak with Gannon via monitor as I had hoped. So I had to make do with telling him that I accepted his invitation via comm. I had expected a delay in his response due to the demands on his time, but only a few moments later, he had replied:

`Talib or Jonah will escort you.`

I scowled. He was underestimating the security coordination required for an ash ceremony of this size and importance.

`No. They have more important things to take care of right now, especially for your family.`

Then his immediate reply:

You're important to me, so important to them as well.

My shoulders slumped as I imagined the firm set of his jaw. Well, I could be stubborn too:

I'll find my own way.

I don't want you traveling alone!

I sighed. Considering the rash of attacks on arc crafts, I didn't like the idea of traveling alone either, but being a burden to him held even less appeal.

I won't.

My comm chimed, echoing in the silence of the lobby. *Tai.* After mistaking him for Gannon the night the high chancellor died, I had changed the sound of Tai's incoming calls from a ping to a series of ringing bells.

With a glance through the glass doors to confirm his arrival, I hiked my bag up onto my shoulder and strode outside, trying to squelch the nervousness that threatened to eat me alive. I would need to be persuasive to get Tai to agree to the request I was about to make.

Tai was waiting for me by the curb in a black hover. It was an industrial-looking machine that seemed fueled by power and aggression. I slipped into the passenger seat. In the darkness of the cab, Tai's hazel eyes warmed as he looked me over. I smiled stiffly and glanced away, taking in the vehicle's interior.

"This is quite the hover," I said.

Tai grinned then faced forward. "The benefits of becoming a commander," he said, his uniform stretching across the muscles of his back and shoulders as he maneuvered the hover up and out of the landing space.

"Thank you for picking me up," I said, fiddling with the fastenings on my coat. "I know how busy you are."

Tai shrugged. "Whatever you need, you need only ask."

I sank deep into the leather seat, wondering if he would be so accommodating when he heard my request.

"Though I have to admit," he added, giving me a sidelong glance, "I'm a little surprised."

"About what?"

His eyes narrowed a fraction. "That you would ask me for a ride home."

I sat up straight and cleared my throat, ready for this. "I forgot to load travel credits onto my comm, and Rhoan said you were in the area," I said, and was relieved that I had delivered the line as smoothly as I had practiced it. The lie wasn't foolproof. Truly, I could have loaded credits at any time, but it was a common enough excuse among my peers. I figured it was best to stick to the tried and true.

Tai raised his eyebrows then nodded slowly. He refocused on his navigation, jabbing here and there at the assortment of shiny buttons on the dashboard. Like most citizens, I had learned how to fly a hover by the age of eighteen, but I'd never had a chance to drive anything even remotely close to this. Tai's vehicle was like a mini arc craft, filled with gleaming bells and whistles, many of whose functions I had no clue about. As I searched for something to say, I absentmindedly admired how adept he was at managing the hover.

"Congratulations on your seniority," he said, breaking into my thoughts.

"Thank you," I said. Rhoan must have reached out to Tai, just as he had said he would. "So you know Rhoan's up for sub rep then?"

He shot me a look. "Has he been confirmed?"

I shook my head.

"Well, it's only a matter of time," he said with a drawl. "Your brother's an asshole, but a well-respected one."

I had to agree — not so much about Rhoan being an asshole, though he *did* have his moments, as about the level of respect my brother commanded among his peers. I frowned, remembering my brother's earlier concerns.

"Do you think it'll be a problem, both Rhoan and me being involved on the special committee?" I asked, still playing with my coat fastenings.

Tai pressed a glowing button with two wavy lines on it. When the hover started to glide on its own, he leaned back, facing me with crossed arms.

"Are you *seriously* asking me whether it's okay for two citizens with family members supporting rebels to be involved in a project aimed at reinforcing the ban on exploration?" He raised an eyebrow. "Which, I might add, is the very thing the factions are fighting for."

I cringed, glancing away. "When you put it that way…"

For a long while, we sat silently within the steady hum of the hover and the low hum of chatter on the radio. A news report was on. Like many others, it was reporting on the high chancellor's murder and spinning yarns of incredible speculation about how something like this could have happened. I tried to block it out by focusing outside.

Snow had started falling, blurring the view through the windshield, but I still made out familiar landmarks. We were near my apartment building. If I didn't ask now, I would lose my chance.

I took a deep breath. "The high chancellor's ash ceremony will be held next week."

Tai nodded, squinting through the blurry glass. He tapped a panel to his left and the windshield cleared, the snow melting away immediately. "I'll be escorting the ambassador," he said.

I had hoped as much. Encouraged, I continued. "Are you taking a communal arc craft or a private one?"

He frowned as he retook control of the steering wheel. "A private one."

"I suppose you have a lot of people in your delegation."

Tai clenched his jaw. For the next minute or so, he focused on navigating the hover's descent into a space in front of my apartment building. When we'd landed, he pinned me with a glare.

"You didn't call me for a ride, did you," he said.

I sat forward in my seat, hands clasped. "I *do* need a ride…but to somewhere else."

"Where?"

"Septima Two?"

His eyes sharpened, the green and gold flecks almost black in the shadows of the cab. "Why?"

I shrugged, glancing down at my hands. "I'm nervous about boarding another arc craft by myself," I said. "Plus security will be very tight; I don't want to run into any trouble on the way."

"You're deliberately misunderstanding my question, Kira," he said. "Why do you *need* to go to Septima Two?"

With a deep breath, I reached into my bag to pull out the envelope. When I handed it to him, he frowned, no doubt instantly recognizing the official seal. After reading the enclosures, Tai gripped the papers so hard, they creased.

"That fucking bastard!" He narrowed his eyes on me. "Doesn't he remember what happened the last time you were there? The high chancellor's ash ceremony is another opportunity for the rebels to attack!"

I cringed. I hadn't thought of that. "They've increased security," I said weakly.

Tai tossed the invitation onto the dashboard. "I can't believe he's demanding this of you!"

"It was a *request*," I insisted, grabbing the document and putting it in my bag.

"Has he no consideration for your welfare?" he yelled.

I stiffened. "Of course he does! He wanted to send his protectors, but I refused. They need to be focused on more important things right now."

"So you turn to your next best option instead," he bit out, glaring at me.

"What?" I said, eyes wide. "It's not like that!"

Tai waved a hand, dismissing that line of argument. "Why not tag along with your minister?" he demanded. "She'll be under high security throughout the trip."

"Mila's not going," I said, sinking back into my seat. "She said something about not believing in belaboring grief."

Tai glowered. "Does Rhoan know about this?"

I shook my head.

He snorted. "Of course not."

"You don't understand," I said, my voice hitching as the words tumbled out. "I *begged* Gannon not to go to Hale Three. His father went to Tork in *his* place because of *me*."

Tai scrubbed a hand over his face. "Fuck, Kira," he said. "Why must you insist on taking responsibility for everything and everyone?"

I blinked. "I take responsibility for actions that are caused by me."

"No," Tai said, dropping his hand into a fist on his thigh. "You take responsibility for protecting those you care about — and gods help me, I love that about you — but I won't have you put yourself in danger for it!"

I wasn't sure what to be shocked by more: that he loved anything about me or that he was accusing me of doing the very thing he had dedicated his life to.

Finally, I threw my hands up in the air. "*This*, coming from a blasted protector!"

Tai wrapped his fingers around the steering wheel as he shot daggers at some imaginary target beyond the windshield. I stared at him, taking in his unyielding posture, and decided I needed to change tactics. Knowing that Tai's own father had been killed in service to the Realm six years ago, I appealed to the one thing he and Gannon now had in common.

"He's racked with grief," I said, scanning the strong profile of his face. "He lost his father."

"Don't, Kira," he said, swiveling to face me. "Don't use that to bend me to your will. You did it when we were on Septima, and I won't stand for it now, not when this could mean putting you in a dangerous situation!"

Tears sprung to my eyes. "I'm trying to make you understand."

"I *understand* that when I couldn't find you after the attack, it felt like it did when I had just heard about my father's death. All Above, I had never felt so helpless." He pounded the steering wheel with a clenched fist, making me jump. "Don't *make* me go through that again!"

My eyes widened, shocked by his uncustomary show of raw emotion, and for *me*, no less. I reached out to take his hand, relieved when he didn't pull away. His hand was large and warm cradled between my palms.

"I'm so sorry," I said. "I should never have brought that up, not at a time like this."

He sighed. The pinched tension between his brows gave way as he peered down at me. Suddenly, he shifted and leaned forward, dipping his head. I inhaled sharply when he lowered his mouth close to mine. Soon his warm, spicy breath blew in light gusts against my lips.

I steadied my pulse with a deep exhalation and waited for the inevitable to occur — or, rather, *not* occur.

Light from a passing vehicle cut through the darkness of ours. Tai blinked, his eyes clearing with the movement. A shadow of regret darkened his face as he pulled away.

Just as I thought.

I shook my head and fell back against my seat, arms crossed. "You know, you told me once that you were afraid," I said, staring out into the night. The snow was so thick now, it had started piling up on the ground. "I thought it was because you were afraid to leave those you cared about behind, like your father did when he died. But that's not it at all, is it," I said, jutting my chin toward him. "You're afraid of being hurt yourself."

Tai recoiled as wariness crept into his face.

I shifted closer to him. "You keep yourself apart from others, pushing them away, so that *you* don't have to deal with the pain of losing *them*."

He stiffened. "You have no idea what you're talking about."

I saw the shutters closing over his eyes, cutting me off from seeing the truth.

I sniffed. "That's the difference between you and me, Tai," I said. "I'm *willing* to be hurt for someone I care about."

He sat still, nostrils flaring. "You think you know me?"

I nodded, narrowing my eyes. "I know you're a *coward*, Tai Commander."

He leaned forward, a curl to his lips. "Just because I once let you come against my tongue doesn't mean you understand me," he sneered.

I flinched but recovered fast. "There you go again!" I yelled. "Pushing people — *me* — away!"

I shoved him so hard in the chest, I toppled back against the door. He sat unaffected except for the barely restrained anger burning in his eyes. He reached for me, but I shook him off, almost strangling myself in the process of slinging my bag across my chest.

I attacked the door, trying to leave, but it was locked. "Let me out!"

Tai cursed. "Kira, stop," he said. "You're asking too much of me. I can't help you with this!"

What did I expect?

"Then let me the fuck out!" I yelled, heat flooding my cheeks. "I'll find another bloody way to Septima."

Tai grabbed my elbow and spun me to face him. "Don't push me on this, Kira," he seethed in a low voice.

I met his challenge with a glare of my own. We were both panting now, our breaths coming in short bursts. An unexpected thrill darted through me as I stared him down.

He searched my face, eyes glittering in the dark. "You really will, won't you," he said, the incredulity in his voice mixed with exasperation. "You'll find your own way."

I squared my shoulders. "I *have* to go."

He dropped his head, shaking it. "I don't know how in the Realm I'm going to explain this to my superiors."

My heart leapt.

He raised his head, scowling at me. "I'll take you. But there's no fucking way I'm letting you out of my sight."

CHAPTER FIVE

I couldn't remember the last time I had visited a Hallowed Hall.

The sacred space for the high chancellor's ash ceremony was nothing like the Halls of my childhood. This Hall was a feat of architectural and engineering design that boggled even my more mature mind. It was a domed structure with a sky-high ceiling and walls built out of stained glass and a basketweave of steel beams. The perimeter of the ceiling curved into one archway then another, giving the impression that there was no end to its breadth and reach. Everywhere around me, candles flickered and chimes tinkled lightly, creating a soft and soothing ambiance. It was a place where only a man with the stature of Gannon's father could be laid to rest.

"Stay close," Tai said to me over his shoulder for what must have been the tenth time since we'd left Prospect.

I hastened my step to fall in line beside him as he led Aresh Ambassador and his large group into the inner sanctum of the Hall. Thankfully, our delegation was nearly fifty people. That made it easy for me to lie low and observe without drawing too much attention to myself.

Tai had told his superiors that he felt a great responsibility to accompany me, a close friend of his family, to the ash ceremony, considering these violent times and the fact that I had survived the attack on Septima mere weeks earlier. It seemed to do the trick because no one had batted an eye at my being part of the ambassador's delegation. Meanwhile, I thanked the gods the Protectorate prohibited video coverage inside the Hall, because I had no idea how I would explain my presence on Septima to my family should they see me on some random newsfeed.

We approached a section reserved for Realm Council members, near a circular dais in the center of the Hall, beneath a sprawling, multicolored crystal chandelier. This was where the Corona sat awaiting the start of the proceedings, between two senators. The hem of her plum-colored dress gathered around her feet, pooling on the ground. She appeared lost in thought even while the senators around her spoke in passionate yet hushed tones.

I hadn't seen our sovereign since the attack on Septima. Though she had been vocal during that time, she had been mostly out of the public eye, making an appearance only after the high chancellor's death to pay tribute and make official addresses in his honor.

As we passed by her, I ran a hand down the front of my embroidered knee-length black dress, straightening it and smoothing the creases from travel. I longed for my bag, to fiddle with its straps, but the Hall's security had placed it in a hold with the belongings of many others.

Tai ushered the ambassador to his seat then scanned the brightly lit area before turning to the protector at his right. He ordered him to stand by over at the main archway, one that led to a majestic, ceiling-high fountain that gurgled above the din.

Not wanting to be any more of a burden to Tai, I searched for somewhere to sit and noticed a large group of subordinates, just as wide-eyed as me, seated at the back of the Hall. Seeking kindred spirits, I started in their direction, but took only two steps before feeling a firm hand at my back.

"You sit with me," Tai said, nodding toward a spot directly behind the ambassador.

I frowned, looking back at the other group. "I think it would be more appropriate if I sat with *them*."

He leaned close to my ear. "I told you, I'm not letting you out of my sight," he said in a low voice. "And if we're to maintain the pretense of you being part of this delegation because of my urgent need to watch over you, then I advise you to sit *here* with *me*."

Oh.

Contrite, I lowered myself into the seat.

Tai made a last scan of the Hall and sat down beside me. He shifted to straighten his black and gray jacket then tugged at the collar, cringing.

"What's wrong?" I asked, hoping he wasn't about to launch into the multitude of reasons I shouldn't be there and the caution I would need to take. I had endured his lectures the entire trip here and had been close to pulling out my hair.

He frowned. "I don't know how they expect anyone to be of any use wearing this blasted thing," he said, fidgeting in his seat.

I looked him over, as I had found myself doing many times on the way from Prospect. He was dressed in a formal, and apparently more constricting, version of his Protectorate uniform. The number of gleaming metallic badges and crests on the left panel of his jacket indicated his rank as Commander.

"I think you look very nice, Tai," I whispered, watching him scowl as I'd expected him to.

"Would you rather I look *nice* or be able to protect you?" he said under his breath.

Despite the solemnity of the moment, I smiled at that.

With a few moments to go before the start of the ceremony, I took the time to peruse the elegant space, pretending with a fluttering heart that I wasn't looking for Gannon. The sacred area was now filled with citizens, but there was a row of empty seats on the other side of the dais directly across from me. By the purple and red satin ribbons strewn along their high backs, I knew they were reserved for the high chancellor's family.

Suddenly, a hush fell across the room, and I saw him.

Gannon entered the Hall with an elegant dark-haired woman in a bright red dress, who I knew was his mother from the photos that had been plastered all over the newsfeed. She gripped her son's wrist as he led her toward their reserved seats. Following close behind them were a graceful woman and a stately man who between them held the hands of three young children. If the woman's coloring was any indication, she was Gannon's older sister, Gillian.

With a remote look that tore into my already broken heart, Gannon nodded to the clergyman who had stepped onto the dais when the family arrived, signaling the start of the ceremony.

Over the next two hours, I watched helplessly as grief worked its way through Gannon's family. Gannon sat stoic between his mother and sister, who dabbed frequently at their eyes. Not once did he look at the urn that sat on a small gilded table in front of the clergyman. Instead, he stared beyond it, through the doors toward the Hall's expansive wraparound terrace that looked out onto a spectacular view of Septima Two's darkening skies.

As the ceremony went on, his family became more drawn into their sorrow, shoulders shaking as they sniffled with heads bowed. Even the children, who at their ages should have been fidgeting incessantly, were silent. Throughout it all, Gannon sat showing no emotion. Only when his mother slumped forward, sobbing terribly, did he move, wrapping an arm around her and pulling her close against his side.

Something soft slipped into my palm. I glanced down and saw that Tai had placed a tissue in my hand. Only then did I realize that I had been crying. I peered up at him and found a bleak cast to his eyes.

"Thank you," I whispered, using the tissue to blot my eyes.

Tai nodded curtly and looked forward again, focused on the proceedings.

At last, the clergyman invited Gannon's mother to the platform for the final goodbye. Gannon had to physically support his mother throughout the act. Together, the three of them walked out onto the terrace and tipped the urn over the balcony railing, sending ashes into the wind.

An expected pall thickened the air when everyone started to leave their seats and exit the Hall.

Tai exhaled deeply and turned to me. "The ambassador will want to say a few words to Gannon and his family," he said. "Will you be all right if I leave you alone for a few minutes?"

"Of course," I said, still using the tissue he gave me to wipe away my tears.

He frowned, looking at the ambassador, who was already standing up. "Stay by the fountain in the common area," he said, his eyes returning into mine. "That's the most public space, and it's filled with protectors."

"All right."

"Message me if you need anything."

"I will."

"Are you *certain* you'll be all right?"

I dropped my hands and leveled him with a look.

He scowled. "Your fathers — *both* of them — are going to skin me alive if they find out I've taken you here," he said in a low voice. "Never mind what your brother's going to do with whatever's left of me."

I shook my head as I stood up. "I'll be fine."

He looked me over, indecision flickering in his eyes, before he accompanied the ambassador to the other side of the sacred space.

I stood on my toes as people bustled around me, trying to catch sight of Gannon around shoulders and above heads. It was no use. He was surrounded by citizens who were more than likely offering him and his family kind words of condolence.

With a sigh, I toyed with my necklace and headed obediently over to the fountain. Following closely behind a small group of swift-moving subordinates, I soon entered the common area, which turned out to be an elaborate indoor garden filled with vibrant flowers and dense foliage. I had to assume the oasis had been created to provide respite from Septima's usual colorlessness to those who visited the Hallowed Hall.

Sitting on a bench under a stained glass, pergola-like structure covered in vines, I thought about messaging Gannon, but hesitated. He was busy. If he needed me, he would reach out. Wouldn't he? Still, I debated what to do. The decision was made for me when a message from him arrived.

`Where are you?`

I responded, smiling.

`By the fountain.`

`Stay there.`

I stood up, straining to locate him among the various leaders walking out from the inner sanctum. Suddenly, Gannon's tall, arresting figure came into view. Every now and then someone said a word or two to him, but he kept to his path. I knew he'd spotted me when his pace quickened, no longer slowing down to acknowledge those who called out to him.

I took a deep breath and prepared myself for our practiced show of polite professionalism. As he came closer, I clasped my hands together tightly to keep from launching myself into his arms, but the effort was unnecessary.

I gasped when Gannon crushed me to his chest and kissed me like it was only the two of us in the Hall. We were partially hidden by the trellis, but there was still a chance we would be seen if someone looked too closely. I stiffened from surprise, but soon fell into him, gripping his waist. After a moment, he pulled away and I rested my head against his chest. With a deep inhalation, I breathed him in and enjoyed the heavy beat of his heart against my cheek.

"Thank you for coming," he said, leaning back to look down at me. The light blue of his eyes was sharp and stark against the paleness of his skin.

"Of course," I breathed, crushing the thick fabric of his jacket between my curling fingers. Tears started filling my eyes as he held my cheek. "I'm so sorry, Gannon."

He shook his head and placed a palm against my cheek. He didn't say a word, but the way his fingers shook told me that he didn't want to talk about his father's death. Instead, he smoothed his palm along my jaw and up into my hair, brushing it back. I had reined my hair into a tight bun at my nape, but coils had come loose around my face and neck.

"Chancellor?"

I stepped back as Gannon turned to Talib. The protector gave me a quick nod of acknowledgment before speaking. I wondered whether it was his training or loyalty that kept him so pokerfaced all the time.

"Your mother will be ready within the hour," he said. "I'll have Jonah take you to the farewell on Dignitas."

"Thank you," Gannon replied, giving the other man permission to leave.

Talib pivoted and strode over to Jonah, who stood a few respectful feet away. They exchanged hurried words before going their separate ways.

I frowned. "Why isn't the farewell here, on Septima?"

Gannon exhaled deeply. "My mother didn't even want an ash ceremony, much less one on Septima, but leadership thought it was the best thing to do since it's our diplomatic core." He shrugged. "The compromise was to have the ceremony here and the farewell on Dignitas."

I nodded slowly, marveling at that. When you were in such high-level positions, it seemed your personal choices had to be based on so much more than preference. The revelation rested heavily in the back of my mind.

"Will you come to the farewell?" Gannon asked, stepping close again.

I shot a look toward the inner sanctum, where Tai was probably wrapping things up with the ambassador. "I-I think I'm supposed to leave soon."

He scanned my face. "It should only be a couple of hours," he said. "My mother didn't want a long, drawn-out affair."

It was a bad idea. I had already taken a risk attending the ash ceremony; an intimate event filled with leadership and Gannon's family members could be too far out on the limb.

"Will *all* ambassadors be there?" I asked, hope filling me. If Aresh Ambassador and his delegation were going, then it meant I would be as well.

Gannon nodded after a slight hesitation. "I believe so."

"All right," I said, a smile coming to my mouth. "I just have to check in with Tai."

He stilled. "Why?"

My breath caught. In my eagerness I had forgotten to break this news with more care. "I came with him as part of the ambassador's delegation."

His eyes narrowed. "That explains why you were sitting with *him* and not in the seat I had reserved for you."

My eyes widened. I had been watching Gannon during the entire ceremony. When in the worlds had he noticed where I had been sitting?

I shook my head. "I-I didn't know," I said. "I knew security would be high, so I asked Tai to —"

"That's why I gave you a printed invitation, Kira," He said. "No one would deny your entry with it."

"I realize that *now*." I sighed, my shoulders slumping. "I was just so nervous about traveling by myself to Septi—"

"And for *that* reason I told you that Talib or Jonah could escort you."

"Gannon," I said, straightening my spine and flinging an upturned hand toward his two protectors, both of whom were running around, taking care of business behind him. "They hardly have time for *you* right now, much less *me!*"

His eyes cooled instantly as he folded his arms across his crisp ceremonial Senate uniform.

"Gannon," came a voice from behind me.

He glanced over my head as I turned, still bristling.

The woman I had suspected was Gannon's sister approached, her shoulder-length dark blond hair shimmering in the candlelight as she moved. She was as poised as Gannon was dominating. I took a step away from Gannon, suddenly conscious of how close we stood together.

"I believe my children have had enough sorrow and tears for the day," she said, coming to a stop in front of us. She smiled at me, but her grief prevented any warmth from reaching her blue eyes. "Alan and I will be taking them home before heading to the farewell."

Gannon nodded in response then looked to me. "Kira," he said, "this is my sister, Gillian Principal. Gillian, may I introduce Kira Metallurgist."

I released a deep breath then offered her my hand. "It was a beautiful ceremony," I said. The remark sounded sorely inadequate, though it was sincere.

"Thank you," she said graciously, shaking my hand with a small smile. "Metallurgist…I believe I've heard that name before."

I frowned, releasing her hand. "Oh, no. I highly doubt that," I said. Why in the worlds would someone in her rank have heard a name like mine?

Gannon cleared his throat. "Subordinate Metallurgist is working on the special committee," he said. "You've probably heard her name in connection with the project."

But Gillian was shaking her head. "No," she said, looking me over. "That's not it."

I shifted the weight on my feet and shot Gannon a look, but he was focused on his sister, his expression inscrutable.

His sister's gaze landed just below my neck. I thought she was about to succumb to her emotions by the way her face seized up. "What a lovely pendant," she remarked, lifting wide eyes to meet mine.

My mouth fell open as I clutched my chest, feeling for the jewelry she had noticed. I must have pulled the ring out while fiddling with it earlier. I tucked it hastily beneath my collar, where it belonged, while cursing the All Above for my carelessness.

I stammered, trying to come up with an appropriate response. I could have said it was a family heirloom, as Gannon had suggested, but his sister would no doubt recognize her own mother's ring.

I looked anxiously to Gannon, but his eyes were still steady on his sister, a moment of silent communication passing between them. She tilted her head and looked at me again, this time through narrowed eyes.

"Kira *Metallurgist*," she said thoughtfully, as if just now truly hearing my name. Her slow perusal of my person was as intimidating in its thoroughness as her demeanor was now cool. "My father did say that Gannon had become quite preoccupied outside of work."

"Gillian," Gannon began, caution in his tone. "I believe you said my nieces and nephew need you."

She slid her gaze back to him. Ten years her junior or not, Gannon held his own, staring his sister down. The time that passed felt like an eternity, but in truth it was only a few moments before she spoke again.

"Yes, they do." She glanced between the two of us before saying pointedly to Gannon, "Will you be coming? Or should our grieving mother make do without you?"

Gannon clenched his jaw. "I'll be there shortly."

Gillian stared at her brother for a moment before releasing a sigh. Then she turned to me. "It was a pleasure meeting you, Kira Metallurgist."

I figured it was her upbringing that compelled her to say so. Nevertheless, I returned the courtesy with a shaky smile.

When Gillian walked away, I gripped Gannon's hand as he faced me.

"I'm *so* sorry," I whispered urgently, searching his face for any anger over my negligence with the ring.

"She already suspected." He shrugged. "Now she knows."

I wanted to kick myself, but instead wrapped my fingers even tighter around his. "I'm sorry," I couldn't help repeating.

"I'm not," he said with such decisiveness, it startled me.

Eyes wide, I stared up at him. "But your sister…"

"I won't publicize our relationship," Gannon said firmly, "but I won't deny it either. I love you."

As he looked down at me, his emotions clear, I struggled to remember why I had been denying my feelings for him. Was I waiting for our circumstances to change? They never would, or at least not any time soon. With uncertainty taking over the Realm, waiting for a brighter tomorrow seemed silly and idealistic. The reality was that we only had this moment, and I should be sharing it — no matter how long it would last — with Gannon, knowing that I loved him.

Dear gods, I love him.

I inhaled sharply, placing my free hand to my chest, trying to catch my breath.

Gannon frowned, placing a hand at my cheek. "Are you all right?"

I smiled as something shifted deep inside me. "Y-yes," I said, ready to tell him how I felt right there and then, but suddenly I thought better of it. This wasn't the time, and certainly not the place. I took his hand from my cheek and grasped it firmly. "I'm just concerned about you."

His eyes shadowed. "I'm fine."

I pressed his hand to my chest. "Are you sure?"

He closed his eyes briefly before looking off into the middle distance. For a moment I was sure he was about to fall apart and, let the Realm be damned, I would hug and kiss him for all to see until his pain went away, but his eyes snagged on his mother, who was entering the common area, and he stiffened.

"I understand if you can't make it to the farewell," he said, still watching his mother, who was now speaking with his sister. "In fact, now that I think about it, you probably shouldn't. My mother can be even more difficult than Gillian."

I followed his gaze and squeezed his hand. He looked down at me, a fine line of worry flickering through his eyes.

"If you want me at the farewell," I said, "I'll be there, Gannon. I can handle it."

He sighed. "I know, but I don't want you to have to," he said, and after a swift kiss, he walked away.

CHAPTER SIX

Ma rummaged inside a colorful bag and pulled out two infant dresses, both of them drowning in lace. Her smile was bright and hopeful as she held them up for me to see. We were in the spare bedroom where Khelan usually stayed when he visited our family home.

"Do you think Sela would like the lavender or the cream?" she asked. "I bought both so you could help me decide."

I walked over to her, biting back a groan. "I'm really not sure," I said. "She's become quite fond of pink as of late."

Ma drew back and frowned, looking the dresses over. "I didn't think of Sela as a *pink* sort of girl."

I had returned with Tai from Septima the day before, and both the time difference and the weight of grief were taking their toll, leaving me sluggish and despondent. Discussing baby clothing for the past hour and a half had done nothing to lift my mood.

I peered into the bag and saw a few items I had bought and a thousand others I hadn't.

How many children does she think Sela's having?

Ma had been throwing herself into preparations for Sela's baby welcoming with wild abandon. It was a good thing Sela's mother and mine were such good friends, or with the way Ma was taking over, I would have worried about the future of their relationship.

"Well, I can't decide," she said, placing the dresses in the bag. "I suppose nothing's wrong with giving her both."

I rolled my eyes and wandered over to the deep-cushioned armchair that Ma had just added to the room. Since our parents had revealed Khelan's true relation to me, the bedroom had been taking on a more lived-in look. The closets and chest of drawers were filled with more of his things each time I visited.

Ma shook out another dress, this one made of thicker fabric and covered in embroidered snowflakes. She tilted her head, running a finger along her jaw, considering it. I knew that look. She was veering toward indecision, ready to ask me for an opinion.

Holy gods. I needed to change the subject, and fast.

"Did Rhoan tell you that I gained seniority?"

She nodded. "He told Khelan and Da too," she said, refolding the dress. "It's no surprise. You're as ambitious as your father." She stopped then glanced at me with an almost imperceptible wince. "I'm sorry. I meant you're as ambitious as *Khelan.*"

I studied her with a frown. I didn't have a problem with her referring to Khelan as my father. He *was* my father. I just couldn't come to terms with calling him that myself.

"You don't have to apologize," I said with a sigh, curling my legs under me in the armchair.

Ma raised her eyebrows then glanced back at the dress in her hands before placing it in the bag.

"Is everything all right?" she asked, approaching me. "Normally you would have taken me to task over that kind of slip, but lately you've been low-key — *amenable*, even. Frankly, it's unsettling." She smiled and sat on the bed across from me.

I took in her warm, open expression, and resisted the childish impulse to fall into her arms and have her soothe my troubles away like she had done so many times before.

The first time I fell in love I was twelve. Well, I *thought* I had fallen in love, and when I had shared my feelings with my fourteen-year-old crush, he laughed and told me he could never be involved with a metalworker's daughter. I was so devastated, I cried for an hour in Ma's embrace, allowing her to brush away my tears and tell me everything would be all right.

I assessed her, the memory making me see her in a different light. Who else in the worlds would understand just how I felt about Gannon? My secret relationship with a senator was one of the few things Ma and I now had in common.

"How —" I hesitated, trying to figure out how to approach the conversation without giving anything away. "How did you know you were in love with Khelan, that you couldn't be without him?"

Ma's eyes widened, filling with such astonishment, I worried I had revealed too much. She leaned forward and clasped both of my hands.

"You have no idea how much I've wanted to have this conversation with you," she said in a rush. There was a sudden sheen to her amber-hued eyes. "I never imagined I would have the chance!"

I exhaled a gust of air and smiled. It seemed she had been desperate for this particular mother-daughter talk. She had told me on many occasions how she met Da and grew to love him, but I saw now that leaving out Khelan, and what he meant to her, had been painful.

Ma inched closer, still holding my hands, so our knees were touching. "Well, I've told you about you Da," she began. "I knew him from such a young age, I never really ever knew myself *not* loving him. Our love was very natural and deep, even from the start." She paused then inhaled deeply. "Whereas Khelan...It's hard to describe. He was completely unexpected. He was just this exciting, untouchable person who made me reach beyond myself. I suppose I knew I was in love because I loved who *I* was when I was *with* him."

I ducked my head and stared at the intricate pattern of the rug beneath Ma's feet. *Hallowed Halls, if that's how you knew you were in love, then I'm far gone.*

"That's beautiful," I said, then raised my eyes to hers. "It must have be hard."

She tilted her head. "What?"

"Having to hide your relationship — or rather, a part of it — for so long."

Ma smiled. "I'd be lying if I said no, but I'd do it all over again if I had to," she said. "Everyone has challenges. Anything worth having tends to take work and sometimes risk."

I nodded, considering that. The easier route would have been for my mother to deny her feelings for Khelan and build her family with Da, but she had taken the more difficult path, one that went against the expectations of her family and friends, as well as threatened her social standing. No matter how frustrating and overbearing I considered my mother to be at times, I had to admire the courage it took for her to have made the choice to include Khelan in our lives.

Ma squeezed my hands. "Now," she said, "*you* tell *me*."

I frowned. "Tell you what?"

"Don't pretend with me, Kira Metallurgist," she said, a twinkle in her eye. "I know you better than you know yourself. You wouldn't have asked such a question if you didn't have strong feelings for someone."

Despite my vagueness, I had given myself away. Up to now, the only person I could speak about Gannon with, guilt-free, was Asher. From my last conversation with Sela, I gathered she wouldn't be too open to hearing about the newfound depth of my feelings for him.

"Well?" Ma pressed.

I gave in a little, heat filling my cheeks. "He's ambitious and generous and…All Above, Ma, he's *so* incredibly smart." I laughed, shaking my head as I thought of Gannon's arrogance. "Of course, with all that, he's supremely confident."

Ma's eyes glowed as she laughed with me.

Oh, yes. How could I forget? "And he's *gorgeous*," I added, warming up to the subject. "Like, *sinfully* gorgeous, do you know what I mean?"

Ma nodded as if she did. "And he comes from a good family."

"Oh, an outstanding one." I stopped myself. I had to be careful here, but the compulsion to share this with her urged me on. "They're very well regarded."

"Do you love him?"

It took me only a second. "Yes," I whispered and lowered my head, enjoying the freedom of admitting what I had only recently come to accept.

"Good." Ma expelled a deep breath and tightened her hold on my hands. "Tai is a wonderful man."

My head snapped up. "Pardon me?"

"I was hoping you two would come to your senses."

"*Who* two?" I blinked. "What senses?"

She beamed. "You couldn't have done better," she said. "He's upstanding, intelligent, successful and kind, and he *loves* you so very much."

"He *loves* me?" I nearly choked on the words.

"That man would do anything for you." Ma released my hands and crossed her arms. "Do you think Tai helped our family and risked his status out of the goodness of his heart?"

I stared at her open-mouthed. "Actually, yes. I do."

Ma gave me a pitying look, but underneath that was a frightening amount of glee.

Oh, dear gods.

"I didn't know you liked Tai *that* much," I said, my voice coming out strangled. "You've never said anything about wanting him for me."

"Why would I?" She snorted with a roll of her eyes. "If I did, you wouldn't have given him the time of day."

"What?!"

"Kira, every time I mentioned someone I think you'd like, you immediately resisted." She shrugged. "I got so frustrated I even tried introducing you to a girl once, thinking I was on the wrong path."

All Above! "Who?"

Ma laughed. "Nara."

My eyes widened. I had always wondered why she had been so keen to invite my exuberant friend over on our weekends home from Primary Academy.

"Good grief, Ma!" I said, dazed. "Nara has not *one* but *two* men. She doesn't like women!"

"Well, I know that *now*." She grinned.

This was blowing me away. "What about Lukas?" I'd been so sure she wanted me to partner with the man who ended up better suited as a friend than as a lover. "You were so desperate to meet him."

"Of course I was," she said, dusting a piece of lint off her dark blue dress. "How else would I get him out of the way?"

I stared at her. Who *was* this woman?

Now that I thought back on it, Ma had never said one word about Tai — stunning, selfless, marriageable and partner-worthy *Tai* — the entire time I knew him. Reluctant admiration of her stealth and cleverness made me smile.

"Ma," I said, shaking my head with a grin, "your skills aren't being put to their greatest use. Had you been born a senator, you would have been an excellent politician."

Ma smiled. "Let's just say Khelan has taught me a thing or two over the years." She stood up and returned to hunting through the bag that was near to bursting with Sela's baby gifts.

Yes, Khelan probably had a lot to share when it came to the art of negotiation. He would have learned everything he knew from his peers in the Senate and could have risen to the highest of ranks had he remained in his caste. My heart squeezed. He had given up so much for Ma and me. He was a man who put family first, above all else, so it baffled me that he would put our family on the line by supporting the factions. I understood the need for vengeance, but I had expected him to back down when his anger cooled.

I came to my feet and approached Ma. "Has Khelan told you anything about what he's doing with Maxim? Or even what Uncle Paol is up to?" I asked.

Ma shook her head, reaching for another bag, this one floral.

"Ma, won't you talk to him?" Her shoulders tensed as I drew close. "Whatever help Khelan's providing Maxim needs to stop before it's too late."

"He's doing what he needs to do," she said, fixated on the bag. "Khelan will do the right thing. He always has for his family."

I shook my head. How could she not see how badly this would all turn out?

"How can you say that?" I clenched my fists. "We're all grieving over Aunt Marah's death, but he can't believe his actions will lead him anywhere except to prison — or worse, expelled from the Realm."

She brushed a wayward curl out of her face, still not looking at me. "I think you're exaggerating."

"Oh? Haven't you seen what's been going on? How terrible things have become across the Realm?" I demanded. "Once they figure out Khelan's helping the factions, expulsion may just be the rosier punishment!"

Ma sighed and finally looked at me. "Khelan is committed to this."

I searched her face. "And Da? Is he all right with Khelan putting you — *us* — in this position?"

Her mouth tightened. "He tries to be supportive, yes."

"What is *wrong* with all of you?!"

Ma stiffened, raising her chin. "Tread carefully, Kira."

I turned my back to her, tamping down my temper. Raging against Ma had never gotten me anywhere before. I doubted it would now.

"Take a lesson from me," she said, "and trust him."

I spun around, wondering at such passiveness on the heels of having learned how cunning she could be. "I can't, Ma," I said. "I'm not like you."

"No, you're not." She smiled indulgently, tugging out yet another tiny dress. "Yet, to some extent, we all become our mothers in the end, don't we?"

* * *

Breathe. Focus on your breathing.

I fell awkwardly into my office chair and forced a breath past the tightness in my chest. Closing my eyes, I went through my usual paces.

Deep breath in. Deep breath out. Calm, bright, open spaces.

This panic attack wasn't strong, at least not yet. I could only hope that it wouldn't progress into something more intense. I pulled out a drawer and searched within it then fought back another wave of anxiety when I realized I didn't have any *solumen* with me. I would have to will myself through this.

Mila hadn't been joking when she said we would stay the course, moving forward on projects already underway. If anything, the Judiciary seemed busier than ever. A week after the ash ceremony, everyone seemed to be energized, filled with a new sense of purpose backed by a firm determination to not let the factions break the Realm down.

I rubbed at my throat and chest as the constriction loosened a bit. I had had busy days before. The heightened activity today couldn't have caused the attack. One moment I had been speaking with Asher about preparations for the special committee meeting scheduled for the following day, and the next I was short of breath and lightheaded, apologizing to him for having to cut our conversation short.

Feeling much better now, I stood up and was about to head back to the work area to search for Asher and pick up where we left off when my comm sounded.

If at first you don't succeed…try, try again.

What in the worlds?

I shook my head, searching for the sender identification. Like the last bizarre message I had received, this one had none. With a frown, I tapped on my monitor to search for a vendor in Merit who could do a quick repair on comms displaying random archaic sayings. I had identified one near the Judiciary when I heard a sharp rap on my office door. On the other side of its opaque glass, Mila's tall, lithe figure paced. I hurried to let her in.

"Well, you live another day, don't you," Mila said as she strode into my office.

I followed her, giving her a questioning look as she sat in the chair on the other side of my desk. "Pardon me?"

Mila smirked. "Once again you've made it out of Septima alive," she said, bracing back and resting her elbows on the arms of the chair. Under her, the furniture appeared more a throne than a piece of stainless steel. "It seems you're still in the gods' favor."

I gave her a weak smile as I sat down. Only Mila could make tragedy and upheaval sound like a battle to be won.

Given that I'd needed to be away from the Judiciary in order to attend the ash ceremony, I had taken Tai's lead and told Mila that I had been asked to attend the ash ceremony on behalf of a family friend. I could have simply told her I was out sick or needed time off, but the fact that I was in the ambassador's delegation took that option away. I'd hate it if she found out

I was at the ceremony by way of a passing comment by the ambassador, revealing my lie.

"I'm sorry I had to cancel our meeting yesterday," she said, hooking her ankle over a knee. "I'm glad I caught you before you left today. I'll be tied up way into the evening, preparing for the special committee meeting tomorrow."

I sat down. "Have I missed something in your briefing package?"

She scoffed. "Of course not," she said. "I have a few updates to share with you. First off, *all* special committee meetings will all be held on Prospect, so need to worry about travel to Dignitas One."

My stomach dipped. Despite my concerns about arc travel, I had looked forward to the chance to spend time in with Gannon, on *his* world.

"Why the change in location?" I asked as nonchalantly as I could.

Mila shrugged. "Your guess is as good as mine," she said. "I was informed by the chancellor himself in a memo."

"The chancellor?" I said with a frown. "I didn't think he was leading the project anymore."

"The Corona has reassigned him to the project."

I considered that. Gannon and I had spoken each night since his father's ash ceremony, but he had never once mentioned leading the special committee. The Corona's direction was logical, based on Gannon's past work on the project, but I couldn't imagine him being anywhere close to emotionally prepared to take on a role that meant essentially filling his father's shoes.

"I also wanted to let you know that Realm Council has approved the special committee members," Mila said.

I sat up straighter. "*All* of them?"

She nodded. "We've decided on the sub rep," she said, watching me with keen brown eyes. "His name is Rhoan Advocator."

My eyes widened, but I managed to suppress my excitement. This was wonderful! *Or was it?*

Rhoan hadn't seemed too enamored with the idea of taking on the position. I sobered, wondering how he would take the news.

I cleared my throat. "I should let you know that Rhoan Advocator's my brother."

She snorted. "We do background checks, Kira," she said. "I'm fully aware of that. Your relationship to him is one of the reasons I specifically recommended him. My hope is that if he's anything like you, he won't fuck things up."

It sounded like a compliment, but I couldn't determine whether I should say thank you.

"I like you, Kira," Mila said, steepling her fingers, elbows on the arms of the chair. "So I feel compelled to be completely honest with you. You must know that this special committee is an exercise of control, a reminder to our citizens to adhere to the ban on exploration."

I nodded.

"Then you must also know that the sub rep position was created to appease the members of your caste and discourage them from siding with the factions."

I nodded again, but this time swallowed a strong swell of anxiety. The absurdity of my brother and I working on this project loomed large in the back of my mind. Perhaps I should have requested to leave the project. But then what about Rhoan? This was an incredible opportunity for him. Should he have to reject this opportunity too?

Suddenly, a spike of anger tore through me. Khelan had told me that I was one of the two most important people in the worlds to him. Yet, as he went behind our backs trying to exact revenge, he was showing me that he had a greater priority.

"I see you understand the significance of this project," Mila said, scanning my face. "I just want you to know that I have all faith in you and your brother. I wouldn't select people I didn't think could handle this project."

"Thank you, Mila."

With a curt nod, she stood up and walked toward the door, but soon slowed to a stop. Standing at the threshold, she glanced about the office.

"One of these days," she said, looking around, "you're going to have to tell me how you came about this office."

I slumped in my chair as she strode out. Considering who had given the office to me, I had to pray that day would never come.

CHAPTER SEVEN

"Do you have everything on your scroll?" I asked, nodding to the tablet cradled in one of Asher's arms.

"I think so," he said, keeping pace beside me. The double doors to the Council building's main assembly room loomed just ahead.

"How about the briefing documents?" I asked.

"Got them." He shifted his messenger bag, glancing down at the device.

"There'll be audio recordings of all the meetings," I said as we navigated through citizens and a few members of the media, "but it's probably best if you take your own notes too. We don't know how soon we'll get access to the files."

"Aye, aye, Captain." I caught Asher's jaunty salute in my periphery.

I slowed to a stop just outside the entrance, taking in his wide grin.

"I'm sorry," I said with a grimace. "It's just that I've forgotten to bring files to a meeting before."

"No worries," Asher said. "Your anxiety makes me feel a whole lot better about mine."

With a smile, I pushed open the large double doors, remembering when I first walked into Prospect Building and was just as awe-struck as Asher was now.

"I gotta say," Asher said as we entered. "I can't remember the last time I had to *push* open a door."

"They put us in the old side of the building, since it's more private. It's ancient, but" — I tilted my chin toward the lecture-style auditorium — "it does have its charms."

Rows of wooden chairs with lap desks circled the perimeter of a room that could hold maybe two hundred people. The skylight was the primary source of light; it provided a necessary warmth and airiness to the drafty space. While the room was old, the technology wasn't. There were monitors of every kind and size on the walls and in the center of a long, wide table, where the committee members would sit.

I spotted seats in a section near to the front and led Asher toward them. We had just settled in when the doors swung open. Mila strode in with my brother at her side, her gesticulations punctuating each of her words. After she took a seat, Rhoan headed over to us, but not before catching the eye of two female subordinates who had been setting up the mics and monitors on the table. They stopped to watch as he made his way over to Asher and me. My brother, as usual, attracted attention no matter where he went.

Asher sighed. "If only I were into men," he murmured.

I gasped, turning to him. *No way. Not Asher too.*

He grinned then winked at me, amusement clear in his eyes.

"Thank gods you're joking," I said. "I thought you'd fallen victim to my brother as well."

Asher appeared justifiably confused.

"Never mind," I said, shaking my head. "Remind me to tell you about my friend Lukas some other time."

"Interesting," he said, grinning.

"Very," I conceded with a grin of my own.

For what felt like the hundredth time that morning, I thanked the All Above for Asher. Taking on the role of director and supporting the subordinate representative — my older brother, no less — was bound to be challenging in every way. Knowing that Asher would be by my side made everything seem much less daunting, and I suspected would be more entertaining too.

"So, what do you think?" Rhoan asked, stopping in front of our seats. "Do I clean up well?"

I sent Rhoan a withering look for his feigned disregard. The truth was, my brother gave everything he did focused attention. The night before, when I went for a glass of water at nearly two in the morning, I'd found him hunched over his tablet in the kitchen with the contents from the briefing package I had prepared for him strewn across the table.

I stood up and looked Rhoan over. He was dressed professionally, as usual. His black suit and shirt were crisp, and I could see he had tried to tame his hair a bit, but just like mine, it wouldn't submit. His curls twisted this way and that, as resistant as ever.

I crossed my arms and smiled. "You'll do," I said, then added, "This is my colleague Asher Analyst. He's working on the project with me."

Rhoan held out a hand to Asher. "Don't let her boss you around too much," he said.

Asher stood up and accepted the handshake. "Oh no, Kira's great," he said quickly, pushing his glasses up the bridge of his nose. "She can boss me around any time. I don't mind."

Rhoan snorted. "Yes," he said, nodding. "Kira tends to have that effect on people."

Irritation crawled up my neck, and I smothered a burning desire to roll my eyes at the smirk on my brother's face. Would he treat me like his little sister even at work?

Rhoan squared his shoulders and scanned the room. It had filled up quite a bit now. He turned to me, all humor gone from his face. "Mila mentioned that you were supposed to update my scroll with the most recent files," he said. "Did you?"

I straightened my spine at his all-business tone. "Y-yes, I sent them to you just before I left the office," I said. "I'll be sitting here with Asher in case you need anything else."

He nodded and shoved his hands in his pockets. "Thanks," he said, and after a quick goodbye to Asher, strode off to take his seat beside Mila.

"Look who's here," Asher said, jutting his chin toward the double doors.

I followed his line of sight. A small huddle of subordinates and senators had walked through the doors. Leading the way were Gannon and Aresh Ambassador. As always, Gannon's presence eclipsed everything and everyone else in the room. My heart stuttered as I fought for calm.

I hadn't had a chance to speak with Gannon since Mila had told me the day before that he would be leading the special committee. He had sent me a message apologizing for having to attend a last-minute meeting, taking away my opportunity to determine whether he was truly prepared to take on the project.

Asher leaned close to my ear. "I didn't know the chancellor would be here," he whispered.

"Mila told me late yesterday afternoon," I said, watching Gannon approach his peers at the table and searching for some lingering sign of grief.

I held my breath as Mila introduced Gannon to my brother. Despite my concern over Gannon's welfare, I smiled, thrilled he was meeting my brother, someone in my family and another part of my life.

Once he'd shaken Rhoan's hand, Gannon glanced about and his gaze immediately found mine. We could have been in the middle of a million people, but when he looked at me like that, with every profound emotion he had for me clear in his eyes, I was the only one in the room. The corner of Gannon's lips tipped up, and I struggled not to respond like the lovesick woman I was.

"You two are going have to dial that down a notch," Asher said, sitting down.

"What?" I said, dragging my eyes from Gannon.

"The electricity," he said, blinking like an owl. "It's hurting my eyes."

I fell into my chair, and Asher laughed when I ducked my head to focus on my tablet.

Soon after, the rest of the special committee members arrived. Dominic, Xavier and Abigail — the ministers representing Dignitas, Hale and Septima, respectively — took their seats. With everyone now in attendance, the ambassador called the meeting to a start with brief opening remarks.

I scanned the room, looking for Tai. If the ambassador was here, he surely should have been too, but I didn't see him anywhere. Instead, I saw a few of the other protectors I recognized from his team, standing off to the side.

When the ambassador handed the floor over to Gannon, I focused on the front of the room. Gannon provided a summary of the actions leading up to this point, which included establishing the position of a subordinate representative on the special committee. Through it all, he appeared his usual commanding self, and I released the breath I hadn't realized till then I was holding.

But my relief had come too soon.

As the meeting went on, it was clear that Gannon was only half-hearted in his focus. While he managed to keep up with discussion, as the ministers presented their ideas and opinions, there were more than a few times when the ambassador had to intervene to follow up on a remark that warranted further consideration. Gannon was well respected by his peers for his decisive and strategic leadership, so it was no wonder that soon everyone in the room appeared mystified by his behavior.

Even more alarming was his fixation on *me*.

Gannon stared at me steadily during the times he wasn't required to speak. I had thought that maybe he simply wanted to catch my eye, tell me something he should have when he had just arrived, but that wasn't it. I soon realized that he watched me for the simple reason that he had wanted to.

"Chancellor?"

Gannon pulled his eyes from me. "Yes, Ambassador," he said, looking now at the older man.

The ambassador scowled, shooting a bothered look toward Mila. It was rare to see either him or her so baffled and ill at ease.

"We're interested in your opinion on the type of sanctions we should consider in support of a ban on exploration," he said, clasping his hands on the table. "Do you want to weigh in?"

Gannon took a deep breath and straightened in his chair. He leaned forward, resting his elbows on the table before him. "No, I don't," he said simply.

The ambassador seemed to be at a loss for words. "I beg your pardon?"

"I've heard the ministers' initial views," Gannon replied, swiveling his chair to face Rhoan. "I'd like to hear from our subordinate representative. Advocator, what are your thoughts?"

My brother had been watching the proceedings with an expression that had gone from skeptical to disillusioned as the minutes had passed by. Every now and then he'd made a note, but most of the time as leadership had tossed out their ideas he had only watched, with disdain clear on his face. At Gannon's question, he took a deep breath and activated his mic with a wave of his hand before clearing his throat.

"May I speak frankly, Chancellor?" he said.

I tensed. Such a question was never followed by anything good.

Gannon nodded, raising an eyebrow. "Your candor would be greatly appreciated."

Rhoan shifted in his seat and shot me a pinched look. Even before he spoke, I knew what he was about.

"All the sanctions in the worlds won't prevent exploration," he said, matter-of-factly.

I cringed as the audience started to speak in hushed voices. A few members of the media perked up and started to take notes.

"Of course, they won't," Dominic Minister grumbled in agreement. He folded his arms across his barrel chest and let his gray-haired head drop against the back of his chair.

Gannon's eyes slid from the minister back to my brother. "Why not?"

Rhoan surveyed the room, seeming to gauge his audience, before continuing. "Because through sanctions, you're attempting to repress free will and subdue curiosity; both are impossible."

It was no surprise that Xavier had a response right on the heels of my brother's remark. "Subordinate, the Realm has done well with sanctions that have prevented exploration and protected our worlds for many years."

Rhoan shook his head. "The sanctions obviously haven't done well enough," he said, bring the murmurs in the room to a higher volume.

Xavier twisted his lips. "Your lack of knowledge and preparation is showing, *subordinate*," he said, making Rhoan stiffen visibly.

Gannon studied my brother. "What do you suggest, then?"

Rhoan squared his shoulders. "Lift the ban and regulate the use of arc travel for exploration," he said. "There's no reason why a system as advanced as ours can't develop protocol that would permit safe travel beyond the Realm."

Oh gods.

Xavier scoffed. "Are you mad?" It wasn't clear whether he was questioning Gannon's or Rhoan's sanity as he looked between the two of them. "Do you have any idea what sign that would send to our citizens? We *expelled* Argon for exploration, and you expect us to turn around and lift the ban? My gods, the Realm would erupt into even more violence, with the rebels killing more innocent people!"

The background chatter from the audience was a loud rumble.

Rhoan leaned into his mic, his voice clear above the noise. "The ban has done nothing but send us down a miserable path," he said, ignoring the voices rising against him. "Over the years, a ban has only served to force this topic underground and enflame belligerent groups."

My shoulders slumped. Rhoan was all but blaming Realm leadership outright for the rebel turmoil.

"Do us all a favor and get off your soapbox," Xavier said, earning a chuckle from some fool behind me. The minister exchanged a smug look with Abigail. "Your role here is to support any decision made by your superiors, who, might I remind you, are leaders of the Realm."

Rhoan clenched his jaw. "Then you've selected the wrong subordinate for the job."

The room erupted into discussion. The ambassador leaned over to speak in Mila's ear as Gannon attempted to quiet the room.

"Whoa," Asher whispered, looking at me, eyes wide.

I shook my head, speechless. Rhoan was driving the entire meeting off the rails. I tapped out a message to my brother on my tablet with shaking fingers.

WHAT ARE YOU DOING?!!!

Rhoan stopped glaring at Xavier long enough to check his device. But all he did was frown and focus back on the heated discussion swirling around him.

"Minister," Gannon said sharply enough to cut through the chatter. Everyone quieted at once. "We've invited a subordinate to this project to offer insight that we might not otherwise have had. *You* were part of the process that approved his participation. It would be wise to show him some respect and, at the very least, hear his opinion."

Xavier narrowed his eyes. "I believe it was your father who said something along the lines of our mandate being not to *debate* the law, but to *enforce* it," he said. "Perhaps you, *Chancellor*, should show respect for his memory, and follow his lead."

I gasped as the blood drained from Gannon's face. The room was so quiet now that when Mila cursed a few feet away, I heard it as clearly as if she sat right next to me.

The ambassador braced his forearms on the table, mouth pinched. "Chancellor," he said, "I respectfully ask that you adjourn the meeting. I believe we all need time to remind ourselves of the purpose of the special committee and the proper behavior of its members." He glowered at Xavier.

The minister shrugged, leaning back without a shred of remorse on his face.

Gannon lowered his gaze and seemed to try to compose himself. Everyone waited, as if suspended in time, for his response. I clenched my fists as tears stung the back of my eyes; I wanted to strangle Xavier Minister with my bare hands.

Gannon inhaled deeply then cleared his throat. "We'll reconvene in two weeks," he said. "At our next meeting, I ask that each minister present a recommendation of the type of sanctions that should be implemented."

The ambassador nodded and expelled a deep breath. "Thank you, Chancel—"

Gannon raised a hand. "I'd also like our subordinate representative to present *his* recommendation on how we could implement regulated exploration," he said, sliding his gaze from the ambassador to Xavier. "If we're to do our job well, then *all* ideas will need to be thoroughly considered."

* * *

"A clusterfuck," Mila said, thumping her mug of *hurim* on the boardroom table and sitting down. She glared at me.

"A cluster what?" I risked asking.

"It's the perfect storm of shit hitting the fan," Mila explained. "A clusterfuck is what people in the old world would have called what went down yesterday."

I quailed, sinking low into my chair and hoping that Asher would arrive for the debriefing soon, so my misery would come to an end.

"Between our preoccupied chancellor and our renegade subordinate representative," she said, bracing back in her chair, "you're probably looking at Prospect Eight's *second* minister who'll be dismissed."

Humiliation rippled through me. "I-I don't know what to say, Mila." I sighed. "My brother...I understand if you're angry with me."

"Why would I be angry with *you*? You're not your brother's keeper." She brushed a hand over her short cropped hair. "It's me who's the fucking fool. I relied on his background profile rather than weighing it against any of his current views. I should have vetted him better." She shook her head and drank her tea.

My heart sank, and my earlier confrontation with my brother came back to mind. By the time I had left work following the debacle of a meeting, I had been vibrating with rage.

"What in the fucking worlds was that?" I'd yelled at Rhoan, hurling my coat and bag on the kitchen table as I walked into our sitting area.

Rhoan shoved up from the couch to his feet. "I could ask you the same thing," he asked, matching my tone.

"What are you *talking* about?" I clenched my fists. "You're the one who decided to go rogue on a project sanctioned by Realm Council!"

Rhoan snorted. "I told you how I felt about this process, Kira. Did you think I would simply play along, hide my opinion?"

"Of course not," I spat. "But the purpose of the entire special committee is to *enforce* the ban — not get rid of it!"

Rhoan scowled. "Everyone in the bloody Realm understands and is familiar with arc travel technology. A ban on its use is like hiding it behind a glass wall," he said. "It's only a matter of time before someone breaks in!"

I tried to make sense of what he was saying. "Haven't you ever heard of diplomacy and tact?"

His eyes narrowed. "Did the Realm have diplomacy and tact when they expelled our family and other innocent citizens of Argon?"

I stared at him, finally understanding where he was coming from. I had never really thought about what role the subordinate representative would actually play. I had been so caught up in trying to establish the position, I hadn't thought about the possibility of the person filling the role having any contrary opinion. Now that I was confronted with it…which subordinate *wouldn't* share Rhoan's opinion? Subordinates were being blamed and castigated for a crime they hadn't committed or even been a part of.

My shoulders slumped as I shook my head. "What are you trying to do here, Rhoan?"

He crossed his arms, frowning. "I'm trying to bring justice, rational thinking and actual dialogue to this blasted project."

I sighed. "All you've done is pit them against you. That's not the way to handle things."

"Funny," he said, stepping toward me, staring me down. "The chancellor doesn't seem to have a clue how to handle things either."

I took a step back. "What do you mean?" I asked, hoping I didn't understand what he was getting at.

"I heard he took after his father," he said, assessing me. "A true leader, strategic, clear-minded and focused. *That's* not what I saw. To be frank, our much-revered chancellor seemed downright disinterested in everything going on around him. Well, not quite *everything*, I suppose." Rhoan's eyes bored into mine.

"H-he's not normally like that," I said.

Rhoan considered me for a long, terrible moment. "Then tell me, Kira," he said in a slow, quiet voice. "What is the chancellor *normally* like?"

I glanced away, avoiding his observation. Rhoan had known that I was involved with a high-ranking senator but not exactly who he was. Gannon's intense focus on me during the meeting had apparently told my brother everything he needed to know.

Rhoan cursed before stalking off into his room.

I cringed at the memory of our argument even now, the morning after.

"Sorry I'm late," Asher said, hurrying into the boardroom. He fell into a seat beside me. "Ana and probably half the people in the office stopped by my desk. They wanted an update on the special committee meeting."

Mila groaned, looking to the heavens. "Of course they did."

I cleared my throat, sitting up. "We were just about to get started," I said, wanting to hurry this debriefing along so that I could hide in my office. Perhaps if I got out quickly enough, Mila wouldn't consider demoting me.

"I'm ready when you are." Asher rolled his tablet flat on the table.

Mila raised the mug to her mouth and made a face against the rising steam. "Unfortunately, Kira won't have the pleasure of joining us as we revisit the horror show that was yesterday's meeting," she said, looking at me. "You've been summoned for a much higher purpose. Our sovereign would like to meet with you."

I started. "Me?"

Again? I almost spoke the thought out loud, but, thankfully, had the wherewithal to keep it in.

Asher's eyes widened as Mila spoke. "The Corona said she wants a word with the support to our wayward subordinate representative."

Dear gods. This was it. The fact that Rhoan and I were working on this special committee together had made her suspicious. She must have found out about our family's connection to the factions. We would both be dismissed as summarily as Gabriel had been. Dread coiled low in my belly and clawed up into my chest.

"I-I didn't realize that she was here," I said, hoping to convey calm. Meanwhile, my mind was going off in a thousand different directions.

"The Corona's been here for the past few days," Mila replied with a shrug. "She has a keen interest in the special committee. She asked for a report from Aresh Ambassador directly after the meeting."

I swallowed. "I don't know what information I could add to the ambassador's report," I hedged.

"Neither do I," Mila said with a sigh, appearing suddenly beleaguered. "I admit it's an unusual request for her to want to meet with you, but this entire project is exceptional. Considering what happened yesterday, she probably just wants to give you advice on how to do your job. It's her favorite pastime. Just nod your head and smile."

I blinked, unconvinced. I had met the Corona on two occasions, and the second meeting had left me feeling more uncomfortable than the first. I thought about refusing to meet with her, crying off for some imagined illness or other, but that didn't sit right with me. That was the coward's way out.

"I'll go," I said with a nod.

Mila appeared amused that I had agreed to meet with our sovereign, as though I had a choice. "Theo will provide you with the directions on your way out," she said, swiping through her tablet, seeming to dismiss me from her mind already.

Kind of her, but I wouldn't need them. I knew how to get to Realm Council's official residences.

I glanced at Asher, giving him what I hoped was a reassuring smile. He appeared more than a little disconcerted by the turn of events.

Mila raised her head as I collected my things. "I know you worked with the chancellor before," she said, eyeing me, "but exactly how long have you known him?"

I hesitated. "Since I started working at the Judiciary."

Mila's eyes narrowed. "And yet you were at his father's ash ceremony."

"Well, I was invited by a friend," I said, compelled to remind her of the fact. "Is anything wrong?"

She shook her head. "It seems you have friends in high places," she said, returning to her scroll.

After a quick glance at Asher, whose eyes looked like they were about to pop out from behind his glasses, I hurried to leave.

* * *

It was like being called into the principal's office. Only it wasn't an academic authority, but the sovereign leader of the Realm who had summoned me, and I faced far greater punishments than detention.

I breathed a sigh of relief when I didn't encounter any problems passing through security at the main entrance of the residences. Having nearly been tossed on my ear after attempting to enter through a private access that Gannon had shown me the first time I had been there, I truly didn't know what to expect this time around.

One of the Corona's female protectors led me through the opulent foyer and into one of the sprawling hallways, its walls lined with paintings and sculptures of leadership from many years passed. She ushered me into the luxurious meeting space where the Corona and I had spoken once before. After handing the protector my coat and bag, I stood in front of the large, blazing fireplace, from which I could see the door. I preferred not to be taken by surprise again by the sovereign's quiet steps. But when she arrived, I startled for a different reason.

The Corona entered the room gripping her protector's arm for support, walking like a woman many years older. I waited, breath held, as she was helped into a chair. The protector positioned a small, white cloth-covered table with a teapot and cups atop it closer to her. Once the protector confirmed that the Corona didn't need anything more, she left the room.

I had known that the Corona had been experiencing some difficulty recuperating from the attack on Septima, but at the ash ceremony, she had seemed fine, though despondent — but then, that was to be expected in the circumstances. Gannon had told me some time ago that the one thing leadership despised was a show of vulnerability. Looking at our sovereign's frail appearance, it was easy to see why she would want to keep out of the public's eye.

The Corona crossed her legs and glanced up at me. "Have a seat," she said, dipping her head toward a chair on the other side of the table.

Her invitation sounded like a command. Nevertheless, I said, "Thank you," and sat down.

She picked up the teapot on the table between us. The ceramic lid clinked prettily as she poured tea into two cups with a steadiness that belied her unsteady gait.

"Here you go," she said, handing a cup to me. I hadn't asked, but I accepted it, of course, watching as she carefully brought her own tea to her lips.

I wrapped my fingers around the warmth of the dainty cup, wishing I knew what line of conversation she wished to go down.

Perhaps I should just come out and ask her?

No. That was a bad idea. Based on my last conversation with her, it was probably best to allow her to get to the point on her own time. I picked up a tiny silver spoon and put two mounds of sugar into my tea.

"Thank you for meeting with me again, Kira," she said, making me look up. The wine-colored jacket she wore made her fair skin appear even fairer. "You must be wondering if I'm making it a practice of meeting with you like this."

I forced a smile to my lips, stirring my tea, wondering that exact thing.

She lowered her cup to the table. "Do you know there are security cameras in the meeting rooms of all Council buildings?"

I stopped stirring as my heart stuttered to a stop. "*A-all* rooms?" My mind raced.

Gannon had propositioned me against a wall in one of the Council meeting rooms. Then we had been in a Council meeting room when Tai, Gannon and I had been talking about Uncle Paol's interactions with the factions. And then there was the time when…*Oh gods, I could go on and on.*

"Well, not *all* rooms," she clarified with a slight toss of her head. "The antechambers don't."

"Oh." I saw stars, my relief was so great. Still, I racked my memory trying to account for each stolen moment behind closed doors.

"That's how I monitored the special committee meeting," she continued. "It was very disturbing."

My eyes widened. *So this meeting is, in fact, about Rhoan's performance.* I placed the spoon and cup on the table and folded my hands on my lap.

"Yes," I said, raising my chin. "I suspect that Rhoan Advocator's views on exploration were unexpected to everyone."

She frowned. "He was only saying what any subordinate would," she said, surprising me, and gave a wave of her hand before tilting her head. "I hear he's your brother."

I nodded.

She leaned back in her chair. "They say the apple doesn't fall far from the tree," she said, assessing me. "I hope I get the chance to meet the parents of two such promising and…*opinionated* children."

I swallowed down the firm grip of fear. It was best to stay remain silent on this point. The last thing I needed was the leader of the Realm looking into my family tree.

"Let me clarify," she continued. "It wasn't your brother I found disturbing. I'm sure you could see that Gannon was not his usual self."

I blinked, taken aback by the change in subject. "Well, I imagine the chancellor has a lot on his mind after his father's death."

"Yes, that's true," she said, curling a blond lock of hair behind her ear. "And when Realm Council appoints Gannon as high chancellor in the next few months, he will only have that much more to focus on."

I closed my eyes briefly, trying to ensure I had actually heard what she said. "I beg your pardon?" I said with a frown.

She studied me. "You look surprised, but you must have expected this," she said. "Gannon's next in line, after all."

I shook my head, stunned by the news. Why would I have expected this? I had assumed that a proxy or some other high-level senator would take on the role in the interim.

"Gann—" I corrected myself. "The chancellor has five more years before he can be appointed to the position."

"That was before his father was killed," she said, drawing herself up in her seat. "I'm able to petition for an immediate appointment to Realm Council under extraordinary circumstances. The death of Gannon's father in these troubling times qualifies, I believe, as extraordinary. Our citizens need someone they know and trust. They need stability, and they need it *now*."

Hallowed Halls, Gannon will be the high chancellor! Though terrible the way it came about, the position was everything he deserved.

"Does the chancellor know about this yet?" I asked, trying to collect my thoughts.

"Of course, he does."

I started. In truth, I had expected her to say no. *Why would Gannon have hidden this from me?*

"I told him a few days ago," she said, further confusing me. "You see Realm Council isn't quite convinced that Gannon should be appointed to high chancellor at this time. They believe he needs time to grieve, and I understand that. But considering the growing strength of the factions, the Realm cannot wait, so I offered a compromise. I reassigned Gannon to the special committee and convinced Realm Council to view his oversight of it as a trial, if you will. His successful management of the project will convince Council to support his early appointment."

I stared at her. It all made sense. I had wondered why the Corona would have thrust Gannon back into the role so soon after his father's murder.

"I see, then, that you understand the repercussions of his not performing well during these meetings," she said.

I took in her satisfied expression and narrowed my eyes. Surely, she wouldn't normally share this type of information with someone in my position! "With all due respect," I began, "why are you telling me this?"

She smiled, plaiting her fingers together. "Yes. Let's get straight to the point," she said. "For Gannon to gain Realm Council's support for his appointment as high chancellor, he cannot have any distractions. *You* are a distraction."

My gut twisted into a knot. "Me?"

"Come now," she said. "Think as far back as only yesterday's meeting and you know what I'm saying is true."

I shook my head firmly. "I think his performance at the meeting had more to do with losing his father than with me," I said, unable to hold back the sarcasm that underscored my tone. "Perhaps he needs time to grieve more than to be put on show for political reasons."

The Corona raised an eyebrow, seeming to take my measure. Finally, she leaned toward me, brown eyes narrowed as she said, pronouncing each syllable, "You need to end your relationship with Gannon Consul."

I stiffened. "The chancellor and I have no relationship beyond working together on this project," I said.

Her shoulders slumped as she sighed. "Please don't pretend with me any longer," she demanded, sounding peeved. "It's very taxing, isn't it?"

I rose from my chair, desperate to leave. "I'm sorry, but I have to go," I said, shaking like a leaf. Maybe I was a coward, after all. "I'm not feeling so well. If you'll excuse m—"

"Please sit down," she said. This time the tone of her invitation revealed the threat it was meant to be.

I sat down heavily.

She shook her head. "You thought you had five years with him before you had to let him go, didn't you," she asked, giving me a pitying look that made me want to...All Above, it made me want to cry. Horrified, I glanced away, trying to take control of the swell of emotion.

The Corona sat back in her chair, fiddling distractedly with a glittering broach on the lapel of her jacket. "Gannon won't leave you," she said. "His father was quite distressed when he told me shortly before his death."

I stared at her. "What?"

She nodded, appearing solemn and moved. "Gannon told Marcus that he would do *anything* to be with you," she said. "I believe that means even disregarding his duties and what he was born to do."

Tears welled as it dawned on me that this was the origin of Gannon's argument with his father, and how his sister had come to know my name.

"Gannon will always do what's best for the Realm." I dropped the pretense of formality and referred to Gannon by his first name rather than his title. The Corona knew the truth. I had no reason to hide it at this point.

"I don't think so," she said, raising an eyebrow. "Tell me. Where was Gannon the night his father was killed?"

I flattened a palm against my chest as the air left my lungs. The ring Gannon had given me that very night shifted beneath my shirt.

"Exactly," she said as if she'd scored a point. "He will put *you* above all things, and I can't have that. Not now."

I didn't know what to say. My body shrank in on itself.

She frowned, her shoulders slumping with a seemingly unbearable depth of compassion. "I hate this, Kira. I *truly* do," she said. "I've been in lust, love, infatuation — whatever you want to call it — once before. And it was difficult because it was unrequited. I can only imagine how hard it must be for you to experience the same thing at such a young age."

I clenched my hands into fists. "It's not unrequited," I said firmly through tears that threatened to choke me. Even though everything she said was testing my confidence, the fact that Gannon loved me stood firm against any and all doubts.

She dipped her head, conceding, and picked up her cup of tea. "No, it's certainly not unrequited, but it's definitely impossible," she said. "Look at this way; now you can focus wholeheartedly on Tai Commander. He's a good man. There was something going on between you two, wasn't there?"

My mouth was trembling so hard from the tears welling in my eyes that I didn't even try to form a coherent response. I couldn't, *wouldn't*, sob like a child in front of the Realm sovereign, but listening to her speak, I realized that this had been her original intent — to break me down.

"I wish our worlds were different, Kira," she said, eyeing me steadily with a frown. "If it's any consolation, even if you and Gannon were in the same castes, I would tell you the same thing. The Realm needs Gannon more than you do him."

CHAPTER EIGHT

I looped a curly length of my hair around a finger and pulled hard before letting it go. It recoiled, snapping back into place, then I did the same thing to the lock beside it. I had been holed up in my room, lying in bed all day, and had no plans to leave it. Each time I made an attempt to get up, a searing pain shot through my heart, leaving me weak-kneed and sick to my stomach.

Are you prepared to be his mistress? Because that's all you'll be.

I squeezed my eyes shut, but Tai's taunting words continued filling my mind. A heavy knock fell against the door.

"Kira?" Rhoan asked. "You all right in there?"

Gannon's a man on his path toward becoming high chancellor. The actions of your aunt and her family are a liability to him.

My lips trembled as I remembered Sela's words. I pressed my face into my palms, holding back the tears as pounding, more insistent now, echoed in the room.

"Kira, open up!" Rhoan demanded.

"Please just leave me alone." My request came out muffled from behind my hands. During the long pause that followed I imagined Rhoan scowling at the door.

"You've been in there all day," he said finally. "What the fuck is going on?"

I inhaled deeply. "I'm…" I lowered my hands to my chest. "I'm just not feeling well."

When he didn't respond, I rolled onto my side. Suddenly, the door slid open, and I struggled to sit up, my eyes narrowing as he entered my room. "How did you open the door?"

"It's my apartment. I have a universal code for all the doors," he said, crouching beside my bed as he looked me over.

I blinked, disbelief fogging my brain. "You have a *what?*"

He made a face. "Deal with it," he said, brows drawn tight. "Why are you crying?"

"I'm not crying," I mumbled, wishing he'd leave me alone. I needed to think, figure things out, find out a way out of doing what knew I had to do.

Rhoan's green eyes darkened. "Which one of those fuckers hurt you?"

I fell back onto the bed and curled onto my side, pressing the heels of my hands into my eyes. "Rhoan…"

"Tell me who to kill."

Gods, I really need to get my own place.

"Rhoan, please just go away," I begged, grabbing a pillow and shoving it over my head.

"Who was it, Kira?" He yanked the pillow from my grip, tossing it on the bed. "It was him, wasn't it, that *senator* of yours."

I glared at him, having had enough of the big-brother tantrum. "No, Rhoan!" I yelled. "It wasn't *that senator of mine!* Now would you please leave me the fuck alone?"

Rhoan clenched his jaw as he shot to his feet and, with a curse, stalked out of the room.

I didn't care where he went — I was just relieved that he had gone. I burrowed back into my bed, pulling the blanket up over my shoulders.

No, it's certainly not unrequited, but it's definitely impossible.

I was trying to erase the Corona's words from my mind when my monitor jingled, signaling an incoming call. I closed my eyes, ignoring it, and started back on the steady assault on my hair.

A moment later, my comm chimed and I groaned. I didn't want to speak to Tai, but after the third time my device sounded, I glanced at his message anyway.

`Activate my call.`

I was in no mood to hear "I told you so" from him. That was the very reason I hadn't reached out to Sela to tell her what the Corona had said. I ignored Tai's message and stared unseeingly at the wall as the device chimed away. After a long while, I checked my comm again and realized Tai was at his wits' end — his spelling had started to deteriorate.

`Pik up my fckin call!!`

When my monitor jingled again, I crawled toward it, voice-activating it on the way.

Tai was in what looked to be a library, books lining the wall behind where he stood. His face was tight as he glared at me.

"Why is Rhoan threatening to kill me?" he demanded, arms crossed.

"What?"

"Your brother just lit into me saying he was going to torture me in ways even the Protectorate doesn't know about."

I sighed. When I'd denied Gannon being the cause for my mood, I had apparently given Rhoan the impression that *Tai* was the one at fault.

"Did he find out about me taking you to Septima?" Tai asked.

"No. It's not that."

"Then what is it?" He leaned into the screen. "And why do you look like you're about to cry?"

"All Above! I'm not crying!"

Tai narrowed his eyes. "I said you were *about* to, not that you were," he said. "What's going on?"

"I don't want to talk about it, Tai."

He took a step toward the monitor, a menacing gleam to his eyes. "Did Gann—"

I shook my head. "Gannon did nothing," I cut in. I needed to change the subject before I broke down. "Why weren't you at the special committee meeting?"

He studied me, and I jutted out my chin, daring him to question my abrupt change of subject. Finally, he dragged a chair into view.

"All right, we'll do it your way," Tai said, sitting down. "I was meeting with the high marshal. He's asked for my help on an investigation into the attacks on Septima and Hale."

I nodded, not listening to much of what he was saying. Instead, I heard the warning he had given me just a few weeks ago.

And what about when he finds out that Khelan, your father — the one who's a senator in hiding — is supporting the factions?

Tai leaned out of view for a moment. He picked up a mechanical gadget of some sort that had been resting off to the side of his monitor. "The Protectorate has strong evidence about who caused the attack on Septima," he said. "We're having a hard time believing that Argon leadership had anything to do with it. However, there's still some connection to an exiled ambassador that's worthy of following up on."

He will put you above all things.

I exhaled deeply as Tai assessed me with a frown. He dropped his gaze and rolled the gadget back and forth in his hands. "The surprising thing is," he continued, "that there are signs that the person responsible for the attack on Septima and the person responsible for killing the high chancellor could be one and the same."

The Realm needs Gannon more than you do him.

"Furthermore," he continued, "no one beyond a tight group has detailed information about leadership's travel itinerary, so someone high-level had to have provided it to the rebels. The question then is who would want to —"

"I'm going to leave Gannon," I whispered.

The gadget Tai was holding thudded onto the desk. He lifted his head. "Apologies?"

I closed my eyes briefly. "You were right. Everyone was. I was a fool to think I could be with Gannon."

Tai raised his eyebrows. "So…you're going to leave him?"

I nodded, unable to speak.

"Why?"

I balked. "*Why?*" I blurted out. "I'm a subordinate who's the illegitimate daughter of a fugitive senator who's supporting rebel groups!"

"*That's* why?"

I stared at him, mouth wide. "Isn't *that* enough?"

Tai eased back in his chair, hazel eyes scanning me. "I've told you all of that before, Kira," he said. "What's changed?"

My muscles slackened under his keen observation. "The Corona," I said, shaking my head. "She asked to meet with me again."

He tensed. "Does she know about Khelan and Maxim?"

"No. Thank gods." I slumped forward and raked my hands through my hair. "It wasn't about that."

Tai cocked his head, waiting.

I released a deep breath. "Gannon's going to be high chancellor," I said. "Not in *five years*, but *now*. The Corona wants him focused on the special committee. His success on it will prove to Realm Council that he's ready to be appointed."

Tai's mind was working as I spoke. "And she wanted to warn you off," he concluded.

I nodded. "Apparently, I'm a *distraction*."

Tai cursed and clenched his fists. "She acts as if the man doesn't have any responsibility in all this!" he said. "She should be focused on figuring out what to do about the fucking upheaval across the Realm, not who leadership wants to be involved with!"

"H-he's not been himself, Tai," I said, wrapping my arms around my waist. "I think she's right about his focus, at least to some degree."

For a few moments, Tai looked to be at war with himself, his mouth tight and shoulders bunched up around his neck. At last, he leaned forward, gaze holding onto mine.

"And you want to do this *now?*" he asked.

My mouth fell open at the accusation in his tone. "Is there some optimal time that I wasn't aware of?" I demanded, my voice rising. "You, Rhoan, Sela — and *now* our system's highest leader — have made it very clear that the longer I continue with him, the worse things will be!"

Tai scrubbed his face with both hands. "I know, I know. That's not it," he said, looking at me now with shadowed eyes. "You know Gannon's not going to accept this, right?"

I faltered. "Well…h-he won't have a choice."

Tai raised an eyebrow. "Gannon Consul's used to getting what he wants," he warned. "I've seen him manipulate situations *and* people to turn them in his favor. He wants you. He'll be relentless."

I bristled. "I can manage him."

"I hope so," he said, arms crossed over the broad expanse of his chest. For a moment his eyes took a slow and contemplative path across my face. "Why *aren't* you crying?"

"What?"

Tai leaned into his screen. The colors in his irises were brightened by an unnerving amount of curiosity. "I'd have thought that considering what you've decided to do, you'd be sobbing right now."

I frowned, coming to a sudden realization. "You don't believe I'll do it," I said. "That I'll actually leave Gannon."

He didn't respond, but then, he didn't have to. His doubtful expression said it all.

* * *

My fingers hovered in front of the digital panel at the side of the door. I clenched my fist and pulled it against my mouth, staring at the device, willing myself to enter the numbers that would grant me entry into Gannon's townhouse.

"Have you forgotten the code?" Talib called out behind me. His words were muffled, the sound buffeted by the wind. "Should I let you in?"

I cringed and peered over my shoulder at the protector. He sat, squinting at me from inside Gannon's hover a few feet away by the curb. Talib hadn't been all too happy when I asked to enter Gannon's townhouse unescorted, but there was no way I wanted a witness to what I had come to do.

"That's all right!" I yelled quickly. "I remember it!"

I took a deep breath and tugged the leather glove from my fingers before reaching for the panel again.

0-5-9-6-8. Enter it, damn it.

I closed my eyes as I began to shake. The tremors weren't from the cold. I pressed my lips together and opened my eyes, ready to try again.

0-5-

The door slid open and I jumped back.

"Why aren't you coming in?" Gannon demanded.

"I-I just got here."

"Talib just sent me a message saying you've been standing here for the past five minutes," he said, dismissing the protector with a wave. Gannon peered down at me, the light reflecting off the snow and into his eyes sharply. "Were you having trouble with the panel?"

Yes. The trouble was that I couldn't bring myself to use it. I shook my head when he looked at me expectantly, and he tugged me into the house, disengaging the door closed behind us.

We stood in the foyer where he enfolded me in his arms. I buried my face into his gray cable-knit sweater and inhaled sharply, feeling the immediate need to memorize every feel and scent of him. My body shuddered as tears pricked at the back of my eyes.

"My gods — you're so cold, you're shivering," he said, running his hands up and down my arms before unwrapping out of the thick layers of my clothing. He placed them in a small closet off to the side then tucked me under his arm as he led me into the sitting area.

The fireplace was ablaze and cast a warm glow about the room; the scent of something delicious hung in the air. Containers of varying sizes — some open, most not — were scattered through the room. The desk on the other side of the room was piled high with what looked like official documents and a small box. I was about to ask about the packages when the newsfeed on the monitor over the fireplace caught my attention. A darkhaired woman was reporting on the special committee meeting, and the delight with which she reported Gannon's handling of it reminded me of what I was about to do.

The knots in my stomach tightened.

Gannon shut off the monitor with a curt verbal command and turned to face me. "Are you hungry?" he asked.

I shook my head, too afraid to speak.

He smiled. "I've been looking forward to these few days before the special committee meeting to spend them with you," he said. "It's been so hard to get a hold of you lately."

Of course, it has been. I've been avoiding this for the past two weeks. I stared at him, fiddling with the ring on my finger.

Gannon ran a thumb along my cheek, concern clear in the pinched lines around his eyes and mouth. "What's wrong?" he asked.

I stared up at him. How did you start a conversation that would lead to a terrible end?

"The Corona asked to meet with me again," I said.

He drew back, all warmth leaving his eyes as he lowered his hand. "Is she still suspicious of you and your family?"

"No," I said, watching for his reaction. "We had a very interesting conversation."

His lips tensed a bit before he said, "I find *most* conversations with our sovereign very interesting."

I frowned. "She had some news to share with me about you."

His eyes slid away from mine as he turned away and approached the desk. "Is that right?"

My shoulders slumped. He obviously had no plans to be forthcoming. "Gannon," I said, and he turned to face me. "Why didn't you tell me about your appointment as high chancellor?"

He crossed his arms. "Because it's not important."

My mouth fell open. "*Not important?* It changes everything!"

Gannon cocked his head. "What does it change?"

There it was. The opening I needed. I swallowed. "Well," I began, "we just can't be running around the way we have."

Gannon assessed me for a long moment. "You knew I was going to become high chancellor at some point, Kira," he said. "Mere weeks ago you said in no uncertain terms that I was meant for the position. You also said you didn't care what others thought about us being together. So what's changed?"

My mind went blank. I stepped toward him. "Gannon, if your appointment doesn't matter, why didn't you tell me?"

He looked away for a moment before coming back to me. "Because most of the time I feel like you're just waiting on the shoe to drop in this relationship," he said. "I didn't want to frighten you away. I'm barely hanging on to you by a thread as it stands."

A rush of air left my lungs as I searched his face. "How can you say that?" I breathed, clasping a hand to my chest. "You have every part of me."

"I have you, Kira," he said, holding my gaze, "but certainly not every part."

How could I argue against that when I had been plotting to leave him? Dear gods, how had my plans to leave Gannon become secondary to defending my feelings for him?

Gannon ran a hand around the back of his neck and turned to face the desk. He picked up the box that sat atop it and pulled out a small bag. As he overturned the pouch into his hand, the sound of metal sliding against metal filled the silence. I went to his side and saw Senate badges of different sizes and shapes laying in his palm. I glanced around the room, noticing for the first time the labels on the boxes strewn around the room. They held his father's belongings.

I peered up at Gannon, but he was still staring at the badges in his palm. "I think your father would be proud to see you take on the role of high chancellor," I said, hating the troubled look that had come over his face, tears welling in my eyes.

"One of the last times I spoke with my father, we argued. He asked me whether or not I truly wanted to be high chancellor, and I didn't answer him," Gannon said before looking at me, the shimmer of tears in his eyes. "I *do* want to be high chancellor, Kira, but my gods, not because my father died — not like *this*."

I inhaled sharply, reaching for him. "Gannon," I said around a sob. I fisted his sweater and he wrapped his arms around me. When we kissed, it was a crush of our lips and the salty taste of tears.

"I was supposed to be there," he whispered against my mouth. "It should have been me."

I pulled back, brushing his hair and the trail of his tears away.

"No," I breathed, forcing air around my shattering heart. "Please don't *ever* say again that it should have been you!"

He shook his head, agony clear in his eyes, as he tightened his hold around me and pressed his face into my neck. I understood then why he hadn't told me about the appointment or even about leading the special committee again: he was torn between his own ambition and taking his father's place.

I held onto him, feeling his tears slip down my chest and between my breasts. Or maybe they were my own tears. I couldn't tell, and it didn't matter one way or the other. His pain was as real to me as my own.

All Above, I can't do it.

I closed my eyes. My gods, Tai was right. He knew me better than I knew myself. I couldn't leave Gannon, not when he was grieving and needed me the most.

After a moment, Gannon eased away, but I held onto the sides of his waist, not willing to let him go. He ran both hands down his face then looked at me with a deep sigh, his eyes dull, lacking their usual vibrancy. My entire body ached to find a way to stop his hurt somehow.

"I'm sorry I made you cry," he said, running the back of his hand down my cheek. I could feel the moisture of my tears on his fingers.

I quirked my lips. "I've been doing that a lot lately."

He frowned and nodded, caressing my jaw. "I know how to fix that," he said with a sudden lift to the corners of his mouth. "A certain dessert named after my favorite subordinate mistress."

I sniffled but managed to smile. "I thought you said it wasn't possible to be both a subordinate *and* a mistress."

"Huh, challenging authority," he muttered, a familiar mischievous gleam filling his eyes. "You must be feeling more like yourself already."

I snorted and he leaned in for a kiss. Then he carefully replaced his father's badges in the box before heading off to the kitchen. As he walked away from the desk, the shift in the air caused a few sheaves of paper fell to the ground. I stooped down to pick them up.

They were official documents, as I had suspected, but there was none of the customary decorative markings that identified them as such. In fact, the papers were filled only with rows of date and time stamps and brief paragraphs of text. I didn't mean to look any closer, but a name caught my eye as I shuffled the documents into order.

Maxim.

Maybe the documents were from the time when Gannon was monitoring my aunt and her family. I frowned: the date stamp at the top of the sheet I held was only the day before.

I glanced up at the sound of Gannon opening and closing drawers in the kitchen. Looking back to the documents in my hands, I sat down, cross-legged, and flipped through the pages before settling on a report from a few weeks ago.

(Start Record)

P8 Date Stamp: 06.07.2558

P8 Time Stamp: 19h 16m 17s

Location: P8(2): Merit

Maxim Noble meets with Khelan Solicitor. No other individuals in attendance. Comm interception reveals that information shared relates to H3 travel authorization; appears nonthreatening. MN returns to Tholos; KS returns to primary residence. Monitoring continues.

(End Record)

I sifted through the sheets again, hands shaking as I saw more reports on Khelan's interactions with both Maxim and some with Uncle Paol.

All Above, Gannon knows Khelan's supporting the rebels!

"Kira…," Gannon said behind me. Wariness threaded his voice.

I twisted around to face him and held up the papers. They quivered in my hold. "You've known everything all along."

Gannon rested a plate filled with flavored toffee on the desk and crouched down to my level. He tugged the papers from my hold, not meeting my eyes.

"You promised me you wouldn't monitor my family," I said to the crown of his head.

He raised his chin, eyes haunted. "That was before my father was killed by rebels," he said. "I knew Khelan had a connection to the factions through your uncle Paol. I couldn't *not* monitor them."

My eyes widened. "So this is for vengeance?" My gods, would everyone in the Realm succumb to that particular motivation?

Gannon looked like I had struck him. "Absolutely not," he said, his gaze locking onto mine. "I'm tracking your family to protect you."

"Me?"

"If your family is doing anything that could harm you in anyway," he said, "I want to know about it, so I can stop it."

My heart stalled at how resolute he sounded. "How can you even *look* at me, knowing that my father could be helping the very people who killed *your* father?" I searched his face. If anything, his determined expression only became more hardened.

"Khelan only became active with the rebels *after* my father was kill—" He paused for a moment then took a breath, collecting himself. "After he died."

"But Khelan is *helping* them," I whispered, staring at him. "I'm so sorry."

"You are *not* your father," he said, jaw clenched as he gripped my hands. "Nothing will prevent me from keeping you safe."

I shook my head, at a loss for words. Dear gods, Gannon was his own worst enemy. He wasn't going to stop making decisions based on his feelings for me. I resented having to admit it, but the Corona had only been telling me the truth. For Gannon, *everything* came down to me. His future as high chancellor was on the line and his relationship with his family had become strained — all because of his feelings for *me*.

Suddenly, I remembered the update Mila had shared with me, and eyed him.

"Why are the special committee meetings being held here, on Prospect, instead of on Dignitas as was planned?" I asked, holding onto a thread of hope that it wasn't in any way tied to me.

He blinked, my question throwing him for a moment. "Because you're on Prospect," he said simply. "I don't want you traveling unnecessarily."

I placed a palm over my mouth, holding back a sob.

Gannon rose to his feet, pulling me up with him. "*Lahra?*" he said, concern shadowing his eyes. He tried to pull me close to him, but I turned out of his hold and walked to the fireplace, a fine tremor working its way through me anew. I searched my mind for paths that would lead me back to the course I had originally set out on.

"Kira?"

I stared into the fire as I weighed my options. I would have to be convincing for him to believe me. Most times Gannon knew what I was feeling before I even realized it.

I turned to him, pulling my shoulders back. "You're putting my family in danger," I said, committing to what I needed to do.

He tilted his head. "What?"

"You're going to be high chancellor, and there'll be even more scrutiny over your actions," I said. "With the way you're watching my family, it's only a matter of time before authorities find out about us."

Gannon frowned. "The only person who knows anything about what I'm doing is Talib. He's the one monitoring and preparing the reports," he said. "Talib would lay down his life for me, and so, for you. He won't say a word to anyone."

I glanced away. "That's not good enough."

"I've been monitoring your aunt and her family for weeks," Gannon said, eyes narrowing. "I arranged for their protection while they were on the run. You more than anyone know I can keep these matters private."

I shrugged, looking at him again. "Much good that did," I said cruelly. "Look how it ended, with my aunt dead and Uncle Paol and Khelan bent on revenge."

He walked toward me, wariness in each step. "Kira, what is this about?"

I crossed my arms as my body started to shake. "You know too much, Gannon," I said. "As high chancellor, now more than ever, your obligation is to the Realm."

"My *obligation* is to *you*," he said firmly, making my heart break.

I took a deep breath, trying to steady myself, but it was no use; I shook like a leaf before him.

"Things have changed, Gannon," I said, trying with little success to numb myself to the suspicion in his eyes. "You know too much, and with you becoming high chancellor…there's too much at stake."

He clenched his fists at his side, standing in front of me. "What are you doing?"

"If I continue on with you," I said, "at some point, my family's secrets will come out, and I…I just can't take that risk."

Gannon paled as he searched my face. "What does that mean?" he demanded.

"I —" My tongue became thick around the words. "I'm leaving you," I whispered, so low I could barely hear my own voice.

His response was immediate. "The *fuck* you are," he bit out so harshly that I took a step back.

"Gannon," I said, "you have to understand. I just can't put my family at risk."

He stepped into my space, bearing down on me. "What did she say?" he demanded.

I walked back again, this time the back of my thighs collided against the desk. "Who?"

He narrowed his eyes. "Our sovereign leader," he said through clenched teeth.

My eyes widened. "This was *my* decision," I said quickly. "The Corona has nothing to do with this."

I prayed he couldn't see through the lie. I wouldn't even consider telling him she had warned me away from him. He would only handle it the way he did everything else: head on. I couldn't have him taking on our sovereign. That could mean losing not only his appointment, but his current rank as well.

"So just like that," Gannon said, scanning me, "after everything, you think *I'm* a threat to you and your family?" Disbelief colored his every word.

I avoided his gaze and stared at his chest. He was standing a hair's breadth away from me; his pulse beat rapidly at his throat.

"I-I've been thinking about this for some time," I said.

"You can't lie to me, *lahra*," he said, gripping my chin and jerking my head up. I had never seen him look so predatory. "You're not leaving me."

I nodded unsteadily. "Yes, I am."

His nostrils flared. "I asked — no, *begged* you not to leave me, with my cock buried deep inside you," he seethed. "And you promised me you wouldn't."

I shrugged, blinking away tears. "What else did you expect me to say?"

I cried out sharply, shocked, when he snaked an arm around my waist, dragging me against him. "I can see right through you, Kira," he said, glowering. "You'll have to do better than act callous for me to believe that you're leaving me."

Of course, Gannon didn't believe a word I said. I didn't believe any of it myself. After everything we'd gone through, the reasons I gave him could only be seen as transparent excuses. The lack of truth behind my words was as evident to him as it was to me.

Suddenly, he wrapped his fingers around the back of my head, his fingers curling into my hair. I winced as strands left my scalp. Gannon glared at me, almost challengingly, as he claimed my mouth so forcefully that he took my breath away. He licked, sucked and bit at my mouth like a man starved.

I couldn't help it. I lost myself in his kiss for a few desperate, heart-breaking moments before catching myself. Then I twisted my head out of his hold, panting.

"Gannon. Please," I begged, but not sure for what.

He gripped my jaw and forced me to face him. "If you want me to stop, then just say the word," he demanded, looking me straight in the eye.

"I…"

Gannon smirked and resumed his assault on my mouth. Like before, I was helpless to him, curling my fingers deep between the thick cords of his sweater, holding on though I needed to let him go.

Dear gods, please tell me what to do.

It was when he slid his hand down my leg and pulled up fistfuls of my skirt that the only thing he would believe came to mind.

"Tai," I blurted out against his lips.

Gannon stilled. "What?"

I shuddered. "Why should I be hiding with someone who can't be with me openly when I can have someone who will?" I asked as the tears I had been holding at bay slid down my cheeks. He stared at me, his hold slackening around me.

"I've wanted Tai forever," I said, a wave of dizziness threatening me at the sight of the transformation coming over his face. "And now…now we're going to be together."

Gannon shook his head as if physically rejecting what I was saying. "He doesn't want you."

I shrugged. "He does," I said as convincingly as I could, but the tears flowed now without restraint. "Tai has always been there for me in ways you never could and will never be able to."

He searched my face, his mouth slack. "But you *love* me," he said.

Oh dear gods. Yes, yes, I do.

I wanted to wrap myself around him, just as he had me moments before. I should have been telling him for the first time how much I loved him, telling him the three words I knew he longed to hear.

I clenched my fists and said instead, "I choose Tai."

He shoved away from me, stiff as a broken marionette, and looked me over. Understanding was a slow tide washing over him. "You're leaving me," he said in a voice devoid of emotion.

My pain was too great to give him a response, but then it wasn't a question. It was a fact. I swiped away my tears in the ensuing silence between us. Still they ran down my cheeks.

Gannon walked over to the spot on front of the desk where we had just been in passionate embrace, consoling one another, expressing how much we loved each other without even saying the words. I covered my mouth with a fist, forcing myself not to take back everything I said.

My lips trembled. "I'm s-so sorry."

Gannon shook his head, his back turned to me as he began tapping on his comm. I could see his hurt in the rigid way he held his shoulders.

A sob slipped between my lips. "Gannon, I —"

"Talib will be here in a minute," he bit out, still focused on his device. "He'll take you home."

I didn't know what to do with myself. I didn't want to go, but I could hardly stay. It was when I ran the back of my hand across my cheeks again that I remembered the ring. I stared at it for a long moment through blurry eyes before approaching him slowly. When I stood beside him, I tugged the ring off my finger and held it out to him in a trembling palm. Gannon glanced down, over his shoulder, at it.

Chest aching from the breath I held, I waited for his response, anticipating the worst — anger, contempt, even cruelty. Instead, he closed his eyes briefly as his face twisted into a mask of bone-deep pain. I caught the bright sheen of his tears before he stalked out of the room, leaving me sobbing and wrapping my fingers around the ring he had left in my hand.

CHAPTER NINE

"I apologize for dragging you over here so late."

I heard the fine line of worry threading through Sela's voice even from where I sat, crouched in the corner of her nursery. The volume of her voice rose as she came closer to the door.

"When I told her I was going to call Rhoan," Sela said to someone, "she became hysterical, begging me not to. I didn't know who else to call."

The low rumble of a response filtered through the doorway, but I couldn't make out the words. But then, I really didn't care.

I wrapped my arms around my knees, watching the shadows shape-shifting on the wall across from me. The only light in the nursery came from just beyond the open door. I had asked Sela to turn off the lights just after I'd staggered in an hour ago. Large silhouettes morphed into one petite figure and another, bulkier one.

"She's in here," Sela said as light flooded the room.

I squinted against the intrusion of light, looking to the door, and found my best friend walking in with Tai.

I glared at her. "You called *Tai?*"

"I didn't know what to do!" she said, cradling her pregnant belly and settling on the edge of the bed, beside me. Meanwhile, Tai eyed me as he removed his coat and rested it on a hook just inside the door. "You appeared at my front door," Sela continued, "with tears streaming down your face and stumbled into my arms, refusing to speak. You scared me!"

Tai came over and looked me over. For some reason the sight of him made me want to start crying again, but I was all cried out. I glared up at him as he studied me. I appreciated his restraint at not jumping all over me and demanding an explanation. My best friend, though, was of a different mind.

Sela leaned into my line of sight. "Did something happen to your family?" she asked, her gray eyes wide.

I shook my head and dropped my gaze to my hands. The space on my ring finger remained bare. Before leaving Gannon's house, I had left the promise ring on the fireplace mantle along with a handwritten note filled with apology and regret and splattered with my tears.

"No," Tai said on my behalf, still considering me. "If something had happened to her family, Rhoan would have called me."

Sela inched closer and took my hand. "Did something happen to *him*, then?" she asked in a voice so low, I knew she was conscious of inquiring about Gannon in front of Tai.

I shook my head and twisted my hand out of Sela's hold. I pressed my palms hard against the sockets of my eyes. The pain in my chest was a fever, aching, spreading throughout my limbs.

Holy fuck, this hurts.

I knew it would, but this was a knife carving out my heart. Maybe I *wasn't* done with the tears yet. They clogged my throat and burned the back of my eyes. I started to bawl then, the strength of my sobs wracking my body, making me shake all over.

Tai gripped my wrists and pulled them from my face. "Kira, you're scaring the shit out me *and* your best friend!" he yelled, crouching now in front of me.

I took a heaving breath, trying to calm down when I caught the tears in Sela's eyes.

She struggled to the floor and wrapped an arm around my shoulders then rested her temple against mine as she spoke to Tai. "Make her tell us what happened."

If I had been in a better mood, I would have laughed at Tai's flabbergasted expression.

He scoffed. "You seem to think I have some magical power that will make your best friend do what I want," he said then shot a look my way. "Kira doesn't listen to me."

Sela sighed, drawing me closer, but I pulled away to lift my head.

"No. Sometimes I do listen to you, Tai," I said to him, bitterness seeping through. "And Sela, Rhoan and everyone else."

Tai stared at me.

"I did it," I said, my voice catching. "You didn't believe that I could do it, but I did."

Tai frowned, confused for a moment, then his eyes widened.

"Did what?" Sela asked, looking between Tai and me.

I couldn't bring myself to put the words together.

"You left Gannon," he said, rescuing me from having to speak.

Sela's mouth fell open, her arm tightening around me.

Suddenly, sharp peals of laughter came in through the door, jarring me. Sela grimaced. "Derek's parents...," she said with a shake of her head.

I reached for her hand, frowning. Sela's in-laws had arrived earlier that day and there I was in a near fetal position, hiding between a chair and a crib in the corner of her nursery. "I'm sorry," I said. "Go. I'll be all right."

Sela made a face. "No, first tell me what happened."

Just then, Derek called out for her. She scowled, mouth set in a peevish line. "You would think the man could entertain his own parents for a few minutes without me." She sighed and used the hand Tai offered her to stand up. Before she turned to leave, she ran a hand over my hair and said, "Kira, I know it hurts, and I know you don't want to hear this, not now, but…leaving him *really* was the right thing to do."

I glowered, watching her waddle out of the room. Sela's comment was the precise reason I had held back from telling her anything when I had arrived.

I had only myself to blame. The first place I had thought to go to after leaving Gannon's in tears was to Sela's. Facing Rhoan in my current state of mind didn't hold any appeal.

"So…," Tai said, and I looked at him. "He just let you go?"

I shook my head. "We argued. He couldn't believe I was leaving him."

He grunted. "Of course not," Tai said. "He thinks he's the gods' gift to both man and woman."

I pressed the pads of my fingers into my temples. I had been crying so hard over the past few hours, my head was starting to hurt. "Tai, please…"

He relented. "So what *did* you say to make him believe you?"

I cringed, dropping my hands to my lap. *Here we go.* "I told him that you and I were going to be together."

Tai seemed to choke on air. "Apologies?"

I shook my head. "I'm *so* sorry I brought you into this," I said. "He wouldn't believe anything else. Please don't be mad."

Tai frowned then ran a thick hand across his mouth before shifting out of his crouched position to sit beside me. I scooted over, but he hardly fit in the cramped space. Nevertheless, he found a spot and wrapped an arm around my shoulder as a fresh round of tears began falling on my cheeks. I pressed into the warmth of him, marveling at the irony of it all. Tai, the man I had always wanted, was consoling me after I'd left another.

I clenched my fists. "Why is it I can't have who I want?" I said, glaring at the wall across from us.

Tai stilled. "You can have *anyone* you want, Kira."

I eased away from him, turning so I could look him straight in the eye. "That's not true, and you know it."

He had the good grace to look chagrined and glanced away as he removed his arm from around my shoulders.

I sighed and rested the back of my head against the wall. "A clusterfuck," I mumbled.

"Apologies?"

I swiveled my head toward him. "That's what my superior would call my life."

The corner of Tai's mouth kicked up as he thumbed away one of my straggling tears.

The fact that Sela had contacted Tai had angered me at first, but now, sitting with him, I was glad that she had. Sela was my best friend, but she didn't know everything I had gone through with Gannon, not the way Tai did.

The sound of chatter had dimmed beyond the door. I checked the time on my comm. It was near midnight, and Tai and I were huddled in the corner of the room where Sela's in-laws were meant to stay. They would need it soon, if they didn't already.

Tai glanced down at my comm. "Do you want to go home?" he asked.

"No," I said. "If I do, Rhoan will take one look at me and want to kill someone."

He snorted. "Since he doesn't know you were involved with Gannon, then that *someone* will probably be me."

I slouched against the wall, shaking my head. "Rhoan pretty much knows Gannon's the senator I'm — I *was* — involved with." Using the past tense hurt so much, I clenched my teeth.

Tai nodded. "Well, you can't stay here," he grumbled, glancing around the room. His eyes snagged on a particularly bright cushion on a chair. "The pink alone will drive you closer to the edge."

A hiccup of a laugh fell out of my mouth followed by a sigh. "I can't anyway. Derek's parents are visiting and supposed to stay in this room," I said. "Good grief! They must think Sela's best friend the most rude and psychologically unstable person in the worlds!"

Tai pressed his shoulders back against the wall and gave me a side-long glance. "So…do you want to go to your parents' house?"

I shuddered at the thought. Ma would know something was wrong on the spot, then prod and poke until I blurted everything out.

"Maybe I could call my friend Nara," I said, but she lived in the next town, and it was already so late. Cade and Ben, her partners, were also my good friends, but I wasn't certain I wanted to be around their triad of unrelenting storybook love at the moment. I slumped. "Or maybe not."

Tai cleared his throat and gave me a gentle nudge with his shoulder. "You could come to my place."

I looked at him sharply. "Oh no. I-I couldn't do that."

"Why not?"

My mouth hung open for a moment then found the reason. "I don't want to be a problem."

He grinned. "Well, like it or not," he said, tugging on a curl of my hair. "It seems you're *my* problem now."

* * *

I had been awake for a while but had yet to open my eyes. I didn't want to face the day. I had slept, but it had been a fitful, torturous event. Throughout the night, I kept hearing the pain in Gannon's voice and seeing the anguish on his face. A few times I jolted awake in the dark, hoping it had all been a nightmare. When I realized that it was my reality, one I had created, I dropped my head in my hands, sobbing, until I fell back into an agitated sleep.

Gods, could I have chosen a worse time to end my relationship with Gannon? The special committee meeting was in a few days. The thought of coming into contact with him again made me want to bury my head under the covers and weep. So I did just that, pressing my face into the tangled sheets, sniffling.

Wait a minute.

My blankets usually smelled of almond oil and vanilla, not... *Tai?*

I flipped onto my back and looked straight into his eyes. I yelped as Tai jumped back, away from the bed.

"Shit!" Steaming liquid sloshed over the rims of the two mugs he held and ran onto his hands.

I sat up, trying to get my bearings. Sunlight poured through the windows of the room — *Tai's* room. It all came back in a rush.

After leaving Sela's, Tai had taken me to his apartment. I had sat on his couch in his sitting area, staring blindly at the wall, as he moved about in his bedroom, readying it for me. After he led me into his room, he handed me one of his shirts then asked if I needed anything else. I had shaken my head then asked him to turn off the lights. He had frowned, kissed my forehead and done as I had asked before closing the door quietly behind him.

I must have put the shirt on at some point before falling asleep, because I was wearing it now. There were drops of what smelled like coffee clinging to the thin gray fabric, splattered across my chest.

Tai placed the mugs on his bedside table and grabbed a small towel from a comfortable-looking upholstered chair. He sopped up the splashes of coffee that had reached his pants and some sections of the bedsheets.

"Apologies," he said, not taking his eyes from his task.

"No. *I'm* sorry," I said. "Y-you startled me. I just didn't remember where I was."

Even with his head bowed, I could see his signature scowl. "It didn't help finding me staring at you when you woke up," he muttered then looked me over, his eyes stopping at the coffee stains across my chest. Tai exhaled deeply then lifted his eyes to mine.

"Here," he said, giving me the towel. "You have some on my shirt, *your* shirt. I mean the shirt." He shook his head, his scowl deepening as he strode off into his bathroom.

I was too caught up with the fact that I was in Tai's room — his *bed*, no less — to wonder at his mood. I had been so emotional and inside my head when I had arrived the night before that the memory of my surroundings was only a blur.

Tai's bedroom was a revelation. The man was disciplined and organized, so it was no surprise to see his living space reflect those traits. What I didn't expect was how *lived in* it looked. The furniture was all dark wood, warm-colored fabrics and an assortment of lush plants — *good grief, plants!* — in every corner of the room. What single male with a busy career that took him all over the worlds had time to care for plants?!

I wiped at the stain on my shirt — no, *Tai's* shirt — barely paying attention to what I was doing while I gorged on more of the room. There were two tablets on the side table, which was no surprise. Tai and his scroll were extensions of one another, after all. Beside them was a book that looked to be filled with no fewer than a thousand weathered pages. I reached for the heavy tome but snatched my hand back when Tai returned to the room and went still as I took him in.

He was comfortably rumpled in a white shirt — similar to the one I had on, in fact — and loose gray pants. Beneath the soft fabrics, his muscles bulged and rippled as he crossed the short space between us. The way his short brown hair stuck up on end made a corner of my mouth tilt up.

"What?" he asked, picking up one of the mugs.

I shrugged and shifted into a better position on the bed, pulling the blanket up around my waist. "Nothing," I said. "I've just never seen you look so...*normal.*"

He raised an eyebrow. "I suppose I've been given worse compliments," he said, shoving the chair closer to the bed with his knee before sitting down on it.

My smile grew. "You just always look…on guard, ready to intimidate and fight at a moment's notice."

He snorted. "Did you think I wear my uniform while I sleep?" he said over the rim of his mug.

"Yes," I said promptly, holding back a laugh when he sent me an intimidating glare.

"Well, that should come as no surprise. Some days I feel like I might as well sleep in the blasted thing," he muttered, indicating the other mug on the table with his chin. "I brought you coffee. Well, whatever's left of it."

"Thank you," I said, reaching for the cup and bringing it to my mouth.

For a few minutes, we drank in silence. The coffee was good, but the entire time I was too conscious of Tai to pay it much attention. He watched me as closely as I suspected he would an alleged criminal or spy. Finally, I couldn't take it anymore.

"You're staring at me again," I said, lowering the mug to my lap.

He blinked, glancing away then winced. "Apologies," he said, looking at me. "Do you want more coffee?"

"No, thank you."

He leaned forward in his chair, resting his elbows on his knees. "How're you feeling?"

I dropped my gaze and ran my finger around the rim of the mug with a frown. "Like someone dug my heart out with a spoon, ran it through a food processor and is trying to shove what's left of it down my throat." I glanced up.

Tai rubbed a palm down his thigh, nodding with an eyebrow raised. "That's pretty much how you *should* feel," he said, pushing himself up to stand. "Come on. I'll make you breakfast."

A sour taste filled my mouth at the thought. "No. I can't eat."

"We'll see," he said, taking the mug from me. My hands were still cupped as he left the room.

With a heavy sigh, I dragged myself out of bed. There was no sense delaying the inevitable. I would have to face the day sooner or later.

Reflexively, I checked my comm for messages, but there were none. I hadn't taken the device off the night before the way I usually did before going to bed. I could argue that I had been too distraught to remember to do it, but the truth was, somewhere in the back of my mind, I had hoped Gannon would call or message, begging me to come back to him. Despite everything, that's all it would probably take for me to toss my good intentions out the door and run back into his arms.

I tugged on the hem of Tai's shirt and it fell past my knees, billowing around me as I walked to his bathroom to take care of my most immediate needs. After that, I scrunched my face in the mirror, not liking the redness in my eyes and the bags underneath. I shook my head. I would have to make do with washing my face and raking my fingers through the knots of my hair. What was I fussing about? Tai had never seemed to care too much about my appearance before, so looking bedraggled shouldn't make any difference now.

Having pulled myself together as best I could, I sought him out in the sitting area then stopped short, staring wide-eyed at the sunny and handsomely appointed room. A deep-seated leather couch and a large, round coffee table sat in the middle of a space filled with potted plants of varying sizes. But it wasn't the furnishings or oversized plant life that held my fascination. It was the walls. Every bit of their surface was covered in floor-to-ceiling shelves, filled to bursting with books.

"Good grief, Tai!" I said loud enough for him to hear me from the kitchen. "This is incredible!"

"What is?" he asked, walking into the room.

"The books!" I approached a shelf and ran a finger along it. Some of the titles were in different languages, but most were in Samaric, Prospect's official language. "My gods, you must have a *million* of them!"

"Not quite a million. There are four thousand, eight hundred and twenty-three," he said, then glanced down at me with humor shimmering in his eyes. "To be precise."

I smiled then a book caught my eye. "Can I?" I asked, pointing at its spine.

He nodded, pulling *1984* by George Orwell from the shelf and handing it to me. "It's about government control and social order," he said. "I think you'd like it."

I turned the book over in my hand, caressing it, holding it like the treasure it was. Books like these were collectors' items, whether first edition or not.

"Tai, all of this must be worth a fortune." I shook my head, staring at him. "Where did you get them?"

"Most of them were my father's."

"So *he's* the reason for your love of reading," I said with a smile.

"For the most part," he said. "Stress relief is the other."

I nodded, remembering he had said something along those lines before. Suddenly I gasped, holding up the book between us. "Should I be touching it like this?"

"It's all right," he said. "The cover and pages have a coating on them."

I looked closer at the book. I couldn't feel or make out the gloss usually found on paper covered in a protective resin. He closed the book in my hand and tilted it a bit so the hard cover caught the light.

"You can't ruin this book, not with the Protectorate-grade technology I applied to it." As he spoke, I caught sight of a barely there, filmy finish. "The coating's almost imperceptible."

Impressed, I glanced up at him to tell him so, but my eyes collided with his, flaring. He had been looking at me instead of the book. He was so close I saw a light dusting of freckles across the bridge of his nose, just beneath a small scar I had never noticed before.

Tai tensed, ran a hand over his hair, ruffling the short strands even more than they already were, and started backing away.

I reached for him, wondering at his reaction, but he was already out of range. "Are you all right?"

"Yes, I'm fine," he said, gripping his nape.

I frowned.

"Why don't you keep looking around?" he said with a heavy sigh. "I'm almost done with breakfast."

As he made his odd retreat, I considered the bookshelf again. The lower shelf was filled with a row of brightly colored books. Intrigued, I placed the copy of *1984* on the coffee table and stooped down to pull one out. It was a child's book. No matter what Tai said about the protective coating, it felt very precious in my hand, and I opened it gently. When I read the handwritten inscription on the first page, I knew I was right to feel that way.

To my son, Tai.

Because with a book, you'll never be alone.

I smiled, my heart warming at the words. What a gift! No wonder Tai had held on to these books, caring for them like a librarian or museum curator. Carefully, I replaced the book and admired a few others, each one revealing more about Tai and his childhood than the one before.

Tai called out for me a while later, and I walked toward the kitchen, spotting a sturdy wood desk on the way. In addition to a large monitor, a shiny, metal gadget sat atop it. Tai had been tinkering with that device when I told him I planned to leave Gannon. Now that I was more focused on it than on other things, I saw that it was an advanced communications device of some sort. I smiled, wondering whether Tai had entered the Protectorate for the sole purpose of accessing the newest technology.

I slid onto a stool in the kitchen and watched as he moved about the small space. It was decorated in the same warm, masculine strokes as the rest of his apartment. He poked around inside each of the cupboards and drawers, searching their contents.

I smirked. "How is it that a man who has a greenhouse for an apartment," I said, "doesn't know his way around his own kitchen?"

Tai chuckled, still hunting around. "I have an automatic water dispenser in each of the plant pots," he said.

I chuckled. *Of course, he does.* Always so organized.

He found cutlery and turned to me with a plateful of something in his hand. Whatever it was, it looked delicious, but it turned my stomach.

"I'm sorry, Tai. I *really* don't think I can eat that right now."

He placed the plate in front of me. "I'm no chef," he said with a grin, "but I can make a decent breakfast."

And then I remembered.

You know, if this high chancellor thing doesn't work out, you could become a chef.

And effectively kill my parents? You're a wicked woman.

I squeezed my eyelids shut at the bittersweet memory of my conversation with Gannon. I willed myself not to cry again, but it was no use. I dropped my face into my palms and, a moment later, Tai's arms were around me. I pressed my face into his chest, and pulled away only when I felt the moisture of his now tear-soaked shirt against my cheeks.

I looked up at him. "I'm so—"

"Don't apologize," he said, squeezing my arms. "I understand."

"You do?"

"I'm twenty-eight years old, Kira," he said before releasing me to return to the stove. "Do you think I've never had my heart broken before?"

His back was turned to me, so it was fortunate that he didn't see the stunned look on my face. Of course, Tai had had relationships before. If Rhoan's tales were any indication, he had plenty of them in his past. But I had tried not to think about that over the years.

Tai started hunting inside the cupboards again as I picked at my meal. He pulled out a couple of glasses, set them on the table, then went to the cooler to take out a pitcher of lime-colored drink. After pouring me a glass, he took a seat across from me and started in on his food.

"Rhoan called," he said.

My eyes widened. *Shit*. I had forgotten to tell him where I was. "How mad is he?" I asked, cringing.

"On a scale of one to ten?" Tai's mouth turned down in thought, still looking at his meal. "Eight."

"Just eight?" Eight I could deal with.

He swallowed a hulking bite and nodded.

I frowned, glancing at my comm. Still no messages or any indication that a call had come in. "Why didn't he call me?" I asked, looking up.

Tai shrugged. "He said he figured you were with one of two people," he said, raising his hazel eyes to mine. "Rhoan must be getting past his resentment of me. He sounded downright relieved to know you were with me and not with..." He frowned.

And not with Gannon, I thought.

I sighed and played with a piece of food with my fork.

"Gannon knows about Khelan and Maxim," I said, glancing up. "He's been monitoring them since his father was killed."

Tai placed his fork on the table and leaned onto his elbows, the short sleeves of his shirt straining around the width of his arms. "What does he know?"

"Everything," I said. "He had reports up to when Khelan recently met with Maxim."

Tai narrowed his eyes. "Khelan *recently* met Maxim? When? Where?"

"Yes. A few weeks ago. Here in Merit."

"I didn't know that." Tai frowned. "Did the report say what they talked about?"

I shifted in my seat, remembering the H3 acronym in the report. "They discussed travel authorization to Hale Three."

Tai's eyes sharpened. "Is his protector, Talib, providing the reports to him?"

I nodded.

"Then the reports should be accurate," he said, blowing out a breath.

"What is it?"

Tai studied me then pushed away from the table. He picked up his tablet and came around to my side of the table before rolling the device out on the counter.

"Yesterday," he began, "I received a report confirming that the person responsible for the attack on Septima is the same person who caused the attack on Hale."

Tai activated his scroll.

"Since this person would have to be at a high enough rank to gain access to leadership's travel itinerary," he said, swiping at the screen, "we've been investigating citizens in the Protectorate and Senate castes. Coming up empty, it occurred to me that our search was too narrow, that we should look even higher. My superior was cagey about me investigating the Elite, but permitted it as long as I did it under the radar. It's by pure luck that I've been monitoring your family's interactions with Maxim or I would have missed it."

"Missed what?" I tried to follow along, but when he had first mentioned this to me, my mind had been elsewhere, preparing to leave Gannon.

Tai glanced up from his device. "His connection to an exiled ambassador."

I frowned. "I don't understand."

"We were thinking of Donal Ambassador as the exiled ambassador connected to the rebels, but he wasn't the *direct* link," Tai said. "Liandra was."

"Liandra?" I searched Tai's face. "She wouldn't orchestrate an attack on the very arc craft that she and her father were planning to be on," I said. The young woman had been tormented, beside herself, after finding her father dead.

Tai shook his head. "She's not who I think caused the attack." He pointed to the tablet, where a report was now displayed on the screen.

(Start Record)

Name: Maxim Noble

Caste: Elite

Citizenship: Hale Dominion, World Five

Age: 30 years
Gender: Male

Family: Father, Edgar Noble (deceased); Mother, Marion Patrician (deceased)

Relationships: Unmarried, partner of Liandra Ambassador of Argon (age: 23; elite female citizen; exiled; recently held for possible involvement in attack on S2, released following investigation; on D1, awaiting transfer to A4.)

(End Record)

Maxim and...Liandra?

My mind started to reel.

If Maxim had been involved with Liandra, he had a motivation to coordinate the attacks on both Septima and Hale. With Argon's expulsion, the system was separating her from him. From the little interaction I had with Maxim, I could tell he wasn't someone who would have taken such a thing sitting down. It made sense now that he and Uncle Paol had become allies. Both of them faced a future without someone they cared about deeply.

Still, something didn't make sense.

"But if Maxim's involved with Liandra," I said, working it through out loud, "why would he plan an attack that would have killed her on Septima?"

Tai shook his head. "I don't think he knew she'd be there," he said, rolling up his tablet. "Liandra said she and her father were invited by the Corona to meet with her on the arc craft, but we have no record of an official invitation being issued."

Liandra had been so adamant that she was invited by our sovereign. No one, especially Tai, had believed her then. I mean, truly, *who* in their right mind would have? Liandra had also been claiming that Realm Council had been secretly exploring the Outer Realm for years and that hundreds of rogue worlds had already been discovered! The woman came across as delusional at best.

Tai scowled. "Our sovereign recently felt inclined to share with the Protectorate that she had, in fact, invited Donal Ambassador to the arc craft, corroborating Liandra's story," he said with a wry twist to his mouth. "I don't know why she didn't simply tell us that she had wanted to speak with Donal privately before the diplomatic meeting."

Yes, that was odd, but I was still trying to connect the dots between one attack and the other.

"So...after failing to kill the Corona on Septima," I said, "Maxim killed the high chancellor on Hale?"

Tai nodded, crossing his arms. "It's just my speculation," he said, face grim, "but I think that's exactly what happened."

I dropped my face in my hands, horror filling me. "Thank the gods I left Gannon!" I cried, raising my head. "Khelan's working with a man who could be directly responsible for his father's death!"

"It wasn't Khelan who did this, Kira, but his ties to the factions *have* to be cut," Tai insisted, jaw clenched. "When the Protectorate confirms that Maxim caused these attacks, it'll only be a matter of time before your father's discovered, and all of his secrets as well."

My body wilted, staring up at him with wide eyes.

Ping.

My heart tripped over itself as I checked my comm.

`You are not leaving me.`

I gasped. Another message from Gannon rolled up:

`I do NOT accept this.`

Then another:

`Do you understand me?`

"Is that Gannon?" Tai asked.

I nodded, still looking at my device. A second later, another message arrived:

`Answer me, damn it!`

"He's angry," I whispered, looking up at Tai as my heart began to race.

He raised an eyebrow. "And you're surprised?"

I swallowed. "H-he was so *hurt* last night."

"There are many stages of grief," Tai muttered. "Last night he was in shock. Today he's rallied."

Oh.

Tai eyed me, contemplative. "Are you going to talk to him?"

I held his gaze as I considered the question.

Earlier, I had been ready to run back into Gannon's arms, just waiting on one message or call from him to do so. But now, after the information Tai had revealed, my resolve had been strengthened. I couldn't go back to Gannon, no matter how angry or persuasive I knew he could be.

"No," I said finally.

He nodded, satisfaction blooming in his eyes. "Good."

CHAPTER TEN

"So, how long do you think you're going last?"

"Pardon me?" I asked, sidestepping a slushy pile of snow.

"You said your brother's being an ass and you don't know whether you can work with him. So my question is," Asher said, tugging his scarf closer around his neck, "how long do you think you're going to last? That'll determine when I implement my exit plan, because there's no freaking way I'm working alone with Mila on this project."

I blinked. "Oh. I'm sorry," I said, struggling to come back to the present. "I got lost in my thoughts."

Asher and I were walking to the Council building for the special committee meeting, talking about what to expect this time around.

Or rather, *Asher* had been talking.

My mind had been preoccupied with trying to find ways not to think of Gannon, which was difficult considering the stream of heated and insistent messages he had been sending my comm. I should have removed the device from my wrist or at least turned it off, but I didn't — couldn't. I seemed to have had some perverse desire to watch his messages arrive one after the other, steadily, over the course of the last few days.

"Hey. You okay?" Asher asked, a frown between his brows.

I glanced away from the concern in his eyes.

Dear gods, I didn't know how I was going to manage sitting through a meeting without breaking down. I had thought for a fleeting moment, as I was getting ready in the morning, that I should cry off, but the longing to simply lay my eyes on Gannon was too powerful to ignore.

"I'm fine," I said, not prepared to explain my mood. The pain was still too fresh and deep. Instead, I opted for an alternate explanation. "I'm just worried about how things will go today."

Asher bobbed his head. "I've been thinking about that," he said after a moment. "You know, your brother had some strong points, don't you think?"

I glanced at him. "What do you mean?" I asked as we stepped up onto the curb on the other side of the street.

He shrugged. "I don't know." He exhaled, his breath frosting in the wintry air. "The more I read up about it, a ban can only do so much when the technology's already out there. I mean, my grandmother knows a guy who can design a safe enough arc craft for as much as it costs to buy a vintage car. A ban just seems kind of…short-sighted."

I raised an eyebrow, considering him.

So Asher too shares Rhoan's opinion.

I shouldn't have been surprised. Still, Asher might be a subordinate, but he worked in the Judiciary. If anyone should be in accord with the Realm, it should have been those working in its legal arm.

As we entered the Council building, I glanced about, dusting snowflakes off the arms of my coat. The lobby was filled with citizens of every caste, but most of them were subordinates, chatting and going about their own affairs. How many of them harbored similar dissenting thoughts?

Perhaps Asher and Rhoan were right. A ban did seem a silly option in light of our system's advancement. However, I couldn't fathom leadership accepting anything less. After overhearing my brother prepare the night before, I knew he had a solid case. But it would take more than a well-delivered presentation to win leadership over.

"Kira Metallurgist?"

Asher and I were almost at the meeting-room doors when the reedy voice called my name.

I looked over my shoulder, and it took me a minute to spot a gangly man with a face that appeared much too young for his height step away from a large clutch of media. He approached me with a small, hesitant smile.

"Can I help you?" I asked, turning to face him.

"I'm Heath. Heath Reporter, that is," he said, offering me a thin hand. "Beth Curator's brother."

Oh yes. "It's nice to meet you." I smiled, taking his hand to shake. Heath had a firm grip despite the timidity of his approach. Now that I looked closer, I saw the resemblance between him and Beth. Heath had the same dark red hair, deep blue eyes and height as his sister.

"Are you covering the special committee meetings?" I asked.

He nodded. "It's my biggest job yet," he said, releasing my hand and shifting on his feet. "I-I was hoping that I could interview you about the process so far. You know, for the newsfeed."

My eyebrows shot up and I glanced at Asher. "Wouldn't you rather interview a minister or at least someone in a higher rank?" I asked, looking back at Heath.

His shoulders slumped. "There's no way I could get an interview with someone *that* important," he said.

Asher was suddenly overcome by a terrible and suspicious coughing episode.

"I'm sorry," Heath said, his eyes widening. "That didn't come out right. It's just that I keep getting shut down by everyone I try to interview."

I felt for him. Heath seemed like a good person, but my job wasn't to *be* the focus of the media — it was to *manage* them on behalf of the subordinate representative.

"How about I ask Rhoan Advocator to speak with you after the meeting?" I didn't know how I was going to convince my brother to do it, but the offer couldn't hurt.

Heath grew a couple of inches. "If you could arrange that, I'd be *forever* in your debt."

I smiled. "No need, Heath. I only promised to *ask*."

"That's a whole lot."

I looked him over as he shuffled away. Heath called out to an older man and started speaking to him with wide and excited gesticulations, his exuberance radiating through his every pore. Heath was *definitely* Beth Curator's brother.

"Come on," Asher said with a laugh, turning toward the double doors. "I just saw Mila and a couple of senators go in."

And just like that I was thrust out of a moment's respite from my misery into the moment I had been both dreading and anticipating: facing Gannon. My heart thumped out of my chest. I inhaled a chestful of air, digging deep for my courage, and followed Asher into the meeting room.

As soon as I walked in, my eyes found him. Gannon stood at the front of the room, arms crossed, in deep discussion with Mila and Rhoan.

I tugged on Asher's sleeve. "Can we sit in the back this time?"

Asher raised an eyebrow. "Ya. Sure."

I ducked my head, avoiding both the front of the room and Asher's assessing gaze, and chose the two seats farthest away from the platform.

I busied myself getting settled, unrolling my tablet and rearranging a few documents — anything to prevent myself from looking up.

Asher put a hand on my wrist, stopping me. "Where's all the heat today?" he asked, flicking a look toward the front of the room. "It's downright frigid between you two."

I slumped and glanced up to find Gannon's gaze on me. Instead of the fire that normally blazed in his clear blue eyes, there was only a cool regard, the blue in his eyes like chipped ice.

I dropped my gaze and shrugged, resuming my inane fidgeting. I wanted to confide in Asher but worried that he would say the same thing everyone else had: that my relationship with Gannon had been doomed from the start.

I shored up my strength over the next few minutes and when Gannon called the meeting to order, I managed to look to the front of the room. He invited each of the ministers to present their views.

One after the other they offered their opinion on how best to reinforce the ban on exploration. Xavier and Abigail cited a need for updated penalties, including imprisonment of citizens even remotely connected to those using arc travel technology for exploration. Mila also suggested a need to update penalties, but nothing so severe as her counterparts had. She preferred fines and hard labor for those in collusion with disloyal citizens. Meanwhile, Dominic proposed a widespread educational campaign, if you will, about the consequences of non-adherence to law.

I tried to listen. I really did, but it was no use. I ate up the sight of Gannon as the ministers went on, my heart sinking at the irony of it. The tables had turned. Unlike the last meeting, Gannon made no effort to catch my eye, hadn't looked at me once. Instead, it was *me* who watched *him*, like a hawk.

It was only when Gannon called my brother to speak that my attention shifted away from him.

Rhoan cleared his throat and stood up. He acknowledged Gannon with a nod before starting. "The reason for the ban on exploration is as familiar to us as the bedtime stories we heard as children," he said. "The loss of citizens on the old world was a terrible and eye-opening event, one that will never be forgotten. Unfortunately, our respect for that memory has held us prisoners. We have let the past haunt us, keeping us from seeing the obvious — that a ban on exploration is a useless and amateurish attempt to control what cannot be controlled."

Gannon crossed his arms. "We know your opinion is that we should allow regulated exploration," he said. "I'd like to hear how you think we could do that effectively."

Xavier puffed out his chest. "Yes, what exactly *is* your solution?" he asked.

Rhoan released a breath as if relieved to have gotten through the hard part. "May I?" he asked, gesturing to his monitor.

When Gannon nodded, Rhoan tapped on the device a few times and a large screen rolled down from the ceiling as the lights dimmed.

"First," Rhoan began, "today we train only protectors in arc travel technology. We need to properly train *all* of our citizens."

Rhoan tapped his monitor again and a 3D display of the worlds within the Realm and those known to the Outer Realm appeared, orbiting the black expanse of the screen.

"Second," he said, "we need to outline boundaries and establish a system of graduated authorization, giving citizens with the appropriate clearance access to certain zones. I anticipate that the farther out we explore, the more clearance levels we'll have to develop, but this system will allow us to monitor exploration while giving citizens an opportunity to travel safely."

Of course, Xavier was the first to speak.

"Pretty pictures, Advocator," he said. "But you're assuming that our citizens even *want* to go out into the unknown. They still understandably carry the horrible memory of what happened on the old world."

"That might have been the case once, but not anymore," Rhoan said. "I read an article in the newsfeed just this morning reporting that citizens would be open to the idea of exploration if provided proper training."

Xavier scowled. "They don't know any better," he said.

"How can they know better if they're not given any information about an alternative?" Rhoan said. "Up to now, our citizens have been told that exploration is a frighteningly bad idea, but they've been told so based on reports hundreds of years old."

Abigail waved a hand over her mic, activating it. "Exploration simply isn't worth the risk," she said.

Rhoan shook his head. "We don't *know* that," he said. "Through regulated exploration and with our advanced technology, we can go beyond the Realm to determine whether it's still actually dangerous."

Xavier exchanged a look with Abigail. "There's no regulation that will be foolproof," he said, sitting back in his chair with the corners of his mouth turned down.

Dominic made a disgruntled sound. "That's true," he said with a huff. "But the same can be said of the ban."

Rhoan acknowledged Dominic with a curt nod then looked around the table. "There has to be some benefit to exploration," he said. "The Realm *was* formed as a result of it, after all."

Xavier's eyes narrowed. "Yes, and the deaths of many our citizens came as a *result* of exploration," he replied. "You're asking us to tempt fate, and invite the same annihilation for the rest of us?"

Rhoan straightened his spine. "We can't leave our heads in the sand," he said tightly. "Our citizens are intelligent and strong-willed. If you deny them this, it's only a matter of time before they invent their own technology and explore on their own — *without* your consent."

There was an audible silence within the room.

Mila cleared her throat. "As you said earlier, Advocator, we limit arc travel training to protectors," she stated, considering my brother closely. "How do you expect other citizens to develop a similar technology?"

Rhoan held her gaze. "We also don't teach our citizens how to form rebel groups that threaten to take over the Realm," he said. "But they seem to be managing just fine."

Mila frowned as Gannon studied Rhoan. I sat, tense, wondering their response. Rhoan had been as eloquent and knowledgeable as I had expected so far, but I knew that he would need to be able to handle their harder questions just as well.

"If we were to implement regulation, how much would it cost?" Gannon asked.

Xavier's eyes nearly popped out of his head. "You can't *seriously* be considering this!" he said, glaring at Gannon.

Gannon slid a look at the minister. "I believe I said that all recommendations would be thoroughly considered by this committee, so we will do so," he said. Then he looked to Rhoan. "The cost?"

My brother stiffened before glancing down at his tablet. After a moment, he raised his head. "Approximately five hundred million *oros.*"

Xavier balked as chatter in the room rose in volume. "Are you planning on mining for precious gems in the Outer Realm?" he demanded with a curl to his lip. "Because that's the only way we could pay such an exorbitant price."

Rhoan glared at Xavier. "Regulation would cost only a fraction of what it does to support leadership's meetings and travel between our worlds," he said tightly. "I'm *sure* the Realm can manage."

Xavier's eyes narrowed. "Are you casting doubt on our sovereign's management of the Realm's financial affairs?" The gleam in Xavier's eyes said he would relish it if Rhoan was doing just that.

Rhoan shook his head. "I'm merely questioning where the Realm's priorities rest," he said, fists clenched — "with its citizens or in its pockets."

I slumped. There were one or two gasps in the audience. Members of the media descended into a flurry of note taking.

Xavier glowered. "If we're going to change the way things are done, why stop there?" he said to no one in particular. Sarcasm was a thick undercurrent to his tone. "Why don't we simply allow citizens to run rampant throughout the galaxy without restriction at all?"

"Don't be a fool," Dominic said, sending his counterpart a withering look.

"Why am *I* the fool?" Xavier asked, hand at his chest as he bored holes into the older man. "Our esteemed subordinate representative is the one bringing us ludicrous ideas. He was asked to present his side of the argument, and he did. We should all pat him on the head for a job well done." He turned to Gannon. "Can we get on to discussing reinforcement of the ban?"

Gannon eyed him. "I've had enough of your condescension, Minister," he said sharply. "If you don't approve of the way I'm running this meeting, I'd be more than happy to arrange your removal from this committee."

Xavier hesitated, mouth open.

Gannon rested a fist on the table and surveyed the room. "I applaud your courage, Advocator," he said to Rhoan. "It's not easy to go against what everyone says is wrong to say what you feel it is right."

Rhoan nodded and exhaled a deep breath. "Thank you, Chancellor."

"Having said that," Gannon said, his eyes skimming his colleagues around the table, "I'm still not convinced either way."

The ministers all spoke at once while Rhoan observed them with a frown.

Gannon simply raised a hand, quickly quieting them. For a moment, he appeared thoughtful, as if weighing his options or what he was about to say. "What I *am* convinced of," he said finally, "is that times are changing and we now have an opportunity to truly consider a law of compromise."

"Thank the gods for the rare combination of youth and wisdom," Dominic said, lifting his eyes to the ceiling.

A few citizens sitting in the row in front of me chuckled. A quick look to my right, and I saw by Asher's grin that he had found humor in the minister's remark as well.

Gannon raised an eyebrow in Dominic's direction before continuing. "I ask each minister to send me a written report," he said. "At our next meeting, we'll review them then go to vote."

* * *

"You okay?"

I glanced up to find Rhoan striding up the aisle with a look of concern on his face.

The meeting had adjourned a few minutes ago. Asher had left, but I had decided to hang back and see whether Rhoan needed any help with anything.

"I'm fine," I said, sitting up in my chair and trying to muster a smile. The meeting had been eventful, but it was more than the heated argument that had left me unsettled. "Why do you ask?"

Rhoan quirked an eyebrow and glanced toward the front of the meeting room. I swallowed and made sure not to follow his line of sight. I didn't have to look to know who he was looking at. Gannon was still in the room, speaking with Mila and a group of senators. Up until then, I had managed to keep my eyes fixed on my tablet, finding it incredibly interesting despite the blank screen.

"Much different meeting this time around, don't you think?" Rhoan asked.

I nodded.

"The chancellor seemed to be a different man altogether," he said.

I shrugged, refusing to take the bait. "Do you need me to prepare anything for your report?" I asked, willing him to let this line of conversation go.

Rhoan frowned, looking me over, and sighed. "As a matter of fact I do," he said, thankfully relenting. "Can you get me a summary on Xavier's and Abigail's voting histories on anything even remotely related to exploration over the past few years? They seem to be the ones most against regulation. Maybe I can win them over with a more detailed report that addresses their concerns."

I studied him, noting the lines of frustration and disappointment around his eyes and mouth. He looked as if he had failed somehow. "You did *really* well, Rhoan," I said, trying to lift his spirits.

He snorted. "I don't know about that," he said, running a hand around the back of his neck. "I have a tendency to get too keyed up over these things."

I smiled.

Just then, the doors opened and Heath entered the room, followed by the older man he had been speaking with earlier and a woman carrying a recorder.

"Rhoan," I said, cringing as I looked up at him. "Would you be willing to speak with the media by any chance?"

His face instantly fell into a scowl. "I'd rather be grilled by the special committee again than by those vultures."

I sighed. I had feared this. My brother's unwavering disdain for authority was mirrored in his disregard for the media. Still, I had promised Heath I would ask, so I would do my best.

"You're the first subordinate representative the Realm has ever had," I pressed. "You're not going to win any votes by being so resistant."

"I'd like to think that to *win* votes, all I would need is common sense," he said, crossing his arms.

I groaned. Rhoan was using his "I'm the defender of equality and justice" voice.

"Does it make any difference if I tell you the interview is with Beth's brother?"

Rhoan shook his head.

I opened my mouth, ready to try again.

"The answer is *no*, Kira," he said, pivoting on his heel and striding off.

Stubborn ass.

It was testament only to how conscious I was of Gannon being in the room that I refrained from rolling my eyes.

Heath's steps faltered as Rhoan crossed paths with him and walk out of the room. "Is he going to prepare for the interview?" he asked, approaching me.

I sighed. "Heath, I'm sorry," I said. "I tried, but it's not going to happen."

His smile slipped. He threw an uneasy look over his shoulder at the man and woman behind him.

Heath swung back to me. "Is there any way he would change his mind?"

"I don't think so," I said. The way Heath hung his head made me feel like I had kicked a puppy. His head snapped up. "How about you?"

Good gods. He must truly be desperate. "As I said earlier, Heath," I said, "it's probably better you interview someone in a higher rank."

"I know, but he's *your* brother," he said, eyes filled with hope. "Two siblings working on such an incredible project is a great story. People would want to hear what *you* have to say just as much as they would him."

I shook my head firmly and began collecting my things from the lap desk and chair.

"Heath, is this happening or not?"

I glanced up to find Heath looking over his shoulder at the man he'd come in with. "Sorry, Gavin, I'm just trying to negotiate an interview."

Gavin strode up, a look of distaste curling his upper lip. "Negotiate?" he said. "You said you *booked* an interview with Rhoan Advocator."

"He's not available," Heath said, a blush coming in high on his cheeks as he looked to me. "So I'm trying to get his support, Kira Metallurgist, to fill in."

I hated to embarrass him, especially in front of someone who appeared to be his superior, but it couldn't be helped. "Heath…," I said, wrapping my arms around my coat and bag. "I-I can't do it."

Gavin shot a look at the woman behind him. Her black hair was braided into two thick plaits, one resting on each shoulder. Threads of yellow and green glimmered throughout their strands, revealing the optic behind the intermittent change in color.

"Why in the bloody Realm did I listen to the rookie?" Gavin bit out, shaking his head. "We could have been interviewing any one of the ministers by now."

The woman rolled her eyes and rested a hand on her hip. I wasn't sure if her irritated look was due to her superior's insolence or Heath's inability to book the interview. Either way, it pissed me off. I knew how it felt to be bullied by someone.

Heath sighed heavily. "Please." He winced, looking at me.

I checked Heath's entourage again. The man looked to the heavens as the woman tapped the side of her leg with a palm, impatient, I supposed, to move on to her next task.

"All right," I said. Gavin and his sidekick looked at me as I lifted my chin. "I'll do it."

Heath lit up like a festival-day bulb. "Okay. Hold on. Just let us get set up," he rushed out, holding up his hands as if afraid I'd make some sudden move or perhaps change my mind. "I'll message you when we're ready."

I nodded as he fumbled to tap his comm against mine to take my contact information then jogged off, his superior and optic-hair lady dragging their feet behind him.

That's when my gaze collided with Gannon's. The senators around him were still engaged in conversation, but his eyes were trained steadily on me. Whereas they had been frigid before, they were burning bright now. My heart tripped up at the look of pure longing and need that blanketed his face. I flushed and, like a coward, ducked my head as I hurried down the aisle to exit the room.

"Kira?" Gannon said sharply before I could leave.

I stood, frozen, facing the dark paneling of the double doors for a few moments before turning to him.

Gods, it was too much to bear. I had committed every feature and line of his face to memory, but seeing Gannon in front of me after so many painful days out of contact with him twisted a knife in my heart. I searched for my resolve and found it after remembering what Tai had told me. The possibility that Khelan could be tied to a man who killed Gannon's father was enough to keep me committed to the decision I had made.

I had taken a step, ready to retreat, when the doors behind me swung open. I spun around and stumbled, nearly falling into Tai. I gripped his wrist to steady myself.

"I've got you," he said, steadying me.

"I-I didn't realize you were here," I said.

"The ambassador just arrived for a meeting," he said then glanced over my head. "With *him*."

I didn't have to look to know who "him" was.

"Gannon's coming over here," Tai said, still looking beyond me. "I imagine he wants to speak with you."

I nodded, staring at the badges glistening on his uniform. Suddenly, Tai cupped my cheek, startling me.

My eyes snapped up to his. "W-what are you doing?"

He bent down, his mouth close to my ear. "Didn't you tell Gannon that you left him so we could be together?"

I frowned. Tai knew very well that I had.

He pulled away and peered down at me. A flicker of something akin to challenge burning in his eyes. "Then don't you think we should act the part?"

My eyes widened.

Tai placed his hand at my waist. "I missed you," he said with a grin, running the back of his knuckles down my cheek. "Waking up with you in my bed after all this time has only made me want you more."

Holy gods.

"Kira?"

I turned at the sound of Gannon's voice. He was standing, fists clenched, only a few feet away. "I need to speak with you," he said, ignoring Tai.

There was an urgent quality to the way he said "need" that made me frown. I was about to step over to him, tossing out my commitment to stay away, when Tai wrapped an arm around my waist.

"Feel free to speak, Chancellor," Tai said. "Anything you have to say to Kira can be said in front of me."

I glared at Tai, mouth slack. He had said the same thing Gannon had when Tai had approached us at a reception weeks ago. Tai had been stunned by Gannon's declaration, so I knew he fully understood the impact of repeating it to Gannon now. It was one thing to maintain the pretense of us being together; it was another to intentionally throw it in his face.

Gannon stepped up to Tai. "I was speaking to Kira," he said through clenched teeth, blue eyes snapping.

Tai raised an eyebrow.

I shot a look at Mila, hoping she and anyone else across the room couldn't hear us. She was still speaking with her peers but glanced toward me before returning to her conversation.

I swallowed. "Gannon," I began, trying to ease out of Tai's grip, but he had tightened his hold, keeping me by his side. "Is everything all right?"

Gannon's gaze fell to Tai's hand at my waist and rose to mine. For an agonizing moment, he studied me with a look filled with such a torrent of emotions, I had to bite the inside of my cheek to stop from going to him.

Tai cleared his throat and I glanced up at him. He tilted his head to the group of senators on the other side of the room. Mila was leading them toward the doors where we stood.

I tensed as she approached.

"Chancellor," Mila said, looking between the three of us, "I've been notified that the ambassador is ready to meet with us."

It was few strained seconds before Gannon released me from his gaze. "Then I suppose we should get going," he said, bracing his shoulders back as he faced Mila. "I can see I'm no longer needed here."

CHAPTER ELEVEN

"Mila wants to see you," Theo said, tapping away on his monitor.

I had just arrived at work the day after the special committee meeting with plans to meet with Asher about doing research for Rhoan's report.

"Did she say why?" I asked, walking to Theo's desk.

Mila, Asher and I had a meeting scheduled for later in the afternoon. The only reason I could think that she would want to meet with me privately before that was to speak about any concerns she had over my brother's presentation. But that didn't seem right. By this point, Mila was more than familiar with Rhoan's strident opinions.

Theo glanced up at me. "Unfortunately," he said with a drawl, "though I'm a senator, I'm not privy to such information."

I frowned, still deep in thought as I walked to Mila's office. The previous name etched on the minister's door had been removed and were replaced by the words Office of Mila Interim Minister of Prospect Eight. The change had been done so quickly and inconspicuously that if I hadn't worked for Gabriel, I would have had a hard time believing he had ever worked at the Judiciary.

I tapped on the panel at the side of her door. When it slid open, I peeked inside. "Mila?"

"Come in," she said from her seat behind the desk. Her head was down, eyes focused on her monitor as she sipped a drink. The scent of *hurim* filled the room. She pointed at the chair to her left, not taking her eyes off of her screen.

I sat down then watched as Mila's dark brown eyes slid across the screen, reading whatever it was that was displayed there. She appeared to be in no hurry to speak, so I plaited my fingers in my lap and glanced around. The office was just as Gabriel had left it. In fact, there was nothing that reflected Mila's personal life or tastes within the space. It was clear that Mila was under no illusion that she would be here very long.

I cleared my throat. "How are plans coming along to elect our new minister?" I asked.

Mila scowled at her monitor. "Too fucking slow," she said, finally looking at me. "I'm trying to hold two worlds together during a time of unprecedented unrest, yet Prospect Council appears to be in no rush to get things started."

I frowned. "Do you at least know who's in the running?"

Mila set her mug on the desk. "There are two senators who are strong candidates so far: the designate ministers from Dignitas Two and Hale Six."

I gaped at her. "Hale *Six?*"

Mila nodded. "Petra Minister."

I slumped in my seat. If there *truly* were gods, then they were surely enjoying a good laugh right now.

Mila looked me over and cocked her head. "Do you know her?"

I glanced away. "Only in passing," I mumbled, reflecting on the chance meeting between me and Gannon's old flame. I quickly plotted out paths to transfer to another world should she become Prospect Eight's minister and, gods forbid, my superior.

"Kira, have I been clear about what your role is in supporting the sub rep?"

I looked up. "Of course."

"When I asked you to handle the media," she said, eyeing me, "I didn't expect you to be the one actually *doing* the interviews."

She reached for her monitor and swiveled it on its axis so I could see the screen. She had been reading a story from the newsfeed with a headline that made me freeze: "The Subordinate Caste Demands Exploration." Beneath Heath's byline was an article filled with fabricated quotes from me, filled with righteous indignation, demanding that leadership lift the ban.

My mouth fell open as I scanned the article. "Mila, I don't know what to say," I spluttered, looking at her. "Rhoan wasn't available. I never said *half* of these things."

Mila raised an eyebrow.

I fisted my hands. *I am going to murder Heath Reporter.* There I was trying to help him out only to have him twist my words.

"I'm so sorry, Mila," I said, shaking my head. "I never should have done the interview."

Mila waved her hand. "Even without your interview, Rhoan's presentation would have resulted in the same headline."

I blinked, shooting a look at the screen. "You're not angry?" Perhaps I would come away from this unscathed.

"At first I was," she said, bracing a hand against the edge of her desk, "but then I thought about it a little more. You doing the interview instead of your brother was probably a good thing. Rhoan is smart and articulate, but abrasive. If he had done the interview, it probably would have been far worse."

She narrowed her eyes. "Though I would like a little notice about things like my support doing interviews. It gives me the false impression that I actually know what the fuck's going on in my two jurisdictions."

I frowned, giving her a tight nod as I started to get up. "Of course, Mila," I said. "I understand."

She eyed me. "So you *do* have friends in high places."

I fell back into my seat. "Pardon me?"

"Tai Commander," she said. "I saw you speaking with him *and* the chancellor after the special committee meeting."

"Y-yes," I stammered. "Tai's the family friend who invited me to the high chancellor's ash ceremony."

Mila nodded. "Things seemed pretty intense between the two of them."

I glanced away briefly. "They're not the best of friends."

"I imagine they wouldn't be if they both wanted the same thing."

I froze again, eyes wide.

Mila sat forward, steepling her fingers on the desk. "You know, Kira, you may not know this about me, but I have a reputation of being a hard-ass, foul-mouthed bitch." If she hadn't said it with a straight face, I would have laughed out loud. "I don't have issues with crossing boundaries from time to time. I just try to ensure that no one gets hurt, *including* myself. Do you understand?"

I swallowed. "Yes. I think so."

She nodded, reaching for the mug of *hurim*. "You're a smart young woman," she said. "I'm sure you do."

I stood up and was out the door before she raised the tea back to her lips.

* * *

Free for lunch?

I leaned against my desk, cringing as I read Khelan's message. He had been trying for the past week to reach me, saying that he wanted us to have some one-on-one time. No doubt, he wanted to speak about where things stood between us since he had revealed that he was my biological father.

I sighed, walking out of my office and typed in a "yes" to his invitation even though the last thing I wanted to do was endure the inevitably awkward conversation. I had found a happy medium of harboring a mild resentment about the whole thing and feared that speaking with him would only bring up a flood of painful emotions. Between dreaming about Gannon at night and living up to my superior's expectations during the day, I had enough to think about.

The irony of it all was that there was no greater time when I could have used Khelan's guidance and support. I longed to speak with him about my new role. As a former senator and a Judiciary employee, he would more than likely have some nugget of advice that would set me on the right path as I navigated the obstacles at work. He always seemed to know what to say.

When I had run for a student leadership position at the Academy, I had struggled to find votes toward the end of my campaign. Students were against my push to spread out evaluation dates to allow more time between them to study. When I had told Khelan about my struggles, he had said, "Stay the course. People have confidence in steady leadership supported by consistent opinions."

Khelan's advice was playing in my mind when I stopped abruptly in the middle of the work area. A few subordinates in their cubicles glanced up at me. Ignoring their inquiring looks, I hurried toward Asher's cubicle on the far side of the room. I was passing the boardroom when I nearly bumped into him.

"Whoa. What's wrong?" Asher asked, glancing in the general direction of Mila's office. He lowered his voice with a grin. "Do I need to activate my exit plan?"

"No," I said, pulling him into the meeting room. The lights came when we crossed the threshold. "I have an idea."

"Thank the gods, because I'm fresh out of those," Asher said with a chuckle, shoving his hands into his pockets.

I smiled. "Do you still have access to the background files on the special committee members that you prepared for Mila?"

"Ya," he said with a bob of his head. "I'm the one who pulled the information up, so I still have access until the end of the project."

I nodded. "How detailed are the reports?"

"I have database authorization up to level twelve," he said. "Beyond that, only the gods and the Corona know what goes on."

I thought about that. "That means you only pulled basic information about their backgrounds."

He nodded, confirming my assumption.

"Rhoan asked me to provide him with a summary on the ministers' voting patterns over the last few years," I said, "but can you access that information about Xavier's and Abigail's special interests further back than that, maybe before they became ministers?"

Asher's eyebrows climbed up his forehead. "I guess so. It all depends on what you're looking for," he said. "The system won't give me more than I ask for. It's not like I can just browse." A frown filled his normally jovial expression. "What's going on?"

I took a deep breath. "If Rhoan's is going to be heard by leadership, then we have to be much more strategic," I said, my idea taking root.

"I'm with you so far," Asher said. "But you have to give me more than that. What exactly are we looking for?"

Truly, I wasn't sure, but I remembered Khelan's advice and said, "Inconsistency."

* * *

I waved a hand to catch Khelan's attention as he walked into the crowded eatery. When he spotted me at a table at the back, he shouldered passed a large group of people waiting by the door and walked toward me.

"Sorry I'm late," he said, shrugging out of his coat with a deep frown. Being late was something Khelan deplored. "A last-minute errand came up."

"That's all right," I said, rolling up my tablet and tucking it into my bag. I had been scanning the article Mila had shown me, plotting ways to wring Heath's wiry neck, when Khelan had arrived. "I went ahead and ordered us something to eat."

"Good," he said, settling into his seat. He ran a hand through his hair, ruffling the wheat-colored strands, then looked at me with a warm but hesitant smile.

I shifted in my seat, wondering what to say. It was odd having him there, where I spent most of my time, a place where I was someone other than my parents' daughter.

He rested his elbows on the wooden table between us and looked around. I had selected the eatery on the ground floor of the Judiciary because it was close and the food was surprisingly good. I had eaten there with Asher a few times, and enjoyed the easy, bright atmosphere and inexpensive menu.

"I've never been to this division of the Judiciary," he said, settling his eyes back on me. "It's a lot busier than where I'm assigned."

I shrugged. "It's the main division, so…"

"So it should be busier," he said.

I smiled and fidgeted with my napkin.

He took a deep breath and flickered a look over me. "Your mother told me about you and Tai."

I froze and glanced up, remembering that Ma was still under that false impression. "What exactly did she say?"

Khelan winced, the movement deepening the lines at the corner of his eyes. "She said that you and he are *involved*," he said. "Isn't that what you young people call it nowadays?"

"Yes…," I said, feeling heat in my cheeks. "But Tai and I aren't involved."

Khelan blew out a chest full of air. "Thank gods," he said. "Tai's a wonderful young man, but I could do without hearing your Ma talk about you two having children any time soon."

My mouth fell open. "She's been talking about us having a *baby?*"

He nodded with a grin. "Just this morning she was planning for your second child."

I groaned as he laughed.

The waitress arrived then and placed our orders on the table. With a pleasant smile, she left after we refused anything else from the menu. I picked up my fork, but instead of eating, used it to poke at the food on my plate.

"So…," I began, raising my head. "You're here because Ma wanted an update on things between Tai and me?"

"Well, not exactly," he said, head down. "It was actually your Da who told me to ask you about Tai."

I cocked my head, surprised Da would be interested.

Khelan clasped his hands around his plate, leaning forward. "Your Da, he's a little uncertain how to talk to you right now," he said. "He doesn't seem to know where he fits in."

I frowned, not liking the sound of that. "What do you mean, 'where he fits in'?"

"Now that you know I'm your father," he said, lowering his voice despite the fact that the din in the eatery was so loud he couldn't possibly be overheard, "he worries that you think differently of him and his role in your life."

I stiffened. "He'll *always* be my father," I said firmly.

Khelan drew back, his eyes clouding over. "Of course, he will," he said.

For a brief moment, I couldn't understand his reaction, then I realized he must think I was trying to make a statement — that *he* could never take Da's place.

I shook my head, hating the strangeness that had become the norm between us. "I didn't say that to hurt you," I said, shoulders slumping.

Khelan searched my face, his blue eyes bleak. "I know," he said with a sigh. "I've become too sensitive, I think. Your Da isn't the only one feeling lost. You and I used to speak so freely. Now I feel like you're always measuring my words, judging their truth."

I placed my fork on the table and ran a finger back and forth across a deep groove in the surface of the table, avoiding his gaze. "I guess it'll take a little time."

When I glanced at him from under my lashes, it was to see him disheartened. His expression was fraught with an uncommon insecurity.

"I just don't want you mad at your Ma or Da," he said.

I scowled. "I'm not *mad*. Well, not anymore. I'm just…unsettled," I said, realizing just how true it was. I shook my head. "I just feel like everything's been tossed up in the air and I don't know where the pieces have landed."

He nodded, seeming to understand, and laid a hand over my wrist. "I hope we can have a relationship like we had before. I'd hate it if the truth were to drive you away," he said, giving me a gentle squeeze. "I want to be a part of your life."

I stared at him, finding myself doing what he had accused me of, measuring his words. I nodded, flipping my hand over to give his own a squeeze in return. He was trying to find his way through this just as much as I was.

"I want that too," I said.

Khelan smiled, his mood lifting visibly. He released my hand to pick up his fork and start back on his meal. I followed suit, happy to have come out on the other side of the awkward conversation feeling better, not worse.

A moment later, he raised his head. "I see on the newsfeed that you're making waves." Khelan chewed, eyeing me.

I sighed. "I didn't say most of those things in the article."

He grinned. "I would have been surprised if you did," he said before raising an eyebrow. "Now, if it was your *brother* who was interviewed..."

I smiled.

"I haven't had a chance to officially congratulate you on your seniority," he said, his grin widening. "I couldn't be more proud of you, Kira."

A soft heat spread up my neck and filled my cheeks. I basked in his praise until the irony of what he said dawned on me: there Khelan was, applauding my career advancement, while everything he was doing with Maxim could make it all go away.

I rested my elbows on either side of my plate. All of a sudden, I was no longer hungry.

"Please," I said, leaning toward him. "You have to let this go."

Khelan frowned. "Let *what* go?"

I stared at him, waiting on him to catch on, so I wouldn't have to spell it out in a public place, in a building that upheld Realm law, no less.

The easy look on his face faded away. "This isn't the time or place to talk about this, Kira."

I lowered my voice, my urgency filtering through it. "You're putting our family at risk."

Khelan tensed. "I would never do anything that would harm my family," he said, steel in his voice. "I'm doing nothing but providing information."

I clenched my fists. "There's only so long you can hide behind that."

He glanced away. "Halls, you sound like your mother," he muttered.

My eyes widened. So Ma *had* spoken to him, after all. I wondered whether it was before or *after* I had spoken with her. Encouraged, I forged ahead.

"Addy's under your care, and Rhoan and I are working on the special committee," I said. "You must see that what you're doing carries consequences that won't impact only you."

Doubt crept in from the corners of Khelan's eyes, but it was a momentary thing. He shook his head, a sharp, decisive movement that let me down.

"My sister was killed as a result of the Realm's decision to expel Argon," he said. "I *have* to do something." He glanced at a neighboring table as he leaned in, closer to me. "If it were Rhoan in my sister's place, what would you do?"

I rocked back in my chair, mouth agape.

Khelan sighed, closing his eyes for a moment. "I'm sorry," he said, regret tempering his unexpected flare of rage. "I just…I just need you to understand."

"I *do* understand," I said. "But you don't know anything about the man you're working with. Do you have any idea what he's capable of? How far he's willing to go?" I couldn't say much more in our surroundings and without giving away the fact that Tai was monitoring him.

"If Paol trusts him, then so do I," Khelan said.

I balked. "Uncle Paol is no longer the man we used to know. He's broken," I said. "You can't depend on him as your moral compass *or* for judgment."

"Kira, leave this alone," he said, tension making his words tight. "I know what I'm doing."

I ignored his warning. "Do you want blood on your hands? On *our* hands?"

He pounded a fist on the table, rattling the cutlery and glasses. "What exactly are you accusing me of, Kira Metallurgist?"

I tensed and shot a look at the table next to us, where one of the two citizens sitting there sent me a furtive glance. The eatery hadn't been noisy enough to cover the sound of Khelan's angry outburst.

I pushed away from the table and grabbed my bag as I stood up. Khelan was right: this wasn't the time or place. I had said too much already, and I was tired of pounding my head against a wall.

"Kira," he snapped, glaring up at me, "sit down."

I shook my head. "You just said that you want us to have a relationship like we had before," I said, watching his expression become crestfallen. "Unfortunately, I don't think that's possible since it's clear where your priorities lie." I ran my comm across the panel to pay for our meal then stalked away.

* * *

There was nothing for it.

No form of entertainment could distract me from the troubles running through my mind. I set the monitor on silent mode and flipped onto my back, watching the light from the screen flicker across the ceiling of the sitting area in my apartment.

I wished Rhoan were home. I could run my conversation with Khelan by him to get his opinion, but he had left hours ago to spend time with Beth. Thank the gods he hadn't invited her over. I wasn't fit for company and had no desire to bear witness to Rhoan's seductive charms yet again. Never mind that *Beth* being around would only remind me of my developing plot to murder her brother.

I sat up and shook my head, trying to clear my thoughts. I had to pull myself together. I had meetings with Abigail and Xavier coming up, and I needed to focus on that.

After I had told Asher about my grand idea about how to help Rhoan, he had thrown himself into background research on the ministers. Before the end of the day, he had walked into my office and plunked two hefty folders and his tablet on my desk. Shortly thereafter, I shut my office door and immersed myself in the documentation, sifting through the details of the ministers' working lives. While Abigail's history was an eye-opener, I had yet to locate anything helpful in Xavier's.

I jolted when the front door buzzed. I voice-activated the monitor's dashboard. In addition to displaying a view of the lobby of my building, it provided each resident with a record of who had arrived and which particular apartment floor was their destination. Usually, visitors had to buzz to gain access to the elevator, but Sela and Tai, being our close friends, had a code.

I scanned the screen. Tai. Why was *he* here?

I pushed up to my feet and approached the door. I hoped he wasn't expecting much. I was dressed for bed, in my favorite beige sweater and pair of flannel pants. When I opened the door, I found Tai on the other side, dressed in his full Protectorate uniform, crests, badges and all, despite the late hour.

I leaned against the doorjamb with a grin. "So you *do* sleep in your uniform," I said.

The corner of his mouth tipped up. "Can I come in?"

I stepped aside. "Rhoan's not here," I said as he entered.

Tai shrugged. "Even if he was," he said, "I'm the last person he would want to see."

I made a face as I disengaged the door. "I thought you were on Rhoan's better side nowadays."

Tai quirked a brow and stood in the middle of the sitting room. He was such a large man, the space seemed to shrink around him. "Does Rhoan *have* a better side?" he said with a drawl.

I rolled my eyes, wondering when the two of them would smooth things out.

Tai's expression sobered. "I'm heading out of Merit tonight. There've been reports of rebel activity in Helios," he said.

My pulse shot up as I met him by the couch. Nara's family lived close to Helios, in a town called Port. I would hate anything to happen to them.

"Is everything all right?" I asked.

"I'm not sure yet."

I had an awful thought. "Do you think it has anything to do with Maxim?"

"I highly doubt it, but I won't know until I get there," he said, glancing me over. "Has Khelan said anything to either you or Rhoan about him?"

I frowned, remembering my last interaction with Khelan. "No, but I've said a lot to *him*," I said with a sigh. I gave him a summary of our argument over lunch. "Khelan's committed to working with Maxim."

Tai crossed his arms. "Did you tell him my suspicions about Maxim, that he may have coordinated the attacks on Septima and Hale?"

I shook my head. "I thought it was best that didn't know he was being monitored," I said.

Tai's gaze turned inward. "Maybe it's time I told Khelan exactly who he's dealing with."

"Tai, I don't know…," I began. I couldn't see the benefit of that. Revealing that Tai knew about Khelan and Maxim working together was risky. "After you talk to him, he could very well stick to his guns but be even more careful of his moves, preventing us from tracking him."

Tai's shoulders stiffened. "I've had enough of him acting like some blasted avenger, with no consideration of anyone else."

I understood how he felt. "I was hoping he would stop by now," I said. "That after he settled into his grief, he would understand how dangerous this was."

Tai scoffed. "I know Khelan, and he's not going to stop," he said. "The longer he's in with Maxim, the worse it will be for him when the rebels are brought in to answer for their crimes."

I shuddered at the thought of Khelan being sent to prison, or worse, expelled from the Realm.

"I didn't stop by only to ask about Khelan," he said, stepping toward me. "I haven't seen you since the committee meeting and wanted to be sure you were all right."

Oh. I wrapped my arms around my waist and forced a smile.

Since Tai's and my performance as a couple, Gannon had been uncommonly quiet. He hadn't sent a message or called. I wasn't sure how to feel about that, but held firm to the belief that it was for the best. What I'd had with Gannon was a fairy tale, a little girl's dream. The reality was that I couldn't be with him. No matter how much I wanted him, with Khelan's ties to Maxim, the fact that Gannon and I were in restricted castes was the least of our problems. I was right to have left him to keep him out of my family's mess. I would find a way to move on. I had to.

Tai was looking at me expectantly.

"I'm fine," I said with a weak shrug.

He reached for one of my hands, tugging it away from my body. "I want you to know that I'm here for you," he said, holding my gaze. "I was serious when I said that if you need anything, all you have to do is ask."

I smiled, trying to ignore the intense way he was looking at me. "Th-thank you, Tai," I said. "You've done so much for my family."

He hung his head so he could look me closer in the eye. "I haven't been doing what I have for your *family*, Kira," he said, placing a hand on my cheek.

I was studying him, trying to read in his expression what he was really saying, when my comm vibrated.

Tai stiffened and lowered his hand as I read the device.

Be careful, Metallurgist. Terrible things happen to subordinates who don't know their place.

I stared at the message, disoriented. Like the others, there was no sender identification, but this one sent a chill up my spine. It referred to me by name.

"Is that Gannon?" Tai asked tightly.

"No," I said, looking up at him.

"What's wrong?"

I swallowed. "I've been receiving some strange messages on my comm lately," I said. "I don't know who they're coming from."

Tai frowned. "Show me."

I held it up so he could see the screen.

"When did the messages start?" he asked after reading it.

I thought back. "A few weeks ago."

"What did the other messages say?"

"Nothing like this," I said, shaking my head. "The first was like a countdown to something, and another was some random old saying."

Tai's shoulders lost some of the tension. "Did you try to get your comm fixed?"

I blinked. "Well, no. I was going to, but…" I frowned, looking back at my comm. "Do you think this is just some sort of error?"

He expelled a deep breath. "Here. Forward all the messages to me at this account," he said, taking my wrist. He tapped his device against my own, transferring the necessary information. "Let me look into it. I'll figure it out."

For as long as I had known Tai, he had been a man of his word. If he said he would figure it out, then I knew without a doubt that he would. Still, I felt unsettled.

My shoulders slumped as I turned toward the couch.

"Don't worry about the messages," he said as I sat down. "You're in the public eye now. It's probably some fanatic with nothing else to do."

I cringed. "You saw the article, didn't you."

He nodded.

"Had I known the article was going to published that way," I said, "I would have asked you to remove every reference to it on the newsfeed." Tai had done it before — modified a handful of media reports that had mentioned me. At that time, I had been worried about drawing attention to myself, and so to my family on the run. While that was no longer as much of an issue, Khelan's actions still loomed large.

Tai raised an eyebrow, approaching me. "Even I can't modify *that* much media coverage."

I smiled, but it felt sad on my lips. The couch dipped under Tai's weight as he sat down. He wrapped an arm around my shoulders and pulled me against the hard, warm wall that was his side, comforting me.

I shook my head. "I thought when I left the Academy months ago that the biggest problem I'd have was deciding which world I wanted to travel to," I said with a small laugh. "I wish I only had *that* to worry about nowadays."

I glanced up to find Tai considering me, a look fast becoming familiar to me in his eyes. The flickering light from the monitor played across his face, bouncing off the strong lines of his jaw and thick curves of his mouth. After scanning my face, he cupped my cheeks, dropping his gaze to my mouth.

I waited, just as I had done before, expecting him to do what he always did — turn away or shut down. Instead, he ran a thumb along my cheek and leaned in, closing the distance between our mouths.

I gasped between his lips when they met mine. "Shocked" was a poor word to describe how I felt. It took me a moment to respond, worried that this was a hallucination brought forth by a mental breakdown. But when I reached up to hold his jaw, he was still there, not pushing me away. This wasn't a fabrication of my troubled mind.

The kiss was rough and searching, as if we were trying to relearn each other since our first time. He sunk his fingers deep into my hair, pulling me close as I fell into his mouth. The few times he had kissed me before had carried a shade of hesitation, but now there was an eagerness that I matched with my own.

I gripped the thick fabric of his jacket at his shoulders, trying to steady myself as he leaned into me. I shifted to face him and allow him to deepen our kiss. My body flushed with heat when he licked his way between my lips to suck at my tongue. I moaned, licking inside his mouth and trying to draw him closer. He grunted and ran his hands down my back and around my waist, dragging me into his lap without breaking our kiss. I straddled him, sliding my fingers between the short strands of his hair, breathing in his bold, spicy scent between my lips.

I needed this, to feel connected this way with someone, with Tai, the person who was always there before I even realized I needed him. I pressed my chest against his and the badges snagged on my top and scratched my skin as he devoured my mouth. Suddenly, there was an buzzing in the background, but I was too lost in the taste of him to pay it much attention.

"Fuck," he ground out between my lips.

I couldn't agree more.

I moaned, grinding down on the thick bulge between his legs.

I hesitated when Tai swore again and realized that he wasn't tell me what he wanted us to do but was angered by something. I frowned as he pulled away and checked his comm. He exhaled sharply and looked up at me, stark need and frustration filling his face.

Oh gods. "You have to go?" I should have known this would have ended before it had even begun.

He gave me a sharp nod, tension radiating in the muscles around his neck. "In a few minutes," he said. "They're waiting for me."

I dropped my gaze to his badges, shoving away my disappointment. "We can do a lot in 'few minutes,'" I said, glancing up at him with a shrug.

Tai sighed. "My first time with you is not going to be quick, Kira," he said, running a hand around the back of his neck as he glanced around the room. "Plus, I'd rather not to be reminded of your brother everywhere I look."

I frowned.

"Hold on," he said, shifting out from under me. "I may not have a lot of time, but I do have enough to watch you." He sat on the coffee table directly across from me.

I tilted my head. "Watch me what?"

Tai's eyes darkened. "Come."

My eyes widened, a flash of heat racing over me. "You want me to make myself *come* for you?"

Good gods.

He grinned. "Well, first, you'll need to remove your clothes, but then, yes," he said. "I want to watch you come."

I stared at him.

"I know you're not shy," he said, smiling. "Weren't you the one seducing me before, in this very room?"

He was challenging me. I swallowed, uncertain.

Suddenly, Tai searched my face then leaned forward, elbows on his knees. "You don't have to do this," he said all hint of challenge gone as he held my gaze. "I know you're hurting right now. I can wait."

My heart twisted. I should have taken him up on his offer. He was right. I was drunk on all kinds of pain. There was so much shit going on in my life, between work and Khelan, but, as he held my gaze, I sensed that he was most concerned about my feelings for Gannon.

I watched the war of emotions flicker through his eyes. He was trying to be strong and maintain his usual cool, giving me an opportunity to decide what I wanted rather than be swayed by his need. I shook my head, wondering at his selflessness — not just for giving me this choice, but for standing by mine and my family's side over the last few months.

After meeting Tai for the first time five years ago, I had spent many afternoons at Primary Academy fantasizing about him with a giggling Sela. So often I had wondered what it would feel like to be with him, and now he seemed willing to give that opportunity to me. Finally, he was allowing his guard to come down, and there I was, holding back, when it was everything I had wanted. I loved Gannon, and always would, but if I was going to be able to move on, I would need to start looking at what was right in front of me instead of in the past.

I inhaled deeply, decision made, and rose to my feet.

I ducked my head as I pulled the shirt over my head and unhooked my bra, letting it fall to the ground while fighting off the compulsion to race through the strip-show portion of our encounter. I clenched my shaky hands and stole a glance at Tai. His expression was tense, jaw clenched with his fists curled on his knees. Encouraged, I hooked my thumbs in the waist of my pants and underwear then slid them to the ground. Then I froze.

Holy shit. What am I doing?

Tai had seen me naked before, but undressing like this before him made it feel like a new experience. It was one thing to lose ourselves in a sudden rush of lust, but another to perform. Now, like the last time I had tried my hand at seduction on Tai, I didn't know what my next move should be. I stared at the floor, naked, trying to figure it out.

He leaned forward and rested a hand on my knee. "Show me," he said.

My eyes locked on his. *Show him. Right.* It was as simple as that.

Biting my lip, I sat down on the couch and, after yet another fortifying breath, parted my thighs.

Tai's eyes ran down the length of me, setting my skin on fire. There was something incredibly arousing about being on display for him while he sat dressed to the hilt, looking over me. I watched as desire grew in his eyes, heightening my own arousal. Slowly, he leaned forward and ran a hand up my leg and along my inner thigh. I took a second to take him in. He was flushed, color high on his cheeks, breath coming out in unsteady, irregular pants.

"Go on," he said, encouraging me, eyes darkening.

I licked my lips, enjoying the unexpected thrill of being with him this way. I was the one who should have felt unsteady, lying before him like a naked feast, just for him. Instead, the fact that I could make a normally controlled person like Tai shake with need empowered me, gave me the urge I needed. I gave in, throwing away any inhibitions I was feeling.

I slid my hands between my legs and gasped at how wet I was when I slipped a finger between the folds of my sex. Tai swallowed hard as a stronger blaze of heat filled his eyes. I found the nub of my clit and rubbed it in the slow and familiar, tight circles, moaning as need rippled through me. I wasn't new to masturbation. It was the only way I'd been able to survive the many weeks of not seeing Gannon after Septima, after all.

My fingers slowed as my thoughts stumbled into a place where they shouldn't have.

"You still with me?" Tai asked, heat in his eyes banked a bit by concern.

I pressed my lips together, angry with myself. *Tai is reality. Gannon was a fairy tale.* "Yes," I said firmly and thrust my fingers deep inside myself.

"Fuck," Tai cursed under his breath, staring at me. His eyes widened as he watched me, his gaze flickering along my body. It was if he didn't know where to focus, wanting to take all of me in.

I bit down on my bottom lip, my breath shallowing, as I fucked myself with my fingers, allowing the heel of my palm to rub against my clit, spreading the ache there wider, thicker and stronger. Hair-raising tingles ran throughout my limbs. For a while, only the lewd sounds of my fingers plunging in and out of my sex filled the room.

Tai groaned long and hard as my fingers searched, reaching for the climax that threatened to come too soon after I had started. But it wasn't enough. My fingers just weren't enough.

I closed my eyes, resting my head against the back of the couch and whimpered in response to my plunging fingers, wishing they were replaced by something longer, thicker, harder. Then I heard movement and opened my eyes to see Tai fall to his knees between my legs. He ran the coarse pads of his fingertips along the lips of my sex, and I knew he must have been reading my mind when he gave me what I was wishing for, what I needed.

Tai nudged my fingers aside then plunged not one or two fingers inside me, but three, the width and coarseness of them sending me to new heights. He curled them up and stroked a part of me so deep, the room tilted on its axis.

"Holy fuck," I breathed as I arched my back, still circling my own clit as Tai's fingers worked within me.

Stars lit up behind my eyelids and I knew I was near. It was when Tai pulled out his fingers to lick them then thrust them inside me again that I fell apart. I cried out his name, shocked by a climax so strong, my sex tightening so hard, that the feel of Tai's fingers inside morphed into a fleeting moment of the sweetest pain, tipping me over into another orgasm. I gasped, panting through the second wave, as Tai kept pumping, wringing every last bit out of me. Slowly, my body released the tension and the familiar woozy, otherworldly sensation took over.

Tai removed his fingers the same time I did. He climbed up onto the couch and clasped my face between his two hands. He kissed me hard, a fine tremor running through his hands.

"That was" — He kissed my cheeks — "the most" — He sucked my lips — "incredible fucking thing I've ever seen."

I panted against his lips, still coming down off the high.

"Do you know how many nights I've thought about you like this?" he said, staring down at me.

I shook my head, catching the wonder in his eyes. "Actually, no."

He smirked. "Let's just say my palm used to be much coarser than it is now."

A laugh slipped out of my mouth as I rested my head against the back of the couch, finally catching my breath.

Tai stroked my cheek, watching me. "Holy shit," he said. "I hate to have to leave you now..."

"...but you have to go," I filled in for him.

He nodded with a look both tortured and regretful. "I promise to make this up to you."

I smiled, studying him. He looked sincere. Nevertheless, I said, "I'm going to hold you to that, Tai Commander."

CHAPTER TWELVE

"Well, *that* was eventful," Asher muttered, tugging the front of his shirt into place as a protector allowed us entry. "I've never felt more violated in my life."

I smiled as we walked through what I hoped was the last round of intrusive high-level security. "So I guess it's safe to assume you've been violated in a similar fashion before?" I asked, heading toward a row of elevators on the other side of the lobby in Septima Nine's Judiciary building.

Asher caught up to me. "That's a story for another day," he said with a wink.

I laughed as we entered the elevator, enjoying the feeling after what felt like a very long time. I could have said it was time that healed all pain, but it wasn't that. Tai had a lot to do with the lift in my mood. Sela had told me Tai would come around, and it seemed she had been right. I straightened my spine, committing to focus on Tai as she had advised and enjoyed a swell of pride at my resolve. *I can do this. I can move on. Leaving Gannon won't have me falling apart.*

The digital numbers on the elevator panel overheard increased as we ascended. The fact that Abigail Minister's office was on the highest floor in the building was a surprise. While she held the highest position on Septima Nine, it was odd to be so removed from the rest of the Judiciary. Even Gabriel, for all his ulterior motives and machinations, had maintained an office that was easily accessible by his employees. Of course, in hindsight, he had probably done that to keep tabs on everyone who worked for him.

We exited the elevator and into a white-walled hallway. The absence of art or plants to break up the monotony of color was so glaring under the fluorescent lights that I squinted.

"This place just keeps on getting better," Asher murmured, glancing around. "Are all Septima's worlds this…*quaint?*"

I smiled. I had had a similar first impression of the dominion. While the only other location in Septima I had visited was World Two, it was clear that World Nine shared the same features or lack thereof. "You mean *dull*," I said.

"Yes. There's that," he said, "but it also just feels *old*."

My first trip to Septima had begun with tragedy but had ended with me becoming closer to Gannon despite the terrible circumstances, so it was hard for me to look at Septima with completely jaded eyes. But as I looked around now, trying to do so, through Asher's eyes, I had to admit he was right. I hadn't noticed that our system's first dominion was showing its age. Perhaps it was because I had been so focused on surviving the attack and being with Gannon without judgment that I hadn't noticed it all before. Septima had a well-used look; the white paint was peeling, and hairline cracks ran across the walls.

"Don't worry," I said, tugging on the sleeve of his coat. "I hear Hale Five is much better."

I led him toward Abigail's office doors, which slid open suddenly. We stepped back as a group of senators and protectors walked out.

I didn't recognize any except one. Jonah, the other half of Gannon's personal protection, strode by. He appeared to be waiting on something or…*good gods* — some*one*.

Was Jonah waiting on *Gannon?*

My heart sped up, and my earlier resolve to move on crumbled like the weak thing it was at the thought of seeing Gannon.

Asher walked into the reception area then turned. He eyed me. "You bailing on me?"

I shook my head and hurried in, praying that Jonah being there was a mere coincidence.

A petite woman in a simple black sheath hurried toward us, her heels clicking on the wide marble tiles. "You're Kira Director," she said, holding out a hand to me.

I shook her hand. "It's actually Kira *Metallurgist*," I corrected with a smile then glanced to my left. "This is my colleague, Asher Analyst. We have a meeting with Abigail Minister."

"Oh, yes. I know," she said. The accent of Septima Nine filtered through her words, making them sound melodious. "I'm Celine Clerk. I'm pleased to meet you. When the minister told us you'd be here for a meeting, there was quite a bit of excitement within the office."

I frowned. It was unusual that someone in my role would request a private meeting with someone in the minister's position, but then, I *was* supporting the subordinate representative on a special committee; my meeting with the minister shouldn't have garnered such interest.

"Why was everyone excited?" I asked.

For a moment, Celine appeared confused, but then she laughed, as if I had made a joke. She indicated a narrow hallway to our left with an upturned hand. "Please follow me," she said.

As Asher and I followed, we passed a number of work rooms filled with mostly subordinates. Each door we passed, people stopped what they were doing to stare. I caught the eye of a young woman who smiled then leaned in to speak into the ear of a male colleague who sat beside her. He appeared equally enthralled by the three of us walking down the hall.

Unnerved, I looked behind me gauge Asher's reaction. He raised an eyebrow and shrugged.

"You'll have to forgive my colleagues," Celine said with a smile, looking over her shoulder at me. "We're not used to having people like you here."

If Celine's eyes weren't twinkling with delight, I would have been offended by her remark. I was about to ask her what she meant when we turned right and found ourselves in front of the minister's office. Like on Prospect Eight, the minister's office was easily identifiable by her name and position etched into her glass door.

Celine pressed a finger onto the digital panel at her right. "Please, go right in," she said as the door slid open.

Abigail's Minister's office was a reflection of the world she lived in. The room was large, but sparsely furnished, with only a large wood and metal desk, a few chairs and a small potted plant begging for light by the single window.

"I'll be back to collect you before the minister's next meeting," Celine said to Asher and me before exiting the office.

Abigail rose from her desk and approached us, her dark green eyes looking sharply between us. The minister was a study in modesty and serenity. Despite the heat outside, she was dressed as though it were the dead of winter. The severity of her black jacket and long skirt were relieved almost resentfully by the red trim required to reflect her caste. And her black hair, threaded with gray, was held back in a tightly coiled bun.

"I hope your trip to Septima was without trouble," she said, nodding toward the three metal chairs in the middle of her office.

"Yes, thank you," I said as Asher and I sat down. "It was."

Abigail crossed her legs at the ankle and placed her hands, one atop the other, on her lap. "How may I help you?" she asked.

I took a deep breath. "Thank you for meeting with us," I said. "I know how busy a time it is for all Realm governance and law officials, especially during these unsettling times."

The minister's cool gaze held steady as she waited on me to continue.

Very well. Straight to the point, then.

"As you know," I said, "my colleague, Asher, and I are supporting the subordinate representative on the special committee."

"Yes," she said. "You're doing research for his report."

I nodded.

The minister's eyes narrowed a fraction. "Everything I have to say on the matter is well documented."

"Yes, I know," I said, shooting a quick look at Asher. He sat quietly, seeming content to have me to take the lead as we had discussed. "But so far, we've not heard the specific reasons why you're against exploration."

"I don't think I need to be any more specific," she said with a shrug. "Exploration is dangerous in every way. Citizens have been killed for the sake of being curious. I think that simply focusing on developing and improving the worlds we know is the safer and wiser approach."

"I understand that," I said, trying to direct the conversation. "But the newsfeed reports each day that more and more citizens are in support of lifting the ban. People are changing their minds."

"Yes, Rhoan Advocator mentioned as much," she said, tilting her head, cool eyes assessing me. "And I note that you're not shy when it comes to encouraging that support."

I stiffened. She too had seen Heath's article.

"I didn't mean to offend you," she said, raising her chin, "but all you and the subordinate representative are doing is confusing citizens. People want to be led, not…entreated or petitioned. There's a reason the Realm was designed the way it was. The Senate and Elite castes have been making sound decisions in the interest of our system for years."

I stifled a sigh. I'd heard that too many times to count. "How many more disgruntled groups will the Realm have to endure before we listen?"

"Are you suggesting we bow to the demands of rebels who've endangered and *killed* so many of our citizens?" she demanded, eyes sharp.

"No. Not at all," I rushed to say. Giving in to rebels was the last thing I wanted to do. "But the law is out of date. There's an opportunity now to think about exploration differently and perhaps prevent future dissension, at least when it comes to this issue."

She sighed. "Subordinate Metallurgist," she said, "I appreciate what you're trying to do, but change such as that is simply too drastic and reckless, especially at a time when the Realm is under attack and experiencing such tremendous upheaval."

My shoulders slumped. I was trying to draw water from an empty well. "I wish you would reconsider, Minister."

Abigail stood up and walked to her desk. "Even if I decided to support regulated exploration," she said, turning to face us with hands clasped in front of her, "Septima would never agree to it. Our worlds are much too conservative to adapt to such radical thinking. Tradition and adherence to rules are a virtue here, not a disadvantage."

I considered her words. She appeared so sincere and confident in her opinion, the role she believed she was born to play. Who would have thought someone so dedicated to tradition and rules would have voted in support of lifting the ban on exploration in her early days, before becoming a minister?

Asher shifted in his chair. When I glanced at him, he raised an eyebrow.

I stood up and met the minister at her desk. "Why did you change your opinion?" I asked.

The minister frowned. "I beg your pardon?"

"Years ago, you were in support of exploration," I said. "Is there something that happened to make you change your mind?"

There was a long, unsettling pause as she stared at me. "How do you know that?" she demanded.

I blinked. "We found a file on your support while we were doing research."

Abigail's expression tightened. "No one except Realm Council has access to information so far back in any minister's history."

"It was registered at level twelve," Asher said, coming up beside me, shooting an uneasy look at me. "I pulled the file myself."

"Who else has seen that file?" she snapped.

I frowned, taken aback by her tone.

"No one," Asher said. "We're the only two doing research for the special committee."

She stared at the two of us through narrowed eyes.

Asher and I glanced at each other. He appeared as baffled as I was by her reaction. Certainly, Abigail shouldn't have been terribly pleased to have us refer to her divergent opinion, but she hadn't yet been a minister, and was new to interworld politics at the time. Many people had changing opinions over their careers. Plus, the information hadn't been difficult to find. It was easily accessible in the database, at our level of authorization.

The minister drew herself up. "I would be greatly in your debt if that file was never seen by anyone else," she said.

Asher nodded slowly, eyes wide. "I can recode it at level twenty-five, if you'd like," he said, referring to the highest level of classification. "After that, even I won't be able to access it again."

Abigail clenched her jaw then swung to look at me. "Are you here to blackmail me?"

I reared back. "I beg your pardon?"

"You heard me," she said.

I could only stare at her.

When I had sought to find inconsistencies in the ministers' backgrounds, I hadn't intended to hold anything I found over their heads. I simply hoped to find an inconsistency in their voting history that would show that their opinions had changed with the times before. When I saw that Abigail Minister had supported exploration in the past, I nearly fell over, thinking it a gift from the gods — the perfect angle from which to help her understand Realm citizens' evolving opinions.

"That was *never* my intention," I said firmly.

Abigail raised her chin. It was a quiet minute between the three of us as the minister assessed us. Finally, her body wilted like the plant on the windowsill.

"Thank gods," she said, lowering herself unsteadily into her chair. "If Septima senators were to learn that I had ever held such an opinion, I would lose my rank."

I frowned. Would leadership really take such drastic action for an opinion held so many years ago?

"I only wanted you to consider supporting exploration again," I said, stepping closer to the desk, hoping she would see my sincerity. "I mentioned your past seeking to understand why you changed your mind."

She raised her chin, assessing me. "Is that right?"

I nodded quickly.

She eyed me then exhaled, resting back in her chair. "When I was young, my mind longed to go beyond the confines of the Realm," she said, looking up at me. "Despite the fact that exploration had led to the death of citizens on the old world, the desire to see the unknown was too strong a compulsion to fight. Then I became minister and learned that things were better off this way, without exploration, and dedicated to advancing the worlds we already know."

I frowned, trying to make sense of what she was saying.

"Minister?"

I glanced over my shoulder to find Celine poking her head into the office. "The chancellor has arrived for your next meeting," she said with a wide smile.

I froze. *Oh good gods.* Gannon *was* here.

I turned to the minister, heart in my throat. "Thank you for meeting with us, Minister," I managed to say as I backed away from her desk.

Asher and I turned to collect our belongings and exited the room with Celine, leaving Abigail deep in thought.

"Do you have a few minutes before you leave?" Celine asked once we entered the reception area. "My colleagues would love to meet you."

I was already shaking my head. "I'm sorry, but we really should be heading back." *As in, right now. This very second.* If I caught sight of Gannon, there was no telling how I would react.

Celine waved a hand. "Oh, it'll only take a second," she said, then hurried off.

I stared after her, trying to figure out how to excuse myself from her last-minute request. "The people here seem to have a fascination with us," I muttered.

Asher snorted. "You mean a fascination with *you.*"

I glanced at him. He must have read the confusion on my face because he soon asked, "You do know you have a following, right?"

"A *what?*"

"Ya. I had a feeling you weren't the gossip-column kind of gal," Asher said with a grin then looked over my head, the smile slipping from his face. "So I take it you and the chancellor aren't on the best of terms right now."

My eyes widened. "Why do you ask?"

He dropped his gaze to me. "Because he's down the hall, glaring at you."

I spun around to find Gannon standing with Jonah across the room. Even from that distance I could see the storm gathering on his face.

"How about I wait for you in the lobby downstairs?" Asher asked, already heading toward the elevator.

Considering the way Gannon's legs were eating up the distance between us, I figured it was a good idea. I nodded to Asher and he slipped into the elevator just as Gannon arrived.

"What are you doing here?" he demanded, looking me over.

Despite the prickle of awareness that ran through me at the sight of him, I took umbrage at his tone.

I crossed my arms and glared up at him. "I could ask you the same thing."

Gannon gave me a look of warning. "I have work to do *here*, and on many worlds," he said between clenched teeth. "I travel, sometimes four times a day, in and out of dominions to meet with various Realm leadership. What's *your* excuse?"

Oh, so arrogant Gannon is in full swing.

I narrowed my eyes. "You're not the only one who has work to do," I said.

"Did Mila send you?" he asked. Concern clouded his face, smoothing away the tight lines around his eyes. "If she did, I'll have to speak with her about sending her support back into the dominion where she was nearly killed."

I stared up at him, realizing that the reason for his overbearing disposition was worry over my welfare. The man had kept special committee meetings on Prospect to prevent me from having to travel across the Realm and there I was doing exactly that. My annoyance subsided.

"Which protector did Mila assign to you?" he asked.

I blinked. "Protector?"

Gannon cursed. "By all that is holy," he said, closing his eyes briefly, "tell me you have protection with you as you travel to these meetings?"

I stiffened. "I don't need protection," I said firmly, but I couldn't help but feel foolish. Mila had offered to send a protector with me; I hadn't thought it necessary, considering all the heightened security across the Realm.

Gannon glanced up when Abigail and three senators entered the reception area. The minister's eyes skimmed over to me before she led her group down the hall. "Did you manage to convince Abigail to support your brother's recommendation?" he asked, looking back at me.

I stared at him. "How do you know that's why I'm here?"

Gannon snorted. "I hardly think you came all the way from Prospect to simply exchange pleasantries," he said, making all the sense in the worlds as he crossed his arms. "So did you convince her?"

I thought back to the meeting with the minister and the inscrutable look on her face as Asher and I left her office. "I don't know," I said, shaking my head with a frown.

Gannon lowered his head, holding my gaze. "Why? What did she say?"

I considered him, and saw his desire to help me fix whatever was wrong burning bright in his eyes. It would have been so helpful to have Gannon's insight. He was leading the special committee I was working on, after all; yet I held back. In addition to Abigail's having appeared so stricken at the thought of her past decision coming out, I was supposed to be putting distance between Gannon and me, not giving him a reason to cling to me.

When he noticed my hesitation, he drew back. "You don't trust me," he said, blue eyes dimming.

I shook my head, reaching for him, but caught myself in time. "That's not it." Nothing could have been further from the truth. "I just don't want you involved."

He raised an eyebrow. "Kira, I lead the special committee," he said. "The moment you stepped foot into the minister's office to discuss this project, you involved me."

Again, he was making a whole lot of sense. I relented a bit. "I found an inconsistency in her voting history that I hoped would make her reconsider her resistance to exploration."

"Good," he said simply.

I wasn't so sure about that. "She thought I was manipulating her," I said with a frown, still disturbed that she would think me capable of such a thing.

Gannon thinned his lips. "Of course she did," he said. "Leadership sees inconsistency as a weakness to be leveraged. It's a chink in the armor, something to be fixed or removed."

Abigail had said something along those lines. Still, I hated the fact that she thought I had come to use a simple change of opinion against her.

He studied me. "Are you planning to meet with Xavier as well?"

When I nodded, Gannon squared his shoulders as if ready for a fight. "I'll have Jonah accompany you to Hale."

I groaned. "That's not necessary."

He glared at me, eyes flashing. "It's either him, or I go with you myself."

Everything about him said he was serious. His fear for my safety tore at my heart.

I shook my head, holding his gaze. "You don't need to watch over me, Gannon," I said quietly, conscious of our environment and the people within it. "Not anymore."

His eyes darkened as he held my gaze. "Believe me," he said through thinned lips. "I'm fully aware of that now."

I glanced away briefly. Apparently, my performance with Tai had brought about the necessary effect. It occurred to me that this was why Gannon had stopped calling or messaging me. I should have been relieved. I was no longer a distraction, a threat to his future. This was what I had wanted. Yet the emptiness I had been fighting off since I left him expanded, warring against my commitment to move on.

Gannon frowned. "What do you plan on saying to Xavier?"

I sighed. "Apparently, not much," I said. Asher and I had come up empty in our research. I didn't think I would ever in my lifetime come across a minister more consistent in his votes and opinions. My meeting with him the next day was doomed to be a silent one.

Excited chatter suddenly filled the reception area, and Celine entered the room with a group of subordinates. They stood by the desk, a few of them gesturing to me as they spoke. I stifled a groan. They appeared more than content to wait for me to finish my conversation with the chancellor.

"I think I know how to sway Xavier's position," he said, pulling my gaze back to his.

I stared up at him, finding his expression appearing suddenly preoccupied. "How?"

"I've learned a lot since my father died," he said. "Now that I'm supposed to take over his position, I've been entrusted with more confidential, higher-level information."

I cocked my head, looking for answers in his face. "Information about what?"

He thinned his lips, flicking a look at Celine and her group before coming back to me. "I can't go into details here, and I can't risk telling you via comm," he said, but I could see as his gaze clouded over that he was still weighing the wisdom of telling me now. Finally, his eyes focused. "When you meet with Xavier, allow him to lead the conversation."

I frowned. "Why?"

How in the worlds would allowing the minister to take the lead help to convince him of anything?

Gannon studied me. "Do you trust me?" he asked, holding my gaze.

I didn't hesitate. "I do."

"Then leave it to me."

CHAPTER THIRTEEN

Hale dominion was said to be built out of granite, steel and unabashed displays of glory. As Asher, Jonah and I walked into Hale Five's Judiciary for our meeting with Xavier, I was inclined to agree.

The building was larger than life, and so met all of my wildest expectations. Within the confines of granite floors, glass walls and steel beams, citizens of every caste strode by, each one appeared to have a clear mission and destination in mind. Hale Three was the Protectorate's headquarters, so I had expected to find the majority of the people there to be protectors. What surprised me, though, was how formidable they all looked when they congregated in one place. It seemed like they fed off one another's dominant energies and overwhelming strengths. If one protector was tall, another was wrapped in an armor of heavy muscle. Then there were the lucky few who had both attributes and wore badges similar to Tai's.

I frowned at a sudden memory as we crossed the lobby. Tai had called me just before I left for Hale, and he had looked drawn and disturbed by his work in Helios.

"You look tired," I had said to him, leaning into the monitor in my office to look at him more closely.

He ran a hand over his head as he sat down at his desk. He was in a poorly lit room, so I could barely see the creases of fatigue around his eyes. People were talking around him, in the background.

"I am," he said, nodding his thanks when someone placed a mug of what must have been coffee by his arm. "Things are worse than we thought here."

I searched his face. "What do you mean?"

He sipped his drink then said, "I wish I could say."

Of course he couldn't tell me — he was conducting an official investigation. "Sorry," I said with a short laugh. "That was silly of me to ask."

Tai shook his head. "No," he said. "What I mean is the citizens of Helios are quaking in their shoes so much they're not willing to speak."

I thought that through. "You think they're being intimidated."

He nodded. "I think so," he said. "On the surface, everything seems normal, calm, as if nothing unusual is going on, but all our reports tell us there's rebel activity here, and a lot of it. They're hiding something."

I didn't like the sound of that. "When will you be coming back?" I asked, anxious to have him back in Merit, safe and sound.

"In a couple days," he said with a smile. "So what have *you* been up to?"

Such a simple question, but I hesitated. If Gannon's reaction to my traveling to Septima was any indication, Tai would fly off the handle when he learned about it as well — never mind that I was just about to head to Hale, another dominion where there had been another fatal attack.

"Work," I said, glancing away briefly with a shrug.

He nodded. "I've messaged Khelan. I told him I want to see him when I get back. I'd actually prefer if your entire family were there when we meet."

I shook my head, wondering how, in the middle of a potentially dangerous situation, Tai could be thinking about my family's welfare. Despite my brother's disdain for Tai, Rhoan would be glad to know that Tai had information that would make a strong case against what Khelan was doing.

"I'll tell Rhoan," I offered.

Tai smirked. "Don't," he said. "I'll do it. Protecting your family is one of the only things your brother and I can agree on."

Asher cleared his throat conspicuously as we neared the elevators, and fell in step beside me. I glanced at him as he tipped his head toward a digital wall that displayed rotating images of protectors, their names and ranks written in Kenaric, Hale's official language, beneath them. At the top of the digital presentation, the Realm motto was lit up by a brilliant, blinding strobe-light display.

"That's a bit much, don't you think?" Asher asked under his breath.

I cringed. *Unabashed displays of glory indeed.*

No wonder Xavier Minister was so full of himself. Had I lived in a place that was unrestrained in its self-adulation, I too would probably think the worlds spun on my very own axis.

As the three of us stepped into the elevator, a moment of panic nearly buckled my knees. *What in the worlds am I going to say to Xavier?* Maybe I was worried for no reason. After all, Asher and I would probably be turned out on our ear the moment we arrived at his office. The man had always seemed to have an ingrained dislike of me, or perhaps it was of just everyone in my caste. He treated Rhoan with the same level of condescension.

I straightened my shoulders and raised my chin.

Gannon had advised me to listen first. He handled meetings like this more often than I did. I would take his advice and see where things led.

The elevator trip was a short ride, stopping a moment later at the second floor.

"Welcome to the Office of Xavier Minister of H5," Jonah said as we passed through the office's thick metal doors and into the reception area.

Asher glanced at me and, with eyebrows reaching for the ceiling, made a big show of mouthing the acronym "H5" for only me to see. I chuckled, unable to stop the laugh that bubbled to the surface. Thankfully, Jonah was so focused on surveying the area that he paid me no mind.

If I had thought Tai a straight and narrow enforcer, Jonah surpassed him in all ways. From the moment he had picked us up from Prospect Judiciary, the young protector had been throwing around Protectorate lingo as though just out of training.

When I had told Asher that Jonah would be accompanying us to Hale for our meeting with Xavier, he hadn't seemed surprised. He was still under the illusion that Gannon and I were living our star-crossed romance and had simply had some lovers' tiff. I couldn't bring myself to tell him the truth.

"Subordinate Metallurgist."

I stopped admiring the reception's stunning combination of dark wood and sleek digital technology long enough to see Xavier crossing the room before he got to us. The minister hurried toward me with a hand stretched out. I stared at his palm, the fact that he had chosen to greet me himself throwing me off for a second.

"Minister," I said, accepting his handshake. Xavier was at least a foot taller than me, so I had to crane my neck to look at him.

Xavier shook Asher's hand and sent Jonah a nod before darting a look behind him. I followed his line of sight and saw Realm Councillor Gaia Ambassador of Hale speaking, head bowed, with a senator across the reception area. Just then the ambassador raised her gaze to me, still conversing with her support.

I exchanged a look with Asher. "Is this still a good time for us to meet?" I asked the minister when he faced me again. Xavier must have had some urgent matter to attend to if the leader of the Hale dominion was at his Judiciary.

"No. Let's get this over with," he said tightly. "We'll meet in my office. Come along."

Asher and I began to follow the minister, but Jonah hung back.

"I'll be out here when you're ready," he said, positioning himself by the elevators. The way he settled into his stance told me that he had no intention of leaving that very spot until I returned.

After traversing the maze that was the Judiciary's work space, we arrived at the minister's office. It was as large and imposing as the man who occupied it.

"Have a seat," Xavier said, taking his behind his desk.

As we did, I scented a familiar pungent aroma. "Is that *hurim*?" I asked without thinking and with a smile. I gestured to the mug of steaming drink on his desk when the minister looked at me quizzically.

He narrowed his brown eyes as he leaned into the arm of his chair. "You're familiar with *hurim*, subordinate?" he asked. The stern set of his face made me realize my error. He was wondering how I, a subordinate, would have come to know about a regulated substance.

"N-no, not me," I spluttered. *Shit.* "I just know *of* it. A senior colleague of mine drinks it, that's all."

Xavier frowned. "It seems you're privy to a lot of things both confidential and restricted," he said.

I frowned. "I'm certain I don't know what you mean."

His face tightened. "I'm referring to the reason you're here, of course," he said. "Whatever else could I be referring to?"

My eyes widened. He must have spoken with Abigail. She and Xavier seemed to be good friends, at least as far as I could make out from their interactions on the task force and, more recently, the special committee. I wondered what she had told him. I couldn't imagine that she would reveal the fact that we knew she had supported exploration in the past, but I could imagine her telling him her suspicion that we had meant to threaten her.

I inched forward in my chair. "Thank you for agreeing to meet with us, Minister," I said. "I know you probably have more pressing matters to attend to."

"I'm sure you don't believe that?" Xavier muttered, looking at me through narrowed eyes.

I frowned and shot a look at Asher. He gave me an almost imperceptible shrug. We hadn't been kicked out yet, so I forged ahead.

I looked at the minister. "We're here simply to better understand your position against exploration," I said, trying to correct any misleading information Abigail might have shared with him.

"Why?" he drawled, steepling his fingers in front of his mouth as he studied me. "What does it matter?"

I sagged into my seat.

What in the worlds am I doing here?

Xavier was an immovable rock — tenacious, abrasive and downright mean on the best of days. What did I expect to come from meeting with him? The research Asher had spent hours pulling together for me had, unfortunately, been no help. I had wasted his time, and now I was wasting the minister's as well. I should have just cancelled the meet—

I sat up, suddenly realizing what I had been doing, or rather had *not* been doing. Gannon had asked me to listen to Xavier, allow him to take the lead. Yet there I was, trying to direct the conversation.

I exhaled deeply, and sat back. "Perhaps there's another matter related to exploration that you'd prefer to discuss, Minister," I said, hoping he would give me some indication of where to go next.

Xavier looked between Asher and me, his light brown eyes becoming darker as the seconds passed. Finally, he lowered his hands to the table, where they fisted. "There's no reason that we can't come to some sort of a compromise," he said.

I blinked. "A compromise?"

"I understand that to someone like you, on a lower rung of the ladder, it may seem like what we're doing here is wrong," he said, angling forward in his chair, "that prohibiting exploration is an injustice to the rest of the Realm. But you must see having now worked with leadership how important it is that we manage these things carefully. Exploration is not for the uninitiated."

I was following so far. "Yes," I said. "That's why the subordinate representative is proposing to *regulate* exploration rather than allow a complete lifting of the ban."

He started. "So a total lift on the ban is off the table?"

I cocked my head, confused. Xavier had been there during Rhoan's presentation. Why would he ask such a question?

"Minister, it was never *on* the table," I said. "We appreciate that citizens shouldn't be traveling across our worlds without a proper process in place. We want regulated exploration."

The minister expelled a gust of air. "Thank the gods," he said, shaking his head. "I suppose it *is* the lesser of two evils, but we'll all need to work together with *accurate* information in order to make it work."

I glanced at Asher, baffled. Xavier was speaking as if he was on board. This was the man who had fought the idea of exploration — even regulated — tooth and nail from the very start!

"That was easy," Asher said under his breath, eyes wide.

I didn't know what to say. "I don't understand," I said, looking to the minister again.

Xavier pushed away from the desk, stood up, then walked over to the low cabinet that ran along a wall. A row of bottles sat atop it. I thought he was about to replenish his *hurim*. Instead he flipped a switch on the wall above the furniture.

The lights in the room dimmed and the shades over the windows closed. Suddenly, a hologram map filled the middle of the room, between the three of us. It was filled with an array of shimmering red and blue dots, which I easily determined identified the worlds in the Realm and those known to be in the Outer Realm.

"This," Xavier said, "is the Protectorate's version of the Realm and Outer Realm, similar to what Rhoan Advocator showed during his presentation." He glanced at me. "But it's wrong."

I stood up and approached the display. "I don't think so," I said, studying the map. It looked right to me.

Xavier leveled me with a look. "Forgive me," he said drolly. "I should have been more precise. It's not *wrong*. It's *incomplete*."

I fought the compulsion to ask him to explain. Listening to him without interfering had revealed a lot so far. Asher, however, was of a different mind.

"What do you mean?" he asked, coming up beside me. "It looks accurate to me."

Xavier's body went rigid. "All right then," he muttered. "I'll show you, if I must."

He strode to his desk and tapped on his monitor before typing in a series of numbers. When he was done, the hologram lit up, swiveled on its axis, then settled back into place, but this time there was something different.

Asher frowned. "What are these?" he asked, pointing to a section in the Outer Realm. It was speckled with a multitude of glowing green dots.

"They're rogue worlds," Xavier said, still watching the dazzling display of light.

I lifted my gaze to stare at the minister.

"Forgive me," Asher said, shaking his head as my own started to swim. "But there should only be *four* worlds in the Outer Realm, yet you have what must be a hundred of them lit up."

"Two hundred and eight to be exact, fifty of them inhabited," Xavier said then glanced up. "But then, you knew that."

My gods, Liandra wasn't delusional. She was right! She had said after the attack on Septima that there were more worlds in the Outer Realm, supposedly discovered as a result of Realm Council's orders that leadership of each dominion explore. If what Xavier was saying was true, it meant that Argon's expulsion was truly unjustified. My pulse raced.

Xavier's eyes narrowed on me. "You *did* know that, didn't you?"

My eyes widened. He thought I *knew* about this. Why?

Gannon.

It all flooded back. This was what he had wanted to tell me but couldn't because of where we were. Now I understood why he couldn't even risk telling me by comm. My gods, should this ever be picked up through our comms somehow, it would create even more of an uproar by the factions across the Realm.

"Y-yes," I said, gathering myself. "Of course we did."

"Uh no…I'm pretty sure I remember my elementary astronomy," Asher said, hands on his hips, as he stared down at the hologram with a frown. "There are only supposed to be *four* worlds in the Outer Realm."

He startled when I staggered over to him and gripped his wrist. "You're mistaken," I said, holding his gaze hard. "We thought there were, what? Maybe a few dozen, but we now see that there are so many more."

Asher's eyes widened, but thankfully, he received my message to stay quiet.

"Thank you for sharing this with us," I said to Xavier, mind reeling.

He folded his arms across his chest. "I trust I have your continued discretion on this, subordinates," he said, eyes narrowed. "I would hate for the media to get wind of this."

"O-of course."

He walked to the cabinet and flipped the switch again. The hologram faded out as the lights came on and the shades opened. "If word got out that you managed to come across this information while looking through Hale's files in the database, my ambassador would have my head. Not to mention the chancellor." His lip curled. "He guaranteed my demotion if I didn't work with you to reach a compromise."

My mouth slackened. "He did?"

Xavier nodded slowly. "He said you were thinking of bringing this information to the subordinate representative to push for full exploration — *without* any form of regulation," he said, scowling. "I'm happy to learn that you've returned to your original recommendation."

Oh gods. All I could do was nod.

Xavier pinned me with a glare, drawing himself up. "You can tell Rhoan Advocator that I'll support regulated exploration at the special committee meeting."

I nodded jerkily.

Face grim, Xavier sat down, effectively ending the meeting.

Asher seemed frozen on the spot, so I tugged on his arm and, after we collected our belongings, led him out. We rushed through the work area and into reception, my hands shaking. Jonah tapped a panel, calling for the elevator. When the doors slid open, Asher and I slipped inside so fast, the protector gave us an odd look. I couldn't blame him, but our behavior couldn't be helped. I was certain that any minute now, the minister would come to his senses and decide to hold us hostage for unearthing government secrets.

The lobby was just as busy as before, but the floors were covered by a smattering of wet footprints. Sheets of rain ran down the glass walls, blurring the view.

"I'll bring the hover up to the front door," Jonah said. I watched, fingers gripping the straps of my bag, as he walked through the entrance doors.

Despite the heavy din in the lobby and rumble of thunder outside, I still heard the faint signal of Gannon's incoming message on my comm.

Did you let him take the lead?

I expelled a breath before I replied:

Yes.

It was a beat before his response:

Meet me after the committee meeting. We have
much to discuss.

* * *

Thank gods, I remembered it.

I reached for the bottle of *solumen* inside the drawer of my office desk and, with unsteady hands, poured a small amount of the clear liquid into a glass. I wasn't having a panic attack, but an hour after our meeting with Xavier, my pulse was still racing and my breath still shallow, so I figured I might as well take a dose of the medicinal herb to find some semblance of calm. I laughed and drops of it fell from the cup to the desk.

How could anyone be calm at a time like this?

Asher and I had been silent during the trip back to Prospect. I had to assume he was as hesitant as me about discussing what happened in the company of our strict chaperone. By the time Jonah had dropped us at the Judiciary, it was near the end of the workday. I needed a minute to catch my breath, so I had asked Asher to meet me after everyone else had left the office. He had appeared more than happy to have a moment to his thoughts.

"Did that *really* just happen?" Asher asked, standing at the threshold of my office.

His question was clearly rhetorical, but I nodded anyway, needing to confirm it for myself.

Asher ran a hand over his head as he shut the door behind him and approached me.

I could only imagine how confused Asher was feeling. I had, at least, received some forewarning from Liandra, but for him, the universe had literally expanded all at once.

I replaced the bottle of *solumen* then stood up to round the desk. "You didn't say anything to anyone, did you?"

He shook his head and slipped his hands into his pocket. "Of course not," he said, then eyed me. "Are you going to tell your brother? I mean, something like this would tip the scales at the special committee meeting."

I exhaled deeply. "I've been thinking about that," I said. "Maybe I should speak with Gannon before telling anyone. We have to be careful. This information is so high-level and controversial it could do more harm than good." I would hate to know that by sharing it with Rhoan, I had put him in a terrible position somehow.

Asher nodded. "Plus, it's not like we don't have Xavier's support anyway," he said. "If he's on board, then Abigail's probably a shoe-in."

I wasn't quite convinced of that, but I nodded all the same.

He shook his head, staring at me in wonder. "The chancellor would do *anything* for you, wouldn't he!" Asher had obviously used our time to collect ourselves to connect the dots and figure out why Xavier had been so willing to support regulation and share the information had with us. Considering all we had learned that day, there was no time like the present to reveal another truth.

I sighed and rested a hip against the edge of my desk. "Gannon and I aren't together anymore, Asher." I managed to say it with only a slight hitch in my voice.

He raised his eyebrows. "Really?" he asked. "Because I don't think he got that memo."

I frowned, a sharp pang darting through me. Asher was speaking directly to one of my worst fears. It was clear after the meeting with Xavier that no matter what effort I had made to put distance between us, Gannon and I were only becoming more intertwined.

"Sorry," Asher said, cringing. "That probably wasn't the most sensitive thing to say."

I shook my head to dismiss his apology and clear my thoughts. "So we'll keep this to ourselves, then," I said, placing a hand on his wrist. "You won't say anything, at least until I learn more, right?"

Asher grinned. "I won't say a word," he said. "I mean, let's face it, Kira, no one would believe me even if I did!"

CHAPTER FOURTEEN

"Exactly how *many* babies is Sela having?" Rhoan asked, joining me at the kitchen table at our family home. He stood by my side as I stared at the mountain of baby paraphernalia mixed in with colorful wrapping paper that was scattered across the tabletop. "One or *twelve?*"

I sighed. "She said something about having four some time ago, but I could have sworn she was joking," I muttered, marveling at the various types of toys that one infant could have. I shook my head and glanced up at him. "There's no way all of this could be for just one child."

Rhoan stiffened, a look of mortification replacing the smirk on his face. "Kira, if the real reason Tai's coming over here is so you two can make a big announcement about something that will come to fruition in the next *nine* months," he said, "I swear I will break his neck with my bare hands."

I stared at him. Was this the same level-headed individual who had articulately debated his opinions with the leaders of our worlds?

I rolled my eyes. "You can save your show of masculinity and brotherly indignation for another time," I said, picking up two of the gift boxes to bring some order to the pile. "I'm not pregnant." As intimate as Tai and I had been, we had never gone *that* far.

Rhoan's puffed-up chest deflated at once. "Thank the gods," he said, raking his fingers through his tightly wound hair with a shudder. "All Above, I think Ma's getting to me. The entire afternoon she's been humming lullabies that've been giving me the chills."

I would have laughed if I hadn't been subjected to a similar treatment. "I just spent the last hour with her looking over a checklist for Sela's baby welcoming," I said, then stopped rolling up lengths of red and purple ribbons to glance at him. "She asked me what my favorite baby names are."

Rhoan laughed. "Better you than me," he said. "After seeing how she's been acting over the last few months, I can now safely say I will never partner, marry or have a child."

I snorted. "Good luck with that."

Rhoan walked to the kitchen counter and picked up a pine fruit from a tray. "Tai should be here soon," he said.

I nodded, knowing that already, but still my heart tripped over itself.

True to his word, Tai had contacted Khelan to arrange to meet with him and the rest of my family. I figured Tai wouldn't wait too long for this, but I hadn't expected him to stop by the *very* moment he returned from out of town.

I placed the last of the baby trappings into a box, one decorated with colorful planets dancing amid an assortment of smiley-faced suns, moons and stars, then expelled a deep sigh.

How in the worlds am I going to face Tai and keep this secret from him?

Tai had been with Gannon and me on Septima when Liandra told us the truth about the Realm exploration. Telling Tai what I had learned — and straight from an official's mouth, no less — felt like the right thing to do. I willed myself to hold out a little while longer. After the special committee meeting the following day, and after speaking with Gannon, I would tell Tai and Rhoan too.

Rhoan eyed me. "What's wrong?" he asked around a bite of fruit.

I smiled tightly and sat down in a chair. "I'm fine."

He frowned. "You know, Kira, Tai talking to Khelan is a good thing," he said, mistaking the reason for my shift in mood. "I know you didn't want Tai involved, but this is the best shot we have of getting through to him."

"I know. It's not that…" I considered my brother, feeling the desperate need to unload some of the weight of my worries. Since I'd committed myself to not telling him about the largest secret in Realm history, I chose the secret he could actually help me with, the one I had wanted his advice a few nights earlier. "Khelan and I had an argument the other day."

Rhoan raised his eyebrows then nodded. "*That* explains why you two were hardly speaking to each other over dinner," he said. "I thought the two of you were making headway."

I shrugged, spooling a ribbon around my forefinger. "It's hard to 'make headway' with a man who says he puts his family first yet is determined to put all of us on the line."

Rhoan tossed the core of his fruit into a receptacle and crossed his arms. "I have to believe that when Tai tells Khelan what Maxim's been involved in, he'll come to his senses," he said.

I shook my head. "What Tai says could make him stop working with Maxim, but it's not going to do much to help my relationship with him," I said. "Khelan already suspects I don't trust him *now*. After hearing what Tai has to say, he'll know that we've been keeping track of him. It'll confirm that I didn't trust him after all."

Rhoan scowled then exhaled a heavy breath. "And he'll know Tai and I didn't trust him either," he said, "but it's the risk we have to take. Look, Tai isn't my favorite person, but when it comes to this type of thing, he knows what he's doing."

He pushed away from the counter at the sound of the buzz at the front door. "That must be him," he said. "Come on. Let's get this over with."

I followed him and entered the sitting area at the same time as Tai. Like the night he'd left town, Tai was an incredible sight in his official uniform. I smiled a quick hello and glanced away, an unexpected flush spreading up my neck and to my cheeks.

Good grief, this was *Tai!* How many times had I seen him here for family functions? But then, the last time I had seen him in person, I had been giving him a wanton show. I avoided his gaze as I skirted the room to sit down on the small couch facing the fireplace.

After the usual round of greetings — a kiss on the cheek for Ma, a handshake for Khelan and a tight nod to Rhoan — Tai took a quick sweep of the room. My eyebrows rose when he stepped past the two available armchairs and came to sit beside me on the couch. It was made for two people, but Tai had such a large build, it would be a tight squeeze.

I shifted over to give him an imaginary amount of additional space then studied his profile, my thigh and shoulder pressed firmly against his in the tight confines of the space. Tai normally tried to keep a well-defined distance between us while around my family. Perhaps he was trying offer me support. He knew I had concerns about telling Khelan about Maxim's true character.

Tai glanced around. "Should we wait on Hugo?" he asked me.

I shook my head. "Da will be out for a while," I said. "He took Addy out for a treat."

Ma frowned as she sat down in an armchair. "Khelan and I tried to tell Adria her mother wasn't coming back, that she passed away," she said. "I don't think she really understands what it means, but, as you can imagine, she's been a little down."

"We thought it best Addy not be around during this conversation," Khelan said, crossing his arms where he stood by the fireplace. "She doesn't know what rebels or factions are, but she could probably pick up on the tension, and that's the last thing she needs."

Tai accepted that with a nod.

Rhoan cleared his throat, eyebrows raised. "So you said you have some news to share," he asked, sitting down in the other armchair.

Tai nodded, looking from Rhoan to Khelan. "I've just returned from Helios," he said. "I've been working closely with the high marshal and his team on a wide-scale investigation to identify members of the factions."

Ma leaned forward in her seat. "Have you heard anything about Paol?" she asked.

Tai shook his head. "He's a subordinate with no record of violence," he said. "The Protectorate doesn't consider him a threat to the Realm. My investigation's focused on tracking down violent dissenters."

Khelan tensed. "And did you have any success?"

Tai nodded, holding his gaze. "It took a quite a bit of coercing," he said, "but we were able to learn the name of the faction leader who has the most control in Helios and the surrounding areas."

I frowned. This was news to me. The last time I had spoken with Tai, he had told me the citizens had been tight-lipped, showing no sign of revealing anything, much less the identity of any rebel leader.

Tai continued. "Once I got a name, I was able to track his interactions and see who he's been in contact with over the last few weeks."

Khelan exchanged an uneasy look with Ma. "And what's this person's name?"

Tai rested his elbows on his knees. "Maxim Noble," he said, watching Khelan closely.

The two of them studied each other for a long moment. Finally, Khelan broke away from his gaze and started to pace.

"What is it?" Tai asked, eyes tracking the older man's steps.

Khelan stopped abruptly and faced Tai. "I had hoped it wouldn't have come to this," he said, shoving his sleeves up his arms. "Weeks ago, Paol came to our home, bringing his daughter and a man, Maxim Noble, with him. When he told us that my sister had been killed in the middle of a fight between factions, I was angry and felt helpless."

"That's understandable," Tai said, still eyeing him.

"It is, but then —" Khelan broke off with a deep sigh, fists clenching at his sides. "Then I did what I thought I needed to do. I…"

"What?" Tai probed, and I glanced up at him. He already had the story, but for some reason was keeping up the pretense that he wasn't in the know. "What did you do, Khelan?"

Khelan's shoulders slumped. "I offered to help the factions."

Tai shook his head slowly, disappointment clear in his eyes. "Why didn't you come to me?" he demanded, brows drawn together. "I could have helped you identify those who killed your sister within *legal* means."

"You've been nothing but generous in helping our family, but you're a *protector*," Khelan said. "You're limited by your obligation to *protect* the Realm. I wanted to get back at our system, and Maxim and Paol presented with me with a way to do it."

Tai stood up and took a step toward him. "I think it's clear that I *can* and *would* protect this family," he said, looking Khelan over with a scowl. "But instead you put your faith in some renegade you'd only just met. What good did you think would come of it?"

Khelan scrubbed his hands over his face. "I put my faith in *Paol*," he said then shook his head, looking at Ma now. She sat peering up at him, tense, her fingers plaited on her lap. "I thought Paol knew the man. But I was wrong. Maxim, he's not who I thought he was."

"What do you mean?" Rhoan asked, coming to his feet to stand beside Tai.

Khelan expelled a heavy breath, dragging his gaze from Ma's. "I understand fighting for justice and even revenge," he said. "But for Maxim…I couldn't pinpoint why he, an elite, would be involved with the factions. I couldn't figure out what was in it for him, what his priorities were."

Tai gave a satisfied nod as if what Khelan was saying confirmed what he already knew. "Maxim's definitely in with the factions for revenge," he said. "But his main priority is avenging the expulsion of Liandra Ambassador of Argon."

His statement met with a round of baffled looks from Khelan, Ma and Rhoan.

Tai quickly filled them in about the connection between Maxim and Liandra, and his suspicion that Maxim was using the factions to retaliate for the Realm's decision to expel Argon, which would separate them from each other.

"This," he concluded, "is why I think Maxim's responsible for the attack on Septima that murdered many of our citizens and nearly killed the Corona."

"And nearly took Kira's life," Ma said, her entire body going slack as she glanced at me, eyes filled with horror. Khelan paled and leaned heavily against the mantel, looking at me as well. Meanwhile, I wrestled with the memory of those terrifying moments during the attack when time had hung, suspended, for what seemed like an eternity. It must have only been a few seconds, but it was long enough for the pressing weight of silence and darkness that fell around me just before I passed out to lodge itself into the farthest corners of my mind.

My hands trembled in my lap and I closed my eyes briefly, trying to stave off a possible panic attack by focusing on the conversation around me.

"But if Maxim was involved with Liandra," Rhoan began with a frown, "why would he attack the same arc craft she was —"

"Maxim didn't know she was there," Tai said with a frown. "And I think failing to kill the Corona only made him more determined."

Khelan studied Tai. "My gods," he said. "You think Maxim's responsible for the high chancellor's death, don't you!"

"Yes, but…" Tai nodded, then studied me so hard I stood up to rest a hand on his arm.

"What is it?" I asked, searching his face.

Tai thinned his lips. "It was a last-minute decision for the high chancellor to go," he said. "Even the Protectorate was turned upside down because we didn't have the most up-to-date travel itinerary. Whoever did this *couldn't* have known Marcus Consul was on board."

There was a breath of silence as we absorbed that.

Rhoan cursed and rounded on Khelan, fists clenched. "Have you heard enough?" he demanded, glaring at him. "You're supporting a murderer! You have to stop working with Maxim! Now!"

Khelan rested a hand on my brother's shoulder. "You have every right to be angry, Rhoan," he said, shaking his head. "But —"

"Yes, he *does* have every right," Tai cut in, eyes hard and pinned on Khelan. He appeared just as enraged as my brother but was doing a better job at keeping control of himself. "It was easy enough for me to make the connection between you and Maxim. If you get out now, I can protect you. I can say you were helping me track Maxim, not helping him, when the Protectorate finally brings him in."

I stared at Tai, speechless. The lengths he would go to for my family knew no bounds. No, not for my family — for *me*.

My gods, how could I have been so blind?

Ma. Sela. They had both been right. Tai loved me.

I should have known, or even *suspected*, but I hadn't allowed myself to entertain the thought since he had always done what he did best: push me away. He had never said the words, but the fact that Tai loved me was now clear as day, easily seen by the lengths he would go for me.

Glancing around the room, I saw that everyone else was just as stunned as me by what he was willing to do. I clenched my fists and glared at Khelan. Dear gods, if he didn't take Tai's offer, he was a fool, and any relationship he said he so desperately wanted to restore with me would come to an end before it even had a chance to start.

"Listen to him," I begged. "Please."

Khelan studied me for a long time before glancing at Ma, who gave him a small, encouraging nod.

He expelled a chestful of air and lowered his hand from my brother's shoulder. "I'm no longer helping Maxim," he said, walking over to stand beside Ma. "I met with Paol this morning and told him that though my sister had died, and I would grieve her death every day, I still had a family who needed me." He held my gaze. "I won't be providing information to him and Maxim any longer."

I stared at him, reading the meaning of his decision in his eyes. He had chosen his family, a relationship with *me*, over avenging his sister's death. I swallowed around the tears that stung the back of my throat.

Khelan clenched his fists suddenly, disgust contorting his face. "I never should have offered to help that man," he said. "To think how much danger I could have brought to my family!"

Tai nodded, bracing back his shoulders. "You did the right thing," he said.

"I just hope that's the last we see of him," Khelan said.

I tensed and glanced at Rhoan, finding a perplexed look on his face. "What do you mean?" I asked.

Rhoan followed up. "Uncle Paol's sole purpose was to avenge his wife's death," he said. "If we're not helping him, then it would only benefit him to stay far away from us."

Khelan shook his head. "It's not Paol I'm worried about," he said with a shrug, but the gesture did nothing to remove the pinched lines around his eyes and mouth. "My role was to provide Maxim with information. To rebels who have little to no access to the system's records or database, information is *everything*. The more of it they can get, the stronger they are."

Ma stood up and came to stand by his side. "Do you think he'll try to reach out to you again?" she asked, placing a hand on his forearm, face tight with concern.

"I doubt it," Khelan said, searching her face as he thought it through. "The information I shared was of little value. He'd do better reaching out to someone in a higher rank, or at least in a better position to get what he needs."

Ma nodded with a smile brimming with relief as Tai and Rhoan exchanged a satisfied look that settled my nerves. It seemed we could rest easy that Maxim was out of our lives.

* * *

"Are you ready to go?"

Ma and I looked up to find Tai entering Da's study. We had been showing Adria a few of her mother's journals. She was too young to read them, but we hoped that by sharing something of her Ma's, we could lift the little girl's mood. It must have worked because Adria launched herself at Tai and wrapped her arms around his knees before peering up at him.

"I'm ready to go, *corranda!*" she yelled, her face bright and full of mischief. Tai's title came out distorted, the big word too much for her tongue, making him smile.

Ma laughed as she stood up and dislodged Adria from Tai's legs. "I don't think he's talking to you, Addy," she said, making my cousin scowl.

Tai placed his duffel bag on a small table by the door and crouched to her level, which was quite an effort for a man of his height and build. Adria seemed to appreciate the effort because her frown flipped back into a grin at once.

I quirked my lips, watching her tug at the shiny badges on his Protectorate jacket. It seemed even little girls weren't immune to gorgeous men in uniforms.

After our family intervention with Khelan, Ma had plied Tai with food. I had almost felt sorry for him. But no matter how much Ma had placed in front of him, it had disappeared within minutes, so I figured he had no need for my sympathy. When Rhoan joined in for what must have been his fourth helping of dinner, I had decided it was time to leave them to it and had gone to the study to clear my thoughts. A few minutes later, Ma had wandered in with Adria and we'd started flipping through Aunt Marah's journals, enjoying the brief smiles the little girl made when she heard her mother's name.

Tai rested an elbow on his knee with a smile. "How about the next time I come by," he said, "I take you out for a ride on that over-the-top excuse for a hover."

It wasn't a surprise when Adria jumped up and down. She had, we'd been told, squealed when she'd first seen the vehicle parked in front of our house after returning home with Da.

Tai held out a hand, a sudden mix of seriousness and mischief sparkling in his eyes. "Just promise you won't tell my superiors," he whispered.

Adria gasped then nodded solemnly before shaking his hand with all the gravitas a two-year-old could muster. I laughed.

Ma winked at me then looked at my cousin. "How about we leave these two alone," she said with a smile.

I frowned as she led a bouncing Adria out of the room. As far as I knew, Khelan had dispelled the myth that Tai and I were involved, but that suspicious wink gave me pause. Even if he had told her, it was clear that Ma wasn't quite convinced.

Tai returned to his full height. "She reminds me of you," he said, crossing his arms.

I snorted and rested a hand on my hip. "What? Blond-haired and blue-eyed?"

"Spirited."

Heat filled my cheeks. "I suppose that's an improvement from — what was it you called me once?" I tapped my chin, pretending to be in deep thought. "Ah yes. *Fucking frustrating.*"

Tai chuckled. "I believe you deserved that at the time," he had the gall to say. "I prefer to think of you now as an overwhelming responsibility."

Responsibility, huh? "Careful," I said with a grin. "We've been doing well so far. I can hardly remember the last time we argued."

Tai glanced away, appearing to consider that, then nodded. "Neither can I," he said, looking at me with a wide smile.

I stood there, frozen for a moment, dazzled by the way that smile softened the hard lines of his face. Then I remembered what he had said to Khelan.

"You lied," I said, stepping toward him.

He drew back. "I did?"

I nodded, studying him. "You told me the citizens in Helios were wary, unwilling to tell you anything," I said, "but earlier you said they told you about Maxim."

He frowned and ran a hand over his head. "I figured a fib was better than telling the truth," he said. When I cocked my head in question, he explained, "I decided it was best for Khelan to think I learned about his connection to Maxim through my work."

It took me a moment to catch on. "So he wouldn't know that we were monitoring him."

He nodded with a shrug. "I didn't want him to think his family distrusted him," he said. "I know things between you and Khelan have been strained."

I searched his face for a long moment then closed the distance between us. "Thank you so much for doing that," I whispered, wrapping my arms around him and resting my cheek against his chest. Tai had once again come through for my family. "You have no idea what it means to Rhoan and me."

He ran a hand up my back, pulling me close. "I knew what it would mean to *you*," he said. "That's why I did it."

I pulled back and found him smiling down at me with everything I had hoped for in his eyes. His hazel eyes darkened with a depth of emotion I was still trying to come to terms with.

"So are you ready to go?" he asked, tightening his hold on my waist.

It took me a moment before I was able to respond. "Where?"

"To my apartment. I've been looking into the messages you've been receiving," he said. "I want to show you what I found."

I blinked. With everything that had been going on, I had completely forgotten about that.

I glanced at his bag by the door. "Can't you bring it up on your scroll?"

"No."

I frowned. "Why not?"

He shrugged. "I forgot the file."

I narrowed my eyes, assessing him, but his expression was indecipherable. Tai never forgot *anything*. Rhoan had once said his memory was like our system's database. Once information went in, it was never erased.

I raised an eyebrow, but he simply held my gaze, unmoved, revealing nothing.

I sighed. "All right," I said. "Just let me tell Rhoan not to wait on me."

He nodded then ran a hand up the length of my arm, the warmth from his palm spreading along my skin. "You really should consider getting your own place," he said, holding my gaze.

"Funny," I said with a smile. "I had that same thought the other day."

* * *

Tai tapped the screen, and I drew a chair up beside him, closer to his desk, to see what he was pointing at.

"Whoever's sending you those messages is using this code," he said, pointing to it.

I nodded, looking at the string of numbers glowing in front of me.

"You see the first three digits?" he said, glancing at me. "They're assigned to employees at the Judiciary on Prospect Eight."

I looked at him sharply. "Does that mean the person sending me the messages is someone who works with *me?*"

Tai shook his head then turned his back to the screen. "It can't be," he said, leaning against the edge of the desk, his thigh resting against my arm.

"Those digits were discontinued weeks ago. More than likely someone on the outside was able to hijack them somehow."

"Who?"

Tai frowned. "I don't know."

My shoulders slumped. "So we're back at square one."

"As I said before," Tai said, reaching for my hand. "It's more than likely just someone who's seen you on the newsfeed."

I stared up at him, hopeful. "You're probably right," I said, the feel of his fingers running along my wrist soothing me. "I haven't received any messages for some time now."

He nodded, holding my gaze. "That's a good sign," he said. His eyes took a lazy path across my face, and stopped at my mouth, which suddenly went dry.

"Tai," I began, eyes narrowing. He raised his eyes to mine. "You could have told me this back at my parents' house."

He nodded, the corner of his mouth lifting. "I made a promise to you, and there's no way I planned on keeping it under your parents' roof." Tai pulled me to a stand and cupped my cheeks. "I'm going to make love to you tonight."

I stilled. *Make love?*

Tai had said he would keep his promise, but based on our past and the craziness of the last few days, I hadn't actually spent too much time considering whether he would actually follow through.

My pulse kicked up a notch as he slid a thumb over my cheek. "Kira?" he said, a flicker of concern blotting out the heat in his eyes. "Do you still want this?"

I almost laughed. Of course, I did. This was it. Tai wasn't running away, making excuses or arguing with me. He *loved* me, wanted to *make love* to me, but…I frowned, staring at Tai's mouth. I shook my head, trying to regain some sense. There shouldn't *be* a "but."

Tai is reality. Gannon was a fairy tale.

I repeated the phrases two more times before raising my gaze. "Yes," I said firmly. "More than anything."

A flash of heat shot through his eyes before he tightened his hold on my wrist and led me into his bedroom. The room looked just as I had left it: warm, masculine and reflecting everything that made up Tai.

I reached for him the second he turned to face me at the foot of his bed. My knuckles skimmed his shirt as I undid the buttons of his shirt, happy I didn't have to battle with the multitude of fastenings on his formal jacket. He had discarded it the moment he had walked into his apartment, looking so relieved to be out of the garment, I had laughed out loud.

I reached the last button and was starting for the buckle of his pants when he gripped my wrists. I glanced up at him. He was wearing a wry grin, his hazel eyes laughing.

"We don't have to rush this time," he said.

I blinked, not realizing that's what I'd been doing. "I'm sorry," I said, the prickly heat of embarrassment crawling up my neck. "I guess I'm worried you'll change your mind."

He shook his head, running his hands up my arms. "Not this time," he said, then wrapped his fingers around my nape before pulling me flush against his chest. When he lowered his head, capturing my mouth with his, I sighed as I licked the salty taste of him from his upper lip and the flavor of the coffee he always drank from his tongue. His flavor was so familiar and sexy, my body hummed.

I thrust my hands into his hair, pulling him closer even though there was no space between us. A moment later when I ran my hands down the front of his shirt, he didn't stop me. The muscles of his chest rippled beneath my palms, enticing me to finally see what lay beneath the garment. I had yet to see Tai naked. During our intimate interactions, I had always been the one in the nude.

My pulse picked up as I shoved the shirt down his arms and to the floor. Tai was everything I had imagined he would be. Thick muscles corded his arms and shoulders and shaped the hard lines of a stomach so firm, my mouth watered. I ran my tongue along my bottom lip and traced a path with my fingers across his chest, enjoying the way the contours of his body shifted when he inhaled sharply.

I ran my fingers along a tattoo of swirling text in a language on the left side of his chest. "*Tolo caro pa nu rai,*" I read, and he glanced down. If I hadn't had my hand on him, I wouldn't have felt him tense, the reaction was so quick. "This is Kenaric, isn't it?"

He nodded then repeated the phrase but with the *c* pronounced as *sh* and the *p* as *f: Tolo sharo fa nu rai.* "It's an optic," he said tightly. "I've just been trying it out."

I stared at the spot, just above his heart. "What does it mean?"

He hesitated then exhaled a deep breath. "It says, 'Everything I do is for my queen.' It's a loose translation," he said then added quickly with a shrug. "Everyone in the Protectorate has something similar."

I raised my eyebrows, smiling. "I hope our sovereign appreciates such loyalty."

A corner of his lips kicked up into a grin. I studied him, trying to read his expression.

I didn't have time to ask him to explain himself because a moment later he snaked his arm around my waist and drew me against me, taking my mouth again. He walked me the rest of the way to the bed and pushed me down onto it, flat on my back, and made quick work of removing my clothes. My skirt and blouse piled up on the floor beside his shirt. My bra and panties offered little resistance to his deft fingers. He looked me over when I was bare, the need shining in his eyes making me shiver. Finally, he reached for his belt buckle, and I hurried to sit up, not wanting to miss a second of him undressing.

He raised an eyebrow. "So I'm the one doing the strip show now?"

I smirked. "Feels a bit different when the shoe's on the other foot, doesn't it."

He looked me over, and then the joke was on me when he removed the rest of his clothing. I stared at him for a full minute before any sensible connections were made in my brain. The man was as thick below as he was above. He was muscular, of course, but the sheer power of him was most evident in the size and length of his cock. I swallowed and glanced up at him to find him grinning. Tai was usually uncomfortable with praise, but I could see he had experience in being admired for how well endowed he was.

He leaned down and crawled toward me, making me reposition my legs so I could fall back onto the bed. He climbed over me and lowered himself to lick and drink from between my lips, making my sex clench and thicken as it flooded with heat. He nudged my legs wider with his knees and kissed his way close to my ear. "This may hurt," he said.

I frowned. "What?"

He lowered himself between my legs and nudged his cock against my sex, telling me without words that he meant his cock.

I laughed. "Good grief! I'm not a *virgin*, you know, Tai."

He frowned, peering down at me. "I just don't want to hurt you."

I brushed my fingers across the freckles I had rediscovered on the bridge of his nose. "I wouldn't mind if you did," I said, and by the way he started, could tell I had surprised him as much as I had myself.

He studied me as I lowered my hand. "You like that? Pain?"

I shrugged, glancing briefly at one of the mammoth plants over his shoulder. "A little."

He searched my face. "I never would have thought...I mean, I suspected you were submissive, but..."

I drew back, pressing the back of my head deep into his bed and staring up at him. "All Above! Is my sexual preference branded somewhere on my forehead for all men to see?"

He smirked. "Not quite," he said, moving deeper between my thighs. "But it couldn't be more obvious, at least to me."

I searched his face. "So…you're attracted to sexually submissive women?"

His broad shoulders rounded as he shrugged. "I don't know. I don't spend much time labeling women," he said. "I'm attracted to you, so I guess so."

My eyebrows raised. *Huh.* "Then you must be sexually dominant, right, to want to be with me?"

He snorted. "Hold gods, Kira. Where are you getting your information?" he asked with a grin. "The twenty-first century?"

I scowled and he instantly fell into a bed-shaking round of laughter.

I had never heard Tai laugh with such lack of restraint. Usually, he just smirked or grunted or did some sexy thing with his mouth that made my insides go all funny and upside down. Who knew all I had to do was display my naiveté to finally crack a full-bodied laugh out of the man?

I frowned. Gannon had done something similar — laughed at my ignorance about my own sexual inclinations. Apparently, I was an absolute riot when it came to the subject.

After a long while, Tai caught on that I wasn't joining him in the resounding laugh at my expense. He cleared his throat, pulling himself together.

"You didn't answer my question," I said, refusing to be cowed by the glimmer of mirth still shining bright in his eyes. "Are you sexually dominant or not?"

Tai smirked. "I'm whatever I need to be to get inside you," he said, running his knuckles along my cheek, then leaned down for a quick kiss. "My health data is clean and up to date."

I rolled my eyes. "Of course it is," I muttered as the stiffness in my shoulders eased at his touch. "Doesn't your caste put protectors on desk duty at the slightest sign of a cold?"

He grinned. "Not quite, but close."

I enjoyed the sight of his thick lips curving into a smile then gasped, remembering myself. "My health data is up to date too." I tapped my comm and showed it to him.

"You're on birth control," he said, reading the device as his grin widened. "Thank gods."

I felt the nudge of the blunt head of his cock against my sex just before he entered me in one hard thrust, erasing any thought I had about making some smart remark.

I moaned around the feel of him thick and pulsing, driving so deep that I felt the sharp edge of pain I had hoped for bloom inside. I groaned, accepting the power of his thrusts by widening my thighs, trying to believe this was actually, finally, happening.

I wrapped my fingers around the width of his arms, watching the tattoo ripple on his skin with every flex he made as he pummeled into me. He captured my mouth with his, groaning as I slid my hands down his back and curled my fingers into his hips so unforgivingly, he was bound to have the shape of the crescents of my nails marking him there for days to come.

Tai fucked the way he did everything else, with purpose and determination, but still I sensed him holding back.

"Harder," I said, panting into his mouth. "Please."

He grunted and forced the full length of his cock into me. I arched my back, enjoying the feel of taking him deeper, of finally being with him the way I had only dreamed about. He plowed into me, relentless, driving me to greater heights as the bed rocked hard beneath us. I closed my eyes, allowing him to lay claim to my body, demanding everything he had held back for years.

He gripped my right thigh and lifted it up and around his waist. Apparently, that wasn't the position he was looking for or needed, because he pushed my thigh back and hooked my knee over his shoulder, sliding home so deep, both our breaths caught. My eyelids flew open, watching the flash of heat morph the need in his hazel eyes into something primal and fierce. He pounded into me like a battering ram, staring down at me with every emotion I had wanted to see there, revealed, open for me to see.

I clawed at his shoulders and he took my mouth again. I sank my teeth into his bottom lip and smiled when he grunted and hardened inside me. The walls of my sex fluttered, the first sign of a dam that was about to break. It was all too much. I gripped the short strands of his hair as he fucked into me, his moves becoming short and irregular, telling me he too was on the cusp. The years of longing and need between us rushed to the surface.

"Harder!" I demanded, holding onto him, begging with my body for even more.

"Fuck, Kira." He hesitated but then strengthened his thrusts and gave me everything I wanted, needed.

"Tai!" I cried out as I fell apart, the intensity of the climax sending me straight into another one.

Tai followed me over the edge, calling out my name around an orgasm that made the veins along his neck and shoulders stand up in sharp relief. I stared at him, riding the tail end of my own release, not wanting to miss a moment of seeing him like this.

Finally, he collapsed onto his forearms, holding himself above me as he gasped for air. He rested his head on my shoulder and I felt the heat and gusts of his breaths against my breasts. My nipples, already hard, puckered at the airy caresses. It was a while before either of us moved. Only when I shifted, my parted thighs starting to ache under the weight of him, did he lift his head to stare down at me with fire still in his eyes.

"I've never known anyone like you," he said. "You're the sexiest woman I've ever met."

I smiled, body humming at the sound of that.

"The way you talk, walk, even the way you *eat* makes me to fuck you so deep, you won't be able to walk for a week."

"Be still my heart," I drawled with a laugh, but soon sobered. He was staring at me. Suddenly, a deep frown marred his face.

"What is it?" I asked, cupping his jaw, alarmed.

He inhaled deeply. "There's something I've been meaning to tell you," he said. "I…"

I studied him, surprised by his apparent loss for words. A flush rode high on his cheeks.

"Tai?"

He exhaled then stared deep into my eyes. "I love you," he said simply, but I felt just how much it meant to him to say those words in the tremor in his hands.

My heart squeezed and started to thump heavily.

Of course, by now I had realized that he loved me, but to hear him say it after all this time was like the worlds as I knew them had suddenly taken different shape and form. I parted my lips, the same words leaping to mind, but — There was that blasted word again.

What in the worlds is wrong with me? I knew the answer but I squashed it, buried it under my usual mantra, determined not to acknowledge how much weaker it was sounding the more I repeated it.

I shook my head, clearing my thoughts, noticing Tai's frown. "You must know I love you too," I said, but his expression didn't improve.

"How could I have known?" he asked, studying me. "Soon after I told you I had feelings for you, you committed yourself to Gannon. And then I watched you cry for the man after you left him, and only because you were forced to."

"I wasn't *forced* to leave Gannon," I said. "It was my choice."

"Tell me," he said after a moment. "If the Corona hadn't threatened Gannon's future, would you have left him?"

I glanced away, a pang blooming in my chest. "I'm not with him now."

"Thank the fucking gods for that," he was quick to say.

My ache deepened. I shifted, suddenly feeling the need for space. Tai moved to rest along my side.

"This is my fault," he said, regret twisting his face into a scowl. "I waited too long. Pushed you away like a fool."

I frowned. "Pushing me away has nothing to do with it. My feelings for Gannon aren't something that could have been prevented."

Tai thought about that then shook his head, seeming to dismiss it. "If I had been less of a coward," he said, "Gannon wouldn't have been able to hurt you the way he did."

I eased away from his touch. "He *never* hurt me," I said, glaring at him. Tai was making me sound like some lamb sent to the slaughter. "Gannon loves me."

Tai drew back, eyes narrowed. "He cares for you, Kira," he said, "but if he truly loved you, he would've let you go, not waited on you to make the decision and bear the weight of the pain. My gods, he was willing to engage in an illegitimate relationship with you, one that would taint your reputation and impact your future, knowing full well it would go nowhere."

I pushed up onto an elbow, making Tai lean back when I met him eye to eye. "Anything Gannon's done has been for my benefit," I said, ignoring the flash of irritation that ran through his eyes. "I chose to bear the weight of leaving him because I wanted what was best for him. I don't give a *fuck* about my reputation and would gladly give it all up because —"

"Because you love him," Tai said, eyes cooling as he assessed me.

My breath caught. What was I doing?

I ducked my head and pulled the sheets up over my breasts. I couldn't believe that I was there, in the middle of Tai's bed, naked, after just making love with him, defending another man's feelings for me and mine for him. It just didn't make sense, and Tai didn't deserve any of it.

"I'm sorry," I said, fighting back tears.

He rolled onto his back and stared at the ceiling. For a long moment, he remained silent as I wondered about my sanity.

"I know what it's like to have your heart broken," he said finally, still not looking at me, "so I'll give you the time you need."

I searched the profile of his face. "Time for what?"

Tai scrubbed his face with his palms then turned his head to look at me. "I made a mistake not committing to you when I should have," he said tightly. "I'll give you time to get over him."

I stared at him, not understanding. Or maybe it was that I couldn't believe what he was saying.

He pushed up onto his elbow, facing me. "I want to be with you, Kira," he said. "I'm not hiding or afraid of that fact anymore. I'm ready to make a commitment, but you're not."

My gods. "You would *wait* for me?"

He studied me for a number of my unsteady breaths, then nodded, although reluctantly.

I shook my head, amazed by him, as the tears I had been holding off fell to my cheeks.

He pulled me against him and pressed his mouth against mine. I kissed him with everything I had, grateful for his compassion, though I knew I didn't deserve it when even then my thoughts turned to another man.

CHAPTER FIFTEEN

There he is.

I quickened my step and crossed the lobby of the Council building, noticing that the number of media seemed to have doubled in the few minutes since I had arrived. With it being the last day of the special committee meetings, it was no surprise that they had come out in full force.

"I'd like a word with you," I said in a tight, low voice, latching onto one of his wiry arms.

Heath glanced at me over his shoulder, eyes flaring wide as he turned around. "Oh. Hi, Kira," he said as friendly as you please.

I leaned into him. "Don't you 'hi, Kira' me," I said. "Would you care to explain why you twisted my words like that?"

He shot a look over his shoulder at the optic-hair woman I had seen him with before. She was a short distance away, enduring some horrifically boring conversation, if the droll look on her face was any indication. Then again, I suspected that expression was one she wore all the time.

Heath swung back to me. "You should be thanking me," he said quietly, an unexpected glint sharpening his blue eyes.

I drew back, mouth slack. "For *what?*" I demanded. "For making my superior call me into her office for a reprimand? She wasn't particularly pleased to see that article. I could have lost my position!"

Heath smirked as he pushed his hands in his pocket, straightening his back. "But you didn't, did you."

I frowned, looking him over. He looked like the same man, but something was off. The Heath I'd met before was the kind of person who would have already been apologizing to me, effusively, for his actions. But there wasn't a lick of remorse in his cool expression.

Heath cocked his head. "It wouldn't serve Mila Minister well to demote the Subordinate caste's media darling."

"*Excuse* me?"

"That article attracted so much attention, the Judiciary is getting words of praise for the first time in years," he said, studying me. "And not *only* from subordinates. I mean, Rhoan Advocator's a big deal and all, but there's something people like about you, Kira Metallurgist."

I stepped forward, poking him in the shoulder as I crowded his space. "I don't need that type of attention, Heath," I hissed. "I just need to do my job."

He bowed his head, looking me straight in the eye. "Don't resent your newfound fame, Kira. Subordinates look up to you whether you like it or not. What you say makes a difference." He grinned. "Enjoy it."

What an obnoxious, ungrateful little... I wanted to hurl something at him so badly, my hands started to twitch.

"Don't look to me to be doing you any more favors, Heath Reporter," I spat. "Just forget you ever met me."

It seemed I had finally gotten through to him because his eyebrows climbed high up on his forehead. I spun on my heel and stalked away from him as fast as I could within the bustling space.

Asher had agreed to meet me here, so I searched for him. Instead I found Tai, on the other side of the lobby. He was speaking with two members of his team but soon glanced up at me. I didn't know what to make of his expression. It was back to being distant and controlled. Then again, what did I expect after the way our first time together had ended?

After promising to give me time to sort through my emotions, Tai had taken me home. He had insisted I stay, but I had felt so terrible about our conversation that I couldn't bring myself to. I had returned to my own bed and stared at the blank screen of my monitor for the rest of the night, trying to understand why everything had turned out so differently from what I had expected. In truth, it wasn't that *everything* had turned out differently. After five long years of wanting Tai, finally being with him had been all I could have hoped for, but we should have spent the hours after making love wrapped in each other's arms, making plans for the future, excited by our commitment to each other, the one we would spend the rest of our lives in. After a night alone filled with a torrent of conflicting emotions, those expectations seemed glaringly naive now.

My comm chimed, signaling a message from Tai.

I want to talk to you. I'll walk you back to the Judiciary after the meeting.

I winced. Gannon had said we would speak at that same time.

I have a meeting. I'm not sure how long it'll go.

Where? I'll come get you.

I looked up. Tai studied me, waiting on my response while his team conversed around him. I shook my head then replied:

I'm not sure where I'll be.

That's all right. I'll find you.

Guilt ate a deep hole in my chest.

I hated hiding anything from him, especially now. As soon as I'd spoken with Gannon, I would bring Tai up to speed about what I had learned on Hale. I frowned, watching as he said a few words to a protector then led the ambassador down one of the halls.

I glanced about. Asher was still nowhere in sight, so I squeezed through a throng of citizens and headed for a passageway that led to the meeting room. When I entered, Rhoan, Dominic and Mila were settling into their seats.

I spotted Asher at the back of the room and, as I made my way to him, noticed Xavier and Abigail sitting beside each other around the table. Neither of them was speaking, which was unusual since normally they'd be sharing quiet words before the start of a meeting.

A tremor of uncertainty ran up my spine. Xavier had said that he would support our recommendation, but who knew what his thoughts were now, days after our meeting with him? His reputation was built on a solid record of unpredictability and brash behavior. There was every possibility that he would turn around and change his mind. Then there was Abigail. I had no idea which way she would go.

Asher smiled at me as I slid into a chair beside him, but the good-humored spirit was missing in his eyes. He too was probably wondering at the outcome of the meeting. We had been so certain about Xavier and so hopeful about Abigail, but time had a way of breaking down confidence and building up doubt.

I sighed and pulled my tablet out of bag. We had done our part. It was up to the ministers now.

A sudden break in the light chatter within the meeting room caught my attention. I raised my head to see Gannon walk in with two senators and Jonah. My heart thumped heavily as he greeted the ministers and my brother then took a seat, but not before finding me and holding my gaze. I told myself it was the anticipation of the outcome of the meeting that had my pulse racing, but it was a lie just as weak as the mantra I had been repeating to myself. With a deep breath, I looked down at my hands, willing myself to rein in my emotions and focus on the task at hand.

The chatter silenced as Gannon addressed the room a few moments later. "As outlined on our agenda, we'll start with a brief review of the reports and then go to vote," he said, leaning onto his elbows. "If there aren't any objections to the speaking order as it's been laid out, we'll proceed."

Xavier leaned over and spoke into Abigail's ear. Meanwhile, Mila exchanged a look with Dominic then glanced at Rhoan. I tensed.

Everyone seemed to be readying themselves for what could be another round of heavy debate. I prayed the information I had given to Rhoan would be enough to help him through.

The day after meeting with Xavier, I had returned home and handed Rhoan a printed report on the ministers' voting history. As he read the document, hunched over our kitchen table, guilt filled me at the uselessness of it. In an effort to keep to my promise not to reveal the secrets I had learned from both Abigail and Xavier, I had left out quite a bit of substantial information. The report had ended up including a multitude of interesting facts, but not much more than my brother already knew.

Xavier ended his brief conversation with Abigail and raised his hand. "If I may, Chancellor?"

The other ministers started. Dominic, in particular, stared at Xavier as if he had never met the man. Gannon, on the other hand, didn't seem surprised. He nodded, giving the minister permission to speak.

Xavier sat forward, taking a moment to adjust his mic. "I would like to request that we bypass the formalities and go straight to vote," he said, causing several members of the audience to start speaking at once.

Rhoan frowned, sitting forward in his seat. "I believe I'm allowed another opportunity to speak," he said, looking between Gannon and Xavier.

The minister nodded with a twist to his lips. "Of course," he said, flicking a glance at Gannon. "But it would be a waste of your time."

Rhoan's frown deepened as he studied Xavier.

"This is completely unorthodox," Dominic said, his entire body bristling with indignation. "We know you're against the advocator's recommendation, Minister, but show good faith to the citizens of the Realm and at least listen to what the subordinate has to say."

The hum of chatter was louder now, expanding the sinking feeling in my gut. This couldn't be a good sign.

Gannon eyes were steady on Xavier, but his remarks were for everyone in the room. "I don't believe the minister's finished speaking," he said. The talk quieted.

Xavier cleared his throat and looked at Rhoan. "I've had a chance to read over your report with a fresher perspective on the matter," he said, shooting a look at Gannon. It was quick, but I saw resentment flash in the older man's eyes before he banked them away. "I think I may have underestimated the Realm's capacity to regulate exploration."

Rhoan sat forward. "In my report, I've explained that the Realm has everything we need to regulate explor —"

"Yes, yes. I know," Xavier said, making a face and drawing himself up in his seat. "Believe me, Advocator, I'm well acquainted with your report. I've read it thoroughly and found that I've changed my mind."

Rhoan blinked, his mouth open. Finally, he found his voice. "What do you mean, you've changed your mind?"

Xavier's expression became beleaguered. "I approve of your recommendation, Advocator," he said, causing the chatter to rise again, this time to new heights.

Asher and I exchanged a look. I released a breath as relief rushed into his eyes. *Xavier* didn't *change his mind. Thank gods.*

With a raised hand, Gannon quieted the noise in the room. "I feel compelled to remind you of the importance of this decision," he said. "Do you have any questions at all on the matter?"

Xavier sat back heavily in his chair. "None at all," he muttered.

If I hadn't known Gannon so well, I would have missed the shadow of a smirk around his lips. He looked at everyone else at the table. "I'm prepared to go straight to a vote," Gannon said, "but only if everyone else agrees."

Dominic piped up. "I'm ready to go to vote."

Gannon accepted his response with a nod then looked to Abigail. "Minister?" Gannon prompted.

Abigail raised her chin. "I'd like to ask the subordinate a question first."

Gannon hesitated a fraction of a second then nodded. He turned to Rhoan, who shifted forward, readying himself to defend his recommendation against any last-minute doubts.

"I'd be happy to respond to any question you have, Minister," he said.

Abigail frowned. "No, not you," she said with a sharp shake of her head before looking to the back of the room.

"*Oh no*," Asher said under his breath, looking at me as he slid down in his seat.

"Her," Abigail said, pointing at me. "Kira Metallurgist."

A heavy moment of silence filled the room before it erupted into chatter once again. I swallowed hard and tried to steady my pulse.

What in the worlds would Abigail Minister want to ask me, and in the middle of the special committee meeting no less? The last thing she should have wanted was to bring attention to me, the person who knew about her past dissident support.

I looked at Rhoan, who, like everyone else, was staring at me, but he was doing so with a mix of growing concern and uncertainty in his eyes.

Gannon swiveled his head from me to Abigail, a fist clenched on the table. "Rhoan Advocator is the subordinate representative," he said to the minister. "He's more than prepared to answer your questions."

"I'm sure the advocator can answer me," Abigail said evenly. "But I want to hear from *her*."

Even from where I sat, I could make out the conflict in Gannon's eyes. He looked at me for a long moment, his body rigid in his seat as he wondered what to do. I sat up in my chair, trying to appear more pulled together than I felt, hoping Gannon would know that I would speak if he needed me to. If Abigail wanted to ask me a few questions, I could certainly handle it…At least I hoped so.

Gannon expelled a deep breath, releasing me from his gaze. "All right," he said, glancing at Abigail, who nodded in response.

Casting what I hoped was a reassuring glance at Asher, I stood up and walked to the front of the room, where a subordinate hurried to position a mic on a small podium for me to speak into. I inhaled deeply and waved my hand over it to turn it on. By the time I looked up, the audience had quieted down.

"Months ago, in the early days of this process," Abigail began, "you said something that struck me. You said that you agreed with others in your caste that Argon's dissension was the failing of Realm leadership."

I blinked. "I don't believe I said it quite like that, Minister."

"You also said," she continued, ignoring my correction, "that Subordinate representation on this special committee would placate the disgruntled groups."

I frowned. "I-I believe I said it could *help*, yes."

"What's your *question*, Minister?" Gannon interrupted. He glared at Abigail so hard, she rocked back in her chair.

"I simply want to know whether the factions will stop their war on our system should this recommendation be passed by Realm Council," she said, eyeing him.

"You go too far, Minister," he warned. "You're asking her to speak for the *factions*."

Abigail bristled. "I'm doing no such thing, Chancellor," he said. "She's been involved in this process from the very start. I know she's not shy in sharing her opinion, whether to the committee or to the masses. Before I make my decision, I'd like to hear what young woman has to say."

The audience came alive, chatting all around me.

Rhoan caught my eye. He appeared ready to jump in at a moment's notice. I shook my head, looking at him meaningfully, hoping he'd see that I was okay. When he sat back in his seat, I knew that he had understood.

I had to think this through. *Why would Abigail expect that I would have anything to offer?* The last time we'd spoken, she had made it clear how little she thought of a subordinate's opinion. While she had been condescending, I had still come away appreciating her obvious dedication to doing what she thought was best for her dominion. Then it dawned on me: she needed reassurance that she'd be doing the right thing.

I leaned into the mic, looking at Gannon. "I'm prepared to answer any questions from the committee," I said loud enough to quiet the room.

He looked at me sharply. For a minute that felt longer, he studied me, appearing uncertain. Finally, he gave Abigail a reluctant nod.

"Thank you, Chancellor," she said, straightening in her seat as she turned to me. "So, is there any chance this recommendation will calm the rebels?"

I stared down at the flashing green light at the base of the mic, trying to think how best to respond. "I think," I began slowly, raising my gaze to Abigail's, "that this recommendation will show the rebels as well as our law-abiding citizens that leadership is willing to listen."

She glanced away with a frown before looking back at me. "You said something like that before," she said. "Yet here we are, still under siege."

I nodded. That was true. "But *approving* a recommendation from the subordinate representative will show that his position wasn't simply a token," I said, holding her gaze. "That the Realm is willing to truly change for the benefit of its citizens, and isn't afraid to hear differing opinions."

Abigail frowned, appearing unconvinced.

Xavier sent Gannon an apprehensive glance before looking at her. "It's the best-case scenario, Abigail. Believe me," he said, glum. "This decision would be for the good of the Realm."

She studied the meaningful look Xavier was giving her. "I hope so," she said, easing back in her chair.

Gannon cleared his throat, looking from me to the other committee members around the table. "Does anyone else have any questions?"

There was a fleeting second of silence during which I thanked the gods for a quick cross-examination. Then someone spoke.

"I do."

I blinked at the voice. Up until then, Mila had been speaking quietly with Dominic every now and then, and watching the proceedings as though deep in thought.

Gannon looked at her, a slight wrinkle in his brows. "Minister?"

Mila swiped through her tablet and raised her eyes to his only when the room was quiet. She sat back in her chair, crossed her arms, then eyed me.

"I prefer to base my decisions on fact and on lessons learned from the past," she said, "not simply on hope and the speculation of a young woman who has yet to reach her first anniversary at the Judiciary."

My eyes widened, uncertain what to say. While Mila's tone was diplomatic, her words were anything but. In fact, nothing in her disposition suggested she held any collegiality toward me.

She leaned forward and rested her elbows on the table. "There's nothing in our history that suggests that our citizens can explore safely," she said. "Yes, our system has progressed over the years. We can implement a rigid safety protocol with authorization levels, as our subordinate representative has recommended, but our citizens could very well abuse the allowances we provide them, couldn't they?"

My belly took a sharp dip, trying to digest her words. I was such a fool. I had been so focused on Xavier and Abigail that I hadn't even considered the opinion of my very own minister.

"I…"

Mila raised an eyebrow, her dark brown eyes holding my gaze.

I swallowed. "Well, I suppose there's always a chance that our citizens will go against protocol, but…that could happen with any rule of law."

Mila balked. "Chance?" she said, shaking her head. "I don't like uncertainty very much, subordinate."

My shoulders slumped. *What in the worlds is she getting at?* I stole a look at my brother. Dear gods. After all the work he put into this project, would whether it was approved all come down to me? Rhoan narrowed his eyes and looked pointedly at his tablet in his hands. It took me a few seconds before I realized what he was trying to tell me. *His report.*

I looked to Mila. "The subordinate representative has stated in his report that we should implement strong measures to prevent citizens from going beyond their authorization and abusing arc travel technology."

She shrugged. "What kind of measures?"

I wracked my brain, trying to remember what Rhoan had included in his report, but came up empty. He hadn't actually stated what they should be. That was the *next* step. If Realm Council agreed to regulated exploration, then it would be up to them to oversee a detailed plan to enact it. How did she expect me to come up with plausible penalties on the spot?

"I-I'm not sure," I said.

Mila's eyebrows drew together, but her expression seemed more disappointed than confused.

I sought out Gannon for answers. He was visibly tense, just an unkind comment or two away from stepping in and stopping Mila's line of questioning, but he was holding back. Like everyone else, he waited for me to respond. I *had* offered to answer the committee's questions, after all.

I inhaled deeply and forced myself to meet Mila's gaze. She narrowed her eyes and considered me, her mouth set in a firm line. The stern expression she wore now usually set Asher back on his heels, but I knew Mila better than he did. Mila was challenging me. For what purpose I didn't know, but I wasn't about to fail Rhoan, not now.

I swallowed and straightened my spine. "Regarding trade, under section two hundred and eighteen on the Enforcement of Fair Practice," I said in a clear voice, thanking the gods my memory hadn't failed me, "our law states that we can implement fines and restrict arc travel up to a lifetime should a citizen go against protocol."

Mila shook her head curtly. "That relates to arc travel for *trade*, and *within* the Realm," she said. "Not for the purpose of discovery beyond our system."

"Then we'll have to borrow from it," I replied quickly, ready for that response. "We've never regulated exploration, so there's no section of law that could speak directly to measures to curb an abuse of our technology for that purpose."

She nodded, crossing her arms. "How would Realm Council go about adapting trade measures for exploration?"

I faltered. "I'm not sure I understand the question."

Mila raised an eyebrow. "As you've just noted, we've never regulated exploration. Realm Council isn't current on the finer details about the law on exploration in order to properly adapt such measures."

She was right. "In similar instances, Realm Council has sought support," I said, thinking it through as I spoke. "We'll recommend that Council recruit an advisor from a Judiciary's Office of Exploration."

Mila appeared intrigued. "And who will this advisor report to?"

I searched my mind, heart thumping in my chest. "A subcommittee," I offered, but cringed even before Mila made a face of distaste in response.

"You're creating process to oversee process," she said, shaking her head and leaning back in her chair. "I don't like it."

I didn't like it either.

I clasped my hands in front of me. "He or she should report directly to the high chancellor," I tried again, "since that position oversees law."

Mila nodded, studying me for a long moment. It was only during that break in her volley of questions and responses that I remembered the rest of the committee members and the audience around us. The room was quiet save for the sound of the media tapping away on their devices. Meanwhile, Abigail considered me quietly and Xavier fidgeted in his seat, appearing eager to be done with the whole thing.

A grave expression took over Mila's face. "Subordinate Metallurgist, are you and the sub rep prepared for your caste to bear the brunt of the responsibility should regulated exploration fail?"

I frowned, my body seizing up at the unexpected concern now shadowing in her eyes. "I beg your pardon?"

Mila glanced at Dominic, whose eyes were on me. "If Realm Council approves regulated exploration, the decision will go down in history as being at the recommendation of representatives of the Subordinate caste," she said, holding my gaze now. "The first time something goes wrong — and believe me, it will at some point — citizens will blame not only leadership, but you as well."

I gripped the edge of the podium to steady myself, lowering my gaze. I hadn't thought of the other side of the coin. Mila was right. If our recommendation was passed, my caste would be among those heralded not only for any success it had, but for any failure too. Dread unfurled in my chest as it dawned on me that Rhoan's and mine would be the first names called. A long moment passed as I measured the strength of my conviction.

So much in my life had been impacted by other people's choices. Intercaste restrictions prevented my birth parents from being together openly, Realm Council's decision to expel Argon had led to my Aunt Marah's death as well as the high chancellor's. Dear gods, the Corona herself had driven me to leave Gannon! I was at a loss to think of anything in my life that hadn't been decided on by leadership in some way, shape or form. Meanwhile, their hypocrisy stunned me.

Leadership promoted adherence to governance and law. Yet they had been exploring for years, against their very own prohibition. I had pushed for the establishment of the sub rep position on the special committee to finally give my caste a voice in a decision that impacted our lives. If accepting blame was the necessary result of being involved at this level, then so be it.

I shot a look at Rhoan, taking strength from his nod of encouragement, before raising my eyes to Mila's. "The Subordinate caste has always wanted representation at higher levels of decision making," I said. "Being part of such a process means making difficult choices and managing the outcomes, good or bad, so…I believe my caste is behind me when I say that regulated exploration is a risk we are willing to take."

The murmurs in the room returned, starting in the penny section, where the media sat, and spreading to the audience behind me. I watched Mila, wondering whether I had answered her question adequately enough to finally escape her interrogation. The sharp edges of the podium on which I had tightened my hold bit into my palms.

Mila raised an eyebrow then turned to Gannon. "I have no further questions," she said, then returned to tapping at her tablet without a glance in my direction.

Gannon looked at me, and for the first time during the meeting, an outright smile came to his mouth. "Good," he said. "Then we'll go to vote."

* * *

"Kira."

I had been weaving through the crowd in the lobby, searching for Gannon but trying not to appear too obvious about it, when my brother called out to me.

"Do you have a second?" Rhoan asked, approaching me.

I didn't have a second — I needed to find Gannon. But I had to remember I also still had a job to do.

The meeting had adjourned over an hour ago. Since that time, Rhoan and I had been tied up with media and citizens of every rank who had questions to ask. After Gannon had called for the committee to go to vote, I had returned to my seat, waiting with bated breath as the committee members went through the process. It went swiftly, with all four voting in favor of recommending regulated exploration to Realm Council. It was an incredible, landmark decision that had everyone abuzz and speculating whether leadership would truly approve such a thing. I understood the excitement, but all I had been thinking about since the vote was meeting Gannon to get answers to a much larger question.

Rhoan dipped his chin to a spot a short distance away, and we walked over to it. On the way, I noticed a young woman with dark blond hair and a flashing mic on the lapel of her black jacket. She sent Rhoan an expectant look as she rested a hand on her hip and shifted her weight from one foot to the other.

"I thought you didn't do interviews," I said, watching as the reporter gave an exaggerated sigh and checked her comm. The only thing left for her to do was tap her shoe against the marble floors. Apparently, her conversation with Rhoan had come to an abrupt or unsatisfactory end.

"I've been trying *not* to do interviews for the last hour," he said, frowning so severely that I knew the media wouldn't be on my brother's good side any time soon.

"Do you want me to send her away?" I asked.

"You're not my support anymore, Kira."

"We still have Realm Council to get through."

"Only for a rubber stamp."

I nodded. I knew from experience how the process would unfold, and that approval at that level was more than likely a certainty.

"I'm proud of you," he said, smiling down at me, then laughed. "You were amazing today. Holy shit. Khelan's going to be over the moon when he hears about this."

I flushed at his praise, pleased to be acknowledged that way by my older brother, one of the few people other than Khelan I'd looked up to for as long as I could remember.

I shrugged, my cheeks still warm. "I only responded to their questions."

He snorted. "You locked in the vote."

I smiled outright then, allowing pride to swell my head, if only for a bit.

"It's quite a momentous day," he said, shoving his hands in his pockets.

I nodded, but my eyes started to wander, searching for Gannon once again. He had only told me to meet him after the council meeting, but he hadn't said where. I was looking across the lobby when Tai and another protector entered with the ambassador.

Is Gannon tied up in a meeting with the ambassador? Is that why he hasn't reached out to me yet?

"It's odd though, isn't it," Rhoan said, bringing my attention back to him.

I frowned, tilting my head in question.

"This is the most significant decision to be made in our worlds' history, and it was just approved for recommendation to Realm Council without even one vote against it."

"Leadership has had more than enough time to think the subject over," I said. "Exploration has been debated for years."

Rhoan shook his head. "But not at this level, and certainly not by Realm Council," he said, his green eyes alight. "Don't you find it suspicious how easily our recommendation was approved? In the short time I've been working with the ministers, Xavier hasn't been anything less than sanctimonious. And he was damn near on his knees before us all today. Abigail, she was a shadow of herself."

I tensed. "Mila put up a fight," I reminded him, trying to determine what path he was on.

"She only took you on because she enjoys playing devil's advocate," he said. "Mila told me during a briefing just the other day that while she doesn't approve of my approach, she never truly understood or cared for the Realm's conviction against exploration."

I digested that. I hadn't realized just how serious Mila had been when she said she didn't have a problem crossing boundaries. "I guess we were very convincing," I muttered, forcing myself to hold his gaze.

A crease formed between Rhoan's brows. "Don't patronize me, Kira," he said, searching my face. "This decision was made because of *him*, wasn't it?"

Heat crawled up my neck. "I don't know who you're talking about," I said, knowing full well who he was referring to.

He gave me a withering look, flicking a wary glance at the reporter, who was still waiting nearby. "You need to end this, Kira," he said in tight voice. He would have come across as threatening if not for the concern filling in his eyes.

I frowned. "I already have."

He drew back. "Are you *sure* about that?"

I glanced away from his skepticism and found the reporter sidling up to us.

"I'm sorry to bother you," she said to Rhoan, though she appeared anything but. She tapped at her lapel mic. "I have to file this interview within the next hour. Any chance you have time for just two more questions?" She held up two fingers as if to demonstrate she could count.

Rhoan groaned and shot me a bothered look before facing the young woman. "Only *two* questions?"

She grinned. "Oh, maybe a few more than that," she said with the right amount of charm. "I hope you don't mind."

He shoved his hands deeper into his pockets and headed off across the lobby beside her. I released a deep breath, grateful for the first time in my life for the tenacity of the media.

I searched the lobby again, absentmindedly noting Tai speaking with the ambassador. After a few minutes, I decided to do what I should have done in the first place: send Gannon a comm message. But I didn't have a chance to do so, since he finally reached out to me.

Ping.

Room 12.

I exhaled, relieved to know where to go. Tai had been sending me glances, each one filled with increasing concern. No doubt, he was wondering whether I had lost my way as well as my mind. Again, guilt over keeping secrets from him flooded me.

I firmed my jaw.

Once I spoke with Gannon, I would tell Tai what I knew, and I wouldn't have to maintain this cloak-and-dagger behavior anymore.

I walked down one hallway, reading the signs on the front of each door. I soon realized that the antechambers there were named after long past Realm leaders, not numbered. *Damn it.* I circled back and found a glass plaque that indicated with a glimmering digital arrow the way to the numbered rooms. As I walked toward them, I made an effort not to look behind me, sensing Tai's eyes on my back. I was passing room 11 when the door to room 12 slid open and Jonah stepped out.

"The chancellor's inside," he said as professionally as ever, with his clipped tone and rigid stance. "He has only fifteen minutes before his next meeting."

I flushed with heat. Jonah probably thought I was heading in for some romantic tryst with his superior. But then why wouldn't he? The fact that Gannon had assigned Jonah to accompany me on the trip to Hale would have done nothing to dispel that assumption. By every indication, I was still involved with Gannon. Somewhere in the back of my mind, I wondered whether the continuing interactions between us were by chance or by design.

I gave Jonah a tight smile as I slipped by him and entered the brightly lit room. As soon as I did, the door slid shut and Gannon was there, in front of me.

I didn't have a moment to fully register the hunger in his eyes before he reached out and thrust his fingers into my hair, pulling me against him. I gasped into his mouth as his lips locked onto mine, but I couldn't catch my bearings enough to do much else. I stood helpless and panting as he took, not caring whether I wanted to give to him or not. Somewhere in the distance, I heard my bag fall to the ground.

He pulled away, still holding the side of my face as he stared down at me. "I hated having to watch you answer to the committee," he said, the blue in his eyes flashing even in the brightness of the room. "But holy gods, I'm glad I did. You were incredible!"

My heart raced.

I opened my mouth, about to tell him stop, but it was crushed beneath another of his kisses. He wrapped his arm around my back and lift me up and against him to deepen the kiss. I found myself opening my mouth wider under his assault. I told myself my palms were on his chest so that I could stop him, but when I fisted the lapels of his jacket, pulling him toward me, not away, I knew it was a lie.

"I need you," he said, and I felt how much he did as he pressed the bulge of his cock at the apex of my thighs.

Dear gods, I have to stop this.

I returned to what had worked for me in the past, my mantra, trying to remind myself that this wasn't real, was a thing of the past, but it didn't work. As I had suspected, each time I repeated my mantra, it had become weaker; it was no longer enough to give me the motivation I needed to push him away.

"Gannon, please stop," I managed to say, but still he licked and plundered my mouth. I panted as the crisp and tangy flavor of him filled my senses.

It was only when he adjusted his position so he could run his hand up my side and cup my breast that I was able to find the strength to pull away. As I staggered out of his hold, my feet hit the ground and I covered my mouth with a shaky palm, staring at him, still tasting him on my lips.

Gannon stood back, fists clenched, panting, watching for my next move. I knew he'd read my indecision when he stepped toward me, need blazing once again in his eyes. I stepped back, making him stop.

"I heard there are cameras in some of these meeting rooms," I blurted out, grasping at straws as I tried to catch my breath. He studied me, and I used time to reach down and collect my bag. When I straightened, I wrapped my arms around it, holding it firmly against my chest.

"There aren't any cameras in this room," he said.

Of course, Gannon would have ensured that we had privacy.

"Nevertheless," I said, shaking my head, "that should not have happened."

Gannon ran his hand across his mouth then glanced away. When he looked back at me, he appeared more in control of himself. We considered each other for a long, fragile moment, in which I engaged in a battle against myself while his face filled with emotion I didn't want to acknowledge.

Finally, he stepped toward me. "I'm sorry I didn't message you as soon as the meeting ended," he said. "The ambassador insisted on speaking with me about the recommendation."

I placed my internal conflict aside. "Is anything wrong?"

Gannon shook his head. "He's just worried about the Corona's response," he said. "He's asked that I speak with her ahead of the Realm Council meeting, so she has the time to get past her initial shock that the special committee is making a recommendation that *doesn't* enforce the ban on exploration."

"Considering that Realm Council has been exploring for years, she should be able to get over her surprise quite quickly," I said, searching his face. "How did you know?"

He raked a hand through his hair and turned to walk to the center of the room. The space was small so the furniture was sparse, with only a nondescript table and two matching chairs. I followed him, anxious to finally hear how he had come across the truth.

"I had heard rumors of more inhabited worlds in the Outer Realm before," he said, "but had dismissed them because they would mean we had been exploring, going against our very own laws." He turned to face me. "After my father was killed, and now that I'm about to become high chancellor, I've been entrusted with more confidential documents. They not only confirmed the rumors, but detailed the full extent our involvement in exploration."

I shook my head, staring at him in wonder. "But how did you know that Xavier would reveal everything during our meeting with him?"

Gannon snorted, crossing his arms. "He's an asshole who likes to hear himself speak," he said. "I counted on him to show his hand early on. It might make me a lesser man, but I thoroughly enjoyed putting that prick in his place."

There was clearly no love lost between Gannon and Xavier. And why should there have been? Xavier had thrown Gannon's late father's words in his face, attempting to belittle him. I only wished I could have been there to see Gannon take him down a notch.

Suddenly, Gannon's eyes sharpened. "You said *our* meeting. Why?"

I blinked then understood what he was asking. "Because I met Xavier with a colleague."

He tensed. "Who?"

"Asher Analyst," I said, watching his eyes darken into a worrying shade of blue. "He won't say anything. He knew about you and me, and he hasn't said a word to anyone."

His eyes widened as he drew back. The tension in his shoulders eased, but only a bit. "I suppose we have no choice but to trust him now."

I studied him, bracing myself for his response to what I was about to say. "We have to tell Tai."

Gannon closed his eyes briefly as he looked away. "I had a feeling you would say that."

I rested my bag on the table as I went to stand before him. "He was there on Septima when Liandra told us the truth about Realm exploration," I said, peering up at him, hands clasped. "We should tell him. Maybe he can help."

"I'm obligated to keep this to myself, not to say a word to anyone," he said. "Not even to my family."

I frowned. "And yet you found a way to tell me."

He nodded, holding my gaze. "I wanted to tell you the moment I found out, but I never had a chance. The last time we were at Abigail's office, and before that…"

"I was with Tai," I said, finishing his train of thought.

My shoulders slumped as I remembered the urgency that had seemed to surround him when I had been trying to keep up the pretense of being with Tai.

He exhaled deeply then reached for my hand. "Just give me a chance to learn more," he said, wrapping his fingers around my own. "I want to be sure I have all the information before we involve anyone else."

"You think there's more to this?"

"There has to be," he said. "The Corona expelled an entire dominion for the very thing she had mandated it to do."

It pained me to admit it, but he was right. There had to be more to the story, but still I wondered how I was going to be able to keep this from Tai.

Gannon stepped toward me, his body a breath away from brushing mine. "Do you have any idea how hard it is for me to stand back and wait until you come back to me?"

I glanced away, hating the hurt I saw in his eyes. "You shouldn't be waiting."

"You belong with *me*, Kira," he said, eyes flashing even in the brightness of the room.

I shook my head. "I don't. I never did."

"Always, Kira."

I studied him. Gannon looked ready to fight this to the end, but I knew that it was an argument that would go nowhere, that it wouldn't change anything.

I pulled my hand from his. "I have to go," I muttered, grabbing my bag from the table and turning my back to him.

"I've been thinking of filing another unconventional recommendation," he said.

I stopped and turned to face him, gripping the straps of my bag. "What *other* recommendation?"

"One that will to do away with intercaste restrictions on relationships," he said, crossing his arms. "What do you think?"

I staggered a few steps toward him, eyes wide. "I think — no, I *know* — you won't be appointed as high chancellor."

He appeared nonplussed. "I would file it after I became high chancellor," he said. "It's the only way I could petition for such a change."

Air rushed from my lungs. "Realm Council would *never* agree to that," I said. "You would be demoted on the spot."

He shrugged.

I stared at him. "What are you doing?"

"What do you think?" Gannon dropped his arms and bore down on me. "I'm trying to get you back!"

I looked him over, mouth slack. "By *manipulating* me?"

"Don't you dare look at me that way, Kira," he said, fists clenched by his side. "You once told me that if I didn't stay in the Senate, you would leave me. If *this* is manipulation, then *that* was as well."

I gaped at him. "I was thinking of *you*, of your future."

He shook his head. "I have no future without you."

Tears stung the back of my throat. "I did that to *protect* you, so that you wouldn't throw everything away for me."

His body suddenly went stock still as he stared me, and I had a sinking feeling that I had revealed something I shouldn't have.

"My gods, *that's* why you left me," he said, eyes narrowing on me.

I stiffened.

"You're trying to *protect* me," he said.

I took a step back, but he followed.

"Are you even *with* Tai?"

There was little space in the room, so my back soon hit the wall. I stood, grasping for words, as he looked me over. By the way his eyes suddenly cleared, I knew the true reason I had left him had clicked into place.

The buzz at the door cut through the tension between us, startling me. Gannon clenched his jaw and watched the doors slide open.

I had expected Jonah to walk in, calling Gannon away for his meeting, but instead it was Tai who entered. My heart sank at the way his eyes darkened as he glanced between Gannon and me.

"I've been looking for you," he said so calmly, I knew he was nothing but. Tai's eyes narrowed on me. "Jonah told you me you were here, in a meeting with the chancellor."

Damn Jonah and his unbending respect for authority. As commander, Tai outranked Jonah. No doubt, Jonah thought nothing of directing Tai to where he could find me, even if it was in a private meeting with the chancellor.

I approached Tai where he stood by the door. "We were talking about the recommendation," I said because it was the only explanation I could give.

"Among other things," Gannon said.

I stiffened and Tai looked at him sharply, over my head.

For a tense moment the two of them glowered at each other, while I wished I had had the good sense to keep track of the time. When Tai had said that he would come look for me after the meeting, I should have known he would make every effort to find me the moment he had the chance.

"Tai," I said, placing my hand on his arm, hoping to prevent the argument that looked like it was bound to happen. "I have to check in with Mila. I'm ready to go now."

Fortunately, Jonah chose that moment to enter the room. "Chancellor," he said, "I can't hold the delegation back any longer."

Gannon's jaw clenched, his eyes snagging on my hand on Tai. He exhaled deeply then nodded at Jonah, turning to leave, but not before tossing me a look full of fierce possession.

When the door slid shut behind them, Tai stared long and hard at the door.

I tightened my hold on his arm, and he looked at me from the corner of his eye. "So you were talking about the *recommendation?*"

I nodded.

He turned fully to me, eyes hard. "When I arrived you were flushed with what could only be described as guilt," he said. "Tell me you weren't moments away from allowing him to kiss you."

I swallowed, staring up at him, wishing I could deny it, but Tai knew me too well.

He stepped toward me. "Or is it that he had just *finished* kissing you?" he demanded.

I lowered my gaze to his chest. "I-I'm just confused."

"I thought you were going to stay away from him."

When I didn't respond, he braced back his shoulders and I met his eyes. "Don't mistake my willingness to give you time as a sign of weakness," he said, anger contorting the strong lines of his face. "I *will* fight for you."

CHAPTER SIXTEEN

"*Tai* said *that?*"

Sela looked at me, awe all over her face, as she eased into a chair beside me.

I nodded, thrusting my hands into my hair, just stopping short from pulling the strands from my scalp.

"I must say," she said, reaching around a centerpiece of exotic red and purple flowers for a dessert dish, "I didn't know Tai was one for such dramatic declarations."

I leveled her with a glare and let my hands drop to my lap. "He was being *serious*, Sela."

"Oh, I know," she said, scooping out a slice of quidberry pie. "I can't tell you how happy I am to hear Tai's finally taking a stand when it comes to you."

I frowned as she placed the dessert in front of me with a sly grin.

Sela and I had been sitting in her kitchen, taking a break from the festivities that had overtaken her home. A baby welcoming was usually a small affair with close friends and family, but Sela's had grown out of control. Between my mother and hers, the event had become nothing less than a grand spectacle, which both our mothers had justified as being warranted since it was Sela's first child. After three hours on her feet, Sela had begged off and dragged me into the kitchen, where I had found a moment to bring her up to speed about Tai and Gannon, noting that the former had finally staked his claim while the latter didn't show any signs of relinquishing his.

"I just don't know what to do," I said, staring down at the pie. It was piled high with layers of pink whipped cream. It looked decadent and rich, the very thing that should make me feel better, but I couldn't bring myself to take a bite.

Sela placed her fork on the table with so much care that I knew she was searching for patience. "You've already done what you're supposed to do, Kira," she said, looking at me. "You *left* Gannon and can now be with *Tai*."

I nibbled on the edge of a nail, watching irritation darken my best friend's eyes.

"He told you he *loves* you," she said, eyes narrowing. "What more do you want?"

Sela and I hardly ever argued, but our conversations were fast becoming tense whenever the subject turned to either Gannon or Tai. The last thing I wanted to do was start an argument now, during her baby welcoming. Like for most complications in my life, I had sought out Sela's advice, but I could see now that she was no longer an objective observer — at least not when it came to my love life.

Turning away from her stiffly, I grabbed up a fork and cut into the pie.

"I'm sorry," Sela said with a sigh. "I know this is hard for you."

I glanced up to find her mouth turned down.

"I just need this baby out," she said with a groan, leaning against the back of her chair and running a hand over her belly. "Between this child and our mothers, I'm at wit's end." She wrinkled her nose the way she used to do when we were younger and was trying to make light of an awkward situation. As usual, it worked to lift my mood.

I rolled my eyes and leaned over to rub her belly, smoothing both the red fabric of her dress and the tension between us. "Stop blaming baby Lahra for your mood swings," I said then smiled. "Our *mothers*, on the other hand, are a different story."

Sela laughed, as I'd known she would.

"Hello, ladies."

Sela and I both turned to the kitchen door to see Nara sweep in. She plopped into a chair beside Sela, slung her bag over the back of it, then fluffed her platinum blond hair before swiveling to face me. She had the usual lift to the corners of her mouth that gave off the impression that she was keeping a secret of some sort.

"I've just enjoyed a very insightful conversation with your mother, Kira Metallurgist," she said.

I snorted. "*That* explains where you've been for the past hour," I said, looking her over with a smile.

Nara had arrived at Sela's house some time ago with an armful of gifts and, soon after, had gone missing. I'd figured she was taking a moment to educate one of Derek's relatives, who had made an awkward remark about multiples within her earshot at a past event. Since becoming involved with Ben and Cade, she seemed to have taken it up as her responsibility to enlighten the "prehistoric few."

I sat up. *That* interaction would have been much less precarious than any private conversation with my mother. "What were you two talking about?" I asked, eyeing her.

Impossible to believe, but Nara's grin grew. "Did you know that your mother has been building up a stash of baby items?" she asked. "It's for when you have your baby, which I understand, on good authority, should be within the next year."

I didn't find it even remotely funny when she and Sela burst into laughter. I folded my arms, allowing them to enjoy their hearty laugh. I knew how to silence at least one of them.

"Did my mother tell you she was hoping *you'd* partner with me?" I asked Nara, delighted when the customary smirk slipped from her mouth.

"All Above!" she exclaimed. "Is she foisting you off on *me* now?"

I grinned and said, "Not anymore," before licking cream off my fork.

"Thank the gods," she said, leaning heavily onto the table. "I can only manage two A-type personalities at once."

Sela laughed, seeming to enjoy the confusion that was more than likely written all over my face.

Ben and Cade were ambitious, smart and charismatic. Well, Cade was charismatic. Ben, he really was a delight after you got to know him. If that was what Nara meant by "A-type," then I would gladly take her remark as a compliment.

Nara sat up. "Congratulations, by the way," she said. "Not only have you gained seniority, but you've managed to get leadership to open their minds about exploration."

I smiled. "Rhoan had a lot to do with that," I said. "He did most of the work."

Nara snorted. "If I know anything about you, then there's no way that's entirely true."

I curled a wayward strand of hair behind my ear, feeling heat on my cheeks. "It still has to go to Realm Council for approval," I reminded them.

"Imagine that," Sela said, her gray eyes sparkling and wide. "My best friend could be the subordinate who actually changes Realm law!"

I shook my head. "Subordinates have influenced law before."

Nara smiled. "Influenced, *yes*. Changed — no," she said, then held out her hand to me. "I'm proud to know you, Kira Metallurgist."

I laughed and accepted her handshake. "Thank you."

"So," she said, leaning into me. "How was it, working with the fair Rhoan Advocator?" She batted her eyes.

I groaned.

"What's that face for?" Nara asked. "Everyone knows your brother's positively divine."

"Divinely *what?*" I asked, wincing, not sure I actually wanted to hear her response. Nara had a very active and colorful mind. Thankfully, her response was only a wink.

"He's got a following," Sela chimed in.

I sighed. There was that word again. "Does he now?"

She nodded, her auburn hair brushing her shoulders. "But yours is much larger."

I shook my head. "I'm sure that's a compliment in some circles," I muttered, baffled by the interest.

Nara looked put out. "Woman, don't you know about the Realm Anarchist?"

"What's that?" I asked, swallowing a bite of pie. "A music group or something?"

Nara looked like I had debunked the theory of quantum relativity. "It's not a *what.* It's a *he*," she said, "and no one knows who *he* is."

"Kira doesn't read the stuff we do, Nara," Sela said, doing a poor job at hiding a grin. "She's much too...*sophisticated* for that sort of thing."

I frowned. "What does *that* mean?"

Sela giggled and took a bite of her dessert.

Nara scrunched her face. "The Anarchist writes about you all the time," she said, reaching behind her to grab her bag from the back of her chair. She dug in, pulled out her tablet and unrolled it flat between us. With a few swipes and taps, she found what she was looking for and pivoted the device toward me. "Look."

My frown grew as I scanned the screen. Within a banquet of neon-colored graphics and over-the-top headlines, there was an article featuring me at the last special committee meeting, with a quote. Fortunately, this time the quote was real, taken directly from *my* remarks.

I stiffened, noticing a poll running alongside the article. It was headlined "Sibling Rivalry: Who has the stronger voice for the Subordinate caste? Kira Metallurgist or Rhoan Advocator?" Apparently, I was in the lead by millions of votes.

Hallowed Halls, who comes up with this shit?

"How have you *not* seen this article?" Nara demanded, waving a hand over it.

I thinned my lips, raising my head. "I've been a little busy working on a law that will hopefully appease those who have been threatening the very fabric of Realm society."

Sela laughed. "See what I mean?" she said to Nara. "*Sophisticated.*"

"Ah, I see," Nara replied with an annoying grin. "So we're our betters now, are we?" She crossed her arms under her ample bosom.

I handed the tablet back to her and shook my head. "All Above, if you're this annoying with Ben and Cade, it's a wonder they're still interested in partnering with you."

Nara made a show of buffing her nails on the shoulder of her light gray blouse. "That's the power of great sex. It's very persuasive."

I scoffed at Nara's boastfulness as Sela gasped, eyes wide.

"The three of you must have a *lot* of great sex," Sela said in a low voice, leaning in. "Though it must make for a tight squeeze in your bed."

Nara's eyebrows reached for the ceiling. "Good gods! Is that you two think we do every night?" she asked, looking between us. "Ménage?"

I snorted. "To be honest," I drawled, "I try very hard not to think about what you do in bed, Nara Architect."

"You should be so lucky," she returned with a haughty toss of her head.

Sela looked perplexed. "I thought *that* was the whole point of being in a multiple," she said. "Doing and sharing *everything* together."

Nara looked to the heavens. "Not *all* multiples do ménage," she said. "I mean, Cade would probably be into it, but Ben — not so much."

"Oh," Sela said, a laughable amount of disappointment dimming her eyes as she slowly took another bite of pie.

Nara smirked then. "But Ben *does* have a thing for watching Cade and me make love."

Sela choked then started coughing.

I sat forward. "Really?" I asked, interested now.

"Please," Sela managed to say once she recovered, "expand on that."

Nara shrugged. "There's not much more to say," she said. "Believe it or not; that's the extent of our kinky behavior."

"But Ben's so…straitlaced," I said.

"Yes," she said thoughtfully. "I suppose that's what make it such a turn-on for all of us."

Sela was looking off to the side, a distant, pensive look on her face. Suddenly, her attention snapped back to Nara. "So what does Ben do?" she asked. "Just sit there or touch himself?"

I drew back, looking at Sela with new eyes. I'd known her most of my life and had never seen her at such a heightened level of curiosity. It seemed my steadfast friend had an unconventional side.

Nara rolled her eyes. "You know, Sela," she said, "you're more than welcome to come join us to see for yourself."

The light in Sela's eyes died a sudden death. "I don't think Derek would approve," she said, surprising me even more.

Nara made a show of commiserating with Sela for a few moments. Meanwhile, I chewed on a corner of my lip, considering more mundane issues.

"How do the three of you make decisions?" I asked.

Nara blinked. "About what?"

I fiddled with the fork in my hand. "Anything. I mean, suppose some-one wants to move to another world. How do you decide whether to go?"

Nara frowned, thinking a moment. "Well, I guess, like in any rela-tionship, we all have to agree."

"But you can't *always* all agree," I said.

Nara nodded. "In those cases, one of us ends up being the tie-breaker, usually me."

"What about bigger issues, like children? Suppose Ben's ready to have a child, but Cade's not."

Sela looked at me sharply while Nara hesitated, seeming to consider a response.

"That's the one thing the three of us *have* to agree on, but we're not even thinking about that yet," she said. "We decided we wouldn't consider that for another few years."

I turned that over in my mind. "They have such different personali-ties," I said. "How do you manage it when they argue?"

Nara took a much longer time to think before responding, running her fingers absentmindedly over the tattoo Ben and Cade had also gotten to confirm their commitment to her. "It's hard being the mediator some-times," she said finally. "Somehow, it all just works."

"It wouldn't work for you, Kira," Sela said, a sharpness to her tone I had never heard before. "Tai has pretty much made that clear."

I flushed, taken aback.

Nara gasped. "Hallowed fucking Halls," she said, her blue eyes twin-kling bright as she leaned into me. "Are *you* in a multiple?"

"No," I said then flicked an irritated glance at Sela, who now looked appropriately contrite. She knew I didn't want Nara to know about Gannon, yet there she was, alluding to my illicit affair! "Believe me," I added, "you'd be the *first* person I'd tell if I was."

Nara studied me as Sela frowned.

"You *want* to be in a multiple?" Nara pressed. There was blood in the water, and she seemed determined to follow its scent.

"No, I don't," I said firmly. Dear gods, I had no plans to follow in my mother's footsteps. I might have flirted with the idea of being in a multiple, but the more I had thought about what my mother had to go through to be with Da and Khelan, the less inclined I felt to go down that path.

"Tai," Nara mused, glancing at Sela before coming back to me. "He's that protector you've been lusting after since we were sixteen, right?"

"Yes," I said with a smile, "something like that."

Nara grinned. "Whoa. He was beautiful then. He must be incredible now!"

"He is," I said readily. "He's perfect."

Nara cocked her head. "Perfect?"

I nodded.

"Huh." Nara ran a finger through the cream on the edge of Sela's plate. "So who's the other guy in this *non-multiple* equation?" She licked the cream from her finger.

Sela's eyes were on me as I responded, "Someone I met at the Judiciary."

Nara raised an eyebrow. "And it won't work out between you two *because...?*"

I studied the petals from the bouquet that had fallen to the table then glanced at her. "He's just not right for me."

Nara nodded. "So he's *not* perfect," she said.

"Something like that."

"Hmm," she said.

I gritted my teeth and sighed. "What is it, Nara?"

"It's just I would never describe either Ben or Cade as *perfect*."

Sela frowned the same way I did. "But you guys are meant to be."

Nara nodded, glancing at me. "Exactly."

* * *

I stopped mid-stride in the Judiciary reception. I had almost passed the desk when I noticed an unfamiliar person sitting there. "Where's Theo?" I asked.

The blond-haired subordinate sat up. "Who's Theo?"

I retraced my steps and narrowed my eyes on the stranger. He looked to be about my age, but his wide-eyed expression made him appear much younger.

I crossed my arms. "He's the senator who usually sits in that chair with a scowl on his face and an overinflated sense of professionalism that comes across as pure condescension." I raised an eyebrow.

"Oh, him." He blinked then stood up. "I'm just getting used to the names," he said then tapped at his monitor, shutting it off. "Give me a second. I'll see if I can find him."

I was about to tell him he didn't need to actually go and track him down that very moment, but he had already hurried off. Asher stepped out of his way quickly as they crossed paths at the double doors.

"What happened to Theo?" I asked as Asher put a folder down on the desk.

He grinned and crossed his arms. "The news is on your dashboard," he said. "Mila gave Theo seniority. Said she didn't understand why a senator was delivering mail and making coffee. Of course, she had a lot more curse words thrown in here and there."

I blinked.

"Ya," Asher said. "Theo was just as stunned as you are. I believe he's humping Mila's leg as we speak."

I laughed, the tension uncoiling a little around my neck. I rubbed at a knot and as we walked into the work area.

"Apparently," Asher said, "he's been telling everyone just how much he despised Gabriel and how glad he was to see him go."

I raised an eyebrow and Asher nodded. "I never worked closely with Gabriel," he said. "He seems to have left quite a reputation around here."

I frowned. "Is that right?"

"Oh ya," he said. "Andres told me they held a small party in the boardroom the day before Gabriel's dismissal was formally announced."

I pressed my fingers into the muscles at my shoulders, still working on the tense spot. I glanced at him out of the corner of my eye. "Why didn't anyone tell *me* about that?"

Asher made a face. "Well, you were supporting Gabriel for a while," he said. "People figured you wouldn't be as happy to see him go as they were. Plus, you were out sick, remember?"

I nodded slowly and kneaded my temples. *Out sick. Right. More like trying to get over Gabriel's assault.*

"Everything all right?" Asher asked.

"I've just had a rough night." For some reason, my conversation with Nara and Sela the night before had kept running through my head, keeping me up until the early hours of the morning.

"You and the chancellor haven't worked things out, huh?" Asher asked quietly.

I had told Asher that Gannon and I were no longer together, but it seemed he had been hoping for the best. "No, we haven't, and we won't."

Asher was silent until we reached my office door. "I guess it was just too good to last," he said, leaning against the doorjamb.

I frowned. "I don't think being *too good* had anything to do with it," I said. "It would have ended anyway."

"Why?"

I balked. "*Why?*" I said. "We can't have a real relationship."

Asher cocked his head, looking me over. "What do you mean by 'real'?" he asked. "Do you think you're the only one who's ever been involved in a restricted relationship?"

I scoffed. *If he only knew.* "*Believe* me," I said, "I *know* I'm not the only one. It's just...interesting to hear you speak about it so casually."

He chuckled. "I know people who've been together for a very long time. Their relationships aren't recognized, and are hidden, but they're committed all the same."

"Need I remind you that Gannon's not only a senator, Asher?" I said, lowering my voice even though we were the only ones in the hallway. "He's the *chancellor*. He'd lose his rank."

Asher thought about that. "And you'd be an outcast," he mused before flashing a wide grin. "But at least you'd be together."

I smiled, shaking my head. The longer I knew Asher, the more I was coming to realize that he was a hopeless romantic. He'd never had a problem with my being with Gannon, but until now, I had figured he had just been indulging me until it all fell apart. I saw now that he had had a lot of hope for our relationship.

"Hey," he said. "How about we round up a few people and head to Drunk Dominion after work? We can celebrate the Office of Exploration's latest great achievement."

"I don't know," I hedged. The new bar had been fun when we had first gone, but considering my fitful sleep and frantic thoughts over the past few nights, I didn't think I'd be good company to anyone now. "I planned on going home and trying to get some rest."

"Ya," Asher said, head bobbing, studying his shoes. "It's a much better idea for you to go to your apartment and wallow in your misery." He glanced up at me. "Alone."

I snorted. "Very subtle, Analyst," I said.

"Come on. Whad'ya say?"

I sighed and turned away, walking into my office. "I'll be there," I threw over my shoulder.

"Solid," he said. "I'll tell Simeon and Andres. I think Ana may want to come too." He eyed me when I faced him by my desk. "She's been really interested in our progress with the special committee. You okay with her coming?"

I activated my monitor as I thought about it. Even if she had been selected over me by Gabriel to oversee the tasks I had been doing for him, Ana had only been doing her job, and it seemed like she was making an effort to be supportive.

I looked up at Asher. "I think that's a great idea," I said with a smile.

He grinned, pushing away from the door. "I'll send you a message with the details," he said then started down the hall.

With a sigh, I sat down at my desk and faced the start of my day. As usual, I reviewed the dashboard to catch up on messages and reminders. I smiled, reading over the message from Mila that informed the office of Theo's seniority. Asher was right: there *were* a lot of curse words. Mila's swearing was apparently no longer limited to her verbal communication. Theo was being assigned to supporting Mila on key projects related to preparations for the election of Prospect Eight's permanent minister.

Despite the grilling she had given me at the special committee meeting, I hated to think about the fact that Mila's time at our Judiciary was coming to an end. I had been able to learn a lot from her, and saw her as a mentor. Compared to Gabriel, she was a gift from above. I would have enjoyed supporting her, if only for a little while longer.

Suddenly, a notification lit up my screen. I tapped the monitor to read the message.

P8 Date Stamp: 07.19.2558

P8 Time Stamp: 09h 33m 56s

Subordinate Kira Metallurgist:

Our Corona, Layla Sovereign, will be on Prospect Eight this afternoon in preparation for Realm Council's review of the special committee's recommendation. She invites you to meet with her at her official residences at 13h 00m 00s to discuss your involvement.

I trust that you will make every effort to attend.

Rhys Baron

Office of the Corona, Layla Sovereign of the Realm

Origin: D1(1): Capita

I stared at the message, jaw slack.

Now I'm getting invitations directly from the Corona's office?

I sat back in the chair as my heart raced. Quickly, I started checking things off my mind's list. She said she wanted to meet to discuss the recommendation, but was that the truth? The last time we'd spoken, she had warned me away from Gannon, nearly driving me to tears.

I forced myself to calm down. If her request was truly to discuss only the recommendation, then she must have also sent a request to Rhoan. *He* was the subordinate representative, after all.

I sent my brother a message via comm, hoping that he would reply before I had to leave to meet with her. His response, telling me she hadn't made such a request, came a few minutes later.

Shit.

I spent the remainder of the morning worrying. My shoulders were stiff as a board by the time I left my office for Realm Council residences.

I was stepping out of the elevator and into the lobby when I thought to contact Gannon. If the Corona wanted to speak with me, then I should let him know. After how we had parted ways, I wasn't certain that he'd *want* to hear from me, but the special committee was his responsibility. I should make him aware of any potential surprises or negative responses to the recommendation should they come up.

Decision made, I tapped out a brief message to him, hoping that I was fretting over nothing.

* * *

"Subordinate Kira Metallurgist," one of the Corona's female protectors said as I entered the main hall of Realm Council residences. "Come with me."

As she led me through the halls, it occurred to me that we weren't going the same way as the last two times I had come to meet with Corona. We wound our way through a maze of passageways before ending up on a much quieter side of the residences. The protector stopped at a broad deep purple door with a brass knob. After tapping a panel to the right of the door, she led me into a room that looked like a private suite, similar to the one Gannon had before he rented a row house nearby.

The young woman stepped back and dipped her head toward the door. "After you."

I swallowed and took a cautious step inside even as I eagerly scanned the room. The suite was luxurious, with dark wood furniture draped in cream upholstery trimmed with gold. On one wall, next to a floor-to-ceiling window, was a large abstract painting of what looked like the orbital rings of the Corona's crown. It dominated the room with vibrant splashes of color and appeared to glimmer in the dimness.

"I'll let the Corona know you're here," the protector said and left.

I pivoted, looking around the suite, and stopped to face the window. The sky had darkened since I'd left the office, and rain had started to fall. A crack of lightning sparked in the distance. We were still weeks away from squall season, but the climate was already shifting, preparing for its violent and stunning displays.

At the sound of movement at the door, I turned to see the Corona walking in. This time she was in no need of support, appearing much more like her cool and composed self. The tentative quality of her movements from our first meeting had been replaced by her usual confidence.

She nodded toward the window as she adjusted the plum-colored shawl around her shoulders. "Pretty, isn't it?" she said, sitting in one of the tanned leather armchairs.

I followed her line of sight just as another crack of lightening streaked across the slate canvas of the sky. "It is," I said, turning to her. "It's my favorite time of year."

She raised an eyebrow. "Is it?"

I nodded, not surprised by her reaction. Citizens on Prospect were known to dread the unpredictability of the season more than the cold of our winters. "After every squall season, the landscape seems to change," I said. "There's always something new to look forward to."

"That's true," she mused, then nodded toward the chair facing her. "Please sit."

When I did, she rested back in her chair, crossing one leg over the other. "I haven't been making very good decisions," she said simply.

I frowned. "I beg your pardon?"

"You left Gannon."

My eyes widened. "I-I did what I thought was best."

She frowned. "At my urging, of course."

I stared at her. *What is she after?*

She sighed, looking down at her hands as she fiddled with a sparkling jeweled ring. "I thought that if you left Gannon, he'd be focused and would put the needs of the Realm first."

"And he has."

She raised her chin. "Yet he's presented me with a recommendation that goes against everything the Realm stands for," she said. "A recommendation that calls for a lift of the ban on exploration."

"But with regulation."

She shrugged. "It amounts to the same thing."

I tensed. Was this why she invited me here, to blame me for the special committee's decision?

A thought struck me, and I sat forward in my chair, the blood draining from my cheeks. "This won't prevent Gannon from becoming high chancellor, will it?"

She narrowed her eyes. "One would think it would," she said. "Instead, region councillors across our worlds are sending Realm Council messages in support of his immediate appointment. In fact, many ministers have been vocal, admiring how well he's handled these affairs."

Since region councillors were all subordinates, I could understand why they would be so supportive of Gannon. He had overseen a process that had seriously considered a recommendation put forward by our caste's first ever subordinate representative. It was the support from the ministers — peers in Gannon's caste — that was more surprising.

"As I had wanted, Gannon has become a sign of stability and progress," the Corona continued. "He's always been admired, but in his father's shadow. Now he stands respected on his own."

I closed my eyes briefly as my shoulders slumped. *Thank gods.*

"Don't worry," she said. "He'll be appointed. Your leaving him wasn't for nothing."

I stared bleakly through the window. It seemed she was planning to leave me near tears like she had before.

"Earlier today," she said, "I had a meeting with the ministers from the special committee. Dominic, in particular, praised Gannon's work, but he was even more impressed with the value that was added to the process by having subordinates involved."

"Thank you," I said absentmindedly. The rain was falling much heavier now. "I'll make sure to share the minister's compliments with my brother."

Her clothing rustled as she shifted in her chair. "You'll be happy to know that I'm considering his request to make the subordinate representative position permanent."

I swung my head around to look at her. There was no way I had heard correctly. "Pardon me?"

She simply stared at me, waiting for me to catch on.

"But the special committee is disbanded," I said, "the process over."

She shook her head. "Let me clarify," she said. "I'm considering making the position permanent at Realm Council."

My mouth fell open. "*Realm Council?*"

She nodded.

I blinked. "But why?"

She tightened her shawl around her shoulders as she stood up. "I was shortsighted, but I learn quickly," she said, moving to stand in front of the window, her back to it. "At first, I regretted my decision to approve subordinate representation in this process, but over the last few weeks, it's become clear that citizens like having someone they identify with to rally around. Subordinates have been demanding a position like this for years. There's no better time to answer that call than during a time of intense strife. This position will be a clear sign of progress in an uncertain time."

I nodded because that all sounded good, but there had to be a catch. "Will the subordinate have the same voting rights as any other councillor?"

She hesitated then nodded. "Yes."

My gods.

"Will my caste have a chance to elect their representative?"

She thought about that a moment, her brown eyes looking off to the side. "Eventually," she said, her gaze coming back to me. "But I'll appoint the first subordinate. I already have someone in mind."

My pulse started to race. Rhoan had thought that he would be a token, that his involvement in the process wouldn't make a difference, but it had, more than even I could ever have expected. She said she already had someone in mind. It had to be Rhoan! He was the subordinate representative, after all.

"This is incredible," I said, standing up and stepping toward her with a smile. "My brother will be pleased."

She tilted her head, considering me with an enigmatic expression. "I would think so."

I turned, believing our conversation over. My mind had already gone ahead, anticipating Rhoan's response when I told him the news.

"I told you before that I haven't been making very good decisions," she said, and I stopped to face her. She held an indecipherable look in her eyes. "It's more than just my decisions in relation to the special committee. People are dead and the Realm is fractured and torn apart because of me. I led our worlds down this path."

I searched her face. I understood why she was taking blame for the division in the Realm. It had all started because of her decision to expel Argon, after all. But why was she bringing this up now? Did she, like Abigail, need reassurance before approving Rhoan's recommendation?

I stepped toward her. "Approving regulated exploration and establishing a permanent position for the Subordinate caste will go a long way in relieving tensions," I said. "I have to believe the Realm will rise above it all in the end."

She nodded, but her gaze was unfocused as if thinking on other matters, not my remark. "I hope you and Gannon find your way back to each other," she said.

If she had told me she wanted to appoint me as her successor, I couldn't have been more stunned.

"*What?*" I blurted out, shock making me forget to temper my tone. One minute she warned me away from the man, the next she was encouraging our relationship! What game was she playing?

She glanced away briefly and ran a shaky hand through her hair. "I made a rash decision to spite someone I loved but who didn't love me back," she continued as if I had never spoken. "I see now that I wasn't in love with him. I couldn't *truly* have been in love to have wanted to hurt him the way I did." The stricken look on her face sent goose bumps racing up my arms. "I don't want Gannon to do what I did."

I clenched my fists. "Gannon would *never* do anything to hurt anyone."

"He's like his father, so I suspect he wouldn't," she said with a morose look that reminded me of her expression at the high chancellor's ash ceremony. "But sometimes you do things you wouldn't expect to because you want something or *someone* so much you can't bear it."

I searched her face, but there were no answers there. She seemed lost in her thoughts as she spoke, as if barely aware of the words she was saying or their meaning.

She inhaled deeply, eyes clearing a bit. "I tried to make things right, but it was too late," she said, turning her back to me and staring through the window. "Hopefully, I still have a chance to correct some of the things I've done wrong."

CHAPTER SEVENTEEN

Meet u @ DD with 3 P8 Judiciary subs @ 18h.

With a smile, I read Asher's heavily coded message on my comm. The short time we had spent with Jonah on Hale had apparently rubbed off on him. After a quick check of the time, I saw that I had fifteen minutes before I had to be at Drunk Dominion to meet up with Asher and three of our colleagues from the Judiciary, and I would need all the time I could get.

After her mystifying remarks, the Corona had dismissed me as summarily as she had summoned me to her side. I had returned to work to find most people already gone for the day, but since I had plans to meet with Asher, I had taken some time to read through the messages I had received on my dashboard while I was away. I tried calling Rhoan on the monitor, excited to tell him about what the Corona had said about the sub rep position, but he hadn't picked up.

An hour later, I stood peering through ribbons of rainwater running down the glass walls of the Judiciary's lobby, mentally mapping out the fastest route to Drunk Dominion. All the public hovers and ground vehicles in sight were occupied, which was no surprise considering the downpour. I'd have to take the underground rail. The nearest station was a good twenty-minute walk away, but I could cut around the back of the building to get there faster.

I messaged Asher as I exited the lobby:

`On my way.`

Because my head was down when I stepped onto the sidewalk, I didn't see the heavily built man in my path. I collided into him, almost losing hold of both my footing and my bag.

I gasped. "Oh. I'm so sorry," I rushed out, but the man either didn't care or didn't hear me over the thunder in the distance, because he ducked his head and shuffled on, with barely a glance in my direction.

All right then.

I frowned and pulled my scarf over my head before turning the corner of the building. The fabric was lightweight and sheer, but it was better than nothing to protect myself from the rain. Of course, as was always the case when I needed my umbrella, it was waiting for me, safe and dry, at home.

It was only because my hand was close by my head, holding the scarf in place, that I was able to hear the ping of my comm. I voice-activated it rather than trying to tap while I walked in the rain. A crack of lightning made me jump and cry out at the same time I answered the call.

"*Kira?*" Gannon said sharply.

I stopped under an awning to catch my breath.

There was another flash in the sky, illuminating the narrow alleyway. A few feet away, a door slid open and three subordinates spilled out. They instantly tried to retreat from the downpour, laughing, but the door had already closed. One smart soul dug into her backpack and pulled out an umbrella. They all huddled underneath it and it widened automatically to provide coverage to them all. They chatted excitedly as they rushed off, crossing paths at the end of the alleyway with an approaching man.

"What's wrong?" Gannon's voice hadn't lost its edge.

"I'm all right," I said, feeling silly, then glanced around, suddenly conscious that I was alone, in the middle of a darkened alleyway, with a strange man. As he came closer, I saw by his clothing that he was a protector and breathed a sigh of relief.

"I just retrieved your message," Gannon said. "You said the Corona wanted to meet with you. Why?"

I started walking again, skirting a puddle as I remembered that I had, in fact, reached out to him before meeting with our sovereign.

I frowned. "Actually, I'm not sure why she wanted to meet with me," I said loudly, knowing that the weather and my scurrying in the rain would make it hard for him to hear me. "At first she seemed to be blaming me for special committee's decision, but then she started speaking about a lot of other things."

"*Blaming* you?" By the terse way Gannon said it, I imagined he spoke with a clenched jaw.

"It doesn't matter," I said, trying to look on the bright side. "I'm just relieved that she isn't planning on rejecting the recommendation. She said she'll approve it."

"I know," he said, surprising me. "But she has no right to call you in for a meeting to blame *you* for a project that *I* oversaw. If she wanted to lay blame at someone's feet, she should have laid it at mine."

As far as I was concerned, the Corona shouldn't be laying blame anywhere but at her *own* feet, considering she was lying to citizens about Realm exploration. I shook my head, turning my mind to even more important matters.

"She wants to make the sub rep position permanent at Realm Council." Even saying it, hours later, sent a thrill of excitement thrumming through my veins.

There was a breath of silence during which I thought that I must have lost our connection or had missed his reply.

"Gannon?" I asked, wincing as I stepped into a puddle, the water sloshing up, ice cold, onto my sheer leggings.

"Why?"

I frowned and explained the Corona's reasoning, but his response was as blunt as his question.

"I don't buy it," he said.

Out of the corner of my eye, I saw that the protector had stopped walking and was staring at me while speaking into his comm even as the rain puddled around his feet.

My steps slowed.

"What do you mean?" I asked Gannon distractedly.

"It's a bargaining chip," he said tightly, but I was so focused on the protector, I didn't respond to his remark.

"Kira?" Gannon said.

The protector lowered his hand and started walking toward me with a determined stride. A frisson of alarm ran up my spine. I swung around to look behind me, squinting through the rain, my brain already trying to decide between fright or flight, when I saw another large figure come into view.

"Gannon…," I began. The other man was the same one who I had bumped into in front of the Judiciary. My blood went cold.

"What's going on?" he demanded, unease making his voice hard.

"I-I think I need help."

I saw the look of intention in the protector's eyes an instant before he lunged for me, but I still managed to dart off to his side, out of his reach. I turned and headed for the door from which I had seen the subordinates exit a minute earlier, but I wasn't quick enough. The thug behind me, though large, was fast on his feet, and intercepted me. I screamed just before his coarse hand slid over my mouth. At the same time, he snaked his arm around my waist and arms, forcing my back against his chest.

In the background, Gannon called for me, his voice barely audible. I yelled his name, desperate to have him hear me, but the hand over my mouth and the thunderous background seemed to drown out my cries.

I kicked out and twisted my torso, trying to break my captor's hold, but it was no use. I felt a surge of satisfaction when I managed to bite down on the coarse skin of his palm. His body flinched as he cursed, but he only strengthened his hold, making me gasp at the pain just below my ribs. I strained to hear Gannon's voice but couldn't. The connection must have been lost. White-hot fear licked inside me.

The protector walked toward me, his wet hair stuck to his forehead and the sides of his face. "Take it easy," he said, grabbing my bag. He opened it and removed my tablet before tossing the bag aside. "Our superior just wants to have a word with you."

I gasped for air around the thug's hand, watching wide-eyed as a hover came into view beyond the protector's head. My heart leapt into my throat.

Good gods. If they get me inside a hover, I won't have a chance!

I screamed and struggled again, panic making me stronger than before, and managed to wrench my arms free of the thug's hold, but it was for only a moment. With a frightening amount of calm, he captured my flailing arms and yanked me against him as the hover lowered to the ground in front of us. Rain sluicing off the darkened windows and the deep blue metal exterior gave it an appearance of a vibrating, living thing. The back door slid open and the thug dragged me over to it. My boots skidded along the slick stones on the ground as I fought to find purchase and stay where I was.

"Wait!" the protector barked, and his accomplice stopped hauling me to the hover.

He came over and took my hand. Reflexively, I yanked it back, but like his friend, the protector was pure strength and gripped my wrist so tightly I whimpered, instantly feeling the bruise his hold would leave behind. The protector yanked off my comm, and dropped it and my tablet on the ground before crushing them under the metal heel of his boot. I watched as pieces of any hope I had of telling anyone where I was and what was happening to me were swept down the alleyway and into the gutter by the driving rain.

Tears sprung to my eyes as I closed my lids.

Suddenly, the thug shoved me into the back seat of the hover. I sat sprawled and disoriented for a moment then snapped into action, lunging toward the door on the opposite side. Of course, it was locked. But panic was a living thing inside me. I pounded against the window, swallowing around the thickness clogging my throat. I gritted my teeth and tried to will the threat of a panic attack away. Getting nowhere in my using my fists against the windows, I repositioned myself so I could try to knock out the glass with my boot heels, but the result was the same: I was trapped.

"It's a Protectorate-issued vehicle," came a voice from the front of the cab. "Only an atomic bomb could get you out of this hover."

I stopped my futile attack and sat up slowly, searching for the owner of the voice with its familiar lilt. The thug was sitting beside me now, focused on something in his palm, while the protector stood outside, looking into the alley, apparently on watch. The person who spoke was in the driver's seat, so I couldn't see his face. When I peered into the rear-view mirror, my whole body went slack.

Maxim turned around, an arm curled around the back of his seat. For a man who was on the run, sitting in the back alley of a government building, he appeared calm and collected.

He frowned. "Her lip is bleeding," he said, sliding an accusatory look to his nearest partner in crime. Without thinking, I ran my tongue along my bottom lip and picked up an unmistakable tangy, metallic taste.

The thug held up his hand, showing red marks where my teeth had sunk into his palm. It wasn't my blood that I was tasting, but his. Bile rose in my throat. I ran the back of my hand across my mouth, wiping any remaining blood away so angrily, my lips felt sore.

Maxim studied me then grabbed a cloth from a compartment. "Here," he said, offering a small towel to me. "Use this to clean up."

I grabbed the scrap of fabric and flung it on the floor of the cab. "What the fuck do you want?"

He looked me over. "I don't plan on hurting you, if that's what you're asking."

"So you kidnap me in the middle of the street, to do what?" I demanded. "Ask me for directions?" I would be happy to tell him exactly where to go.

Maxim shifted so that he faced me fully, his back to the windshield. "I have a favor to ask of you."

I glared at him, fists clenched on my lap. "Why would I do *anything* to help *you?*"

"Come now," he said. "Your family and I were friends before."

"Khelan is a good man who was torn apart by grief," I said, glaring at him. "He had no idea what he was doing when he offered to help you."

"He left a big gap in my plans when he chose to stop working with me," he said, crossing his arms over his thick navy blue coat, studying me. "Khelan made a promise to me. I don't like when people go back on their word."

I considered him, realizing my error. I had thought that, with Khelan's ties to Maxim cut, it would be the last I heard of the dissident elite, but I had been wrong.

"Stay away from Khelan," I said, fists clenched. "We all know what kind of monster you are."

Maxim's eyebrows raised. "So that's why he retracted his offer," he said, then held a hand to his chest, just above his heart. "I truly despise what I've been forced into doing, Kira, but I won't allow citizens to be treated as they have been by the Realm."

I narrowed my eyes. If he thought he could play the virtuous avenger with me, he was sorely mistaken. "What you're doing has *nothing* to do with citizens or the Realm," I spat. "I know about you and Liandra Ambassador."

He lowered his hand slowly, brown eyes hardening. "What did you say?"

I swallowed, the shift in his mood from cool to menacing making me inch back. "You heard me."

His lip curled. "You know *nothing* about Lia and me."

"I know you killed her father on Septima."

The air in the cab stilled. Even the storm outside seemed to go silent.

Maxim's eyes glittered as he lunged forward. "I had no intention of killing Donal Ambassador," he hissed through clenched teeth. "The *Corona* should have been the one the Realm laid to rest."

I covered my mouth with both hands, staring at him. As Tai had suspected, Maxim must not have known that Liandra and her father were on the arc craft. Nevertheless, even if Donal wasn't his target, Maxim had intended to take the Corona's life.

My heart skittered into a race. He had just confessed to the attempted murder of our sovereign. There was no way he was going to let me go.

I searched for some miraculous way out of the cab, panic rising thick and fast, when I noticed the thug check his comm.

"We need to wrap this up," he said to Maxim. His voice was gravelly, as though hardly ever used.

Holy gods, what did that mean? Were they going to kill me now?

I sat forward, gripping the back of Maxim's seat, in front of me. "What do you want?" I demanded, trying to buy some time.

Maxim exhaled deeply. "I need access to information," he said. "A recent contact has high-level authorization, but only up to a point. He's not on the inside anymore. As a result, any information he can acquire isn't always current or accurate."

I balked. "I'm not going to try to convince Khelan to help you again."

Maxim shook his head. "The information Khelan provided was useless," he said. "I've been watching you. You've gained a lot of influence over the last few weeks, which means you have access to people and information that a person in your position wouldn't normally have. I'm banking on you this time around. I have a feeling you'd know how to get what I want."

I stared at him, coming to understand. "You want *me* to get you information?"

He nodded.

He was delusional. "Fuck you."

Maxim stiffened. The protector beside me shifted in his seat, the rustle of his clothing reminding me that he was still there. Maxim slanted a look at him then returned to me.

"You wouldn't want me to kill *more* innocent people by accident, would you?" he said, leaning forward. "First Donal Ambassador, then Marcus Consul. They're examples of what a lack of accurate information can cause. Had I known the correct whereabouts of Gannon Consul, we probably wouldn't be having this conversation right now."

My entire body shut down, the bottom of my belly hollowing out. "Y-you meant to kill Gannon."

"I did," he said simply. "It wasn't anything personal, completely transactional, but I did what I had to do."

I lunged forward, striking him just below his left eye. The protector jumped into action, snaking an arm around my waist. My nails scraped down the side of Maxim's face as he pulled me away from his superior.

"You fucking murderer!" I yelled, struggling against the protector's wrought-iron hold.

Maxim glared at me, eyes narrowed as he rubbed the rising welts along his jaw. He should have been angry. Instead, he appeared intrigued.

Barely holding back a scream of frustration, I dropped my face into my palms, curling my fingers into fists against my cheeks. My hands shook as tears seeped through my fingers. A moment later, Maxim chuckled. I raised my head and found him considering me.

"So *you're* the one," he said with a smirk. "I *knew* he had a bone to pick with someone. I thought it was the chancellor, but no. It was *you*." He ran his eyes down the length of me. "My gods. What did you *do* to him?"

I shook my head, searching his face. "I don't know what you're talking about."

Maxim smiled. "Tell me," he said, leaning toward me. "Have you been receiving any strange messages over the last few weeks?"

I froze. "*You* sent them?"

Maxim gave me a withering look, turning to face the front of the vehicle. "I just abducted you outside of a government building within earshot of the good citizens of Merit," he said. "Do you truly think I would hide behind messages filled with riddles?"

"Then how did you know about them?" I demanded, not believing a word.

"I don't play games," he said, pressing a button on the dashboard. It lit up as the window on the other side of the vehicle lowered. "But I happen to know someone who would be into that sort of thing." Maxim leaned toward the now open window. "Micah, get in!"

I looked between Maxim and the protector who was now entering the hover. "What are you doing?" I asked, my voice rising as I yanked at the door handles. "Where are we going?"

Maxim ignored me and began plotting out an uncongested route out of Merit. Meanwhile, the thug beside me flexed his wounded palm, watching me with a dark look in his eyes.

I drew back into the corner of the cab, trying to get as far away from him as I could. The only hope I had of getting out of this was Gannon. But then what could he do? He had heard me being taken on the streets, but other than that, he had no idea where I was or who had taken me. After tracing my position through my now battered comm and tablet, the most he'd be able to figure out was that I had been in the back alley of the Judiciary.

I was on my own. I had to think, to figure this out.

But thirty minutes later, I still had no answers. Hopelessness filled me as I peered through the window.

The rain had let up, but the sky was still painted with angry purple and orange streaks. The number of buildings and lights had started fading away, becoming less dense the farther we traveled. It must have been another half hour before another built-up area came into view. It was smaller than Merit, but it should have been bustling with activity at this time of day. Instead, there wasn't a citizen or a vehicle in sight. Most of the street lamps and the businesses' lights appeared either to not be working or to have been shut off, casting an eerie pall over the town.

Soon we moved closer to ground level and I searched the darkened buildings and street signs for some indication of where we were. My eyes snagged on a large digital billboard. Though it was unlit, I could make out the words by their dusky silhouette.

Welcome to Helios.

I straightened in my seat, placing my palm on the window as the sign slid by. Helios was the name of the town from Tai's reports. It was a command center for the factions. Tai had pretended to learn about Maxim from his investigation here, but apparently his fib held water.

A surge of hope shot through me. Nara's family lived in Port. If I could escape, then I could find my way there, but I would need help.

"Where is everyone?" I asked as nonchalantly as I could. Perhaps I could beg a ride into the neighboring town from a local.

Maxim's brown eyes met mine in the rear-view mirror. "I pretty much own this town, Kira," he said. "No one will help you, or they'll pay the price."

I shrank back as he turned the vehicle down another street. *That's right.* Tai had said as much.

I thought hard. If no one would help me then I would go to Port by foot. It would take me hours, but I was riding on pure adrenaline, so I had more than enough energy to spare.

"We're here," Alexei said into his comm.

I watched, mind calculating escape routes, as he and Maxim navigated the way to a tall, warehouse-like building. A few hovers and ground vehicles and a handful of protectors and subordinates were standing around in front of it. One of the protectors raised a hand, indicating a space into which Maxim soon lowered the hover.

"Wait here," Maxim ordered Micah, then turned to the thug beside me. "Alexei, you come with me."

The asshole otherwise known as Alexei gripped my wrist and hauled me out of the vehicle. I barely managed not to fall face first onto the wet ground, but did manage to wrench my arm out of his hold. Apparently, there was no longer much concern about me getting away, because he released me without a fight.

I cut him a look and followed Maxim, keeping my eye on the citizens around me. Though most of them were in my caste, I picked up no sign of camaraderie. Hostility fairly radiated at me as I entered the building. It was an old factory by the looks of it, and there must have been fifty or so subordinates and protectors milling about inside in a flurry of activity. All of them came to a silent stop, watching as we crossed the wide and drafty workspace that was filled to the rafters with an astonishing array of advanced equipment. I swallowed, avoiding their aggressive gazes by keeping my eyes focused on Maxim's back.

Maxim stopped in front of a metal door then swiped his comm across a panel on the right. The door slid open, revealing a small box of an office with no windows. Inside were only a few wooden chairs and a desk with a monitor sitting atop it. The room looked as inviting as a prison cell.

"I have gift for you," Maxim announced as he walked in.

Alexei shoved me in the small of my back when I hesitated at the door, and I stumbled forward. I was too busy trying to steady myself to see who Maxim was speaking to.

"Metallurgist?"

I tensed, my body registering the sound of his voice before my mind caught up. The hairs along my arms and at the back of my neck stood on end as I turned around to face a person I had never expected to lay eyes on again.

Gabriel?

His gray eyes were wide as he approached me.

Maxim stopped in the middle of the room, looking between us, hands on his hips. "I was right," he said. "You *do* know her."

Gabriel's eyes narrowed as he stopped in front of me. Like Maxim, he seemed to be faring better than expected considering his circumstances. I saw by the deep blue of his hair and gold-colored nails that he was still a fan of optics. His red and black uniform was as crisp as his eyes were sharp.

"*You're* the one who's been sending those messages," I breathed, staring up at him. "Why?"

Gabriel raised a finger to me like I was an errant child. "First thing's first," he said then turned to Maxim. "What's *she* doing here?"

Maxim shrugged out of his coat and placed it on the back of a chair. "When you first came to me, I asked why you wanted me to kill Gannon Consul. You said because the best way to get at your enemy was to strike at her heart," he said then dipped his head toward me. "You should have seen this one's reaction when I told her I meant to kill the chancellor, not his father. She nearly disfigured me. Only someone who cared that deeply would have had such a reaction."

Gabriel frowned. "But why were you talking to her in the first place?"

"I told you I had another source for up-to-date information," he said, then shrugged. "She's it."

Gabriel raised a sleek brow, turning to look at me. "What are the odds!"

My hands started shaking as I began putting the pieces together. "You asked him to try to kill Gannon to get back at me."

"Much good it did," Gabriel said. "He's still running around like the captain of a ship, and no doubt soon to be appointed high chancellor."

I balled my fists, ready to pounce and rip Gabriel apart with my bare hands. However, Alexei, who had been standing silent and watchful behind me, had faster reflexes this time around and held me back before I could do any harm.

"Is *this* what you're doing now, Gabriel?" I demanded, struggling to get out the thug's hold. He let me go, no doubt confident in the strength of the cement walls surrounding us to keep me from getting away. "Isn't helping rebels below even someone like you?"

"To be honest, at first, I couldn't care less about the rebels and their cause," Gabriel said with a dismissive wave of his hand. "When you're demoted as unceremoniously as I was, you become an outsider, someone respected citizens shun." Gabriel glanced at Maxim. "But you *do* attract other misunderstood and embattled souls."

Maxim slid a look to me. "Believe it or not, leading a resistance requires a lot of resources, so I tracked Gabriel down, figuring he'd be more than willing to provide information and resources in exchange for getting back at those who had done him wrong," he said, crossing his arms. "I gather that I have *you* to thank for Gabriel's dismissal."

I stared at him as tears rose to the surface. "So you sent me the messages to taunt me? Is that it, Gabriel?"

He shrugged. "I thought it was a nice touch."

I swiped away the tears on my cheeks with both hands. "So what now?"

"What now, indeed?" Gabriel said, looking me over. "I asked myself that very question after Marcus Consul died. I decided that I should think bigger than simply trying to exact revenge." He walked toward me slowly. "You see, living on the fringe of society has its benefits. It's grown on me. There aren't as many rules or the same need for balance and order. Maxim and I make a surprisingly good pair. With his and my knowledge of the ins and outs of leadership and our castes, we have more power than we could have ever had as an elite or a senator."

My entire body began to shake. Not only was Gabriel a lunatic, he was a determined one. He had left the Judiciary a pariah and turned into a rebel, more of a threat than before. And, dear gods, now he was aligned with the man who knew about my fugitive family.

I shot a look between him and Maxim, taking a halting step backward. "Let me go." I meant for it to come out forcefully, like a demand, but it came out instead as a whispered plea.

Maxim narrowed his eyes. "We will," he said, "*after* you agree to what I asked. We need someone on the inside."

I shook my head. "Even if I *wanted* to help you, I couldn't," I said. "I don't have authorization to access the type of information you'd need."

Maxim shot a look at Gabriel. "Is that true?"

Gabriel raised his chin, looking down at me. "Theoretically," he said, "but I should be able to instruct her how to get it. Furthermore, that analyst who used to pant after her around the office like a lost puppy is more than capable of accessing the information. I know how skilled he is. I recruited him, after all."

If he thought I was about to bring Asher into this, he was further along into madness than I had first thought. "I won't do it," I said firmly.

Gabriel cocked his head. "I see on the newsfeed that you've gained seniority and have become quite popular," he said, drawing himself up. "Tell me, Metallurgist, are you and our future high chancellor still fucking? Because if you don't agree to our demands, I'll ensure that everyone in the Realm knows that the lauded voice of the Subordinate caste is nothing but a whore."

I would have laughed if I hadn't been so stunned. The fool thought *that* was something that would matter to me! I stepped close to him so I could hold his gaze when I said, "I would rather be thought of as a *whore* than help you."

For the first time, Gabriel's haughty disposition slipped. "Take it from me," he said, glaring at me, his body appearing as tight as a coil, "that's a storm you don't want to weather, Metallurgist. The worlds aren't so rosy on the way down."

For a few interminable seconds, Gabriel and I stared each other down. I had learned long ago that Gabriel despised being confronted or challenged in any way, so I steeled myself for the worst. He would lash out at me verbally, physically or both. Maybe he would go even further. Both Gabriel's and Maxim's records proved that they would go as far as to commit murder. Yet there I was, taking them on in the middle of some rebel compound filled with citizens who would think nothing of killing me at their word. I clenched my fists. I had no intention of giving in, so I stood firm even as my heart pounded so hard, I could hear it in my ears.

Maxim exhaled deeply. "Don't worry, my friend," he said to Gabriel, turning to pick up his jacket. "She'll do it. There's no way she'd want her family to endure the level of scrutiny such a rumor could bring. They've got a list of infractions to rival my own that she'll want to keep quiet."

Gabriel drew back, looking the elite over. "Explain," he demanded with a frown.

Maxim shrugged into his coat. "Do you remember me telling you about a subordinate I met in Tholos? Paol Auditor?" he prompted, buttoning up the garment. "His wife was a fugitive senator who was killed by rebels?"

Gabriel nodded, his frown deepening, seeming to wonder what this had to do with anything. Meanwhile, my shoulders sagged as my worlds came crashing down, meeting in a terrible place that would only strengthen Gabriel's resolve against me.

Maxim smiled and tipped his head toward me. "That fugitive senator was *her* aunt."

Gabriel blinked, returning his gaze to mine. "Hallowed Halls, Metallurgist! You're a treasure trove of secrets, aren't you!"

I closed my eyes briefly as tears filled them.

"Now it all makes sense," Gabriel said, his eyes taking on a forbidding gleam. "I've been racking my brain trying to figure out who got you the position at the Judiciary. It was your *aunt*."

I glared at him, stopping just short of correcting him. He already knew too much, but Maxim soon filled in the blanks.

"Probably not," he said. "Her aunt was a teacher. The aunt's brother, *Khelan*, is the one who works at the Judiciary."

Gabriel's eyebrows raised. "Two senators in hiding within your family, and one still working to uphold law," he said, tilting his head. "The funny thing about secrets is they *always* have a way of coming out, don't they."

I glanced away, focusing hard on the steel beams behind him through tear-filled eyes.

"Perhaps we should bring this Paol Auditor in," he said to Maxim. "A good threat to his welfare should make young Metallurgist a lot more receptive to our ideas."

I tensed. *How in the worlds can I refuse them if my uncle stands before me, his life on the line?*

Maxim shook his head. "It's a good idea, but he's gone silent for the past few weeks," he said. "I don't even know where he is."

Thank the gods. I exhaled a shuddering breath and wrapped my arms around my waist, trying to keep myself together. They discussed my future and that of my family with as much care as they would a strange turn in the weather.

"Very well," Gabriel said, eyeing me. "It's quite clear that she has more than enough reasons to comply with our requests."

Maxim nodded, walking toward the door. "We've given her enough to think about today."

I watched, stunned, hopeful, as Maxim spoke with Alexei about their route out of Helios and back to Merit. *Were they truly letting me go?*

Alexei stepped away from the door and disengaged it. When the door slid open, Maxim turned to me. "Come on, Kira," he said. "I'll take you home."

If the man hadn't just abducted and threatened me, I would have thought he was a friend offering me a ride.

I stood there, gripped by fear, wondering whether he was trying to fool me into some false sense of security before taking my life.

Gabriel came up beside me. "He's not going to kill you, Metallurgist," he said, and reluctantly I looked at him. His gray eyes brimmed with his usual arrogance but were now sharpened by his newfound knowledge about me and my family. "You're *much* too valuable to us now."

I narrowed my eyes, trying to convey the depth and strength of my contempt. I had never thought of myself as someone who could commit murder, but looking at Gabriel, I knew that if I had a weapon in my hand, I would have done it without a hint of remorse or hesitation.

Gabriel tutted. "I'd be much more agreeable if I were you, Metallurgist." He said my name as if tasting a fine wine. "With Maxim on my side, I have the ability to destroy *everyone* you know and love."

CHAPTER EIGHTEEN

My wrist didn't hurt very much, but the skin there was darkening rapidly. Ironically, it was the same wrist that had been injured on Septima during the attack on the Corona. It seemed as if my light therapy kit would come in handy once again.

After heading out of Helios, Maxim and his goons had left me unceremoniously at the curb in front of my apartment building. I didn't try to figure out how it was they knew where I lived. It was obvious that they had been keeping tabs on me.

My hands trembled as I entered the elevator, or maybe it was my whole body that shook. I couldn't tell the difference. I gripped the metal railing that was clamped onto the mirrored wall so hard, my fingers cramped when I released it a moment later to step out.

When I reached my apartment door, I came up short. How was I going to get in? I needed to swipe the code from my comm on the digital panel on the side to enter, but the device was now swirling at the bottom of Merit's sewage system along with fragments of my tablet. The only reason I'd been able to access the elevator was that I had slipped in at the same time as a fellow resident exited.

The door suddenly slid open, and I gasped, staggering back when a large figure appeared and reached for me, wrapping himself around me. Arms as thick and strong as the men who had abducted me pulled me firmly against his chest. My body had gone rigid, about to fight or scream, probably both, when I recognized his familiar scent — spicy, warm and safe. My body wilted as I leaned heavily into Tai, too relieved to wonder why he was there, but so thankful he was.

"Holy fuck, Kira," he said into my hair. I could hear his heart thudding behind his ribs. "We've been looking everywhere for you."

He pulled back and looked me over, gripping the tops of my arms. I swallowed down a sob, still shaking from the surprise at seeing him at my apartment on top of what I had just been through. He leaned in, his mouth closing in on mine, then I heard a familiar name. I angled my head, looking beyond Tai into the apartment, at the wall-to-wall monitor in my sitting area. A newsfeed was running, announcing an upcoming media conference to be held by the Corona. The reporter speculated that the reason for the event was the appointment of the Realm's next high chancellor.

"I have to tell him," I said, distracted, moving away from Tai.

"Who?" he said behind me.

I crossed the threshold, hurrying to the monitor. I tapped at and swiped the screen, searching through my contact codes.

"Kira, tell me what happened?" Tai demanded.

I shook my head. "I will, but I have to contact Gannon first," I said, still facing the monitor. "I have to tell him I'm all right."

Tai came up beside me and placed his hand over mine, stopping me, just at the moment it occurred to me that Gannon's contact information wouldn't be available on my monitor. I hadn't added it to the contact list, not wanting Rhoan to come across his name by accident.

"Gannon knows you're all right," he said.

I startled, looking up at him. "He does?"

Tai studied me. "He's the one who told me something happened to you," he said. "Then I told Rhoan. Both your brother and I have been out looking for you for the past three hours. The only reason I'm here is that I volunteered to check the apartment on the off chance you might've returned."

I slumped, turning to lean heavily against the screen. *Thank gods.*

"I was moments away from notifying your parents and rounding up my team," he said, tightening his hold on my wrist, eyes hardening. "Now tell me. What happened?"

I shook my head, trying to figure out where to start. "Maxim and Gabriel," I blurted out after expelling a tight breath. Just saying their names turned my stomach.

Tai searched my face. "What does one asshole have to do with the other?"

"Maxim took me...then Gabriel was in Helios...and they *killed* them," I said, my voice rising as I spoke. I gripped his hand. "You were right."

There was so much to tell, but I was too keyed up. Everything was jumbling around in my head.

"Take it easy," Tai said, pulling me toward him.

I took a deep breath, resting my forehead against his chest as he wrapped his arms around me. When I felt his comm vibrate against waist, he pulled away to check the device.

"Shit. It's Rhoan," he said, wincing. "I was supposed to tell him whether you were here or not."

While Tai tapped at his comm, I thrust my fingers into my hair and approached the couch, noticing absentmindedly that the monitor had reverted back to the dashboard. As usual when in default mode, it displayed live footage of the entrance of the building.

I lowered my hands to my sides, turning fully to the screen as the large lobby doors slid open and three tall figures strode in. They were dressed in black with heads covered in what looked like wool skullcaps. Their clothing was so nondescript that they shouldn't have caught my attention, but something about them, especially one, looked familiar.

I stepped closer to the monitor to try to make him out, but like the two behind him, his head was down as he passed by the camera. He stood with his back to me, arms crossed, as one of his companions started tapping at the panel. I cocked my head, returning my attention to the figure who carried himself like the leader of the three, wondering why they didn't simply access it with a comm. It was when the elevator doors slid open and he swiped his hand over his head, removing his cap, that I saw the head of blond hair that I would know a mile away.

Gannon!

I gasped, placing a hand on the screen.

Heart racing, I pivoted and raced to the door. I yanked it open and was halfway down the hall when the elevator doors opened. When Gannon saw me, he shoved past Jonah and Talib to meet me in the middle of the narrow corridor.

"*Lahra,*" he said hoarsely, cupping my cheeks and pressing hot kisses against my lips and cheeks. Then he pulled away and stared down at me. That's when I saw his bloodshot eyes and the paleness of his skin. I placed a palm on his cheek, a sharp pang spreading through my chest. It occurred to me then how horrifying it must have been for him to have overheard my abduction. He had lost his father only a few short weeks before, and had been so concerned about my safety since. I couldn't even imagine the thoughts that had gone through his head.

"I'm all right," I said, peering up at him. He didn't look convinced, so I said it over and over until some of the worry left his eyes.

When he wrapped his arms around me, drawing me against his chest, I peered around his shoulder. Jonah and Talib were still standing behind him. I pulled myself together with a deep breath and backed out of Gannon's hold with a glance down the hallway, toward my apartment. Tai stood by the door, watching me, his expression shuttered, remote.

He cut a look to Gannon. "You shouldn't be here," he said simply. "I told you I would keep you up to date."

Gannon's eyes narrowed on him. "If you thought for a moment that I would sit back, not knowing what happened to her, and wait on your reports," he said, "then you're out of your mind."

Tai frowned then threw a troubled look down the hallway, and I suddenly became conscious of our surroundings — anyone could see or hear us. The fact that the chancellor was in my building was bound to draw a lot of questions. Suddenly, it occurred to me why he, Jonah and Talib were all in plain clothing and had been wearing caps: they were trying to conceal their identities.

I looked between Gannon and Tai. "We should go inside."

Tai stepped into the hallway. "Actually, *he* should *leave*," Tai said, pinning Gannon with a glare.

Gannon leveled Tai with a look filled with cool disregard. "I'm not leaving until I hear what happened and I'm certain she's all right."

When Tai tensed, I raised a hand stopping him from saying what he looked like he was about to. I had experienced enough hostility in one day to last me a lifetime. "Gannon *should* be here," I said. "He needs to hear what happened, since it involves him too."

Gannon's gaze dropped to me, confusion clear in the knot between his brows.

A door down that hall slid open and the muted sound of voices floated into the narrow passageway. I caught the anxious looks Jonah and Talib cast at Gannon, but he was busy studying me.

"I'll explain," I said, "*inside*."

Tai blew out a tight gust of air then stalked into the apartment ahead of me. Gannon followed after instructing the two protectors to wait for him in the hallway.

I stood, waiting, in the sitting area as Tai paced the room and Gannon did a quick scan of my apartment. The closest Gannon had come to being in my home was my bedroom, but that had only been via monitor, so it didn't really count.

Tai finally rounded on me, hands on his hips. "What happened?"

Gannon slid a questioning look from Tai to me, arms crossed, waiting on my response.

"Maxim and Gabriel are working together," I said.

Tai scowled as Gannon blurted out, "What?"

I took a deep breath, and by the time I finished telling them the harrowing story about how I was abducted, threatened and manhandled, they were both seething, looking ready to wage a war.

Gannon swung around, eyes flashing, focused on Tai. "We should go after them. Now!" he yelled, hands clenched at his sides. "I have Jonah and Talib here. If we take my hover, we'll be in Helios in less than an hour."

Tai circled the room, his gaze inward as he thought things through. "I assure you," he said, "they're long gone by now."

Gannon cursed and spun away, stalking the short length of the sitting area.

I fell into the couch, wiping the tears that had fallen to my cheeks when I had told Gannon that Gabriel had tried to kill him to get back at me but had killed his father instead. As I spoke his eyes had hollowed, his face becoming drawn, etched in tight lines of anguish. Only after I told him about Gabriel's threat to hurt me or the people I cared about did his expression shift from torment to fierce determination.

I watched blindly as Gannon and Tai retraced their steps. "Please tell me I don't have to help them," I said.

Tai stopped pacing and looked at me. "Of *course* not," he said, his stance defiant. "There's no fucking way you're going to become some informant for the factions."

"But they know about Khelan and Paol," I said, my earlier resolve to not help Maxim and Gabriel slipping away. As I had relayed what had happened to me in Helios to Gannon and Tai, it had become clear to me that I truly was the one who had the most to lose. "If Maxim and Gabriel talk, my entire family will be considered dissidents and will pay the price."

Gannon came over and knelt before me. "I won't let that happen, Kira," he said then shot a look at Tai. "It's our fault this is happening, so we'll come up with a plan to fix this."

I drew back, looking between them. "How is this *your* fault?" I demanded. "It was *my* Uncle Paol who connected with Maxim and brought him into our lives."

Tai appeared grim as he crossed his arms. "But *we* arranged for him to be beaten up and then removed from his position," he said and fixed his eyes on Gannon. "I *knew* I should have killed that fucker when I had the chance."

There was a sharp glint in Gannon's eyes that told me he was in complete agreement. My shoulders slumped, too overwhelmed to argue against that remark. But then why would I? Hadn't I too felt close to murder when face to face with Gabriel?

I sat up, registering what Tai had just said. "You assaulted him before he was dismissed," I said, fear roiling through me. "Doesn't that mean Gabriel will target you the way he did Gannon?"

Good gods. Was Gabriel at this moment plotting Tai's death?

Tai shook his head firmly. "I was undercover and careful," he said. "He couldn't have known it was me."

I studied him, praying I could truly take comfort in that, then had an idea.

"We should tell my family," I said to Tai. "In case Maxim approaches them."

Tai considered that then shook his head. "Khelan will just hunt Maxim down and either offer himself up to provide the information or murder the man himself."

That very well could happen. "But what about Rhoan?" I pressed, staring up at him. "He'll kill you if you don't tell him."

Tai appeared disheartened at the thought, but refused to give in. "He'll want to tell the authorities."

"But maybe we should."

"We *are* the authorities, Kira," he said, gesturing toward Gannon. "It doesn't get much higher than our future high chancellor here. And, I'm a commander; I know exactly what the next steps will be if we get them involved. They'll want to investigate who you're connected with and your family's background."

That's right. My shoulders slumped.

Gannon pushed into a stand. "It should have occurred to me that Liandra and Maxim were involved," he said.

Tai studied him. "Why?"

Gannon looked from Tai to me. "In the files I received after my father's death, there was a reference to a connection between Liandra's and Maxim's families," he said, shaking his head, "but it wasn't detailed. I was so focused on trying to wrap my mind around the fact that she had been right about Realm exploration that I didn't think to probe."

Tai scowled and stepped toward him. "Right about *what* Realm exploration?"

I stood up, approaching Gannon with a frown. "I thought you wanted to wait until you learned more," I said quietly, searching his face.

Gannon grimaced then exhaled deeply. "If Maxim's connected with Liandra, it means he probably knows about the Realm's involvement in exploration." He turned to Tai. "If we're going to work together against Maxim, then you should probably know everything."

Tai crossed his arms, listening with a deepening scowl as Gannon told him everything he had told me about the Realm exploration and the true number of rogue worlds. When Gannon was done, Tai studied him with an indecipherable expression on his face.

"Fascinating," he said.

I started at his response, or lack thereof, as Gannon stepped toward him.

"Is *that* all you have to say?" he said to Tai. "Do you have any idea what this means, what upheaval it would bring to the Realm if this got out?"

I inhaled a shuddering breath at the gravity of what he was saying. Realm Council had expelled a dominion, causing an uprising of factions and the death of innocent citizens. People would be up in arms in every world across our system, strengthening the rebels' position against authority and creating further distrust of their leadership.

Tai raised an eyebrow. "It would certainly shake things up, wouldn't it."

Gannon assessed him as I tried to make out his shift in mood.

Suddenly, a buzzing filled the silence. Tai read the message that had arrived on his comm. "Rhoan's almost here," he said, glancing at me.

Gannon braced his shoulders back. "I should go," he said, but he appeared torn, looking at me. Finally, he turned to walk to the door, I followed him to disengage it, but before I could, he reached inside his coat pocket and pulled out a small pouch. After shooting a furtive glance at Tai, he handed it to me. "This belongs to you," he said.

As soon as my fingers closed around the small circular object in the bag, I knew what it was: the promise ring.

Gannon held my gaze then looked over my shoulder to Tai. "I'll be in touch soon," he said.

Tai nodded after a brief hesitation, a pensive look on his face.

Gannon thinned his lips then looked me over before leaving the apartment.

I returned to the sitting area, lost in my thoughts.

"What's that?" Tai asked.

I blinked, focusing on him, seeing that he was looking at my hand. "I-It's something I forgot at his house," I said, hoping that would be enough of an explanation. I tightened my hold on the pouch and held it at my waist.

"I thought you said you weren't going to answer his calls," he said, "that you were trying to stay away."

"I was. I mean, I *am*," I said, studying him. "What are you trying to say?"

Tai's eyes narrowed. "This *entire* time you've been in contact with him, haven't you."

My eyes widened. "N-no, I haven't."

"Yet you and he managed to be harboring the largest secret known to the Realm," he said. "Why didn't you tell me?"

"I wanted to," I said, glancing away briefly, "but…he asked me not to." It sounded so lame, I cringed.

Tai snorted. "Of course, he did," he muttered, shaking his head. "So let me get this straight. All of a sudden Gannon's come across some *magical* information that keeps you in contact with him."

I stared at him. "He's not lying."

"His timing is incredible," he said, ignoring me. "Do you even realize what he's doing? I warned you, Kira. I told you he could be manipulative, that he'd find ways to keep you."

"I said, he's *not lying*," I repeated loudly this time. "Xavier Minister confirmed it."

Tai faltered at that, but continued. "You're not *supposed* to be with him," he ground out. "When are you going to understand that?"

I expelled a long breath. "I do understand."

"No, you don't."

I searched his face, not trusting myself to speak. I could have tried to convince him that I had finally accepted that Gannon and I couldn't be together, but then that would have been a lie, one he would see through just as easily as any other I had ever tried to tell him.

Tai considered me quietly, staring at me for a long moment, then said, "You let him kiss you."

"What?" I blurted out. It was the last thing I expected him to say.

"When Gannon showed up," Tai said evenly. "You let him kiss you."

I thought back, searching my memory. "I-I was emotional, just reacting."

His eyes narrowed. "Yet when *I* tried to kiss you, you turned away."

Had I?

Tai shook his head then ran a hand around the back of his neck. "I'll go as soon as Rhoan gets here," he said, turning from me. "I have a lot to sort out if we're going to track Gabriel and Maxim down." The way he avoided my gaze stabbed deep in my heart.

"Tai," I said, reaching out to hold his wrist with my free hand. "It's not like that."

He turned to me. "It's not?" he asked me before dipping his head toward my other hand, the one holding the pouch. "Then what's that?"

I tightened my hold on the small bag, and the ring slid around inside. "It's just a keepsake."

"Show me," he demanded.

I swallowed hard, considering my options. I could lie or flat out refuse him. But I didn't like either choice. Tai would know in a second that I was lying, and a refusal would simply make me look guilty, leading us into an argument that would end with me right where I was now, staring him down, figuring out my next move.

With a sigh, I turned the pouch over, allowing the jewelry to fall into my palm. The ring glittered mockingly between us.

Tai cursed and pivoted away.

"You don't understand," I said, following him, tears pricking the backs of my eyes.

He swung around to face me. "I'm trying to be understanding, Kira," he bit out, anger now glinting bright in his eyes, "but there's only so much I can fucking take!"

I searched the hard lines of his face, alarm rocking me. "W-what are you saying?"

Tai's nostrils flared. "This has gone on long enough, Kira," he seethed, leaning into me, "it's time for you to make up your blasted mind."

~

BONUS SCENE

Want more?

Subscribe to my Rebel at Heart newsletter to receive the *free*
bonus scene from *Promising*.

Read when Kira wakes up in Tai's bed — this time from *his* point of view.

Here's a preview of the bonus scene. Enjoy!

TAI

I rolled onto my side, but it wasn't any better. My couch was made for sitting, not sleeping, especially for a man my size.

I kicked off the sheet, shouldered up and hitched my elbows on my knees.

Who was I kidding? I hung my head, giving in to the truth. It wasn't the couch that had been keeping me up. Kira was here, in my apartment, in my bed. And because the gods were spiteful, they had given me too much integrity to take advantage of it. *Fuck.*

I scrubbed my face with both hands then checked my comm. It was almost seven in the morning, a late start for me, but Kira probably needed more rest. I cocked my ear, glancing at the bedroom door, to hear any movement on the other side of it. While I had fought with my makeshift bed last night, I had heard her crying but had managed to stop myself from going to her. She needed time to herself.

I snorted. That actually sounded noble. I had almost convinced myself that the real reason I wanted to go to her wasn't to catch sight of her laying in my bed…long legs tangled in my sheets…wearing my shirt. Hallowed Halls, everything I owned in the room would smell like her, that mouthwatering scent that always surrounded her!

She tasted and felt good way too. Her mouth, her pussy,…everything in between.

I stood up. I had to get a fucking grip.

The woman had just ended a relationship and was a bloody mess, and there I was, imagining the taste and feel of her. I picked up the sheet from the couch and folded it before leaving it on a small table on my way to the kitchen.

I needed coffee. I'd make some, get my head focused and wait for her to get up.

Ten minutes later, I came to my senses. *When am I ever going to have the chance to see Kira in my bed again?* I grabbed two mugs of coffee — one for her, in case she was awake — and strode to my room…

Read the rest of this bonus scene by visiting www.rebelmillerbooks.com and subscribing to the Rebel Miller newsletter.

COMING SOON

Book Three of Kira's Story
The Riveting Conclusion

As the factions gain strength, secrets are revealed that compel Kira to do
what she must to protect those she loves — including Gannon and
Tai, who work together to stop her enemies, even as they
battle to own her heart.

~

The Realm Series

Coming-of-age romances about strong female characters living in
a futuristic society called the Realm.

~

Visit www.rebelmillerbooks.com and subscribe for news on
upcoming book releases.

Follow Kira Metallurgist between books at @TheRealm_Kira.

ABOUT REBEL MILLER

Rebel Miller is an author who overindulges in Pinot Grigio, caramel popcorn and an eclectic mix of movies, music and angst-filled romance novels.

She earned a graduate degree in Communications and Culture from Ryerson University and an undergraduate degree from the University of the West Indies.

Rebel lives in the outskirts of Toronto, Canada, with her husband and two sons.

~

Follow Rebel on Twitter and Facebook.